T0359848

SUSAN MALLERY

The Perfect Ending

MILLS & BOON

MIX
Paper | Supporting
responsible forestry
FSC® C001695

Published by
Mills & Boon
An imprint of Harlequin Enterprises (Australia) Pty Limited (ABN 47 001 180 918), a subsidiary of HarperCollins Publishers Australia Pty Limited (ABN 36 009 913 517)
Level 19, 201 Elizabeth Street
SYDNEY NSW 2000
AUSTRALIA

® and ™ (apart from those relating to FSC®) are trademarks of Harlequin Enterprises (Australia) Pty Limited or its corporate affiliates. Trademarks indicated with ® are registered in Australia, New Zealand and in other countries. Contact admin_legal@Harlequin.ca for details.

Printed and bound in Australia by McPherson's Printing Group

CONTENTS

Finding Perfect

CHAPTER ONE

"WHAT DO YOU mean she left me the embryos? I'm supposed to get the cat." Pia O'Brian paused long enough to put her hand on her chest. The shock of hearing the details of Crystal's will had been enough to stop the strongest of hearts, and Pia's was still bruised from the loss of her friend.

She was relieved to find her heart still beating, although the speed at which her heart was pumping was disconcerting.

"It's the cat," she repeated, speaking as clearly as possible so the well-dressed attorney sitting across from her would understand. "His name is Jake. I'm not really a pet person, but we've made peace with each other. I think he likes me. It's hard to tell—he keeps to himself. I guess most cats do."

Pia thought about offering to bring in the cat so the lawyer could see for herself, but she wasn't sure that would help.

"Crystal would never leave me her babies," Pia added with a whisper. Mostly because it was true. Pia had never had a maternal or nurturing thought in her life. Taking care of the cat had been a big step for her.

"Ms. O'Brian," the attorney said with a brief smile, "Crystal was very clear in her will. She and I spoke several times as her illness progressed. She wanted you to have her embryos. Only you."

"But I…" Pia swallowed.

Embryos. Somewhere in a lab-like facility were frozen test tubes or other containers and inside of them were the potential babies her friend had so longed for.

"I know this is a shock," the lawyer, a fortysomething elegant woman in a tailored suit, said. "Crystal debated telling you what she'd done. Apparently she decided against letting you know in advance."

"Probably because she knew I'd try to talk her out of it," Pia muttered.

"For now, you don't have to *do* anything. The storage fees are paid for the next three years. There's some paperwork to be filled out, but we can take care of it later."

Pia nodded. "Thank you," she said and rose. A quick glance at her watch told her she was going to have to hurry or she would be late for her ten-thirty appointment back at her office.

"Crystal picked you for a reason," the attorney said as Pia walked toward the door.

Pia gave the older woman a tight smile and headed for the stairs. Seconds later, she was outside, breathing deeply, wondering when the world was going to stop spinning.

This was not happening, she told herself as she started walking. It couldn't be. What had Crystal been thinking? There were dozens of other women she could have left the embryos to. Hundreds, probably. Women who were good with kids, who knew how to bake and comfort and test for a fever with the back of their hands.

Pia couldn't even keep a houseplant alive. She was a lousy hugger. Her last boyfriend had complained she always let go first. Probably because being held too long made her feel trapped. Not exactly a sterling quality for a potential parent.

Her stomach felt more than a little queasy. What had Crystal been thinking and why? Why her? That's what she couldn't get over. The fact that her friend had made such a crazy decision. And without ever mentioning it.

Fool's Gold was the kind of town where everyone knew everyone else and secrets were hard to keep. Apparently Crystal had managed to break with convention and keep some huge information to herself.

Pia reached her office building. The first floor of the structure held several retail businesses—a card store, a gift shop with the most amazing fudge and Morgan's Books. Her office was upstairs.

She went through the plain wooden door off the side street and climbed to the second story. She could see a tall man standing by her locked office door.

"Hi," she called. "Sorry I'm late."

The man turned.

There was a window behind him, so she couldn't see his face, but she knew her schedule for the morning and the name of the man who was her next appointment. Raoul Moreno was tall, with huge shoulders. Despite the unusually cool September day, he hadn't bothered with a coat. Instead he wore a V-neck sweater over dark jeans.

A man's man, she thought unexpectedly. Which made sense. Raoul Moreno was a former professional football player. He'd been a quarterback with the Dallas Cowboys. After ten years in the game, he'd retired on top and had disappeared from public view. Last year he'd shown up in Fool's Gold for a pro-am charity golf tournament. For reasons she couldn't figure out, he'd stayed.

As she got closer, she took in the large dark eyes, the handsome face. There was a scar on his cheek—probably from protecting an old lady during a mugging. He had a reputation for being nice. Pia made it a rule never to trust nice people.

"Ms. O'Brian," he began. "Thanks for seeing me."

She unlocked her office door and motioned for him to go inside.

"Pia, please. My 'Ms. O'Brian' years are looming, but I'm not ready for them yet."

He was good-looking enough that she should have been distracted. Under other circumstances, she probably would have been. But at the moment, she was too busy wondering if the chemo treatments had scrambled Crystal's brain. Her friend had always seemed so rational. Obviously that had been a facade.

Pia motioned to the visitor chair in front of her desk and hung her coat on the rack by the door.

Her office was small but functional. There was a good-size main room with a custom three-year calendar covering most of one wall. The squares were half dry-erase material and half corkboard.

Posters for various Fool's Gold festivals took up the rest of the wall space. She had a storage room and a half bath in the rear, several cabinets and a filing system that bordered on compulsively organized. As a rule she made it a point to visit rather than have people come to her, but scheduling-wise, having Raoul stop by had made the most sense.

Of course that had been before she'd found out she'd been left three very frozen potential children.

She crossed to the small refrigerator in the corner. "I have diet soda and water." She glanced over her shoulder. "You're not the diet type."

One dark eyebrow rose. "Are you asking or telling?"

She smiled. "Am I wrong?"

"Water's fine."

"I knew it."

She collected a bottle and a can, then returned to her desk. After handing him the bottle, she took a seat and stared at the yellow pad in front of her. There was writing on it, very possibly in English. She could sort of make out individual letters but not words and certainly not sentences.

They were supposed to have a meeting about something. That much was clear. She handled the city festivals in town. There were over a dozen civic events that she ran every year. But her mind didn't go any further than that. When she tried to remember why Raoul was here, she went blank. Her brain was filled with other things.

Babies. Crystal had left her babies. Okay, embryos, but the implication was clear. Crystal wanted her children to be born. Which meant someone was going to have to get them implanted, grow them and later give birth. Although that was terrifying enough, there was also the further horror of raising them.

Children weren't like cats. She knew that much. They would need more than dry food, a bowl of water and a clean litter box. A lot more.

"Oh, God, I can't do this," she whispered.

Raoul frowned. "I don't understand. Do you want to reschedule the meeting?"

Meeting? Oh, right. He was here for something. His camp and he wanted her to...

Her mind went blank, again. Right after the merciful emptiness, there was panic. Deep to the bone, intestine-wrenching panic.

She stood and wrapped her arms around her midsection, breathing hard and fast.

"I can't do this. It's impossible. What was she thinking? She had to know better."

"Pia?"

Her visitor rose. She turned to tell him that rescheduling was probably a good idea when the room began to spin. It turned and turned, darkening on the edges.

The next thing she knew, she was in her chair, bent over at the waist, her head between her knees with something pressing down on the back of her neck.

"This is uncomfortable," she said.

"Keep breathing."

"Easier said than done. Let go."

"A couple more breaths."

The pressure on the back of her neck lessened. Slowly, she straightened and blinked.

Raoul Moreno was crouched next to her, his dark eyes cloudy with concern. She took another breath and realized he smelled really good. Clean, but with a hint of something else.

"You all right?" he asked.

"What happened?"

"You started to faint." Raoul met her gaze as her eyes widened, and, despite the bigger things crowding her thoughts, she couldn't miss the zing of interest.

She blinked, and shook her head. "I don't faint. I never faint. I—" Her memory returned. "Oh, crap." She covered her face with her hands. "I'm so not ready to be a mother."

Raoul moved with a speed that was a credit to his physical conditioning and nearly comical at the same time.

"Man trouble?" he asked cautiously from a safer few inches away.

"What?" She lowered her hands. "No. I'm not pregnant. That would require sex. Or not. Actually it wouldn't, would it? This is so not happening."

"Okay." He sounded nervous. "Should I call a doctor?"

"No, but you can go if you want. I'm fine."

"You don't look fine."

Now it was her turn to raise her eyebrows. "Are you commenting on my appearance?"

He grinned. "I wouldn't dare."

"That sounded almost critical."

"You know what I meant."

She did. "I'm okay. I've had a bit of a shock. A friend of mine died recently. She was married to a guy in the army. Before he was shipped off to Iraq, they decided to do in vitro, just in case something happened to him. So she could have his kids."

"Sad, but it makes sense."

She nodded. "He was killed a couple of years ago. She took it really hard, but after a while, she decided she would have the babies. At least a part of him would live on, right?"

Pia rose and paced the length of the office. Moving seemed

to help. She took a couple of cautious breaths, to make sure she was going to stay conscious. Fainting? Impossible. Yet the world really had started to blur.

She forced herself back to the topic at hand.

"She went to the doctor for a routine physical," she continued. "They discovered she had lymphoma. And not the good kind."

"There's a good kind?"

She shrugged. "There's a kind that can usually be cured. She didn't have that one. And then she was gone. I have her cat. I thought I'd be keeping him. We have a relationship. Sort of. It's hard to tell with a cat."

"They keep to themselves."

There was something about the way he spoke. She glared at him. "Are you making fun of me?"

"No."

She saw the corner of his mouth twitch. "Don't mess with me," she told him. "Or I'll talk about my feelings."

"Anything but that."

She returned to her desk and sank into the chair. "She didn't leave me the cat. She left me the embryos. I don't know what to do. I don't know what she was thinking. Babies. God—anyone but me. And I can't ignore it. Them. That's what the attorney hinted at. That I could let it go for a while because the 'fees' are paid for three years." She looked at him. "I guess that's the frozen part. Maybe I should go see them."

"They're embryos. What's there to see?"

"I don't know. Something. Can't they put them under a microscope? Maybe if I saw them, I would understand." She stared at him as if he had the answer. "Why did she think I could raise her children?"

"I'm sorry, Pia. I don't know."

He looked uncomfortable. His gaze lingered on the door. Reality returned and with it, a sense of embarrassment.

"I'm so sorry," she murmured, standing. "We'll reschedule.

I'll compose myself and be much better next time. Let me look over my calendar and give you a call."

He reached for the door handle, then paused. "Are you sure you're going to be all right?"

No, she wasn't sure. She wasn't sure of anything. But that wasn't Raoul's problem.

She forced a smile. "I'm great. Seriously, you should go. I'm going to call a couple of girlfriends and let them talk me down."

"Okay." He hesitated. "You have my number?"

"Uh-huh." She wasn't sure if she did, but she was determined to let him escape while she still had a shred of dignity. "The next time you see me, I'll be professionalism personified. I swear."

"Thanks. You take care."

"Bye."

He left.

When the door closed, she sank back into her chair. After lowering her arms to the desk, she rested her head on them and did her best to keep breathing.

Crystal had left her the embryos. There were only two questions that mattered. Why, and what the hell was Pia supposed to do now?

RAOUL ARRIVED AT Ronan Elementary shortly before two. He parked in the lot by the playground. No surprise—his was the only Ferrari in the parking lot. He was a guy who liked his toys, so sue him.

Before he could climb out of the car, his cell phone rang. He checked his watch—he had a few minutes before he was due inside—then the phone number on the screen. As he pushed the talk button, he grinned.

"Hey, Coach,"

"Hey, yourself," Hawk, his former high school football coach, said. "Nicole hasn't heard from you in a while and I'm calling to find out why."

Raoul laughed. "I talked to your beautiful wife last week, so I know that's not why you're calling."

"You got me. I'm checking on you. Making sure you're moving on with your life."

That was Hawk, Raoul thought with equal parts frustration and appreciation. Cutting right to the heart of what was wrong.

"You had some bad stuff happen," the older man continued. "Don't wallow."

"I'm not wallowing. I'm busy."

"You're in your head too much. I know you. Find a cause. Get personally involved in your new town. It'll distract you. You can't change what happened."

Raoul's good humor faded. Hawk was right about that. The past couldn't be undone. Those who were gone stayed gone. No amount of bargaining, no sum of money, made it better.

"I can't let it go," he admitted.

"You'll have to. Maybe not today, but soon. Believe in the possibility of healing, Raoul. Open yourself up to other people."

It seemed impossible, but he'd been trusting Hawk for nearly twenty years. "I'll do my best."

"Good. Call Nicole."

"I will."

They hung up.

Raoul sat in his car for a few more seconds, thinking about what Hawk had told him. Get involved. Find a cause. What the other man didn't know was how much Raoul wanted to avoid that. Getting involved is what had caused the problem in the first place. Life was much safer lived at a distance.

He got out of his car and collected the small duffel he'd brought with him. Whenever he visited a school, he brought a few official NFL footballs and player cards. It made the kids happy, and that's why he was here. To entertain and maybe slip in a little motivation when they weren't looking.

He glanced at the main school building. It was older but well-kept. He usually spoke to high-school-aged kids, but the principal and class teacher had both been persistent to the point of stalking. He was new to small-town life and was figuring out the rules as he went. As he planned to settle in Fool's Gold permanently, he'd decided to err on the side of cooperation.

He stepped toward the main walkway, then made his way into the building. Unlike the inner-city schools he usually visited, there weren't any metal detectors or even a guard. The double doors stood open, the halls were wide and well-lit, the walls free of graffiti. Like the rest of Fool's Gold, the school was almost too good to be true.

He followed the signs to the main office and found himself in a big open area with a long counter. There were the usual bulletin boards with flyers for book drives and after-school programs. A dark-haired woman sat at a desk, typing on an ancient-looking computer.

"Morning," he said.

The woman—probably in her midthirties—looked up. Her mouth fell open as she stood and waved her hands. "Oh, God. You're here. You're really here! I can't believe it." She hurried toward him. "Hi. I'm Rachel. My dad is a huge fan. He's going to die when he finds out I met you."

"I hope not," Raoul said easily, pulling a card out of the bag and reaching for a pen.

"What?"

"I hope he doesn't die."

Rachel laughed. "He won't, but he'll be so jealous. I heard you were coming. And here you are. This is just so exciting. Raoul Moreno in our school."

"What's your dad's name?"

"Norm."

He signed the card and passed it to her. "Maybe this will help him deal with his disappointment."

She took the paper reverently and placed a hand on her chest. "Thank you so much. This is wonderful." She glanced at the clock, then sighed. "I suppose I have to take you to Mrs. Miller's class now."

"I should probably get started talking to the kids."

"Right. That's why you're here. It's been wonderful to meet you."

"You, too, Rachel."

She came out from behind the counter, then led him back into the hallway. As they walked, she chatted about the school and the town, all the while glancing at him with a combination of appreciation and flirtatiousness. It came with the territory and he'd learned a long time ago not to take the attention seriously.

Mrs. Miller's class was at the end of the hall. Rachel held the door open for him.

"Good luck," she said.

"Thanks."

He entered the room alone.

There were about twenty young kids, all staring wide-eyed, while their teacher, an attractive woman in her forties, fluttered.

"Oh, Mr. Moreno, I can't thank you enough for speaking with us today. It's such a thrill."

Raoul smiled. "I'm always happy to come talk to kids in school." He glanced at the class. "Morning."

A few of the students greeted him. A few more looked too excited to speak. At least the boys did. Most of the girls didn't seem impressed at all.

"Fourth grade, right?" he asked.

A girl with glasses in the front row nodded. "We're the accelerated group, reading above grade level."

"Uh-oh," he said, taking an exaggerated step back. "The smart kids. You going to ask me a math question?"

Her mouth curved into a smile. "Do you like math?"

"Yeah, I do." He looked up at the class. "Who here really likes school a lot?"

A few kids raised their hands.

"School can change your life," he said, settling one hip on

the teacher's desk. "When you grow up, you're going to get jobs and work for a living. Today most of your responsibilities are about doing well in school. Who knows why we need to learn things like reading and math?"

More hands went up.

His usual talk was on staying motivated, finding a mentor, making a better life, but that seemed like a little much for the average nine-year-old. So he was going to talk about how important it was to like school and do your best.

Mrs. Miller hovered. "Do you need anything?" she asked in a whisper. "Can I get you something?"

"I'm good."

He turned his attention back to the students. The girl in the front row seemed more interested in the pretty scenery outside of the window. Oddly enough, she reminded him of Pia. Maybe it was the brown curly hair, or her obvious lack of interest in him as a person. Pia hadn't gushed, either. She'd barely noticed him. Not a real surprise, given how her morning had started. But he'd noticed her. She'd been cute and funny, even without trying.

He returned his attention to the students, drew in a breath and frowned. He inhaled again, smelling something odd.

If this had been a high school, he would have assumed an experiment gone bad in the science lab or a batch of forgotten cookies in home ec. But elementary schools didn't have those facilities.

He turned to Mrs. Miller. "Do you smell that?"

She nodded, her blue eyes concerned. "Maybe something happened in the cafeteria."

"Is there a fire?" one of the boys asked.

"Everyone stay seated," Mrs. Miller said firmly as she walked toward the door.

She placed a hand on it before slowly pulling it open. As she did, the smell of smoke got stronger. Seconds later, the fire alarms went off.

She turned to him. "It's only the second day of school. We haven't practiced what to do. I think there really is a fire."

The kids were already standing up and looking scared. He knew they weren't very far from panic.

"You know where we're supposed to go?" he asked. "The way out?"

"Of course."

"Good." He turned to the students. "Who's in charge here?" he asked in a voice loud enough to be heard over the bells.

"Mrs. Miller," someone yelled.

"Exactly. Everyone get in line and follow Mrs. Miller as we go into the hall. There are going to be a lot of kids out there. Stay calm. I'll go last and make sure you all get out of the building."

Mrs. Miller motioned for her students to move toward the door.

"Follow me," she said. "We'll go quickly. Everyone hold hands. Don't let go. Everything is fine. Just stay together."

Mrs. Miller went out the door. The children began to follow her. Raoul waited to make sure everyone left. One little boy seemed to hesitate before leaving.

"It's okay," Raoul told him, his voice deliberately calm. He reached for the boy's hand, but the child flinched, as if expecting to be hit. The kid—all red hair and freckles—ducked out before Raoul could say anything.

Raoul went into the hall. The smell of smoke was more intense. Several kids were crying. A few stood in the middle of the hallway, their hands over their ears. The bells rang endlessly as teachers called for their students to follow them outside.

"Come on," he said, scooping the nearest little girl into his arms. "Let's go."

"I'm scared," she said.

"I'm big enough to keep you safe."

Another little boy grabbed hold of his arm. Tears filled the kid's eyes. "It's too loud."

"Then let's go outside, where it's quieter."

He walked quickly, herding kids as he went. Teachers ran back and forth, counting heads, checking to make sure no one was left behind.

When Raoul and his group of kids reached the main doors leading outside, the children took off at a run. He put down the girl he'd been carrying and she raced toward her teacher. He could see smoke pouring into the sky, a white-gray cloud covering the brilliant blue.

Students flowed out around him. Names were called. Teachers sorted the groups by grades, then classes. Raoul turned and went back into the building.

Now he could do more than smell smoke. He could see it. The air was thick and getting darker, making it hard to breathe. He went room by room, pushing open doors, checking under the large teacher desks in front, scanning to make sure no one was left behind.

He found a tiny little girl in a corner of the third room he entered, her face wet with tears. She was coughing and sobbing. He picked her up, turned and almost ran into a firefighter.

"I'll take her," the woman said, looking at him from behind a mask and grabbing the girl. "Get the hell out of here. The building is nearly seventy years old. God knows what cocktail of chemicals is in the air."

"There might be more kids."

"I know, and the longer we stand here talking, the more danger they're in. Now move."

He followed the firefighter out of the building. It wasn't until he was outside that he realized he was coughing and choking. He bent over, trying to catch his breath.

When he could breathe again, he straightened. The scene was controlled chaos. Three fire trucks stood in front of the school. Students huddled together on the lawn, well back from the building. Smoke poured out in all directions.

A few people screamed and pointed. Raoul turned and saw flames licking through the roof at the far end of the school.

He turned to head back in. A firefighter grabbed him by the arm.

"Don't even think about it," the woman told him. "Leave this to the professionals."

He nodded, then started coughing again.

She shook her head. "You went back inside, didn't you? Civilians. Do you think we wear the masks because they're pretty? Medic!" She yelled the last word and pointed at him.

"I'm fine," Raoul managed, his chest tight.

"Let me guess. You're a doctor, too. Cooperate with the nice lady or I'll tell her you need an enema."

CHAPTER TWO

THERE WAS NOTHING like a community disaster to snap a person out of a pity party, Pia thought as she stood on the lawn at the far end of the Ronan Elementary playground and stared at what had once been a beautiful old school. Now flames licked at the roof and caused glass windows to explode. The smell of destruction was everywhere.

She'd heard the fire trucks from her office and had seen the smoke darkening the sky. It had only taken her a second to figure out where the fire was and that it was going to be bad. Now, as she stood on the edge of the playground, she felt her breath catch as one of the walls seemed to shudder before falling in on itself.

She'd always heard people talk about fire as if it were alive. A living creature with cunning and determination and an evil nature. Until now, she'd never believed it. But watching the way the fire systematically destroyed the school, she thought there might be seeds of truth in the theory.

"This is bad," she whispered.

"Worse than bad."

Pia saw Mayor Marsha Tilson had joined her. The sixty-something woman stood with a hand pressed against her throat, her eyes wide.

"I spoke with the fire chief. She assured me they've gone through every room in the building. No one is left inside. But the building…" Marsha's voice caught. "I went to school here."

Pia put her arm around the other woman. "I know. It's horrible to see this."

Marsha visibly controlled her emotions. "We're going to have to find somewhere to put the children. They can't lose school days over this. But the other schools are full. We could bring in those portable classrooms. There must be someone I can call." She glanced around. "Where's Charity? She might know."

Pia turned and saw her friend standing by the growing crowd of frantic parents. "Over there."

Marsha saw her, then frowned. "She's not getting any smoke, is she?"

Pia understood the concern. Charity was several months pregnant and the mayor's granddaughter. "She's upwind. She'll be okay."

Marsha stared at the destruction. "What could have started this?"

"We'll find out. The important thing is all the kids and staff got out safely. We can fix the school."

Marsha squeezed her hand. "You're rational. Right now I need that. Thank you, Pia."

"We'll get through this together."

"I know. That makes me feel better. I'm going to talk to Charity."

As the mayor moved off, Pia stayed on the grass. Every few seconds, a blast of heat reached her and with it the smell of smoke and annihilation.

Just that morning she'd walked by the school and everything had been fine. How could things change so quickly?

Before she could figure out an answer, she saw more parents arriving on the scene. Mothers and some fathers rushed toward the children huddled together, protected by their teachers. There were cries of relief and of fear. Children were hugged, then searched for injuries, teachers thanked. The school principal stood by the children, a stack of pages on a clipboard.

Probably the master roster, Pia thought. Given the circumstances, parents would probably have to sign out their kids, so everyone was accounted for.

Two more fire trucks pulled up, sirens blaring. The school fire alarms were finally silenced but the noise was still deafening. People shouted, the truck engines rumbled. A voice over a megaphone warned everyone to stay back, then pointed out the location of the emergency medical vehicles.

Pia glanced in that direction and was surprised to see a tall, familiar man speaking with one of the EMT women. Raoul's hair was tousled, his face smudged. He paused to cough and despite it all, the man still looked good.

"Just so typical," she muttered as she crossed the playground and went toward him.

"Let me guess," she said as she approached. "You did something heroic."

"You mean stupid," the medic told her with a roll of her eyes. "It's a gender thing. They can't help it."

Pia chuckled. "Don't I know it." She turned to Raoul. "Tell me you didn't race into a burning building in an attempt to save a child."

He straightened and drew in a deep breath. "Why do you say it like that? It's not a bad thing."

"There are professionals here who know what they're doing."

"That's what I keep getting told. What happened to a little gratitude for risking my life?"

"Odds are, you would have been overcome by smoke, thereby giving the firefighters *more* work to do instead of less," the medic told him. She pulled some kind of measuring device off his finger.

"You're fine," she continued. "If you have any of the symptoms we talked about, go to the E.R." She glanced at Pia. "Is he with you?"

Pia shook her head.

"Smart girl," the medic said, then moved on to the next patient.

"Ouch," Raoul said. "This is a tough town."

"Don't worry," Pia told him. "I'm sure there will be plenty of women who will want to fawn all over you and coo as you retell your tale of bravery."

"But you're not one of them."

"Not today."

"How are you feeling?" he asked.

For a second she didn't understand the question. Then reality returned. That's right—he'd witnessed her breakdown earlier in the day. Talk about an emotion dump.

"I meant to call you," she said, moving beside him as they walked away from the medics. "To apologize. I usually have my meltdowns in private."

"It's okay. I'd say I understand, but you'll probably bite my head off if I do. How about if I tell you I'm sympathetic?"

"I would appreciate that."

She hesitated, wondering if she was supposed to say more. Or if he would ask. Not that she had anything to say. She was still grasping the reality of her friend's bequest and hadn't made a decision about what to do next. Despite the attorney's promise that she had at least three years before she needed to decide anything, Pia felt the pressure weighing on her.

Not that she was going to discuss her dilemma in front of Raoul. He'd already suffered enough.

"What were you doing here?" she asked. "At the school."

He'd come to a stop and was staring back at the school. His gaze moved from one firefighter to another. The chief stood on a garden wall about three feet high, yelling out orders to her team.

"Are you worried about the kids?" Pia asked. "Don't be. I've sat through plenty of preparedness meetings. They're great to attend if you're having trouble sleeping. Anyway, there's a plan for each school, and a master list. Attendance is taken daily and sent by computer to the district office. A list of who is out that day is brought to the disaster site. Trust me. Every student is accounted for."

He looked at her, his dark eyes bright with surprise. "They're all women."

"Most teachers are."

"The firefighters. They're all women."

"Oh, that." She shrugged. "It's Fool's Gold. What did you expect?"

He appeared both confused and lost, which on a tall, good-looking guy was kind of appealing. Assuming she was interested, and she wasn't. If her natural wariness about guys wasn't enough, Raoul was famous-ish, and she didn't need the pain and suffering that came with that type. Not to mention the fact that she might soon be pregnant with another couple's embryos.

A week ago her life had been predictable and boring. Now she was in the running to be a tabloid headline. Boring was better.

"There's a man shortage," Pia said patiently. "Surely you've noticed there aren't a lot of men in town. I thought that was why you'd moved here."

"There are men."

"Okay. Where?"

"The town has children." He pointed to the few students still waiting to be picked up. "They have fathers."

"That's true. We do have a few breeding pairs, for experimental purposes."

He took a step back.

She grinned. "Sorry. I'm kidding. Yes, there are men in town, but statistically, we don't have very many. Certainly not enough. So if you find yourself exceptionally popular, don't let it go to your head."

"I think I liked you better when you were having your breakdown," he muttered.

"You wouldn't be the first man to prefer a woman in a weakened condition. Full strength, we're a threat. Being as big and tough as you are, I'd hoped for something more. Life is nothing if not a disappointment. You didn't answer my question from before. What were you doing here?"

He looked distracted, as if he were having trouble keeping up. "Talking to Mrs. Miller's fourth-grade class. I speak to students. Usually they're in high school, but she wouldn't take no for an answer."

"She probably wanted to spend the hour looking at your butt."

Raoul stared at her.

She shrugged. "I'm just saying."

"You're certainly feeling better."

"It's more a matter of not being on the edge of hysteria," she admitted.

She turned her attention back to the school. It was obviously going to be in ruins when all this was over. "How big is your place?" she asked. "You seem like the mansion type. Could they hold classes in your foyer?"

"I rent a two-bedroom house from Josh Golden."

"Then that would be a no. They're going to have to put the kids somewhere."

"What about the other schools in town?"

"Marsha said they were thinking about bringing in those portable classrooms."

"Marsha?"

"Mayor Marsha Tilson. My boss. You know Josh Golden?"

Raoul nodded.

"He's married to her granddaughter."

"Got it."

He seemed less stunned now, which probably made him feel better. With the smoke smudges on his face, he looked pretty attractive, she thought absently. Not that he hadn't been devastatingly handsome before. He was the kind of man who made a woman do stupid things. Thank goodness she was immune.

A lifetime of romantic failures had a way of curing a woman of foolishness.

"We should make another appointment," she said. "I'll call your office and set things up with your secretary."

"There you go, assuming again. I don't have a secretary."

"Huh. Who sets up your calendar and makes you feel important?" she said with a wink.

He studied her for a second. "Are you like this with everyone?"

"Charming?" She laughed. "As a rule. Just ask around."

"Maybe I will."

He was teasing. She knew he was teasing. Yet she felt something. A flicker. Maybe a quiver, down low in her belly.

No way, she reminded herself as she waved and walked toward her car. Especially not with a man like him. Successful, handsome men had expectations. Blonde ambitions. She knew— she read *People* magazine.

Life had taught her many important lessons. The greatest of which was not to depend on anyone to be there for her. She was a strong, independent woman. Men were optional and right now she was going to just say no.

RAOUL SPENT THE next hour at the school. The firefighters got the fire under control. The chief had told him they would have a presence for at least the next twenty-four hours, to control any hot spots. Cleanup would start when the remaining structure had cooled and the investigation was complete.

It was the kind of disaster he'd read about in the paper and seen on the news a dozen times over the years. But even the best reporting hadn't prepared him for the reality of the heat, the destruction and the smell. It would be months, maybe years, before the campus was even close to normal.

The kids had all gone home, as had most of the spectators. Eventually he turned to walk back to his office. His car wasn't in any danger, but it was blocked in by several fire trucks. He would return later and collect it. In the meantime, the center of town was only about twenty minutes away.

Raoul had grown up in Seattle, gone to college in Oklahoma, and then been drafted by the Dallas Cowboys. He was a big-city kind of guy, enjoying the restaurants, the nightlife, the possibilities. At least he had thought he was. Somewhere along the way, going out all the time had gotten old. He'd wanted to settle down.

"Don't go there," he told himself firmly.

Revisiting the past was a waste of time. What was more important was the future. He'd chosen Fool's Gold and so far he enjoyed small-town life. Walking nearly everywhere was one of the advantages. So was the lack of traffic. His friends had joked that he wasn't going to have much of a social life, but since his divorce, he hadn't been that interested, so it was all working out.

He reached his office, a first-floor space on a tree-lined side street. There was a restaurant—the Fox and Hound—around the corner, and a Starbucks nearby. For now, it was enough.

He reached for his keys only to see the lights were already on. He pulled open the door and stepped inside.

The three-thousand-square-foot office was more than he needed, but he had plans to expand. His summer camp was just the beginning. Changing the world would require a staff.

Dakota Hendrix, his lone year-round employee, looked up from her computer. "Were you at the fire? Didn't you mention you were going to the school?"

"I was there."

"Did everyone get out okay?"

He nodded and briefed her on what had happened—leaving out the part where he went back to check that all the rooms were empty.

Dakota, a pretty woman with shoulder-length blond hair and expressive eyes, listened carefully. She had a PhD in childhood development and he'd been damn lucky to find her, let alone hire her.

One of the reasons Raoul had moved to Fool's Gold had been because of the abandoned camp up in the mountains. He'd been able to get it for practically nothing. He'd updated the facility and this past summer End Zone for Kids had opened its doors.

The camp's mandate was to help inner-city kids be a part of nature—hardly a unique idea, but one that was appreciated by those who lived in the urban center of broken cities. Local kids came as day campers, and the city kids stayed for two weeks at a time.

The initial reports had been favorable. Raoul had an idea to expand the camp into a year-round facility, a challenge Dakota had understood and wanted to take on. In addition to planning and running End Zone, she'd started writing a business plan for the winter months.

"I heard the fire was awful," she said when he was done. "That there was a lot of damage. Marsha called me a few minutes ago." She paused. "Marsha's our mayor."

He remembered Pia mentioning her. "Why would she call you about the fire?"

"Mostly she was calling about the camp." This time the pause was longer. "The city wants to know if they can use the camp as a temporary school. Marsha, the head of our board of education and the principal would like to see it first, but they think it would work. The only other place big enough is the convention center. But it's pretty much booked and the layout isn't really suitable. The acoustics would be awful—the noise of one class bleeding into another. So they're very interested in the camp." She paused for a third time, drew a breath and looked hopeful.

Raoul pulled out a chair and sat across from her. Hawk's words about getting involved echoed in his head. This was one way to get involved—but from a very safe distance.

"We don't have classrooms," he said, thinking out loud. "But we already have all the beds stored so the bunkrooms could be classrooms. They would be small but workable. With the right kind of dividers, the main building could house a dozen or so classrooms."

"That's what I thought," Dakota said, leaning toward him. "There's the kitchen, so lunch wouldn't be a problem. The main dining hall could double as an assembly area. No one knows how much is salvageable in terms of desks, but they're putting out the word to other districts. We should have some solid numbers in the next couple of days. So they can use the camp? I'll take care of the details and act as liaison."

"If you're willing to take that on." There would be liability issues, but that's why he had lawyers.

"I am."

He and Dakota tossed around potential problems and solutions.

"This will give us a lot of practical information about having the camp open all year," she told him. "Dealing with the weather. We get a lot of snow in the winter. Can we keep the roads open, that sort of thing."

He chuckled. "Why do I know all those displaced kids will be hoping we can't?"

She smiled. "Snow days are fun. Did you have them in Seattle?"

"Every few years." He leaned back in his chair.

"I'll take care of everything," she told him. "Earn the big salary you've given me."

"You're already earning it."

"I was over the summer. Less so now. Anyway, this is great. The town will be grateful."

"Will they put me on a stamp?"

The smile turned into a grin. "Stamps are actually a federal thing, but I'll see what I can do."

Raoul thought about the kids he'd met that morning. Especially the little redheaded boy who had flinched, as if someone hit him. He didn't know the kid's name, so asking about him would be problematic. But once the school reopened, Raoul could do some checking.

He remembered Pia's teasing comment about moving the school to his house. This was close. It would be moving to his camp.

"Want to drive up to the camp with me?" he asked. "We should go and see what changes have to be made."

"Sure. If there's anything more than basic cleanup and refurbishing, I'll have Ethan meet with us."

Raoul nodded. Ethan was Dakota's brother and the contractor Raoul had used to refurbish the camp.

Dakota stood and collected her handbag. "We can have a couple of work parties, for general cleaning and prepping. Pia has a phone-tree list that would make the CIA jealous. Just tell her what you need and she can get you a hundred volunteers in about an hour."

"Impressive."

They went out, only to pause on the curb.

"My car is at the school," Raoul said.

Dakota laughed. "We'll take my Jeep."

He eyed the battered vehicle. "All right."

"You could sound more enthused."

"It's great."

"Liar." She unlocked the passenger door. "We can't all have Ferraris in our garage."

"How about cars built in the past twenty years?"

"Snob."

"I like my cars young and pretty."

"Just like your women?"

He got in. "Not exactly."

Dakota climbed in next to him. "I haven't seen you date. At least not locally."

"Are you asking for any particular reason?" He didn't think Dakota was interested. They worked well together, but there wasn't any chemistry. Besides, he wasn't looking to get involved, and for some reason he didn't think she was, either.

"Just to have something to share when I sit around with my friends and talk about you."

"A daily occurrence?"

"Practically." She shifted into First and grinned. "You're very hot."

He ignored that. "Pia was saying something about a man shortage. Is that true?"

"Sure. It's not so bad that teenage girls are forced to bring their brothers to prom, but it's noticeable. We're not sure how or when it started. A lot of men left during the Second World War. Not enough came back. Some people attribute it to a rumor that the site of the town is an old Mayan village."

They drove through town. Dakota took the road that headed up the mountain.

"Mayan? Not this far north," he said.

"They're supposed to have migrated. A tribe of women and their children. A very matriarchal society."

"You're making this up."

"Check the facts yourself. In the 1906 San Francisco earthquake, part of the mountain opened up, revealing a huge cave at the base of the mountain. Inside were dozens of solid-gold artifacts—Mayan artifacts. Although there were enough differences between these and the ones found down south to confuse scholars."

"Where's the cave now?" He hadn't seen anything about it in his travels or research.

"It collapsed during the 1989 earthquake, but the artifacts are all over the world. Including at the museum in town."

Something he would have to go see for himself, he thought. "What do matriarchal Mayans have to do with the man shortage in town?"

She glanced at him, then turned her attention back to the road. "There's a curse."

"Did you hit your head this morning?"

She laughed. "Okay, there's a rumor of a curse. I don't know the details."

"That's convenient."

"Something about men and the world ending in 2012."

"Dr. Hendrix, I expected better from you."

"Sorry. That's all I know. You might ask Pia. She mentioned something about doing a Mayan festival in 2012."

"To celebrate the end of the world?"

"Let's hope not."

Talk about a crazy history. A Mayan curse? In the Sierra Nevada mountains? And to think he'd been worried that small-town living would be boring.

PIA CAREFULLY COLLECTED cat food, dishes, cat toys and a bed that Jake had never used. Jo, the cat's new owner, had said she'd bought a new litter box and litter. After making sure she hadn't forgotten anything, Pia got the pet carrier out of the closet and opened it.

She expected to have to chase Jake down and then wrestle him into the plastic-and-metal container, but he surprised her by glancing from it to her, then creeping inside.

"You want to go, don't you," she whispered as she closed and secured the front latch.

The cat stared at her, unblinking.

Crystal had said he was a marmalade cat—sort of a champagne-orange with bits of white on his chin. Sleek and soft, with a long tail and big green eyes.

She stared back at him.

"I wanted you to be happy. I really tried. I hope you know that."

Jake closed his eyes, as if willing her to be done.

She picked up the tote holding his supplies in one hand and the pet carrier in the other. She took the stairs slowly, then put Jake and his things in the backseat of her car.

The drive to Jo's only took a few minutes. She parked in front of the other woman's house. Before she could get out, Jo had stepped out onto the front porch, then hurried down the steps.

"I'm ready," the other woman called as Pia got out of her car. "It's weird. I haven't had a cat in so long, but I'm really excited."

Jo opened the back door of the car and took out the carrier. "Hi, big guy. Look at you. Who's a handsome kitty?"

The cooing singsong voice was nearly as surprising as the words. For a woman who prided herself on running her neighborhood bar with a combination of strict rules and not-so-subtle intimidation, Jo's sweet baby talk was disconcerting.

Pia collected the tote and followed Jo into her house.

Jo had moved to Fool's Gold about three years ago and bought a failing bar. She'd transformed the business into a haven for women, offering great drinks, big TVs that showed more reality shows and shopping channels than sports, and plenty of guilt-free snacks. Men were welcome, as long as they knew their place.

Jo was tall, pretty, well-muscled and unmarried. Pia would guess she was in her midthirties. So far Jo hadn't been seen with a man, or mentioned one from her past. Rumors ranged from her being a mafia princess to a woman on the run from an abusive boyfriend. All Pia knew for sure was that Jo kept a gun behind the bar and she looked more than capable of using it.

Pia stepped into Jo's and closed the front door. The house was older, built in the 1920s, with plenty of wood and a huge fireplace. All the doors off the living room were closed and a sheet blocked the entrance to the stairs.

"I'm giving him limited access for now," Jo explained as she walked through to the kitchen. "The sheet won't work for long, but it should keep him on this floor for a few hours."

Pia trailed after her.

Jo put the carrier down on the kitchen floor and opened the door. Jake cautiously stepped out, sniffing as he went.

"The house is really big," Jo explained. "That could scare him. Once he gets to know the place, he'll be fine."

"He must have loved my apartment," Pia murmured, thinking of how small it was.

"I'm sure he did. Cats like upstairs windows. They can see the world."

Pia set the tote on the counter. "You know a lot about cats."

"I grew up with them," Jo said wistfully, then leaned down and petted Jake's back.

Pia half expected the cat to take off one of Jo's fingers with his claws. Instead Jake paused to sniff her fingers, then rubbed his head against them.

He'd never done that to her, she thought, trying not to be offended. Apparently being a cat person helped.

Jo set out dry food and water on a place mat in the corner of the kitchen. Jake disappeared into the laundry room. A minute or so later, there was the distinctive scratching sound of litter being moved.

"He found his bathroom," Jo said happily. "He's all set. He'll figure out the rest of it. Come on. Let's go sit in the living room while he explores. I've been working on a new peppermint martini recipe. I'd like it ready for Christmas. You can tell me what you think."

A martini sounded like an excellent plan, Pia thought, trailing after her friend.

They sat on a comfortable sofa, across from the huge fireplace. Jo poured liquid from a pitcher into a shaker, shook it, then tipped the startlingly pink liquid into two martini glasses.

"Be honest. Is it too sweet?"

Pia took a sip. The liquid was icy cold and tasted of peppermint. It was more refreshing than sweet, with a hint of something she couldn't place. Honey? Almond?

"Dangerously good," she admitted. "And I'm driving."

"You can walk home and get your car in the morning," Jo told her. Her gaze sharpened. "Are you okay?"

"I'm fine." Pia took another taste of her drink. "Just feeling kind of strange. Giving up Jake and all."

"I'm sorry," Jo said. "I didn't mean to steal your cat."

"You didn't. He's not my cat. I thought we were getting along great, but you've had more contact with him in the past five minutes than I've had in the last month. I don't think he likes me."

"Cats can be funny."

As if to prove Jo's point, Jake jumped up on the back of the sofa. He stared at Pia for a moment, then turned his back on her. He dropped gracefully to the seat cushion, stepped onto Jo's lap, curled up and closed his eyes. As he lay there, he began to purr.

Pia found herself feeling snubbed, which hurt a whole lot more than she would have guessed.

"He never purred for me."

Jo had begun stroking the cat. Her hand froze. "Did you want to keep him?"

"No. I would say he hates me, but I don't think he put that much energy into it. I just never thought of myself as giving off the anti-cat vibration."

"You weren't raised with pets."

"I guess."

Apparently Crystal had made the right choice in leaving her cat with Jo. The only question was why her friend hadn't given Jo the cat from the start. No, she reminded herself. That wasn't the only question.

She felt a slight burning in her eyes. Before she could figure out what was going on, tears blurred her vision. She set down her drink and looked away.

"Pia?"

"It's nothing."

"You're crying."

Pia fought for control, then sniffed and wiped her cheeks. "Sorry. I don't mean to. I'm feeling all twisted inside."

"You really can have Jake back. I'm sorry to have upset you."

Jo sounded earnest and caring, which Pia appreciated. She

gulped in a breath. "It's not the cat. Okay, yes, part of it is he obviously thinks I'm an idiot. It's just…"

The embryos. She knew that's what it was. That if she couldn't get Crystal's cat to like her, what hope did she have with actual children? Every time she thought of giving birth to her friend's babies, she started to freak.

She was totally the wrong person. She had no experience, no support system, no nurturing abilities. She couldn't even bond with a cat.

But she wasn't ready to talk about that. Not until she'd made up her mind about what to do.

"I miss her," she said instead, mostly because it was true. "I miss Crystal."

"Me, too," Jo said, sliding toward her.

They hugged.

Pia gave in to her tears. Jo held on, patting her back, not saying anything—just being a friend. Oddly enough, Jake stayed where he was, as well. His warm body and the vibration of his purring offered their own kind of comfort.

Pia allowed the caring to heal her, just a little. But even as she started to feel better, somewhere deep inside, she heard the call of three yet-to-be-born children.

CHAPTER THREE

PIA STOOD ON THE SIDEWALK, trying to breathe. The sense of panic was becoming familiar, as was the blurring of the world around her. Determined not to faint, she drew in deep, slow breaths, supporting herself by putting a hand on the brick building.

Think about something else, she commanded herself. Cookies. Brownies. Ice cream.

Chocolate-chip brownie ice cream.

After a few seconds, her vision cleared and she no longer had the sense that she was going to collapse—or run screaming into the bright, warm afternoon. Everything was fine, she told herself. And if it wasn't, well, she would fake it until it was.

She straightened, determined to return to her normal professional self. She had a meeting and this time she was going to get through it without doing anything to embarrass herself. No one would know that she'd just—

"You okay?"

She looked up into Raoul's warm, dark eyes. He stood by an open side door she hadn't noticed. His expression was both wary and concerned, despite which he looked plenty handsome. Which was pretty rude of him, if you asked her. The least he could do was be forgettable. Especially when she was feeling vulnerable.

Slowly, she turned toward the glass windows next to her and held in a groan.

"You saw that?" she asked cautiously.

"The part where you clutched your chest, bent over and nearly passed out?"

Oh, God. Heat burned her cheeks. "Um, that would be it."

"Yeah, I saw it."

She wanted to close her eyes and disappear. But that would violate her mature mandate. Instead she squared her shoulders, sucked in a breath and curved her lips into what she hoped was a smile.

"Sorry. I was distracted."

He motioned for her to step into his office. "It seemed like more than that."

"It wasn't," she lied, firmly clutching her oversize handbag. "So, as you can see, I'm here and ready for our meeting. I have several ideas for linking the camp with existing festivals. Either with a booth, or as a sponsor. A nonpaying sponsor. We force our corporate friends to cough up the big bucks to get their names on a banner, but we're more forgiving with the nonprofits."

"Good to know."

His office was large, with plenty of windows. There were four desks and lots of open space. She glanced around at the blank walls, the few boxes pushed next to a copy machine and the lone visitor chair.

"I guess decorating isn't in the budget," she said.

"We're still settling. Currently, it's just Dakota and me. We had more people working in the summer, but they were mostly up at the camp. I wanted room to expand."

"Apparently. It's nice. I would have expected a few football posters on the wall."

"They're not unpacked yet."

"When you do get them out, they'll add plenty of color."

He motioned to a square folding table in the corner.

Once they were seated on the plain chairs, she withdrew a file folder from her bag and set it on the table. She was aware of him sitting close to her but was willing to pretend she wasn't. One crisis at a time, she told herself.

"In case you haven't heard," she began, "Fool's Gold is the festival capital of California. We have a major event every single month. By major I mean we draw in over five thousand people and we fill at least fifty percent of the hotel rooms. The result is a nice influx of cash for our city."

She paused. "Do you want this level of detail?"

"Sure. Information is never bad."

She thought about some of the very tedious city council meetings she'd sat through—especially the budget ones—and knew he was wrong. But she kept that thought to herself.

"Currently tourism is our largest source of income and employment. We're working to change that. In addition to the existing hospital, we'll soon have a new facility that will include a trauma center. We also have the university campus. Those three sectors provide a lot of employment, but in this town, service jobs rule. One of the long-term goals of the city is to bring in more high-paying manufacturing jobs, so we're not constantly exchanging the same tired dollar, week after week. But until that happens, the festivals bring us both jobs and money."

She opened the folder she'd brought. "In addition to the major festivals, we have smaller events that draw a regional crowd. No 'heads in beds,' as the chamber of commerce likes to say. As in no one spends the night. That's less money for the town, but also less work."

Raoul took the list of festivals and scanned them. She'd marked the ones that would get the most family interest.

"If we can come up with a good angle, say a famous football player headlines the right event, we can draw some media attention," she said. "I'm guessing we can get TV here based on your celebrity, but it would be nice if we could find a good tie-in and maybe get on one of the morning shows."

"Bringing money to the town and donations and sponsorship to the camp?" he asked.

"Exactly."

This was good. Focusing on work helped her stay calm. Because if she thought about that morning...

Without warning, the trembling began again. Her chest got tight and she had to consciously deepen her breathing.

Raoul glanced at her over the papers. "You okay?"

She nodded because speaking seemed iffy at best.

He dropped the sheets. "What's going on?"

"Could I have some water?" she managed.

He stood and crossed to a small refrigerator. After collecting a bottle, he returned to the table and handed it to her.

"Thanks."

"What's going on?" he asked again as he settled across from her. He took her free hand in his and lightly pressed his fingers to the inside of her wrist.

The contact was light, yet warm. She felt something. A little tingly sensation. Right. Because she had time for that now.

"Your pulse is way too fast," he announced. "You're upset about something."

The tingling disappeared. She snatched back her hand and opened the water.

"I'm fine. It's nothing."

He didn't look convinced. "Is it about the embryos?"

She closed her eyes and nodded. "I went to see them this morning."

"How?"

"I drove to the lab and asked if I could see them." She opened her eyes and sighed. "They said no."

"Did that surprise you?"

"A little. I knew they were small but I thought maybe I could peek at them through a microscope or something." She shifted in her seat, trying not to remember the incredulous look the lab guy had given her. As if she were an idiot.

"Apparently that's not possible without thawing them. And if they're thawed without being implanted, they die." She drew in a breath. "When I explained why I wanted to see them, he gave me a bunch of info on IVF."

"You told him about your friend?"

"Uh-huh. Then I read the material." She pressed a hand to her stomach, hoping to ward off another wave of nausea. "Apparently the body has to be prepared." She set the bottle on the table and used her fingers to indicate air quotes. "Which takes a whole lot more than a stern talking-to. An assortment of hormones are sent into my body. After that, there's the implantation procedure." She swallowed. "I won't get into detail."

"I appreciate that."

She managed a slight smile. "Then you wait. Or I wait. In two weeks, I take a pregnancy test. With luck, there are babies."

She felt the panic surging inside of her again. "I don't understand. Why would she trust me with her children? Do you know that Jake can purr? He gets all fluffy and relaxed and purrs."

"Jake's a cat?" Raoul asked cautiously.

"Yes. I've had him over two months. He never purred for me. He barely even looked at me. Then he goes to Jo's and purrs like his life depended on it. Which maybe to him it did."

She shook her head. "I don't get it. Crystal wanted those kids more than anything. After her husband was deployed to Iraq, she talked about getting pregnant when he got home. I went shopping with her and we looked at nursery furniture. She was so excited. After Keith died, she was still determined to be a mother. But that didn't happen. Now I'm supposed to raise her children? And the whole in vitro thing. It's not a hundred percent. Some or all of the embryos might not take. Which is a polite way of saying they'll die. What if that's my fault? What if there's something wrong with me? What if they're the same as Jake and they just plain don't like me enough to hang on?"

She could feel herself slipping past panic and into full-on terror. She glanced at Raoul to see if he'd completely freaked out, only to find him staring at her. Intense staring, she thought, feeling a little awkward and exposed.

"TMI?" she asked softly. "Too much information?"

"You said Keith and Crystal."

She nodded.

"Keith Westland?"

Now it was her turn to stare. "Yes. How did you know?"

He stood and walked the length of the office, then returned to stand in front of her. He was tall enough that it was uncomfortable to stare up at him. She stood.

"Raoul, what's going on?"

"I know him," he said flatly. "Knew him. Keith is a pretty common name, but he talked about his wife, Crystal. He talked about this town. That's why I came here in the first place. He's the reason I agreed to play in the celebrity golf tournament last year. I wanted to see where he'd grown up."

"Wait a minute. How could you know Keith? Crystal never said anything." Pia was reasonably confident that her friend would have mentioned being friends with someone like Raoul Moreno.

He looked out the window, as if he was remembering a long-ago event. "I was in Iraq. A few players go in the off-season. Just to hang with the troops. Help morale. That kind of thing. We were all assigned a soldier to keep us out of trouble. Keith was mine. We traveled all around the country, to the different bases. We bunked together, got shot at a few times. He saved my ass."

Raoul rubbed his hands over his face. "That last day, we were heading for the airport. It was a big convoy. The players, a few VIPs, some politicians. There was an ambush. IEDs in the road, a couple of snipers in the hills. Keith was shot." He shook his head. "I held him while he died. He couldn't talk, couldn't do anything but gasp for air. And then he was gone."

She sank back into her chair. "I'm sorry," she whispered. "I didn't know." Crystal hadn't known, either.

"Reinforcements came and they helped us get home. When I got the invitation to the golf tournament, I came here. I guess to pay my respects to a place Keith had loved. I liked it, so I stayed."

Pia hadn't thought there would be any more surprises, but she'd been wrong.

He crouched in front of her. "I wanted to talk to Crystal, but I didn't know what to say. I knew her husband all of two weeks and I was there when he died. Would that have comforted her?"

She felt his pain and lightly touched his shoulder. "The man she loved had died. I don't think there was any comfort to be had."

"I wondered if I'd taken the easy way out. I didn't want to intrude or get involved." He smiled faintly. "Now you're responsible for Keith and Crystal's babies."

"Don't remind me."

He returned to his chair and stared at her. "You okay?"

"Trying to recover from the latest bombshell." She winced. "Sorry. Bad word choice. Hearing that you knew Keith, that you were there when he died, feels oddly cosmic. Like the universe wants to make sure I have these babies."

"You're reading too much into it."

"Am I? Don't you think it's just a little strange that we're even having this conversation?"

"No. I moved to town because I met Keith. If he hadn't been assigned to me, I never would have agreed to do the golf tournament and I wouldn't be here, having this conversation with you."

He made sense, but Pia still felt as if she was being pushed into a decision she wasn't ready to make.

There was so much on the line. The three embryos meant she could have triplets. That was three babies. She had a tiny apartment. How could they all fit?

She grasped the water and held on as if the act of squeezing would prevent her from slipping over the edge. But after hearing about Raoul and Keith, even questioning the act of having the children seemed monumentally selfish.

"You don't have to decide today," he reminded her. "Or even this year."

"I suppose. When I start to freak, I tell myself that I'm focusing on the wrong thing. This isn't about me. It's about Crystal and Keith and their children. Who am I to question whether or not I should have their children? Doesn't that make me a bad person? Shouldn't I already be on the hormones, buying cribs and reading that *Expecting* book everyone says is so great? If I was a good person, I wouldn't be hesitating."

Raoul stared into Pia's hazel eyes, amazed by the kaleidoscope of emotions. She was possibly one of the most honest people he'd ever met. Crazy, but honest. Appealing, as well, but thinking she was hot wasn't exactly appropriate.

Slowly, he took the water from her hands and set it on the table. Then he pulled her to her feet and wrapped his arms around her.

"It's okay," he told her.

She stood rigid in his embrace. "No, it's not."

He continued to hold on, moving one hand up and down her spine, enjoying the feel of her body next to his. Not that he was going to do anything about it. "Take a deep breath. In and out. Come on. Breathe."

She did as he requested. A little of the tension eased out of her.

He couldn't begin to imagine what she was going through. He was thrown by the fact that he'd known Crystal's husband. For her, the connection was a thousand times more powerful.

Moving his hands to her shoulders, he stepped back far enough to see her face.

"You're not a bad person," he said firmly. "A bad person would walk away from the embryos without a second thought. As to taking your time to make the decision, why wouldn't you?

Having Crystal's babies will change everything about your life. You're allowed to have a plan."

"But she's my friend. I should…"

He shook his head. "No. Crystal didn't give you a head's up. This was dumped on you, Pia. Give yourself a break."

She drew in another breath. "Okay. Maybe."

Her eyes were large and filled with concern. Her mouth trembled. There was something vulnerable about her. Part of him wondered why Crystal *hadn't* warned Pia in advance. Had it been the other woman's advancing illness or something else? Had she not wanted to give Pia a choice?

Instead of finding an answer, he became aware of them standing very close together. He could feel the warmth of her body, the delicate bones under his fingers. She was tall but still had to look up to meet his gaze. Her curls brushed the backs of his hands. Her lips parted slightly, which made him want to lean in and—

He moved back with the speed that had gotten him signed by the Cowboys, then carefully tucked his hands into his jeans pockets.

Where the hell had that thought come from? Pia wasn't for kissing. No one here was. He planned to live in Fool's Gold for a long time. If he wanted entertainment, he would take it somewhere else. Not here. Besides, since Caro, he *hadn't* been interested. This was not the time for that to change.

Apparently Pia hadn't noticed. Instead of being hurt or annoyed, she gave him a smile.

"Thanks. You've been great. I'm sorry I keep freaking out on you."

"You're dealing with a lot," he said carefully.

"I know, but this is business. For what it's worth, I really am a calm, rational person. Professional even. You probably don't want to take my word for it, but you can ask around."

He forced a chuckle. "Don't worry about it."

"I will, because I believe in worrying early and often. I'd

promise to let you speak to my assistant next time, only I don't have one. And with the fire and all, the town can't afford to pay for one."

"I can talk to you, Pia."

"At least I didn't faint this time."

"Improvement."

She sighed. "You're nice, aren't you? I don't trust nice men." She winced, then held up a hand. "Don't take that wrong."

"There's a right way?"

"I'm just saying…" She shook her head, then grabbed her bag. "I'll leave you with the paperwork. We can talk about the festivals and your camp later, if that's okay. I really need to gather the tattered remains of my dignity and move on. Next time we meet, I swear I'll be totally calm and rational. You'll barely recognize me."

He didn't want her to go. For reasons he couldn't explain, he wanted to pull her close again and tell her—

What? What was he going to say? He barely knew her. She had other things to deal with. The meeting didn't matter.

But the problem wasn't the meeting, and Raoul knew that. There was something about Pia. About how she got right to the heart of the problem. She was an intriguing combination of determined, vulnerable and impulsive. If she wasn't careful, life would beat the crap out of her. Only the strong survived, and even they had to take a hit now and again.

Not his problem, he reminded himself. Nor did he want it to be.

"I'll recognize you," he told her. "You're making too much of this."

"So speaks a man who likely has never been hysterical even once in his entire life." She met his eyes. "Thanks for being so…nice."

"Even though it makes you not trust me?"

She winced. "I'm going to regret saying that forever."

"No. I'm sure you'll have other, bigger regrets that fill your mind."

"Ouch. That's not very encouraging."

"We all have regrets. Things we want to change or undo. Nothing about today is worth a second of your worry."

She hesitated. "I thought you'd be different. Cynical. Self-absorbed. You know—a sports star."

"You should have met me ten years ago."

Her mouth curved into a smile. "Wild and impetuous?"

"A typical college jock. My high school girlfriend dumped me my freshman year. I spent a few months feeling sorry for myself, healed and returned to my sophomore year only to discover I was a god."

"Did you perform miracles?"

"I thought I could."

"I'm glad to know you went through a bad-boy period."

"Mine lasted several years."

Right through his signing with the Cowboys and beyond. He'd been on the team just over a year when Eric Hawkins— otherwise known as Hawk—had burst into his hotel room, waking Raoul and the twins he'd been sleeping with.

Hawk had been his high school football coach and mentor. He'd ushered the girls out of the room, nearly drowned Raoul in coffee, then had taken him to the gym for a workout that had no pity on Raoul's impressive hangover.

But that hadn't been the worst of it. The really bad part had been the disappointment in Hawk's eyes. The silence that said he'd expected better.

"What changed you?" she asked.

"Someone I care about had expectations and I let him down."

"Your dad?"

"Better than my dad. It's impossible to have nothing to lose when someone loves you."

She blinked. "That was profound."

"Don't tell anyone."

"You saw the light and let go of your bad-boy ways?"

"Pretty much."

After the workout, Hawk had taken Raoul to the poor side of Dallas, driving past people living out of shopping carts.

"Get over yourself," was all his former coach had said.

Raoul had gone home feeling like the biggest jerk in the world. The next day he'd moved out of the hotel, bought a house in a normal neighborhood and had started volunteering.

Two years later he'd met Caro at a charity ball, which had proved life wasn't perfect.

"So you believe people can change," she said.

"Don't you?"

"I'm not sure. Does the meanness go away or does it just get covered up?"

"Who was mean to you?"

She sighed. "And here I was supposed to gather up my tattered dignity and just go. You've been great. I'll be in touch, Raoul. Thanks for everything."

She walked out of the office.

Not sure if he should go after her, he hesitated. Then Dakota stepped in from the back and stared at him.

"Did I hear that right?"

Raoul shifted uneasily. "It depends on what you heard."

"You knew Keith Westland?"

He nodded.

She crossed toward him and sank onto the chair Pia had used. "I won't say anything, of course. About you knowing him or the babies. This is a lot to take in. Talk about responsibility. I guess I knew that Crystal would have to leave her embryos to someone, but I never really thought about it. Did Pia know before?"

He remembered his first meeting with her. "I don't think so. She thought she was getting the cat."

"Right. She was taking care of Crystal's cat." Dakota looked stunned. "What's with Crystal not warning her? You can't just leave someone potential children and not even give them a hint.

Or maybe she knew Pia would freak and didn't want to be talked out of it." Dakota glanced at him. "Is she okay?"

"She's dealing. She's surprised Crystal picked her."

"Really? I'm not. Pia might not be the obvious choice, but she makes sense. She would do the right thing." Dakota laughed. "After some serious kicking and screaming. Wow—Pia's going to have Crystal's babies."

"She hasn't decided that yet."

Dakota glanced at him. "Do you really think she'll walk away from those babies?"

He shook his head. He couldn't see it, but then he'd been wrong before.

He took the chair behind the desk. "You and Crystal and Pia all grew up in town together?"

"Oh, yeah. Crystal was a few years older, but she was one of those really nice people who wanted to take care of the world. She worked at the library after school. She was always there to help with school projects." Dakota wrinkled her nose. "I can't believe I'm old enough to remember when there wasn't an Internet."

"You're twenty-seven."

"Practically ancient." She laughed. "Pia was a grade ahead of me and my sisters, but we knew her. Or at least of her." Her eyes brightened with humor. "Pia was one of the popular girls. Pretty, great clothes. She had the boyfriends everyone else wanted."

The humor faded. "Then her dad died and her mom went away. Everything changed for her. Back in high school I would have sworn Pia was taking off for New York or L.A. Instead she stayed here."

Which meant something had happened to her.

"I guess it's where she belongs," Dakota murmured.

"You came back, as well," he said. "There must be something about this place."

"You're right." She laughed. "Be careful, Raoul. If you stay too long, you'll never escape."

"I'll keep that in mind."

But the truth was, he wanted a place to call home. Somewhere that felt right.

There had been a time when he'd wanted it all—a wife and a family. Now he was less sure. Back when he'd married her, he would have sworn he knew everything about Caro. That nothing she did would ever surprise him.

He'd been wrong, and in finding out the truth about what she'd done, a part of him had been destroyed. Pia had asked if he thought people could change. He did, because he'd seen it over and over again. But broken trust was different. Even if it was repaired, it was never the same again. There would always be cracks.

CHAPTER FOUR

ONE OF THE perks of her job was that although Pia was a part of city government, she didn't have to participate in any of the really boring stuff. Sure, once a year she had to present a budget, and she was accountable for every penny. But that was easily done on a good spreadsheet program. When it came to the city council meetings, she was strictly a visitor, not a regular.

So when the mayor called Pia and asked her to attend an emergency session, she found herself feeling a little nervous as she took her seat at the long conference table.

"What's up?" she asked Charity, the city planner. "Marsha sounded less than calm, which is unusual for her."

"I'm not sure," Charity admitted. "I know she wanted to talk about the school fire."

Which made sense, but why would Pia have to be there for that?

"How are you feeling?" she asked her friend.

Charity was about four months along. "Great. A little puffy, although no one seems to notice but me." She grinned. "Or they're lying. I'm good with either option."

Charity had moved to town in early spring. In a matter of a few weeks, she'd fallen for professional cyclist Josh Golden, gotten pregnant and discovered she was the mayor's long-lost granddaughter.

Josh and Charity had slipped away for a quiet wedding and were now awaiting the birth of their first child. Marsha was thrilled at the thought of a great-grandchild.

Just another day in Fool's Gold, Pia thought cheerfully. There was always something going on.

Pia glanced around at the other women at the meeting. There were the usual suspects, along with a few surprises including Police Chief Alice Barns. Why would the police chief need to attend a city council meeting? Nancy East sat close to the front. No doubt the superintendent of schools would have information they all needed.

Before Pia could ask Charity, Marsha hurried in and took her seat at the head of the table.

The mayor was as well-dressed as always. She favored tailored suits and wore her white hair pulled back in a tidy bun.

"Sorry I'm late," Marsha said. "I was on the phone. Thank you all for coming on such short notice."

There was a murmur of people saying it was fine.

"We have a preliminary report on the fire," Marsha said, glancing down at the pages she held. "Apparently it began in the furnace. Because of the unusually cool few days we had earlier in the week, it was turned on before it was serviced. The fire spread quickly, as did the smoke."

"I heard that no one was hurt," Gladys said. The older woman had served as the city manager for several years and was currently acting as treasurer.

"That's true. We had a few minor injuries, but everyone was treated on the scene and released." Marsha looked at them, her blue eyes dark with concern. "We're still assessing the damage, but we're talking millions of dollars. We do have insurance and that will help, but it won't cover everything."

"You mean the deductible?" one of the council members asked.

"There's that, which is sizable enough. But there are other considerations. Books, lesson plans, computers, supplies. As I said, some will be covered, but not everything. The state will offer assistance, but that takes time. Which leads me into the next topic. Where to put all those children? I refuse to let this fire disrupt their education. Nancy?"

Nancy East, a bright, plump woman in her late thirties, opened a notebook in front of her.

"I agree with Marsha—keeping the children in school is our first priority. We considered splitting them up among the other three elementary schools, but there simply isn't enough room. Even with portable classrooms, the infrastructure can't support that many additions. There isn't enough space in the cafeteria or on the playground. There aren't enough bathrooms."

Some of the tension in her face eased. "Fortunately, we have a solution. Raoul Moreno has offered his camp. I toured the facility yesterday, and it's going to work beautifully for us."

Pia leaned back in her chair. The camp was an obvious choice, she thought. It was big and had plenty of buildings. It was closed in the winter, so they wouldn't be displacing anyone.

"There are some logistics for our classes," Nancy continued. "Our maintenance staff is up there right now, figuring out the best configurations. There is a main building where we'll have assemblies and where the cafeteria will be. Calls have gone out to schools all around the state for extra supplies, including desks, blackboards, dry-erase boards, buses. We're making an appeal to the commercial suppliers. As Marsha mentioned, the state will be offering some assistance."

She turned to Pia. "I need your help, Pia."

"Sure. What can I do?"

"I want to mount a supply drive for this Saturday. We'll hold it in the park. We need everything from pencils to toilet paper. Our goal is to have the children back in school by Monday."

Pia remained calm on the outside, but inside there was a very loud shrieky voice. "It's Wednesday."

"I know. That's the challenge. Can you pull something together by Saturday?"

The clear answer was no, but Pia swallowed that. She had a phone tree that rivaled anything created by the government and access to an impressive list of volunteers.

"I can get the word out tonight," she said. "Beg mention in tomorrow's paper, along with Friday's. Do media Friday and get it set up by, say, nine Saturday morning." Even thinking about it was enough to make her woozy. "I need a list of what you need."

Nancy had come prepared. She passed a folder to Pia. "If people would rather give money, we won't say no."

"Who would?"

Pia flipped open the folder and stared at the neatly typed sheets. The list was detailed and, as Nancy had promised, listed every possible need, from chalk to china. Well, not china, exactly, but dishes for the camp.

"I thought the camp already had a working kitchen," she said. "Why would they need plates, glasses and utensils?"

"End Zone for Kids housed less than a hundred campers, even with the day campers," Marsha told her. "We're sending up close to three hundred."

"That's a lot of napkins," Charity murmured. "I'll stay after the meeting and you can tell me what I can do to help."

"Thanks."

It wasn't the size of the project that worried Pia, but the speed. She would need a full-page ad in the local paper. Colleen, her contact at the *Fool's Gold Daily Republic,* wasn't going to be happy.

"I need to make a call," she said, then excused herself.

Once she was in the hall, she pulled out her cell phone and dialed.

"Hi, it's Pia," she said.

Colleen was a woman of a certain age—only no one knew exactly what age that was. She was a hard-drinking, chain-smoking newspaper woman who didn't believe in chitchat and had never met an adjective she didn't want eliminated.

"What do you want?" Colleen snapped.

Pia sucked in a breath. Talking fast was essential. "A full page tomorrow and Friday. Saturday we're going to be collecting donations for the school that burned down. For a new school and supplies."

Damn. Talking to Colleen always made her nervous. The worst part was the other woman didn't have to say anything to get Pia feeling frantic.

"The kids will be going up to the camp while the burned-out school is repaired. They'll need everything from books to pencils to toilet paper. I have a list. Money donations are fine, too."

"Of course they are. Anything else? How about a kidney? I was told I have two. You want I should cut that out and send it along?"

Pia leaned against the wall. "It's for the children."

"I'm not competing in any beauty pageant. I don't have to give a fig about kids or world peace."

There was a long pause. Pia heard the other woman exhaling smoke.

"Get me the material in fifteen minutes and I'll do it. Otherwise, forget it."

"Thanks, Colleen," Pia said, already running for the fax machine on the second floor.

She made the deadline with eighteen seconds to spare. When the copy and the list of needed supplies had gone through the fax machine, Pia returned to the meeting only to find out they hadn't actually been as busy as she had.

"Charity, is there any chance you've *seen* Raoul's butt?" Gladys asked hopefully. "Could you get a comparison?"

Pia sank into her seat. "Yes, Charity. You should ask Raoul for a private showing, and I'd like to be in the room when you do."

Charity rolled her eyes. "I haven't seen his butt, I'm not going to ask to see it. As far as I'm concerned, Josh is perfection, and that can't be improved upon."

"You're his wife," Gladys grumbled. "You have to say that."

Marsha rose from her chair. "Debating which of our two celebrity athletes is more attractive can be a thrilling way to pass an hour. However, we still have things to discuss. Pia, you got the ad?"

"Yes. Colleen will run the time, the list and all the contact information tomorrow and Friday. I'll get the phone tree up and running tonight. We'll set up tables for those who want to host a bake sale or whatever. The usual stuff."

Marsha passed her a paper. "Here are the local businesses that will be providing drinks and snacks. I told them not to deliver before eight on Saturday." She glanced around the table. "I would be grateful if those of you with a close and personal relationship with God spoke to Him about the weather. Warm and sunny on Saturday would be best."

Gladys looked shocked at the request, but everyone else laughed.

Marsha sat back in her seat. "There's one other item I need to discuss. I was hoping it wouldn't be an issue, but no such luck. I realize that when compared with the unexpected fire that destroyed the school, this will seem small and unimportant. However, it is going to impact our town and we have to be prepared."

Pia glanced at Charity, who shrugged. Apparently Marsha hadn't talked to her granddaughter about the mystery element.

"A few of you may remember Tiffany Hatcher," Marsha said. "She was a graduate student who came to Fool's Gold in the spring. Her field of study is human geography. As in why people settle where they do, why they move, etc."

Pia vaguely remembered a petite, pretty young woman who had been very interested in Josh. As he'd only had eyes for Charity, nothing had come of her flirting.

"I tried to delicately discourage her from writing about the town, but I wasn't successful," Marsha continued. "Her thesis is being published. She called to let me know there is a chapter on Fool's Gold. Specifically about the ongoing shortage of men. She has sent out excerpts of the chapter to many media outlets and there has been, as she so happily put it, interest."

"No," Chief Barns said forcefully. "I'm not going to have a bunch of media types mucking up my town and parking where they're not supposed to. Isn't there enough real news in the world without them paying attention to us?"

Pia's thoughts exactly. But she had a bad feeling that a town with a man shortage would be exactly the right kind of story to capture a lot of attention.

"I don't suppose telling the media we don't want them here will help," Charity said.

"If only," Marsha told her. "I'm afraid in the next few weeks we're going to have to deal with the problem. And not just the media, either."

Pia stared at her boss. The mayor nodded slowly.

"When word gets out, we'll be flooded with men looking for a town full of lonely women."

"That could be fun," Gladys said, looking intrigued. "A few of you need a good marrying."

Pia suspected Gladys meant her, so she was careful to stay quiet. With less than three days to pull together a massive event, getting married or even meeting men was the last thing on her mind. And even if she wasn't so busy, considering the whole embryo issue, getting involved wasn't just unlikely, it was impossible.

SATURDAY MORNING DAWNED perfectly clear. The temperatures were supposed to be in the low seventies. Apparently God had come through, Pia thought as she arrived at the park a little after seven to find work under way.

The city maintenance crew was already setting up the long tables and collection bins. Several signs had been donated by a printer, and ones that had been made by hand were sorted and in place. Pia had drawn up a floor plan of sorts, showing what would be collected where.

Her miracle phone tree had worked perfectly, and she'd heard back from over fifty people with promises of books, supplies and even cash. Liz Sutton, a Fool's Gold native and a successful author who had recently returned to settle in town, had quietly promised five thousand children's books to start the library. When Pia had offered to shout about the donation from every rooftop in town, Liz had insisted on being anonymous.

She wasn't the only one giving big. Local hero Josh Golden had already handed in a check for thirty thousand dollars, again with instructions to keep quiet about him giving it. A cashier's check for ten grand had arrived in her office the previous morning. Just a plain envelope slipped under the door. No return address and drawn on a busy Sacramento bank, so there was no way of tracing it.

Pia had turned the money over to Nancy, along with a list of what else she knew was being donated.

Now as she sipped her coffee, she went over the events that would happen during the day. The city yard sale would begin at eight. Donations had been delivered the day before, and her volunteers were already sorting through the bounty. To keep things simple, the items would be grouped according to price, at one-, three-, five-and ten-dollar tables.

The bake sale would start at noon, giving the last-minute bakers time to get their goodies finished. The auction was at three, and Pia was still waiting on the list of what would be offered.

Throughout the day, local bands would play, the hospital was offering a mini-clinic for blood pressure checks and the high school senior class was holding a car wash. Pia was less sure about their "Naked for a Cause" theme—even though the class president had sworn that meant bathing suits, not actual nudity, but at this point, she was willing to take every dollar they raised.

By seven-thirty there was a steady stream of volunteers showing up. They checked the master directory Pia had posted and went to their assigned areas. Charity arrived fifteen minutes later, looking pale.

"Sorry I'm late," she said, tucking her hair behind her ears. "I don't get sick in the morning much, but today was one of those days. The good news is the guys did a very nice job installing the floor tile."

Pia winced. "You got a close look at it?"

"For nearly an hour. My knees hurt." She pressed a hand to her midsection. "Not to mention other parts of me." She handed Pia a folder. "The final auction info."

"Thanks for doing this."

"I'm happy to help. There are some great prizes." Charity paused. "Is it a prize if you have to buy it?"

"I'm not sure."

Pia flipped through the list. There were the usual gift cards from local restaurants and shops. She would bundle those into a couple of baskets, so the value was greater. That should up the bidding price. Ethan Hendrix had offered five thousand dollars' worth of remodeling. There were weekends in Tahoe and up at the ski resort, ski lessons, and a weekend in Dallas compliments of Raoul Moreno. His package included airfare, two nights at Rosewood Mansion on Turtle Creek, dinner at the hotel and two tickets to a Dallas Cowboys home game...on the fifty-yard line.

"There's some money in that prize," Pia said, impressed by Raoul's generosity.

"I know. My eyes nearly bugged out," Charity said. "The guy's already donating his camp. That's more than enough."

"He's nice," Pia said absently. "He can't help it."

Charity laughed. "You say that like it's a bad thing."

"It can be." Although Raoul had claimed to have a dark past. Something that should have bothered her but instead made him seem more human.

"He's very good-looking," Charity told her.

Pia looked at her friend. "Don't even go there."

"I'm just saying he's here, he's handsome, successful, rich. I don't think he's dating anyone. He and his ex divorced a couple of years ago."

Pia raised her eyebrows. "You've been checking up on him?"

"Oh, please. I'm with Josh."

As if that explained everything. Which it probably did, Pia thought with only a hint of envy. It wasn't that she'd ever had a thing for Josh, it was more the way he looked at Charity that made Pia feel a little lost and sad. Josh didn't just adore his wife, he worshipped her. It was as if he'd been waiting his whole life to find her and now that he had, he was never letting her go.

Not that Pia would trust that kind of adoration, but it was nice to think about.

"I'm not interested," she said firmly.

"How do you know? Have you spent any time with him?"

Pia wasn't ready to talk about the embryos, but the truth was getting pregnant with them would change everything. Very few men would be interested in raising someone else's kids. Especially triplets. The thought was beyond daunting. And even if there was a guy like that out there, she knew Raoul wasn't him.

"We've spoken," Pia said. "Like I said—he's nice enough. Just not for me."

She eyed her friend's belly. Charity was barely showing, but she knew a whole lot more about being pregnant than Pia. But asking anything, as in finding out what it really felt like, meant answering a lot of questions. Pia wasn't ready for that.

The clock from The Church of the Open Door chimed the hour. Pia glanced at her watch and winced.

"I need to run," she said. "I have fifteen places I need to be."

"Go," Charity told her. "I'll handle the auction. Don't even think about it."

"I won't," Pia told her. "Fool's Gold owes you."

BY ELEVEN IT was apparent the town had come through to support the school. The items brought in for the yard sale had been snapped up, with most people insisting on paying two or three times the posted price. The donation bins were overflowing, as were the tables, and people just kept on coming.

Pia went from area to area, checking on her volunteers, only to discover she wasn't needed. The event ran so smoothly, she started to get nervous.

Over by the mini food court, she bought a hot dog and a soda, telling the kid manning the cart to keep the change.

"Everyone's doing that," he said with a grin, stuffing the extra bills into a large coffee can nearly overflowing. "We've had to empty this twice already."

"Good news," she said, strolling over to one of the benches and taking a seat.

She was exhausted, but in a good way. Right now, in the middle of a sunny day, surrounded by her fellow citizens, she felt good. As if everything was going to be all right. Sure, the school had nearly burned down, but the town had pulled together and order had been restored. Order had always felt really good to her.

Three boys came running down the path. The one in back, a slight redheaded boy, plopped down next to her and grinned.

"There's free lemonade over there," he said, pointing across the park.

"Let me guess. You've already had a couple of glasses."

"How'd you know?"

"I can see the happy glow of sugar in your eyes. I'm Pia."

"I'm Peter." He wrinkled his nose. "I go to the school that burned down. Everybody's doing all this so we can get back to class."

She held in a smile. "Not your idea of a good time?"

"I like school, I guess."

Peter looked to be about nine or ten, with freckles and big brown eyes. He was skinny but had a wide smile that made her want to grin in return.

"What would you rather do than go to school?" she asked.

A shadow crossed his face then cleared. "I like to play baseball. I used to play T-ball when I was little."

"Are you in Little League now?"

He shook his head. "My foster dad says it's too expensive and takes too much time."

That didn't sound good. "Do you like other sports?"

"I like to watch football. They have those funny things they do with their hands. I try to watch what they're doing, but it's hard to see."

"You know they make those up," she told him. "There's not just one right way."

His eyes widened. "For real?"

"Uh-huh. Come on." She put her soda on the ground and tossed her hot dog foil and napkin in the trash, then she faced Peter. "We'll make one up now. I'll do a step, then you do a step."

She made a fist with her right hand. He did the same. They bumped top and bottom, then fist to fist, followed by an open-palm slap and a back-of-hand bump. He added two finger wiggles, and she ended with a double clap.

"All right!" Peter stood in front of her. "Let's do it really fast."

They went through the sequence twice, without a mistake.

"You're good," Pia told him.

"You, too." He glanced down the path and saw his friends. "I gotta go."

"Okay. Have fun. Don't drink too much more lemonade."

He laughed and took off at a run.

Pia collected her drink and stood. It was time to get back to work. As she grabbed her paperwork, she saw Jo crossing the lawn, headed for the auction postings.

Her first thought was to chase after her friend and ask about Jake. Did he seem to miss her? Was he settling in? Then she remembered how the cat had crawled onto Jo's lap and started purring within ten minutes of arriving at her house. Of course he was doing well.

She turned and ran into someone tall, broad and strong. Jostled soda spilled out of the paper cup and trickled down the front of the man's shirt.

Pia groaned and raised her eyes only to encounter Raoul's amused gaze.

"Small-town initiation?" he asked.

"Sorry." She stepped back and brushed his chest, which proved to be more enjoyable than she would have expected. "It's diet. It won't stain or anything."

"I'm fine." He took her hand in his and stilled the movement but didn't release her fingers. "Are you all right?"

"I'm fine. You're the one who got doused."

His touch was light, barely noticeable, yet she couldn't seem to focus on anything else. His skin was warm. She could feel individual calluses, the power he kept contained.

The power he kept contained? What was this—a bad movie script? Who thought like that?

Apparently her, she realized as she looked back into his eyes and discovered she didn't want to turn away. Which made her immediately pull free of his hold.

"So, thanks for your donation. It's very impressive. You really did enough with donating the camp."

"It wasn't a big deal," he said easily. "I was happy to help."

"Good. We should all help, especially now. With the whole burned-down-school thing."

His dark eyebrows pulled together. "Are you sure you're okuy?"

"Yes, of course. Why wouldn't I be?"

No way she was going to mention that the feel of his skin on hers had thrown her. Not only was it irrational, a declaration like that put her into the scary-stalker category.

She searched around for another explanation.

"I saw Jo," she said quickly. "The friend who took the cat?" He nodded.

"I wanted to ask if Jake missed me, which is dumb, right?

He obviously adores her. I was just a way station in the feline road of life. She's a destination. I just..."

"What?"

"I keep thinking if I can't make a cat happy, what chance do I have with kids?"

His expression sharpened. "You're going to have them?"

"Yes. No. I'm not sure." She sighed. "Maybe. I know that's what Crystal wanted. And no matter how many times I tell myself they're not my responsibility, I feel they are. I'm female. I'm going to go out on a limb and assume I have all the working equipment."

She could do more than assume, she reminded herself. She knew for sure.

Don't go there, she told herself. Not today. Not now. Wasn't there enough going on without a side trip to Guilt Land?

"You'll have someone else's children and then raise them?" he asked.

"It's not like I'm going to have them and give them away."

"Why not?"

She stared at him. "Excuse me?"

"Why wouldn't you give them away? There are hundreds of couples who are longing for children of their own. Infants are easy to place, aren't they? You could handpick the couple yourself, be sure the babies are going to be well taken care of."

That had never occurred to her. Give Crystal and Keith's babies away? Despite the warm afternoon, a shiver raced through her.

"No," she said firmly. "If that was what she wanted, she would have mentioned it in the will. Crystal took the trouble to pay for three years of storage. She wanted to give me time."

"She didn't warn you about what she was going to do."

"I know and that confuses me, but it doesn't change reality. If I have the babies, I'll keep them. And raise them." No matter how the thought of it made her stomach flip over and over.

He stared into her eyes as if searching for something. "I don't know many women who would be willing to take that on."

"Really? Because I don't know many who would refuse."

"You can't believe that."

She thought about her friends—how they looked out for each other. "I'm fairly sure."

"As sure as Crystal was of you? You're the one she picked."

"Which raises the question why," she said with a laugh that was almost real. "Okay—enough personal stuff for today. I have to compulsively check on things, and you need to stand in the sun so your shirt can dry."

She took off before he could do something really dangerous, like put his arm around her. That would probably get her to babbling like a starstruck fan.

It was the strangest thing. Usually people made her nervous when she first met them. Over time, the feeling went away. With Raoul, it was the complete opposite. She was more tense every time she saw him. At this rate, in a month, just seeing him would send her into catatonic shock. And wouldn't that give Fool's Gold something to talk about?

RAOUL STOOD BY the main building and watched the kids arrive for their first day of school at his camp. The parking lot was organized chaos as teachers sorted the children into classes.

In less time than he would have thought possible, the camp had been transformed. There were desks and chairs, playground equipment, books, papers and people prepping lunch.

Dakota joined him, a clipboard in hand.

"This is great," she said. "Like the first day of school, only better."

"The kids would have probably enjoyed more time off."

She laughed. "You're right, but education is important." She glanced at him out of the corner of her eye. "Everyone thinks you're amazing for giving the town this place. Such a nice guy."

"There are worse things to be."

She looked surprised. "Most guys don't want to be nice. It keeps them from getting the girl."

He'd never had much trouble getting the girl. "A nice guy changed my life. Being like him would make me a happy man."

Hawk wasn't a pushover. He was a tough guy who did the right thing. Raoul doubted his old friend would have been fooled by Caro. The irony was Raoul had done his best to make sure he *was* choosing the right person. But he'd still managed to screw up.

"I need to check with a couple of teachers," Dakota said and excused herself.

Three more cars pulled up and parked. Pia climbed out of one and waved in his direction.

She wore a dark skirt and boots. Her sweater was the color of her eyes. Not only did he notice, he found himself wanting to walk toward her. Meet her halfway. That image morphed into his mouth on hers, hands everywhere and a whole lot less clothing.

Not a good idea, he reminded himself. Pia was headed in a whole different direction. Besides, he had rules about small towns and the female residents. Pia might tempt him, but making her an exception would be a disaster...for both of them.

"Isn't this the best?" she asked as she approached. "There was actual traffic coming up the mountain. I love it when a plan comes together."

A bus pulled up. When the door opened, kids spilled out. One boy, skinny with bright red hair, ran over to Pia.

Raoul recognized him as the kid who had flinched when he'd tried to help the boy out of the smoky classroom. As he watched, Pia and the kid greeted each other with a complicated handshake.

"You remembered!" the boy crowed. "I know you would."

"It's our thing," Pia told him with a laugh. "You'd better get to class. Have fun."

"I will."

He turned and ran off.

"You know him?" Raoul asked.

"Peter?" Pia shook her head. "We met Saturday at the park. He was there with his friends. Why?"

He thought about the smoke-filled classroom. Maybe Peter had been scared of the fire instead of him. Maybe he'd imagined the whole thing.

Even as his gut told him he hadn't, he knew he wasn't going to say anything. Not until he had more information.

"I think he was in the class where I was speaking," he said. "When the fire started."

"Oh. Maybe. He's the right age." She shifted her handbag onto her other shoulder. "What's your calendar like over the next couple of days? Technically I still owe you a meeting."

"How about today?"

"What time?"

"Noon. We'll have lunch."

She hesitated. "You don't have to buy me lunch."

He raised an eyebrow. "I was going to let you pay."

She laughed. "Oh, well, in that case, sure. We'll go to the Fox and Hound. They make a mean salad, and you look like a guy who enjoys lettuce."

"I might surprise you."

Something flickered in her eyes. As quickly as it appeared, it faded. She nodded.

"You might at that."

CHAPTER FIVE

PIA LOOKED AT THE handsome man sitting across from her in the restaurant and told herself to focus on business. She was here in a purely professional capacity—not to enjoy the view. Though Raoul was pretty enough to dazzle anyone.

They'd already placed their orders and their drinks had been delivered. Pia had chosen diet soda, with the passing thought that if she went ahead with the pregnancy, she could kiss her artificial-sweetener habit goodbye, at least for nine months.

"You grew up in Seattle, right?" she asked, thinking a little chitchat was in order. She was allowed to be friendly.

"Until college," he told her.

"I've never been, but I'm guessing it's nothing like Fool's Gold."

"It's a lot bigger and there's a lot more rain. Seattle has mountains, only they're not as close."

"Why didn't you move back there?"

He flashed her a grin that made her pulse do a little cheer. "Too much rain for me. It's gray a lot. I like to see the sun." He picked up his iced tea.

"Is that why you abandoned them during college? You could have gone to the University of Washington."

"The other offers were better and Coach thought I should

get out of the state and see the rest of the country. Except for him and his wife, and my girlfriend, I didn't have all that much I was leaving behind."

"What about your family?"

He shook his head. "I never knew my dad. One of my brothers died when I was a kid. He was shot. My mom—" He shrugged. "I spent a lot of years in foster care."

There was something about the way he said the words. Bad things had happened, and she wasn't sure she wanted to know what. "I spent a year in the system," she admitted. "Here."

"You?"

"My senior year of high school. My dad died and my mom left to live with her sister in Florida. She said it would be better for me to stay here so I could graduate with my friends, but the truth was she didn't want to be bothered." Pia frowned. "I haven't seen her since. She didn't come back for my graduation and she made it clear I wasn't welcome there. So I stayed. Went to community college for a couple of years before transferring to a four-year university. Got a job with the city when I came back."

She forced a smile. "They tried to offer me a football scholarship, but those uniforms don't really suit me."

"This is your home," he said, his dark eyes serious. "Where you belong."

"You're right. Every couple of years I think I should go somewhere else. L.A. or San Francisco. Phoenix, even. But I won't leave. Which probably seems pretty boring to you."

"No. It's what I want, too. I thought I'd settle in Dallas. The fans are great and I enjoyed the city. I came here because of what Keith had said about his hometown. He made it sound like something out of a movie. When I got here for the golf tournament, I found out he'd been right. I liked everything about Fool's Gold. So I came back and then I decided to move here."

She wondered if he was running to something or from something. Not exactly a casual question.

"So this is your first small town," she said. "Then you need to know the rules."

"Didn't I get them in my welcome packet?" The corner of his mouth twitched as he spoke.

She did her best not to smile in return. "No. But they're very important. You mess up even a little and your life will be hell."

He leaned toward her. "What are the rules?"

"There are the expected things—keep the living room and kitchen picked up. You never know when you're going to have company. Don't mess with a married woman." She paused. "Or man, depending on your preferences."

"Thanks for the news flash."

"Don't favor any one business over another. Spread the wealth. For example, the best places for hair are owned by two sisters. Bella and Julia Gionni. But you can't go to just one. Trust me. Just alternate. When you're at Bella's, she'll trash Julia and vice versa. It's kind of like dinner theater, with highlights."

He looked more wary than amused. "Maybe I should go out of town for my haircuts."

"Coward."

"I know my limitations."

"You're the one who bought the camp here. Now you're stuck."

His face was handsome, in a rugged man's man sort of way. She liked the stubborn set of his jaw and the way his dark hair fell across his forehead.

"Can I get those rules in writing?" he asked.

"I'll see what I can do."

Their server arrived with their meals. Pia had chosen the barbecue chicken salad, while Raoul had picked a burger.

"How did you find the camp?" Pia asked, reaching for her fork. "I've lived here all my life and I barely remember knowing about it."

"I went for a drive," he told her. "I followed some old signs and found it. I'd had this idea about doing something with kids, but I wasn't sure what. When I saw the camp, I knew it was what I'd been looking for."

He held his burger but didn't take a bite. "The summer program is where we're starting, but I'm hoping we can do more. Be year-round. Bring kids in for intensive two-and three-week sessions where we focus on one or two subjects. Mostly science and math. Not enough kids are excited about those subjects."

"You'd have to coordinate with school districts," she said. "To complement their current curriculum."

"That's what Dakota's working on. We're thinking middle-school-aged kids. Get them excited before high school."

He had plenty of passion about the subject, she thought, taking a bite of her salad. What was he like when he was with a woman? Was the same passion there?

An interesting topic, she thought, but not one she would pursue. Even without the potential pregnancy in her future, she knew better than to get involved with a high-powered guy like him. Or any guy. For some reason, men made it a habit of leaving her. If they hadn't wanted to stick around before, what luck would she have getting them to stay when she had three kids?

Three kids? Her head started to swim. She forced herself to think about something less frightening.

"Having the school use the facility is an interesting way to work out any problems," she said. "And here everyone thought you were just being nice."

He chuckled. "It's a win-win for everyone."

"Even if it wasn't, the camp is a great idea. I know a lot of the kids in town appreciated being able to head up there every day this past summer. Or should I say their moms appreciated it. Summer can be a very long three months."

PIA'S HAZEL EYES danced with amusement. Raoul found himself watching her rather than eating. He liked her, which was a good start. He wanted to get to know her better, yet even if he ignored the foolishness of getting involved so close to home, there was the issue of the embryos.

"Why did you want to work with kids?" she asked. "Because of the coach who helped you?"

"How'd you know?"

"The way you talk about him."

"Yeah, it was him. He saw something in me I couldn't see in myself. His wife, too, although they weren't married at the time." He smiled at the memory. "My senior year of high school I was one of the football captains."

"Of course you were," she muttered.

"What?"

"Nothing. Go on."

"Each captain was supposed to bring doughnuts to practice. Once we started two-a-days, I had to quit my summer job. I was living in an abandoned building and didn't have any money."

"Time-out. You were homeless?"

"It wasn't so bad." It had been a whole lot better than dealing with his foster father. The man had never met a kid he hadn't wanted to hit. One day Raoul had hit him back. Hard. Then he'd left.

"It can't have been good," she said, sounding worried.

"I'm fine."

"But you weren't."

"I got by. My point is, I tried to steal them."

"The doughnuts? You stole doughnuts?"

"I didn't get away with it. The lady who owned the bakery caught me and she was pissed." She'd also toppled him with a crutch, a fact he still found humiliating.

"I ended up working for her, then eventually I went to live with her. Nicole Keyes. She liked to think she was tough, but she wasn't."

"You loved her," Pia said softly.

"A lot. If I'd been ten years older, I would have given Hawk a run for his money." He chuckled. "Maybe not. I had a girlfriend at the time and she would have objected." He glanced at Pia. "My girlfriend was Hawk's daughter."

"You're making that up."

"It's true." They'd had a lot of plans, he remembered. Marriage. A dozen kids. "We lasted through my first year of college. Then she dumped me. I got over it."

"Are you still friends with Hawk and Nicole?"

"Sure. They got married and are really happy together. I even keep in touch with Brittany."

"Does he know about your crush?"

"Probably."

"Interesting. I can't begin to bond with a story of my own."

"Your best friend left you three embryos. You'd win." He picked up his burger again. "Hawk and Nicole taught me to do the right thing. What's that phrase? They're the voice in my head, telling me what to do next. I don't want to let them down."

"They're your family," Pia said wistfully. "That's nice."

He remembered she didn't have much of a family. A dead father and a mother with the nurturing skills of an insect. If she had the kids, she would belong, he thought. But he would bet she hadn't considered that. Pia would choose to carry the embryos because it was the right thing to do. She didn't need an example—she just knew.

She pushed aside her salad and drew a folder out of her large bag. "Go ahead and eat," she told him. "I'll tell you what I've come up with and you can think of reasons to tell me I'm brilliant while you chew."

"I like a woman with a plan."

PIA GLANCED AT her watch and was stunned to see it was already after two. "Yikes. I have a three o'clock I need to get to," she said, opening her wallet and pulling out a couple of bills.

"You're not buying me lunch," Raoul told her, picking up the check.

"But you said—"

"I was kidding."

"Too macho to let a woman pay for your food?"

"Something like that."

He tossed money onto the bill, then stood. When she rose as well, he moved close and placed his hand on the small of her back as they walked out.

She was aware of every millimeter of contact. Her faux-cashmere sweater only amplified the sensation of heat and pressure.

When they reached the sidewalk, she turned to face him. "I'll get back to you with a schedule of deadlines," she said. "I think coordinating with a few of the festivals will work out well for the camp."

She found herself wanting to babble, even if she avoided looking directly at him. What was wrong with her? This wasn't a date. They weren't at her door and she wasn't debating whether to invite him in. This had been a business meeting.

"Thanks for your help," he said.

She drew in a breath, squared her shoulders and met his gaze. "You're welcome. You know Robert, our former treasurer, was the kind of man everyone thought was nice, and he ended up stealing millions."

"You're saying I'm a thief?" He sounded more amused than insulted.

"Not exactly. But how much do we really know about you? People should ask questions."

"You think too much," he told her.

"I know, but that's because there aren't enough distractions in my life."

"How about this one?" he asked, right before he leaned in and kissed her.

The contact was light enough—barely a brush of lip against lip. Hardly worth mentioning.

Except every cell in her body froze from the shock. The fingers holding her bag tightened into a death grip on the handle.

Before she could figure out what she was supposed to do, he straightened.

"Thanks for lunch," he said, then turned and walked away.

Leaving her gasping and alone. And very, very confused.

RAOUL ANGLED AWAY from the mirror as he slowly raised and lowered the weight in his hand. He'd been working out long enough that he rarely needed to check his form or speed. The movements were automatic. Unlike some guys, he didn't get a kick out of staring at himself.

Next to him, Josh Golden worked his triceps. Both men were dripping sweat and breathing hard. It had been a hell of a workout.

"In case you were wondering," Josh said as he lowered the weight to the bench in front of him, "I'm the only hero in this town."

Raoul grinned. "Worried, old man? Or should I say, threatened?"

"I've been here a whole lot longer than you. The town adores me. You're some newcomer. The question is, can you last through the long term?"

"I can outlast you."

Josh grinned. "In your dreams." He grabbed a towel and wiped the sweat from his face. "Everyone appreciates that you offered the camp. Without that place, there wouldn't have been a school."

"I'm happy to help."

"Good. That's what we do around here. Those who have more, give more. Life in a small town."

More rules, Raoul thought, remembering the ones Pia had listed. Something about where he was supposed to get his hair cut. Or not. He hadn't really been listening. He enjoyed listening to her speak, watching the emotions chase across her face. Her eyes were expressive. Her mouth…tempting.

"Earth to Raoul." Josh waved his hand. "Who are you thinking about?"

"A friend."

Josh picked up the weight again. Raoul set his down.

"You had lunch with Pia the other day," Josh said flatly.

Raoul raised his left eyebrow. "You're married."

"I'm not interested in keeping her to myself," Josh said firmly. "I've known Pia for years. She's like a sister. I'm watching out for her."

Raoul was glad someone was. From what he could see, Pia was pretty much on her own. "We're working together. Some of the festivals tie in with the work we're doing up at the camp."

Josh bent forward, keeping his upper arm still, moving the weight up and down to work his triceps. "You're getting tied in here. Sure you're ready for what small-town life really is?"

"I'll figure it out as I go. What's your concern?"

"Pia talks tough. She's smart, she's funny, she pretends nothing gets to her. But that's not true. Crystal's death hit her really hard. Before that…" He set down the weight again and straightened. "She's had some tough breaks. Her dad died, her mom left. There were a few bad boyfriends. Nobody wants to see her get hurt. You mess with her, you won't just answer to me. You'll answer to everyone."

Raoul had been a football star since he was sixteen. He was used to being the person everyone wanted to be with. The one who was liked.

"You're saying I'll be run out of town?"

"That'll be the least of it."

"I like Pia," he said at last. "I'm not going to hurt her."

Josh didn't look convinced. "You can't be sure."

"I don't want to hurt her," Raoul amended. "I care about her, too."

"I guess that will have to do for now. But if that changes, you'll answer to me."

"Think you can take me?" Raoul asked, not bothering to hide his amusement.

"Absolutely."

Josh was in good shape and they were about the same height, but Raoul had a good twenty pounds of muscle on him. Not to mention years of playing football. Cycling wasn't exactly a contact sport.

"I'm glad you're looking out for her," he said, because it was true. "Pia needs more people on her side."

Josh studied him. "Nearly everyone would tell you she has the whole town on her side."

Raoul had his doubts. "She's a local girl and they like her. But who does Pia have that she can really depend on? One-on-one? She's all alone in the world."

A reality that was going to complicate her life when she decided to have Crystal's babies. Babies no one else seemed to know about.

He thought about the soldier he'd known—the soldier who had died in his arms. What would Keith think about all this? Raoul had a feeling he would be pleased that his children were being given a chance but suspected he, too, would worry about Pia being on her own.

"You looking to change her situation?" Josh asked.

"I don't do long term."

"You were married. That the reason?"

Raoul shrugged and set the weight back in the rack.

Josh did the same, then hesitated. "I was married before Charity. It didn't go well. Sometimes it's not supposed to."

Raoul nodded because he wasn't going to have the conversation and agreeing moved things along. If he mentioned a bad first marriage, people assumed he'd been cheated on. Or had discovered Caro had married him for his money. Either would have been a whole lot easier than the truth. Hell, he would have preferred if she'd left him for a woman. But the real reason their marriage had ended gnawed at him. It woke him at night and left him wanting to scream at the heavens.

There were things that couldn't be fixed, he reminded himself. Actions that couldn't be undone. Like throwing a rock in a pond. There was nothing to be done but to wait out the ripples and hope no one got hurt.

He and Josh walked to the locker room. After showering and dressing, they agreed to work out together the following week. One of the things Raoul missed most about playing football was working out with his teammates. Josh could be counted on to push him. Sometimes Ethan Hendrix, a friend of Josh's, joined them.

Raoul knew it took time to fit in a place, but he was willing to take things slow. He liked Fool's Gold, so he was being careful not to make any missteps.

He left the gym, intending to go back to the office, but instead found himself walking home. He couldn't get Pia off his mind. Kissing her had probably been a mistake but was worth it, he thought with a grin. Not only because he'd enjoyed the feel of her mouth against his, but because of the look on her face when he'd done it. *Surprised* didn't come close.

He reached the small two-bedroom he'd rented and went into the study and booted his computer. When it was ready, he sat down and logged on to the Internet, then typed IVF into the search engine.

An hour later he had a clearer understanding of what Pia was going to go through. Two hours later, he knew there was no way he would ever agree to something like that. Not that it was physically possible, but still. Not only was Pia going to have to chemically prepare her body for pregnancy, she would be carrying triplets. Assuming all the embryos took. If they didn't, she would have to deal with the loss and, he assumed, the guilt that went along with it.

Hard enough to be pregnant, but how much worse was it to

be pregnant and alone, with no one to depend on? It wasn't like there was a dad she could go after for help or financial support.

Crystal had asked a lot from her friend. He was still convinced Pia would go through with having the babies, even if she hadn't figured that out yet. But he wondered if she really knew what she was getting into.

THE FUNDRAISER FOR the school might have technically lasted only a day, but it had put Pia behind by an entire week. An amount that probably didn't sound like much, she thought as she stared at her scheduling board. But Fool's Gold had a festival every single month. Some were smaller than others, but work was always involved. With success came hours of behind-the-scenes planning.

Summer was the busiest time, but fall was a close second. The city Halloween Party was barely six weeks away, and before that was the Fall Festival. The Thanksgiving Parade was after the Halloween Party but before the Christmas Gift Bazaar. The Saturday Day of Giving led into the Live Nativity outdoor service, which was the Sunday before Christmas. Then there was New Year's and so on.

One project at a time, she reminded herself, making notes on her dry-erase calendar. That's how she got through. It's not as if any of the events were new. The plans pretty much stayed the same. She had master lists that were cross-referenced, decorations stored all over town. If this ever got old, she could probably apply to run the world. There were—

She paused and stared at the calendar square. Instead of noting when she needed to arrange to have chairs and booths pulled out of storage, she'd drawn a string of little hearts. Although sweet, it wasn't exactly helpful. Worse—she knew the cause.

Raoul's kiss.

No matter how many times she told herself he hadn't meant anything by it, she couldn't get her gut, or her heart, to believe it. That one little second of contact had changed everything.

Suddenly he wasn't just Raoul, someone she knew, he was a *guy*. And because he was a guy, she had to be careful around him, which she didn't like.

Awareness was everything, she thought grimly. Two days ago, he'd been everyone's definition of tall, dark and handsome, but she hadn't really cared. He'd witnessed her at her hysterical best, had dealt with it winningly and she'd thought of him as a friend.

Now she found herself thinking about that stupid kiss two or three hundred times a day. She'd wondered why he'd done it, wished he would do it again, imagined him doing more than kissing her. It was pathetic, not to mention a waste of time.

She didn't have a type, but if she did, it wasn't him. He was too perfect. In all her "happily ever after" fantasies, the guy in question had been normal. Maybe even boring. Boring was dependable. With boring, a girl had a shot at the guy not leaving. But Raoul? He was heartbreaker material even when he wasn't trying.

"It was just a kiss," she whispered to herself. "Let it go."

Good advice. And someone, somewhere, would probably take it. Just not her. Not when she could feel the light brush of skin on skin, feel the heat of him and wish…

She lightly bumped her head against the wall, hoping to gently pound some sense into herself. Maybe the problem wasn't that Raoul was not her type, maybe the problem was more generic than that. Maybe if she'd had more kissing in her life, she wouldn't feel like she had to read too much into what had happened. Maybe she should date.

Pia rolled her eyes. "Oh, please. Like *that's* going to happen."

If she went ahead with the embryos implantation, her dating days were long over. Besides, she'd never exactly excelled in the man department. They always left, and for the life of her she couldn't figure out what she was doing to drive them away.

The door to her office pushed open. Pia glanced up and was surprised when Raoul strolled in.

He looked good, she thought, telling herself to make sure *she* looked cool and sophisticated. Barring that, she should try to avoid appearing desperate or needy.

"Hi," she said, going for cheerful. "I haven't had an emotional crisis today so we can't possibly have an appointment."

Instead of seeming impressed by her sparkling wit, he stared at her with an intensity that made her wonder if she'd dropped a bit of breakfast on the front of her shirt. As casually as she could, she glanced down. All seemed well.

"Pia," he said, moving toward her. "We have to talk."

Not exactly words one expected to hear from a macho guy. "Okay," she said slowly. "What about?"

Maybe he'd been as rocked by the kiss as she had been. Maybe he wanted to kiss her again and make her his love monkey. A week or two of intense male attention would probably cure her allergies.

"I've been doing research on in vitro fertilization," he said.

She plopped down on her chair and held in a sigh. So much for the love monkey invitation. "That's more than I've done," she admitted. "Is that what we're going to talk about? Because if it's anything gross, I don't want to know. I have a weak stomach."

He moved toward her desk. "It won't be bad. You take some basic tests, then your body is prepared to receive the embryos."

She hadn't liked the sound of that when she'd read the brochures the lab guy had given her, and she didn't like it now. "Prepared, how?" She quickly raised a hand. "Never mind. Are you going to sit?"

He placed his hands on her desk and leaned toward her. Apparently sitting wasn't on the schedule, either.

"Pia," he said, his dark gaze intense. "You can't go through this alone. You need someone to take care of you, and I want to be that person."

CHAPTER SIX

THE WORDS SWIRLED around in Pia's head. This was even crazier than the kiss.

"I haven't decided I'm going to have the babies," she whispered.

"Sure you have. Are you going to walk away from them?"

"No, but…"

If she hadn't been sitting, she would have collapsed. Was Raoul right? Had she already made her choice?

She closed her eyes. There was no way she *couldn't* have them, she thought with some finality. Whether or not she was the best person, she was the one Crystal had picked. It was crazy and scary and life-changing, but it had to be done. Her friend was depending on her.

She opened her eyes. "Oh, God. I'm going to get pregnant." She sprang to her feet, as her chest tightened and her heart rate zoomed into triple digits. "I can't breathe."

He came around the desk, took her hands in his and held on tight. "I'll help."

"This has nothing to do with you."

"I want to help. Be your…" He seemed to be searching for a description of what he was offering. "Pregnancy buddy. I'll drive you to the doctor, go get you pickles, whatever you need."

"I don't need pickles," she told him, ignoring the warm feeling of his skin against hers. This was not the time to indulge in weakness. "I don't really like them. Not enough to binge on them." A pregnancy buddy? "Maybe you took too many hits to the head when you were playing football."

Despite her tugging on her hands, he didn't release them.

"Pia, I'm serious. You don't have any family here. You have friends, but they all have lives. You need someone to depend on for the next nine months. I'm offering to be that guy."

Did kissing come with the offer, she wondered, before pushing the thought away.

She managed to free her hands and take a step back. "You can't know what you're saying. Why would you give up nine months of your life to help me?"

"Why would you offer to have Crystal's babies?"

"That's different. She was my friend."

"Fair enough. I didn't know her, but I did know Keith. These are his kids, too. The man died in my arms, Pia. I was there. I owe him. Helping bring his children into the world seems like the least I can do."

That almost made sense, she thought. Given that everything about their conversation was beyond believable.

"Okay, maybe," she conceded, "but maybe you could just donate something to charity instead. You're a rich, famous guy. You have a life. Probably a girlfriend."

"I don't have a girlfriend. I wouldn't have kissed you if I did."

Which begged the question of why he had, but she would deal with one weird incident at a time. "Raoul, you're really sweet, but no."

"Why? Don't you trust me?"

She frowned. "What do you mean?"

"I'm not going to offer this, then change my mind. I'm not going to leave."

She did her best not to wince at his words. He knew enough about her past to guess that being left was one of her issues.

Slowly, she returned to her chair and sank down. After drawing in a breath, she looked at him, as if she could find the answer in his handsome features.

There was nothing new there—just the same large, dark eyes, high cheekbones, perfect mouth.

He pulled up a chair and sat facing her. "I mean it, Pia. I want to help. For you and for Keith. You should let me try. I'm good at getting stuff done. All that quarterback training. What you're doing is important. Let me help."

She might not be willing to accept a man she barely knew would do this for her, but she could almost get that he would do it for Keith.

"What does being a pregnancy buddy mean?" she asked cautiously.

"Whatever you want it to mean. Like I said, I'll drive you to the doctor, go on craving runs, listen to you talk about how your ankles are puffy."

Something passed through his eyes—a dark, scary emotion that made her wonder about his past. But before she could ask, the emotion was gone.

"I'll be there for you, Pia. In whatever capacity you want. No expectations, no rules. You won't have to go through this alone."

That sounded perfect, she thought wistfully, wondering if it was possible. Could she really depend on him, trust him, know that he would be there for her?

Leaning on other people hadn't been a big part of her life. Not since high school, when both parents had left her—in one way or another. As she and Raoul weren't involved emotionally, the situation was completely different from what it had been with her boyfriends. If he chose to leave, it wouldn't be a big deal. Right?

Which was what it came down to. Depending on someone she wasn't sure would come through for her.

"It's an interesting idea," she began. "And I appreciate it. But why would you do this? What's in it for you?"

"I'll be there," he said firmly, "because I like you. And because you're doing a good thing. Maybe because there are things in my past that didn't work out the way I wanted them to, and this will make me feel better about them."

"How do you know what I'm thinking?"

"I just do, and I'll be there."

A part of her wanted to believe. Being able to depend on someone, especially while she was pregnant and worried about giving birth to three kids and raising them, would be heavenly. But the rest of her knew that leaving was what most people did best.

"Look at it this way," he said. "Use me shamelessly. Then if I do walk away, you get to be right. A win-win."

An interesting point. He sounded really sincere. Not totally sane, but sincere.

"Okay," she said slowly. "Maybe."

"I'll take it." He leaned in and brushed his mouth against hers.

Again, the light kiss had her entire body reacting. She wanted to haul him against her and have him put some back into it. Instead, she contented herself with remembering to breathe.

He stood. "Let me know when it all starts and I'll be there."

She wasn't clear on the implantation process, but she was pretty sure it was something she didn't want him to see.

"In the waiting room," he amended at her look of squeamishness.

"Okay. That would be fine. I'll let you know."

He left.

She continued to sit on her chair, feeling both stunned and a little relieved. Maybe this would be for the best, she told herself. Having someone else to help. Having someone else looking out for Crystal's babies. And if he got bored or distracted and walked away, so what? She'd been abandoned in ways Raoul couldn't begin to imagine. He couldn't possibly hurt her. So she was safe. And being safe was really what mattered most.

RAOUL TRIED TO be up at camp nearly every day. He timed his visits for recess or lunch so he could spend time with the kids on the playground. It was fun to toss a ball around with them. For the most part they were a little small to throw or catch a football, but a baseball worked well and Josh's sporting goods store had donated several balls and mitts.

When he arrived, the kids were still eating lunch. He went to see Dakota.

She was one of those neat people who had trays and color-coded, arranged files. Sort of like Pia's office, but without the huge calendar or the posters proclaiming Founders Day and Kissing Booth—$1 a kiss.

"How's it going?" he asked.

"Great." She motioned for him to enter.

He took the chair next to her desk.

"All the classes are in place and the kids are settled. We're okay on desks, still a little short on blackboards and books. So there's some creative sharing going on. It's probably good for the students to see that life means being flexible."

He chuckled. "Disaster as a teachable moment."

"Sure. Why not?" She pulled out a folder and glanced through it. "We should have an estimate on the cost to repair the school by the end of the week. If you hear a collective groan about ten Friday morning, it's the school-board-and-city-council joint meeting, where they get the actual numbers. I don't think it's going to be pretty."

"Isn't there insurance?"

"Sure, but it's unlikely to make the school whole again. I'm sure there's state money, too, but I see a lot of fundraising in our future."

He remembered the fun Saturday afternoon in the park. "Pia puts on a good party."

"She has a lot of experience."

A group of yelling kids raced past her open office door. "Lunch must be over," he said.

"Apparently."

More kids ran by.

"Does the noise bother you?" he asked. "Do you want an office somewhere else?"

Dakota laughed. "I'm one of six. I'm used to noise."

"Loud, happy childhood?"

"Absolutely. The boys came a couple of years apart, but when we were born, Mom got smacked with three babies at once. I can't imagine how she did it. I know my dad helped and the neighbors pitched in, but triplets? Somehow she managed."

He thought of Pia. She would have the three embryos implanted at the same time. If all of them survived, she would be looking at triplets, as well.

"So you're used to the chaos," he said.

"I don't even notice it. There are complications with a lot of kids, but as far as I'm concerned, the positives far outweigh the negatives."

"Planning a big family?" he asked.

She nodded and laughed. "I should probably get started, huh?"

"Is there a guy in all this?"

"I'd prefer it that way." She wrinkled her nose. "I know—how boring. I want to be traditional. Get married, have kids, a yard, a dog. Not anything a famous football guy would find interesting."

"What makes you think I don't want the same thing?"

"Do you?" she asked, tilting her head as she studied him.

"It would be nice."

"You were married before." She made a statement rather than asked a question.

"It didn't take."

"Is there going to be a next time?"

"I don't know," he admitted. Like Pia, he found it difficult to trust people. In his case, it was specifically women that were his problem.

"It can be different," she said. "Better."

He was less sure. "What about you? Any prospective husbands on the horizon, or are you waiting for the perfect guy?"

"He doesn't have to be perfect. Just a regular guy who wants an ordinary life." She shook her head. "Finding that is harder than you'd think. We have something of a man shortage here in town."

"I've heard that."

"You could ask some of your single football buddies to visit. As a gracious gesture to the lonely women in town."

"Donating the camp was my good deed for the week."

He stood and glanced out the door. A group of boys walked by, including Peter.

Raoul turned back to Dakota. "There's a kid in Mrs. Miller's class. Peter. He got scared during the fire. I went to take his hand, to lead him out. But when I stretched out my arm, he flinched, like he thought I was going to hit him."

She frowned. "I don't like the sound of that." She wrote the name down on a pad of paper. "I'll talk to his teacher and do some quiet investigating."

"Thanks. It's probably nothing."

"It probably is," she agreed. "But we'll find out for sure." She glanced at the clock. "You'd better go. Your fans are waiting."

He shifted uncomfortably. "They're not fans."

"They worship you. You're someone they've seen play football on TV and now you're on their playground, throwing around a baseball. If that's not fan-worthy, what is?"

"I'm just hanging out with the guys. Don't make it more than it is."

"Caring *and* unassuming. Be still my heart."

"I'm not your type."

"How do you know?"

Because from the second they'd met, there'd been no chemistry. Besides, Dakota worked for him. "Am I wrong?"

She sighed theatrically. "No, you're not. Which is why I'm very interested in your football friends."

"I doubt that. You're going to find your own guy."

"Want to tell me when?" she asked with a laugh. "So I can put a star by that day on the calendar?"

"When you least expect it."

PIA SAT ACROSS from Montana Hendrix in Pia's small office. She'd known the Hendrix triplets her entire life. The family had always been a prominent one and could trace its lineage back to the founding of the town.

People who assumed that the three sisters acted alike because they looked alike had obviously never met the triplets. Nevada was the quietest, the one who had studied engineering and gone to work with her brother. Dakota was more like a middle child—wanting everyone to get along. Montana was youngest, both in birth order and personality type. She was fun and impulsive, and the one Pia was closest to.

"So everything sold?" Montana asked, folding a letter and putting it into an envelope.

"Yes. The auction was a huge success. Despite the fact that there weren't any minimum bids, we made nearly twice what we'd hoped for."

The letters were going out to the successful bidders at the school fundraising auction. It provided information on how to pay and when to claim the prize.

"Everyone wanted to help," Montana said.

"Like you today." Pia grinned. "Did I thank you yet?"

"You're buying me lunch."

"Oh, yeah. I forgot."

They talked about what was happening in town and with their friends.

Montana picked up another letter, then put it down. "I've been offered a full-time job at the library."

Pia raised her eyebrows. "That's great. Congratulations."

Montana didn't look very excited. "It's a big deal, right? I've been working there nearly two years part-time. They're giving me a nice raise and I'll have benefits."

"But?"

Montana sucked in a breath. "I just don't want to." She held up a hand. "I know, I know. What am I thinking? This is a great opportunity. They'd want me to go back and get my master's in library science, and they'd even help pay. I love living in Fool's Gold. Now I'd have job security."

"But?" Pia asked again.

"It's not what I want to do," Montana admitted in a small voice. "I don't love working at the library. I mean, I like it. Books are great, and I like helping people and I enjoy working with the kids. But full-time? Every day for eight hours?"

She leaned her arms on the desk and slumped in her seat. "Why can't I be like everyone else? Why can't I know what I want to do with my life?"

"I thought you liked the library. You were really excited to help set up Liz's book signing last summer."

"That was fun. I just..." She motioned to Pia's office. "You knew what you wanted to do."

"No." Pia remembered trying to pick a major in college. "I didn't have a clue. I went with business because it seemed to give me a lot of options. I started in this job as an assistant, then I found out I liked it. I was lucky. This wasn't a plan."

"I need to get lucky," Montana muttered, then grinned. "I was going to say 'not in a boy-girl way,' but that would be fun, too." Her smile faded. "I feel so stupid."

"Why? You're not. You're smart and funny."

Montana lowered her voice. "I think I might be flaky."

Pia did her best not to smile. "You're anything but."

"I can't pick a career. I'm twenty-seven and I don't know what I want to be when I grow up. Shouldn't I already be grown up? Isn't the future *now?*"

"You sound like a poster. This isn't about the future. This

is about making yourself happy. There's nothing wrong with trying different careers until you find one you like. You're supporting yourself. It's not like you're living with your mom and watching TV all day. It's okay to explore the possibilities."

"Maybe," Montana said. "I never meant not to know what I wanted to do."

"Better to keep trying until you find something that makes you happy rather than choose something now and hate your job for the next twenty years."

Montana smiled. "You make it sound so easy."

"Fixing someone else's life isn't hard. The one I have trouble with is my own."

Montana raised her eyebrows. "Does any of this trouble have to do with a certain tall, very muscled ex-football player?"

Pia warned herself not to blush. "No. Why do you ask?"

"You had lunch with him."

"It was a business lunch."

"It didn't look like a business lunch," Montana told her.

Small-town life, Pia reminded herself. "How do you know? Did you see it for yourself?"

"I got the play-by-play from three different people." Montana leaned toward her. "One of them claimed there was a kiss, but I can't get confirmation on that."

Pia sighed. "I swear, we need more channels on cable around here. People are starved for entertainment."

"So there's nothing going on with you and Raoul?" Montana asked, looking disappointed.

Pia hesitated.

"There is!" her friend crowed.

"Don't get too excited. It's not what you think. It's not romantic." How could it be? Her soon-to-be pregnancy would scare off any sane man and most of the ones only flirting with sanity.

Pia drew in a breath. "Crystal left me her embryos."

Montana's eyes widened. "I thought you had her cat."

"I did, until I found out about her will. Jo got the cat."

"And you have her babies? That is amazing." Montana blinked. "Oh my God! You have her babies. You have to decide what to do with them. Did she leave you any instructions?"

"Not specifically. I know that having them is sort of implied in the bequest. It's not like she wants them frozen forever. She left money to help cover some of the medical expenses and to start a college fund."

"You're going to have them?"

Pia nodded slowly. Reality hadn't completely sunk in, and she was okay with that. Accepting that kind of truth *should* take a little time.

Montana jumped up and ran around the table, then bent down and hugged Pia. "I can't believe it. This is so amazing. You're going to have Crystal's babies."

She dropped to a crouch and stared at her friend. "Are you terrified?"

"Mostly. There's a lot of confusion and worry to go with it, as well. Why on earth did she pick me? There are a lot of other people here who have more 'mom' potential."

Montana straightened and returned to her seat. "That's not true. Of course you're the one she wanted to have her babies."

"You say that like this all makes sense."

Montana looked confused. "How doesn't it?"

"I don't know anything about having a baby or raising one. Or possibly three. She didn't talk to me ahead of time, warn me. I was supposed to get the cat. It turns out he never really liked me, so that's probably for the best, but still…" Pia bit her lower lip. "Why did Crystal pick me?"

"Because she loved and trusted you. Because she knew you'd make the right decisions."

"She can't know that. I sure don't know that. What if something bad happens? What if the embryos hate me as much as Jake did?"

"They're not in a position to make a judgment call."

"Okay, not now, but they will be. After they're born."

"Babies are hardwired to bond. That's what they do. They'll bond with you because you're wonderful. But even if you weren't, they'd still bond with you."

"I'd feel better if they liked me for me and not just because of biology."

"That's going to happen, too," Montana assured her. "You'll be a great mom."

"How do you know?" Pia asked, feeling both worried and desperate. "I don't come from a happy gene pool. My boyfriends always leave. Even the cat didn't want to live with me. What do I have to offer to a baby?"

"Your heart," Montana said simply. "Pia, you'll do everything in your power to take care of those kids. You'll sacrifice and worry and be there when they need you. It's who you are."

"The whole single-mom thing scares me," she admitted.

"You might be single, but you won't be alone," Montana reminded her. "This is Fool's Gold. You'll be taken care of by the town. You'll have all the help and advice you need. Speaking of which, if I can do anything, please let me know."

"I will."

Pia knew that Montana was right about the town. If she needed help, she only had to ask. Then there was Raoul's strange "pregnancy buddy" offer. She wasn't sure exactly what he was putting on the table, but it was nice that he was willing to be there.

"I just wish Crystal had talked to me before she died. Explained what she wanted."

"Would you have told her no?" Montana asked.

Pia considered the question. "I probably would have tried to talk her out of it, but in the end, if this was what she really wanted, I would have agreed. But at least I would have had the chance to find out why."

"You really can't figure that out? You're genuinely confused as to why Crystal left you her embryos?"

"Yes. Aren't you?"

Montana smiled at her. "No. Not in the least. I guess that's what you're going to have to come to terms with. And when you do, you'll know why you were exactly the right person for her to pick."

CHAPTER SEVEN

DR. CECILIA GALLOWAY was a tall, large-boned, no-nonsense kind of person who had gone to medical school back when women were expected to be homemakers or secretaries. She believed an informed patient was a happy patient, and that until a man experienced mood swings and menstrual cramps, he was in no position to say whether or not they were in a patient's head.

A mother of one of Pia's friends had gently suggested Pia consider visiting a gynecologist before starting college. Pia hadn't imagined ever having sex, but she'd taken the advice and gone in for her first pelvic exam.

Dr. Galloway had made the experience more interesting than scary, explaining the details of Pia's reproductive system in language the teen could understand. She'd also offered blunt advice about fumbling boys and their lack of expertise. She'd told Pia how to find her clitoris and G-spot and suggested she tell the boy in question to spend some quality time with both before having his way with her.

Now, a decade later, Pia sat in Dr. Galloway's office. She had a meager list of questions, which had made her realize she didn't know enough to know what to ask. Rather than hit the Internet and get a lot of half-truths, she'd come to the source of all knowledge.

At a few minutes after ten, Dr. Galloway walked into her office. She wore a white coat over casual knits. Her steel-gray hair was cut short. She didn't bother with makeup, but her steady blue eyes were warm behind her sensible glasses.

"Pia," the doctor said with a smile as she crossed the spacious room and settled next to Pia, rather than sitting across from her on the other side of the big wood desk. "I was a little surprised when I saw you were coming in today."

When Pia had made the appointment, she'd said she needed to talk to the doctor before being examined and had explained why.

Now, Dr. Galloway put down the folder she held and studied her. "You're young and healthy. Are you sure about this? It's an extreme measure at this time in your life. Wouldn't you rather wait and be in a relationship? Or even if you don't want to be involved with the father, we can look at artificial insemination rather than IVF."

It took Pia a second to realize the problem. "I'm not trying to get pregnant," she said with a shake of her head. "Okay, I *am* trying to get pregnant, but it's not what you think."

Dr. Galloway leaned back in her chair. "What shouldn't I think?"

"Crystal Westland left me her embryos."

The older woman's expression softened. "Did she? I wondered what Crystal would do. Poor child, to have suffered so much. It's a loss for all of us." She drew in a breath. "So you want to have Crystal's babies, do you?"

Want was kind of a strong word, Pia thought. She'd accepted the shift in her life path and was dealing. Maybe *want* would come later.

"I'm going to have them," Pia said firmly, holding in the need to wince at the words. "What's the next step?"

Dr. Galloway considered her for a moment. "We do an examination to make sure you're healthy. Draw a little blood, that sort of thing."

She got up and walked around to the other side of her desk.

After sitting, she pulled out a pad of paper and started making notes. "How many embryos are there?"

"Three."

"You'll have them all implanted at once?"

"I don't know. Should I?"

"It's probably for the best." The doctor raised her head. "The process is very simple. The embryos thaw naturally until they come to room temperature. They're put through several solutions to wash away any lingering cryoprotectant that was used during the freezing. Then they're warmed to body temperature and implanted. I can do that. It's a simple procedure, relatively painless."

She pulled several brochures out of a drawer. "Then you lie on the examination table for a few minutes, giving the embryos time to settle. Two weeks later, we test you to see if you're pregnant."

That didn't sound so bad, Pia thought. "Will I have to take any drugs? The guy at the lab talked about preparing my body."

"It depends. We'll monitor your cycle with a series of ultrasounds. When you're ready, in they go." Dr. Galloway leaned toward her. "It is possible not all the embryos will have survived the freezing process."

Pia hadn't realized that. "We'll know when they're thawed?"

"Yes, they're checked before they're implanted."

The doctor passed her several brochures. "You can read these over. They give more details about what will happen. Implantation is safe and quick. There's no reason to think this will be anything but a normal pregnancy."

Pia opened her mouth, then closed it. She glanced down at her hands, then back at the doctor. "What if I did something bad?"

Dr. Galloway shook her head. "There is nothing immoral in having Crystal's children, Pia. It is an act of love."

"I don't mean that. I mean..." She swallowed. "When I was in college, I had a boyfriend. I got pregnant."

"You had an abortion." Dr. Galloway sighed. "It happens all the time and has no impact on—"

"No," she said quickly. "I didn't. I was so scared, I couldn't believe it was really happening. There was no way the guy I was seeing would marry me, assuming I'd wanted that, which I didn't. I kept wishing the baby would go away. One morning I woke up and I was bleeding. I got my period."

She felt the wave of guilt, the shame that washed through her. "I wished my unborn child would die and it did."

The doctor rose and pulled Pia to her feet, then held her hands tightly.

"No," she said in a firm voice. "You don't have that much power, Pia. None of us do. A significant percentage of pregnancies end spontaneously. It is impossible to predict exactly when it will happen or even know why. Something went wrong inside the embryo. That is why you lost the baby. Not because you wished it so."

Tears filled Pia's eyes. "I prayed so hard."

"God didn't answer your prayer, child. Have you felt bad all this time?"

She nodded, then swallowed. "I don't deserve to have Crystal's babies. I'm a bad person."

"A bad person wouldn't care. You are young and healthy and you will be an amazing mother. Come on. We'll do the exam. We'll rule out any specific physical problems. Then you can decide. As for the child you lost, it's time to let him or her go."

Pia knew in her head that the other woman was right, but in her heart and her gut, the guilt lived on.

AN HOUR LATER, Pia dressed. She'd been poked, prodded and gone through her first ultrasound.

"Everything is fine," Dr. Galloway told her when Pia returned to her office. "You are ready. Based on when you last had your period, you're within five or six days of peak thickness in your uterine lining. So within the week if you want to go ahead this month."

"That fast," Pia said, hanging on to the back of the chair.

"You can wait for as long as you want."

Medically, yes, but if she waited, she might chicken out.

"How is your insurance?" Dr. Galloway asked. "You might want to check out how much it will cover."

"I'm with the city plan." The pregnancy itself would be covered. "Crystal left money to cover the implantation." There was also some money in trust for each of the children and a small annuity to help Pia with monthly expenses.

"Then the choice is yours." Dr. Galloway studied her. "Let the past go, child. It's time to think about the future. Whenever you're ready, I'll be here to help."

"Should I do anything special as far as food or vitamins?"

The doctor shook her head. "We've done a blood draw. I'll have the results in a few days. You'll go on prenatal vitamins then, along with any additional supplements you might need. For now, relax." The older woman smiled. "No, I take that back. Go find a good-looking man and have sex."

Pia felt herself flush. "Is that medical advice?"

Dr. Galloway laughed. "Yes. You're going to be pregnant with triplets, Pia. Your body won't be your own for much longer. Enjoy it while you can. Is there anyone special in your life?"

She immediately thought of Raoul—her hunky pregnancy buddy. "Not really. I'm not dating."

"My advice stands. Just make sure you take precautions. Then when you're ready, we'll take the next steps." She rose and walked around her desk. "You're doing an extraordinary thing, Pia. I'm so proud of you."

Pia thanked her and left. Information swirled around in her head. She was pleased that the implantation could happen relatively easily, and she appreciated Dr. Galloway's attempts to reassure her about what had happened in the past. Pia knew logically that she wasn't to blame for the loss of the baby she'd

carried before, but she couldn't help feeling that being terrified rather than happy had been wrong. And that she would be
punished later.

Which meant what? Did she give in to the fear and not have
Crystal's children? That didn't seem right, either. If she went
forward with this, she was going to have to take a leap of faith.
On her part, she would do everything right. Take the best care
of herself, live perfectly. It would be up to the babies to take
care of the rest. A reasonable plan, she told herself. A rational
response.

But she couldn't help but wonder if Crystal would have left
her the embryos if she'd known the truth.

PIA HAD BARELY been back in her office five minutes when
Marsha called.

"They're here," the mayor said, sounding desperate. "I knew
they were coming, but still."

"Who's here?"

"Reporters. They're everywhere. I need you to come to City
Hall and dazzle them."

"Is this where I tell you I don't feel especially dazzling?"

"No, it isn't. We're desperate. Charity is going to take questions, as well. I need young, confident and sexy. Anything that
doesn't scream pitiful spinster."

Despite everything that had happened that morning, Pia burst
out laughing. "I don't think we use the 'S' word in this century, Marsha."

"They're going to use it. Count on it. You'll come?"

"I'll be there. Give me fifteen minutes."

"Make it twelve."

PIA MADE IT to City Hall in ten minutes, only to find that the
mayor wasn't kidding. There were several news vans parked
along the street, with reporters setting up for outdoor shots. It

was a perfect fall day—crisp without being too cold, blue sky, the changing leaves adding bursts of red and yellow.

She could see Charity talking to two reporters at once, and a crowd of residents starting to gather. Sucking in a deep breath and reminding herself to speak in coherent sound bites, she stepped toward the cluster of reporters.

"Hello," she said as she approached. "I'm Pia O'Brian. I work for the city. Mayor Tilson asked me to come by and see if you have any questions."

Immediately three cameras focused on her. Bright, blinding lights clicked on. Pia did her best not to blink like a mole in the sun.

"What's your name?" one guy asked. "Can you spell it?"

She didn't think Pia was a tough one, but she did as he requested.

"What's with the man shortage?" a young male reporter asked. "How are you driving them away?"

"Is it a sex thing?" another man asked. "The women in town not putting out?"

The assumption being they *must* be doing something wrong, Pia thought, but she did her best not to let her irritation show.

"Demographically, we're not as balanced as other communities," she said calmly. "There are fewer males born per one hundred births than in other places. As the father determines the gender of the child, you'll have to speak to the men in town to get your question answered."

The youngest of the three reporters around her blinked, as if he couldn't remember what he'd asked. All the better for her, she thought.

"Fool's Gold is a family community," she continued. "We have an excellent school system, a low crime rate and are a popular tourist destination. Businesses thrive here. We've recently signed a contract that brings a second hospital to the area. This one will include a trauma center, something this part of the state needs."

"Are the women in town excited about the man invasion?" the second reporter asked. "Maybe some of you will get lucky."

"Oh, joy," Pia murmured, knowing slapping someone when on camera was never a good idea. "Tourists are always welcome."

"We've heard there are busloads of men coming this way. From all over the country."

That couldn't be good. Busloads? What were they supposed to do with them? The kind of men who could drop everything, hop on a bus and travel to a place they'd never seen with the hopes of finding women didn't sound especially stable. Or community oriented. If this was true, it was a nightmare in the making.

"Lucky us," she said. "Fool's Gold is always ready to make visitors feel at home. Families especially."

"But you're short on men," the older of the three said. "So you'll be personally interested in the guys coming. You can't get a date, right?"

Pia raised her eyebrows, fighting a sudden flash of temper. "Do I look like I can't get a date? Is that what you're implying? That we should be *grateful* for anyone who comes here and gives us the slightest hint of affection? Do you really think we're desperate and—"

"There you are," a smooth male voice said, as a hand slid against the small of her back.

She turned and saw Raoul had joined her.

He gave her a warning glance, which was totally unnecessary. Obviously it was dumb to try to best a reporter while on camera. They had the last word in the editing room. But the assumption that she or any of the women in town were dying for a busload of guys from who knows where to show up was beyond insulting. Sure, many of the women in town wanted to meet someone special and get married, but that was a far cry from being desperate for any man who happened to glance their way.

Raoul extended his right hand to the reporters. "Raoul Moreno. Nice to meet you."

Pia had the satisfaction of watching two of the three guys' mouths drop open.

"The football player?" the youngest guy asked. "You played for Dallas. Jesus, you live here?"

"Fool's Gold is a great town. Family friendly, supportive of businesses. I've opened a camp for kids up in the mountains. There's a new hospital being built and a cycling school run by Josh Golden."

The oldest reporter frowned. "That's right. Josh Golden *does* live here. Hey, I thought there was supposed to be a man shortage."

Pia felt smug but was determined not to let it show. "We might have some demographic challenges, but we're still a thriving, happy community. If single men want to be a part of that, great. If they're thinking they've just entered the land of desperate women, they're sadly mistaken."

As she spoke, she was aware of Raoul's hand still pressing against her back. His touch was sure and warm and very, very nice. She found herself wanting to lean in, maybe rest her head against his chest, but that wouldn't be her smartest move. They weren't involved. Although there was a teeny-tiny chance she was thinking about asking him for sex.

How far did the pregnancy-buddy offer extend?

"There's a lot of regional industry that might interest you," Raoul told them. "We have a local contractor who builds wind turbines. He and his staff are designing some cutting-edge blades using special materials."

The reporters exchanged glances, as if wind turbines didn't exactly get their hearts beating faster. But Pia saw what Raoul was doing. Focusing on all the businesses owned by men, trying to get the reporters confused enough that they wouldn't have a story.

"If you're looking for local color," Pia said in her most helpful voice, "there's Morgan's Books. He's been around for years. When I was little, he always made sure the next Nancy Drew book was in stock for me."

Raoul pulled a business card out of his shirt pocket. "If any of you want to contact me about an interview, I'm available."

"Great," the youngest reporter said. "I'll call you. We can do a feature. Life after football, that sort of thing."

"Sure."

The three men drifted away. Pia watched anxiously, then had to hold in a cheer as the bright lights were extinguished and the cameras turned off.

She spun toward Raoul and grinned. "You did it. You saved the town."

He guided her away from the crowd. "Don't get too excited. They've been fooled, but it won't last long. This problem isn't going away."

She didn't want to think about that. "How'd you know to come here?"

"The mayor called and asked me to help. She's worried about the kind of men who will show up based on a news story."

Pia grinned. "She begged, didn't she?"

He shrugged. "It was uncomfortable. Besides, I'm not looking for bad press, either. This is my home, too." He glanced at the milling reporters. "We've bought ourselves some time. But if there really are busloads of men heading in this direction, the reporters will be back."

Not exactly a happy thought. "I guess we'd all better figure out what we're going to say when they return. Not to mention the logistics of herds of single men. What are we going to do with them? Do you think they're here to settle down or just hoping to get lucky?"

His gaze met hers. "That was rhetorical, right? You weren't actually looking for an answer."

She laughed. "You've saved us for the moment and that's enough. But if you get any brilliant ideas . . ."

"You'll be the first to know."

They stared at each other. He really *was* good-looking, she thought. Talk about an excellent gene pool. And those hands. They seemed…large.

Dr. Galloway's teasing words filled her brain. On a practical level, Pia knew that once she had Crystal's babies, her dating days were long over. Not that she'd been going out all that much before, but still. There had always been the promise of a great guy. Instead she would be the single mother of triplets.

"What?" Raoul asked. "You're thinking something."

It would be asking too much. On some level, it was probably wrong. Still, he was tempting.

"Would you like to come over for dinner?" she asked before she could stop herself. "So we can talk about the pregnancy some more? I saw my doctor today and she gave me a lot of good information."

"Sure. Want me to bring something?"

"Wine would be nice. If I'm going to get pregnant, then there won't be any in my future for nine long months."

They settled on a time and she gave him her address. As he walked off, she stared after him. Between now and dinner, she had several hours to decide if she really was going to ask Raoul for one last fling before she started down the pregnancy road.

The thought of being with him made her feel all squishy inside. Based on what she knew about his past, he had plenty of practice when it came to the wild thing. It would probably be the night of a lifetime. Which was about how long the memories would have to last her.

PIA HAD NEVER been much of a cook. Yet another skill she would need to be a successful mother, she thought as she climbed the two flights of stairs to her apartment. She'd bought a rotisserie chicken from the grocery store, along with a couple of different salads. She would steam broccoli and serve berries over ice cream for dessert. Assuming they got that far in the meal.

The more she thought about asking Raoul for a single night of wildness, the more she liked the idea. Of course that same thought was accompanied by stomach-clenching panic, but that was a problem for another time.

She put the groceries in the refrigerator, showered quickly, then smoothed on jasmine-scented lotion. She kept her makeup light, then chose a simple green dress that buttoned up the front. The scooped neck wasn't so low as to be obvious, but it hinted at curves.

She'd changed her sheets the previous day, so that was good. She checked the box of condoms she kept around, mostly because she felt she should rather than because of actual need. There were still three inside, and according to the box she had a whole month until they expired. Lucky her.

Now it was just a matter of waiting until Raoul showed up then deciding if she should proposition him. The downside was if he said no, it would be awkward between them and she could kiss the whole pregnancy-buddy offer goodbye. Not that she was counting on it, really.

She had no idea what he thought of her. He probably liked her, but liking and wanting were two very different things. The last thing she wanted was mercy sex. Being pitiful was about the worst outcome possible.

There was also his past to consider. All those groupies throwing themselves at him. They'd probably been a lot more perfect than she could ever hope to be. On her best day, she was pretty, but most of the time she was firmly average.

She spent the next ten minutes making herself crazy by deciding she wasn't going to ask, then changing her mind. The back-and-forth reasoning was making her dizzy, and she was grateful when she heard a firm knock on the door.

She pulled it open, "Right on time."

That was as much as she got out. Raoul stepped into her small apartment and seemed to fill the space. He was tall and broad and suddenly there wasn't enough air in the room.

"Hi," he said, handing her a bottle of white wine, then leaning in and kissing her cheek. "You look great."

There were probably words she was supposed to say, but speaking was impossible.

He'd changed for their evening. Maybe even showered. His knit shirt was casually tucked into khakis, but the fabric seemed to cling to every muscle. He smelled clean and sexy and looked so tempting he was probably flirting with breaking the law. Her mouth watered.

"Thank you," she managed. She thrust the wine back at him. "You want to open this?"

"Sure."

He glanced around, found the kitchen and made his way there. She followed, then fished the wine opener out of a drawer and handed it to him. She collected glasses and set them on the counter.

"I saw my doctor today," she said. "We talked about the next steps and I got my physical."

He turned to face her. "What did she say?"

"That there's no reason why I can't deliver Crystal's babies to term. Apparently getting them implanted isn't too bad."

Saying the words made it all seem a little too real, she thought, feeling a bit light-headed. "Two weeks later, I take a pregnancy test."

His dark gaze never wavered. "You'd have all three done at the same time?"

"She thinks that would be best. Apparently there's a chance some of them might not survive the thawing process. But even if they all do, three is considered okay."

He handed her a glass of wine. "You ready for this?"

"No, but it's not like I'm suddenly going to get ready. I think plunging ahead is the best plan. I don't want to talk myself out of this."

"You don't have to do it. You don't have to have Crystal's babies."

She clutched her wine in both hands. "Yeah, I do. It's what she wanted and she's my friend. I would have done anything to save her. Bone marrow, a kidney, whatever. None of that would have helped, so I'm going to have her children and raise them as my own."

Emotions moved through his eyes, but she couldn't tell what he was thinking. "You're a helluva woman, Pia O'Brian."

"Not really, but thanks for thinking I am."

She led the way into the living room. She curled up in one corner of the sofa, and Raoul sat at the opposite end. He faced her.

"Nervous?" he asked.

She was, but not for the reasons he thought. "Yes, but I'm dealing."

He looked around at her bright apartment. "How many bedrooms do you have here?"

She blinked at him. "One." Reality hit her. "I'm going to have to move, aren't I? I'll need more bedrooms." She thought of the two flights of stairs she went up and down several times a day. There was no way she could deal with them and a stroller... or three.

He reached his arm across the back of the red sofa and patted her shoulder, then left his fingers lightly resting against her. "You don't have to move today. Don't worry about it. When the time comes, I'll help."

"I've lived here six years," she murmured, aware of the heat of his touch. "I don't want to move."

What other changes would there be? How many things hadn't she thought of?

"Can we please change the subject?" she asked. "I'm starting to freak."

"Don't freak. You're not even pregnant yet."

"Yet" being the key word.

She forced herself to breathe slowly, then she took a sip of her wine. "I can do this," she said, more to herself than him. "I'm strong. The town will help."

"Don't forget me," he added. "Your pregnancy buddy."

She still thought there was something odd about that, but why spoil his fun?

"Have you been a pregnancy buddy before?"

His expression tightened, then he relaxed. "No, but my girl-friend in high school thought she was pregnant."

"What did you do?"

"Offered to marry her."

"Of course you did."

"What does that mean?"

"It's the nice-guy thing." She sighed. "I'm sure everyone adored you in high school."

"I wouldn't say adored."

"Sure they did." She sipped her wine. "I was a cheerleader."

He raised an eyebrow. "Still have the uniform?"

She laughed. "Yes, but that's not the point. A lot of people don't like cheerleaders. It's the whole popular-girl thing."

"Were you popular?"

"Sort of." At least until her life had crashed in around her. "I wasn't exactly humble and caring," she admitted. "The phrase 'mean girl' has been tossed around."

"You're not mean."

"I was. I made fun of people, flaunted what I had. I know now it was an uncomfortable combination of immaturity and insecurity, but it's not as if that information will make any of my victims feel better."

"You had victims?"

"I had people I picked on." They were having the last laugh now, she thought sadly. Most of them had wonderful lives, while she lived in a one-bedroom apartment and couldn't even get a cat to like her.

"You're pretty hard on yourself," he said.

"Maybe I deserve it."

"Maybe everyone gets to screw up every now and then."

"I'd like it to be that simple."

"Why does it have to be complicated?" he asked.

An interesting question, she thought, allowing herself to get lost in his eyes.

Raoul was one of the good guys. Around him a girl could let herself feel safe. Not to mention a lot of other things that were a lot more yummy than safe.

A flash of courage swept through her. She set down her wine, braced herself for flat-out rejection and said, "Do you want to have sex?"

CHAPTER EIGHT

Raoul felt like a cartoon character. He wanted to shake his head to make sure he was hearing right. Assuming he was, he was pretty sure his eyes were about to bug out.

"Excuse me?" he asked, standing and staring down at her.

Pia sighed. "Do you want to have sex? With me. The doctor mentioned it. Not that it was important for the implantation procedure, because it isn't. Her point was I'm about to be pregnant and then I'll have babies and little kids and it's probably going to be a long time before a guy finds me the least bit desirable, assuming that even ever happens again. So having sex now, sort of a last fling, makes sense."

She'd said most of that without drawing in a breath. She did so now, then stared at him, her hazel eyes wide and wary. "You don't have to if you don't want to. I have no idea what you think of me. I'm not hideous or anything, but it's not like I have a plaque proving I'm really great in bed. I thought maybe it would fall under the pregnancy-buddy umbrella, but maybe not."

She tilted her head. "Fall under the umbrella. Is that a mixed metaphor?"

She was asking him if he wanted to have sex with her and then had switched the conversation to grammar?

She stared at him with wide eyes. Hope fluttered there, along with a hint of apprehension. He would guess she was braced for rejection.

Sex with Pia? He definitely found her sexy and attractive, but he'd never planned to go further than looking. There were plenty of reasons *not* to do this—the biggest of which was they would be living in a very small town together. There wasn't much room for awkward.

She bit her lower lip. The vulnerable movement hit him like a fist to the gut. Pia was pretty. The proud set of her shoulders, the faint glow on her cheeks. The way her brown curls tumbled to her shoulders.

He'd always been the kind of guy who tried to look past external appeal to the person inside. The fact that Pia was going to have someone else's children, simply because she'd been asked, made her one of the best people he'd ever known. And he'd really liked the kisses they'd shared.

The idea of sex—no, making love—appealed more and more with every passing second. He knew this was a one-time deal. That after she had the babies, she would have other things on her mind. But something inside him told him a single night with Pia would be a night worth remembering.

He took a step toward her. "I did offer to be your pregnancy buddy," he said quietly. "To do anything you asked, to take care of *all* your needs."

"This isn't exactly the same as running out for ice cream in the rain."

He pulled her to her feet, then put his hands on her shoulders and stared into her eyes. "It's a whole lot more fun than that."

She swallowed. "You really don't have to do this. I shouldn't have asked. I don't want you to feel pressured or like it's—"

He leaned in and pressed his mouth against hers. The act cut off her words, which wasn't a bad thing. Sometimes silence was better.

Her lips were soft and yielding. Tempting. Her arms wrapped around him. She was warm and slight, but tall enough that he didn't have to bend too far to kiss her again. A good thing, because he found he liked kissing her and wanted it to go on for a good long time.

Pia had expected something of a discussion, or at the very least, ground rules on the whole pregnancy-buddy-sex thing.

Apparently not, she thought as Raoul's warm mouth claimed hers. The kiss was both hungry and tender, his lips making her want to melt into his tall, strong body.

He held her against him, her body pressing against his. He was all broad shoulders and hard planes. He smelled as good as he looked—masculine, but clean. There was a slight rasp of stubble on his cheeks, but not so much that she minded.

It had been a long time since a man had swept her away, she thought as she wrapped her arms around his neck and gave herself over to his kiss. She slid her fingers through his dark hair. The short, layered strands felt like cool silk. He moved his hands down her body to her hips. One had slipped to her rear.

When he cupped the curve, squeezing gently, her stomach clenched. She surged closer, bringing her belly up against him. She was immediately aware of the hard thickness—proof that he wasn't doing this out of pity. Thank God!

He touched his tongue to her bottom lip. She parted for him, then rested her fingers on his broad shoulders. He slid into her mouth, moving with slow, languid strokes designed to make her beg for more.

She held in the whimper and gave herself over to the kiss. Everything about this moment felt right. Hunger filled her, burning hard and hot, making her want to get closer, to touch him and be touched.

She moved her tongue against his, going faster than he had, urging him on. The hands holding her hips tightened, then began the slow journey up her sides. She held her breath until he cupped her breasts in his hands, then she exhaled slowly. He moved from underneath, squeezing her breasts gently, then rubbed his thumbs against her already hard nipples.

At the first brush, she felt a jolt all the way down to her toes. At the second, she had to hold back the need to cry out for more. She reminded herself not to beg—men found it very unattractive. But it was difficult to stay rational and focused when every whisper of contact against her sensitized breasts made her want to scream.

He lowered his head to her jaw and kissed his way to her ear. Then he dipped lower, nibbling along her neck to her collarbone. He paused there to taste her skin, an openmouthed kiss that was surprisingly arousing. Or maybe it was the way he continued to tease her breasts, or the feel of his body so close to hers.

Before she could decide, he'd cupped her face in his hands and was kissing her again. Deep, soul-stirring kisses that made her ache with longing and need. Without realizing what she was doing, she found herself unbuttoning the front of her dress. Suddenly the fabric gapped open to her waist.

Before she could figure out how to stop or what to do next, he'd straightened and pulled her arms free, leaving the dress to pool at her hips. He ran his fingers from wrists to shoulders, then down over her breasts and behind her. With an expert flick of his fingers, her bra came undone and fell away.

In less than a heartbeat, he'd replaced the silky lace with his bare hands. Skin on skin, she thought, her eyes sinking closed. He touched her gently, exploring her curves.

She focused on every stroke, each brush of finger and palm. He moved closer and closer to her nipples but didn't touch them. The contact heightened her arousal, making her knees weak and her body hungry. Then, when she was about to grab his hands in hers and place them where she wanted, he bent down and took her left nipple in his mouth.

The hot, wet, openmouth kiss made her breath catch. He sucked deeply, making her arch against him. A ribbon of erotic connection tugged deep in her belly. Between her thighs she felt herself swelling, wanting.

He shifted to the other breast. She touched his head, then his shoulders, feeling his strength. Wanting poured through her, making her feel delicious and alive.

He straightened. "We should move the party," he whispered, unbuttoning his shirt, then shrugging out of it.

She nodded, even as her gaze was caught by the sight of his broad chest. She wanted to touch and taste, to explore, but he was already moving away. As she followed, she undid the rest of the buttons on her dress and stepped out of both it and her shoes as she walked.

By the time they met up again in the bedroom, he was naked. She'd never gotten the concept of male beauty before seeing him, but she did now. His chest was a series of defined muscles, his waist narrow, his legs strong. He was hard and ready, his expression intense and focused. Just looking at him made her tremble. As she moved toward him, he grabbed her around the waist and they both tumbled onto the bed.

"You have condoms, right?" he asked, right before he kissed her.

She nodded.

"Good. We don't want my sperm swimming around with Crystal's embryos. It would get crowded down there."

He grinned as he spoke, his eyes alive with humor and desire. It was an irresistible combination. Then he was kissing her again. She let herself get lost in the feel of his mouth on hers.

Their tongues tangled in an erotic dance. Then he moved to her neck, as he had before. The man had skills, she thought dreamily, feeling every part of her heat and melt. When he took her earlobe into his mouth and sucked, she had to bite her lower lip to keep from crying out. When she felt the weight of him as he stretched out next to her, it was all she could do to keep her legs from falling open in a shameless invitation. She wanted him...all of him...on top, inside, pleasuring them both into madness.

He moved to her breasts, and it was just as good as it had been before. With each tug of his mouth on her nipples, she felt an answering shiver between her legs. She could feel herself swelling for him.

His mouth moved lower. He paused long enough to pull off her panties in one smooth, easy move. She waited for the feel of his kiss on her belly, but there was nothing. Her heart beat once, twice, a third time. Then she felt the warmth of his lips on the inside of her ankle.

"What are you doing?" she asked.

She felt as well as heard him chuckle. "And here I thought you were pretty *and* smart."

He kissed his way up to her knee, then moved between her legs and nibbled higher. Up and up until he pressed an open-mouthed kiss on the very inside of her thigh.

She opened her legs even wider, knowing it was either that or plead. Then his mouth was on the most sensitive part of her. She exhaled as warm, soul-stirring pleasure flooded her.

He moved slowly, as if discovering all of her. The touch was perfect—quick enough to excite, gentle enough that everything he did was magic. He paused to tell her how good it felt to do this to her, which was nearly as arousing as the finger he slipped inside her.

As he stroked her, he settled his mouth on that one tight and swollen spot. He brushed it with his tongue, which made her squirm. He moved in tandem, his tongue keeping time with his finger. Back and forth, in and out. She couldn't remember the last time a man had done this to her. The last time she'd felt that liquid heat flowing through her body, the promise of release only seconds away.

She tried to hold back, wanting to savor the moment for as long as possible. Although the end would be great, there was something to be said for anticipation. But it was like swimming upstream. Exhausting and ultimately impossible. Every flick of his tongue pushed her closer. When he closed his lips around her very center and sucked, she lost herself to the explosion.

Muscles clenched and released. Every cell in her body quivered as the pleasure crashed into her, through her. She surrendered to the sensations, arching back her head and gasping as she came again and again.

When she could think again, she managed to open her eyes and saw Raoul smiling at her, his expression self-satisfied.

"You're not all that," she told him breathlessly.

"Sure I am."

He leaned in and licked her nipple. She shuddered and had to resist the need to draw him closer so they could do it all again. Instead she pulled open the nightstand drawer and removed the box of condoms.

Raoul frowned. "Is this it?"

"What do you mean? Are they the wrong kind?"

One corner of his mouth turned up. "There are only three."

Her mind went blank. "Only?"

"This is supposed to be your last fling. Shouldn't it be memorable?"

"I figured once was enough."

He pulled out a condom and tossed the package on the nightstand. "Then I'm going to have to show you otherwise."

PIA LAY ON THE BED, doing her best to catch her breath. Her mind was still fuzzy, her body unable to obey even the slightest command. Apparently the body had involuntary systems for a reason. Something had to keep her heart beating. Otherwise, a session with a guy like Raoul could be deadly.

Had she been able, she would have turned her head to look at him. But that would have required more energy than she could muster. Blinking was about all she could manage. As he'd predicted, they'd used all three condoms. She'd come in ways she hadn't known were possible, in positions that were at the very least questionable. In the last five hours, she'd had more orgasms than she'd probably had in her entire life. If doing him was wrong, she didn't want to be right.

He rolled toward her. His handsome face came into view,

along with a bit of bare shoulder. His skin had a golden cast and looked as good as it tasted. Talk about temptation. She was exhausted and still shuddering through her recovery, but the thought of being with him again was enough to cause her nerve endings to cheer.

"You okay?" he asked.

She managed a smile. "Fishing for compliments?"

"Maybe."

"The earth didn't just move—it did a two-and-a-half somersault with a twist."

"Good." He brushed the hair off her face, then lightly kissed her. "Can I stay?"

She swore softly. Of course he would ask to stay. Because he was perfect. Funny, smart, good-looking, great in bed and sensitive. Oh, and rich. The man had money. So why wasn't he involved with someone? Why wasn't he married? She knew there was a divorce in his past, but why hadn't some enterprising woman snapped him up?

Not that she cared, she reminded herself. She had embryos to worry about.

"Earth to Pia," he said, still gazing down at her.

"You can stay," she whispered.

Under normal circumstances she would have forced him out in the name of self-preservation. Having him around could be dangerous to her heart. But that wasn't going to be an issue. In a few days, she would return to her doctor's office and possibly be implanted with Crystal's embryos. Then she would be pregnant. Falling in love wasn't going to happen to her—at least not in the romantic sense. No guy would be interested in a woman with three kids who weren't even hers, and she couldn't imagine having even an extra ounce of energy left over for anything close to dating.

So it was perfectly safe to roll on her side and have him slide in next to her. She snuggled against his warm body, feeling his strong arms circle her waist and pull her close. She closed her eyes and allowed herself to believe it was all real. At least for tonight. No matter what, she could count on reality to return in the morning.

FOOL'S GOLD HIGH SCHOOL sat above town on the road that led up to the ski resort. The campus was only about five years old, with a state-of-the-art science building, a large stadium and an auditorium that held five hundred.

Raoul stood onstage, facing the students filling every seat. He'd pushed aside the podium, preferring to walk back and forth.

"I didn't start out rich and famous," he told the kids. "When I was your age, I was in foster care, fighting the system responsible for feeding and clothing me. I knew no one cared about me. Not as a person. I was a case number to the social worker and steady income for my foster family."

He paused and met the gaze of several of the younger guys in the audience.

"Some families really do care about the kids they take in, and I applaud them. I've heard the stories, but I didn't see it much in action. The social workers I knew were overworked. They tried their best, but they weren't given the tools or the resources. So I got involved in some things that I should have avoided."

He walked to the edge of the stage and stared out at the students. "Gangs can look pretty good from afar. They give you a place to belong. You get status from being with the right crowd. You're around people who accept you. If they're crazy enough, you never know what's going to happen next and that can be fun, too."

He shrugged. "It can also leave you worse off than you ever thought. Pregnant. In jail. Or dead." He let the words hang there for a long time.

"When you're sixteen, the future seems a long way away, but I'm here to tell you the value of thinking long term. Of knowing what you want and going after it, regardless of how many people tell you it's not possible. I spent the first few months of my senior year homeless, living in an abandoned building. I had friends who helped out, but what made the biggest difference was I found someone who could believe in me. And he taught me to believe in myself. That's what you have to do. Believe you can make it."

He crossed to the other side of the stage and looked out at those kids. "The dictionary tells us a mentor is a trusted coach or a guide. Be what you want to see in someone else. Find a younger kid and get involved. It's like throwing a rock in a lake. The ripples stretch out forever."

He talked a little more about the importance of doing the right thing, then said he would answer questions.

There were the usual ones about playing for the Cowboys and what it had been like to take his college team through two undefeated seasons.

"I didn't do it," he told them honestly. "I was one member of an excellent team. Everyone did his part and that's why we won. Football isn't golf. It's not just you and the ball. It's everyone around you. Any team is only as strong as its weakest player."

A small girl in the third row raised her hand.

He pointed to her. "Yes?"

"Have you ever been a Big Brother? My uncle has a boy he's been helping for a couple of years now."

"Good for him," Raoul said. "As for being a Big Brother, it's hard for a guy like me to help someone one-on-one. The media finds out and it gets messy. So I give back this way—talking to schools, sharing ideas, working with teachers."

He rattled on for a couple more minutes and was relieved that the students seemed to buy it and the teachers in the room were nodding.

He wanted them to stand up and yell at him. On what planet would a former football player be so damned famous that he couldn't take a kid bowling? Guys way better known than him had private lives.

The truth was less pretty. He didn't want to get personally involved. He didn't want to care. The price was too high. Better to keep things superficial. That way no one got burned, including him.

A philosophy Pia wouldn't agree with, he thought as he finished the speech. She was the kind who would leap in first and ask questions later. That's what she was doing with the embryos. Talk about a woman with conviction and courage.

And a way about her, he thought as he finished up and smiled as they applauded. Three nights ago, he'd stayed with her. Ever since his bed had been a little colder, a little more empty.

But he knew the value of going it alone and the danger of making something more than it was. He knew how a heart could be ripped apart and left for dead. No way he was going through that again.

PIA WAITED NERVOUSLY on the padded table.

"It's okay," the tech told her. "Ultrasounds don't hurt."

Pia eyed the wand. "There has to be a downside."

"Sorry, no. We even heat the goopy gel we use on your tummy. This is one of the easiest medical tests."

"It beats a barium enema."

The other woman, Jenny her name tag said, laughed. "Have you ever had a barium enema?"

"I've heard rumors. They can't be fun."

"No, they can't, but this is easy."

Jenny pulled up Pia's paper gown and squirted warm gel onto her lower stomach. Then she lowered the wand and rubbed it along Pia's skin.

There was no pain at all. Just a sensation of something warm and flat moving across her. Okay, she thought. Note to self—ultrasounds aren't bad.

A few minutes later Jenny covered her then excused herself. Pia lay there in the dimly lit room, doing her best to breathe. Soon she would find out if she was ready for implantation.

If she was, then it was crunch time. Was she really going to go through with this? Have Crystal's babies? Once they were thawed, there was no backing out.

Before she could scramble from the table and run screaming through the building, Dr. Galloway appeared.

"I heard you're ready," the doctor said with a smile. "Let's see."

She squeezed on fresh gel and studied the monitor.

"Very nice," she murmured. "Yes, Pia. I would say we could implant tomorrow, if you want." The doctor touched her arm. "We can also wait a month, if you need more time."

Ready, as in ready? As in now?

Pia opened her mouth, then closed it. Her chest got tight, as if something heavy pressed down. She felt nauseous and light-headed. Ready.

"The e-eggs can be ready by tomorrow?" she asked, her voice faint.

"Yes. We'd schedule you back for right after lunch." Her doctor put down the wand and wiped Pia's belly. "You don't have to decide today. You'll be just as ready next month."

True, but a month was a long time to wait. Pia was afraid she would freak out even more, or at the very least, try to talk herself out of moving forward.

She sucked in a breath and braced herself. "What time tomorrow?"

APPARENTLY DR. GALLOWAY'S definition of painless and Pia's weren't exactly the same. Having a catheter inserted was a borderline creepy experience, but Pia did her best to relax and keep breathing.

"All done," her doctor told her seconds later. She stood and drew the gown down over Pia's legs, then put a blanket on her. "Lie here for about twenty minutes to let things settle. Then you're free to go."

"And I don't have to act any different?" Pia asked. "Avoid strenuous activities, that sort of thing?"

"I'd stay quiet for the next few hours. You have the vitamins I gave you?"

Dr. Galloway had given her samples the previous day, along with a prescription she'd already filled. She'd taken the first prenatal vitamin that morning, downing the pill with a disgustingly healthy breakfast.

"Yes."

"Then that's all you need for now."

The doctor dimmed the lights and left the room. Pia tried to get comfortable on the padded table. She closed her eyes and placed her hands on her lower stomach.

"Hi," she whispered. "I'm Pia. I knew your mom. She was amazing and wonderful and you would have really loved her."

Thinking about her friend made her eyes burn. She blinked away tears and drew another deep breath.

"She, ah, died a few months ago. Over the summer. It was sad and we all miss her. Your dad is gone, too, which might make you think you're getting off to a rough start. But you're not. You see, both your parents wanted to have children. Your mom especially. She wanted to have all three of you. But she couldn't, what with being dead and all."

She groaned. Talk about screwing up the conversation. "Sorry," she murmured. "I should have planned this better. What I'm saying is she really wanted this. She wanted you to be born. I know I'm not her, but I'm going to do my best, I swear. I'm going to read books and talk to women who are good moms. I'll be there for you."

She thought about her own mother abandoning her to move to Florida. "I'll never leave you," she vowed. "No matter what, I'll be there for you. I won't run off and forget about you." She pressed lightly on her stomach. "Can you feel that? It's me. I'm right here."

Fear lurked in the background. The possibility of cosmic

punishment for wishing away her pregnancy in college. But the truth was, she couldn't change the past. She could only pray that the souls of the innocents were protected. That if anyone was to be punished, it would only be her.

"I'm sorry about that, too," she whispered. "I was wrong." Despite Dr. Galloway's promise that it hadn't been her fault, she couldn't help wondering if it was.

She heard a light knock on the door.

"Come in."

Raoul entered, looking impossibly tall and male. "Hey. The doc said it's done."

Pia tried to smile. "That's what they tell me. I don't feel any different."

"Not hearing voices?" he asked with a grin.

"I don't think hearing voices is ever a good sign."

He pulled up the stool and sat, taking her hand in his. "Scared?"

"Beyond terrified. I was telling them to hold on tight and that I'd be here for them."

He gazed into her eyes. "I'm going to tell you the same thing, Pia. Keep holding on."

Once again she was fighting tears. "For Keith?"

"And for you. I need to do this."

She managed a quivering smile. "So it's all about you? Typical male."

"That's me." He leaned in and kissed her forehead. "What happens next?" he asked.

She tried not to focus on the warmth of his skin and the way he made her feel safe. Even if Raoul lasted through the pregnancy, there was no way he was sticking around for anything else. Getting used to having him around wasn't an option.

"I stay here until the nurse kicks me out. In theory I can go back to work, but I'm heading home. I'm going to spend the afternoon on my sofa. It's the whole gravity thing. I want to give these little guys a real shot."

"Okay. What are you in the mood for?"

For a second she thought he meant sex. The part of her that had been dazzled and satiated wanted to beg for a repeat performance. But there was no way they could do it. Not right after the implantation.

"Italian?" he asked. "Mexican? I'll get takeout."

Oh, sure. Food. "Either. I'm not that hungry."

"You will be in a few hours, and you have to eat."

"For the babies," she said, keeping her free hand on her belly. "Do you think I should sing to them?"

He chuckled. "Do you want to?"

"I'm not very good."

"You could give them a cheer. Do you remember any from high school?"

She laughed. "I appreciate the thought, but it's even too weird for me."

He stroked her cheek. "Look at you. Having babies. What would your friends say?"

"My current friends will be completely supportive. The ones who know aren't even surprised. But my friends from before…" She sighed. "As I told you before, I wasn't exactly the nicest girl in high school. Too much attitude and money. Not enough compassion."

He looked interested rather than judgmental. "When did that change?"

"Early in my senior year of high school."

The door opened and the nurse looked in. "You're free to go, Pia. When you're dressed, stop by the desk. We've made an appointment for two weeks from now."

"Thanks."

She sat up. Raoul brushed her mouth with his.

"I'll wait outside for you," he said.

"Okay."

She watched him leave, then carefully slid to her feet and

started to dress. As she pulled on her jeans, she realized she trusted Raoul to be there for her. At least for now. After all this time, it was nice to have someone to depend on.

CHAPTER NINE

PIA SAT AT A table in front of the high school stage. "You're kidding, right?" she asked the mayor.

Marsha rested her elbows on the table and dropped her head to her hands. "I wish I was. I went to the bathroom. I swear I was gone all of two minutes. By the time I got back, they'd voted to have a talent show featuring the single women in town. I guess they want the busloads of men to get a good look at what's available."

When Pia had been asked to attend an audition, she'd had no idea what she was getting into. At least fifty women were here, which she found stunning, and not in a happy way. They were dressed in everything from tutus to shepherdess costumes. A few wanted to start by listing everything they could cook and/ or bake. One woman even smiled broadly, saying she had all her own teeth and not a single cavity.

"Like that makes her good breeding material?" Pia asked, eyeing the crowd. "Tell me this isn't happening."

"I wish I could."

"When did we get desperate? I've always known there was something of a man shortage, but so what? We're happy—things get done. There are more women doing traditionally male jobs in town than probably anywhere else in the country. Isn't that a good thing?"

Marsha raised her head and sighed. "I've been told that there are women who want to settle down—get married and have a family. That's more difficult here. The choice is to pick from the limited stock on hand or move."

"Stock on hand?" And women complained that men objectify them. "I don't understand this."

"Me, either, but it's too late for us to stop the flood. Men are arriving daily."

A young woman in her twenties got up onstage. She wore a pale pink leotard and a short, wrapped skirt. She nodded and music poured out of the hidden speakers. Within seconds, the contestant was singing and dancing to a popular Broadway musical.

"She's good," Pia murmured. "What am I supposed to do? Make notes on who I like best? Are we really going to have a talent show?"

"I don't see any way around it. I'm just so humiliated."

"Um, no. That honor goes to the woman who juggled pies she'd baked." Pia had always loved Fool's Gold. The town had traditions and polite residents. People cared about each other. Had a single chapter in a thesis and a busload or two of men really changed everything?

Maybe there was something in the air, she thought. Something promoting change. Look at her. Just two days ago, she'd had embryos implanted. She'd been there for the procedure and had spent the rest of the afternoon lying on her sofa, and she still couldn't seem to wrap her mind around the concept. Being pregnant was just a word. More concept than reality. How could she possibly be pregnant?

Yet Dr. Galloway had put the embryos in her. Were they hanging on as she'd asked them to? Were they growing, getting bigger and stronger?

She touched her hand to her belly, as if she could feel them inside of her.

Scattered applause brought her back to the auditions. She clapped as well, then turned to find Marsha staring at her.

"Where did you go?" the mayor asked. "She was pretty good, so it can't have been the singing and dancing."

"Sorry. I'll pay attention." Pia picked up her pen and pulled the notepad closer. "Who's next?"

Marsha continued to study her. "Is everything all right?"

"I'm fine."

The mayor didn't look convinced.

Pia drew in a breath. "Crystal left me her embryos."

Marsha's face relaxed into a smile. "Did she? I knew some-one would get them. You must be very touched, and equally terrified. That's a lot of responsibility."

"Tell me about it. It's not about owning the embryos. Crystal expects me to have her babies."

Marsha nodded. "That's a lot to ask of a friend. Are you going to agree?"

"I..." Pia drew in a breath. "I had them implanted two days ago. There were three embryos. They all survived the thawing, which I guess doesn't always happen. We'll know in two weeks if they were able to embed or implant or whatever it's called."

Marsha looked stunned for a moment, then hugged her. "Good for you. What an amazing thing to do. I'm so proud."

The words made Pia feel good. "I'm mostly in shock," she admitted. "Nothing about this is real to me."

"That will take time."

"I have nine months." A number that she couldn't relate to. Knowing the facts about a pregnancy was very different than it actually happening to her. "I guess even now my body could be changing, but I don't feel any different."

"You will. Especially if you have triplets."

Pia winced. "Don't say that. I can't comprehend one baby, let alone three. I'm going to have these babies by myself."

Marsha squeezed her hand. "We'll all be there for you, Pia. You know that, don't you?"

She nodded. "Everything is surreal. I keep going back to the same question. Why would Crystal pick me?"

"Because she loved you and trusted you."

"I guess."

The mayor smiled. "I have a personal request."

"Sure."

"Can you please have boys?"

Pia laughed. "That part is already determined. Sorry. You should have had the talk with Crystal."

"I hate being late to anything." She turned back to the stage where a couple of guys were dragging on two-dimensional cardboard trees. "Dear God, what now?"

RAOUL WALKED THROUGH the main building of the camp. Less than a month ago, the last of the summer campers had headed home, and the cleaning crew had begun the process of winterizing the structures. Now, several hundred kids filled the various rooms, pinning flyers to walls and driving away the silence with their laughter.

He still had ideas for a year-round camp, but until he could make that happen, using the facility for the temporary elementary school was the right thing to do.

The preliminary meeting on repairing and rebuilding the burned school had been grim at best. The damage was extensive, the funds limited. Realistically, the new elementary school wouldn't be ready for occupancy for nearly two years. Which put his plans on hold for at least that long. His biggest concern was keeping Dakota Hendrix working for him. She was smart and capable. He had a feeling headhunters called her regularly. All he had to offer her was a good salary, work close to her family, running the summer camp and the promise that when they got the camp back she would be in charge of the new program.

The school had contracted her services for a few hours a

week. She provided counseling and acted as the liaison between the school and the camp. So far there hadn't been any problems, and while Raoul didn't anticipate trouble, he'd learned it was always best to be prepared.

He glanced at the big clock on the wall. It was a few minutes before noon. Now the hallway was relatively quiet, but in about two minutes the bell would ring and children would explode out of their classrooms and head for the cafeteria.

He knew because he was here most school days. Somehow he'd gotten roped into playing ball with a group of kids during the lunch hour. He didn't mind too much and he was careful not to spend more time with any one kid. In a group they were great, but he didn't want any of them getting too attached.

He was willing to get involved—to a point. But some distance was a good thing.

When the bell rang, releasing the kids for lunch, doors opened and slammed into the wall. High-pitched voices broke the silence. In a matter of seconds, he found himself surrounded by a dozen or so boys, all clamoring for him to have lunch with them.

He was about to refuse them all—with the promise that he would meet them on the playground after—when he spotted that skinny redheaded kid. Peter, Pia had said his name was.

"You know my friend Pia," he told the boy.

Peter grinned. "Yeah. We met in the park. She's really cool, you know, for a girl."

"I'll pass along the compliment."

"You gonna have lunch with us?" Drew, Peter's friend, asked. "We'll save you a seat and everything."

Raoul hesitated, then nodded. "Sure. I can do that." Maybe he would get a chance to talk to Peter and find out if there was any kind of a problem at home.

They headed for the cafeteria and got in line. Raoul grabbed a tray with the rest of the kids, then smiled at the older woman scooping out mac and cheese.

"I won't take any if there's not enough," he said.

"Oh, we always make extra. Most of the teachers eat here, too," she said and dumped a portion of the pasta onto a plate.

Green beans followed, along with fruit. He passed on very green pudding, grabbed two cartons of milk in one hand, then had to hold in a grin as the boys with him tried to do the same.

Their hands were too small to pick up both cartons at once, so they settled for one and followed him to a low table by the window.

He stared for a second, not sure he would fit on the bench, then realized all the tables were scaled down. Kid-size, he thought humorously, wondering if he was heavy enough to tip one. He lowered himself carefully, centering his weight on the bench. Things seemed steady enough.

The kids gathered around him, pushing to sit closer, until he was crammed in on the bench seat. He picked up the first carton of milk, opened it, then drained it in three long swallows. When he set the carton back down, every boy at the table was staring.

He wiped his mouth self-consciously. "So, ah, how are you guys liking the new school?"

"It's great," one boy said. "When it snows, my mom says we're going to have trouble getting up the mountain. Maybe we'll have snow days."

"Sweet!" another boy crowed.

"Tell us what it was like when you played football," a third boy pleaded. "My dad says you were the best ever."

"Tell your dad thanks," Raoul said with a grin. "I was good, but I'm not sure about being the best. I always tried to do better. That's what defines success."

"I'd like to play football," Peter said. "But I'm small."

"You're not short," his friend told him. "Just skinny."

"Don't worry about being small," Raoul told him. "You'll grow. Now's the time to work on basics. Running, coordination. You can get that from any sport. You can also start learning about the game."

"I want to play football, too."

"Me, too!"

Raoul made a note to talk to the principal about starting a spring football program. Nothing too physical—just some practice with kids split into teams. To give them a taste of the possibilities.

"My sister says she wants to play football," the dark-haired boy sitting next to Raoul said. "I keep tellin' her, girls don't play football. But she's bigger than me and when she gets mad, she hits me."

A couple of the guys laughed. "Then maybe you should stop saying it," Raoul suggested.

"I guess. But you could tell her. She'd have to listen to you."

He held up both hands. "No, thanks. Your sister can do anything she sets her mind to."

The boy sighed heavily. "That's what Mom says, too, and Dad just keeps quiet."

A smart man, Raoul thought.

"My parents are divorced," the boy on Peter's right announced. "I live with them on different weeks. They have houses right across the street from each other."

"How's that working?" Raoul asked.

"I dunno. It's kind of stupid. If they can live that close, why can't they live together?"

"Marriage can be tough," Raoul told him. "The important thing is that your parents love you. Do you have anyone to talk to, like an older brother or an aunt or uncle?"

"My uncle Carl is really nice. He listens."

"Then keep talking to him. Don't let stuff build up inside. That's never good."

"My parents are divorced, too," another boy said.

"I have five sisters," the kid on the end said. Most of the boys at the table groaned.

"That's a lot of girls," Raoul told him. "Are you the youngest?"

"No. I'm in the middle. They're everywhere. My dad built me a tree house so I'd have my own man cave."

"Good for you."

During the conversation, Raoul had been watching Peter. The boy finished his lunch without saying much. Just when Raoul was about to suggest they head to the playground, Peter spoke.

"My parents are dead," he said, staring at his plate. "They died in a car crash two years ago."

"I'm sorry," Raoul told him.

Peter shrugged. "It was bad, but stuff like that happens."

Peter's friend Drew leaned toward Raoul. "He was in the car when it happened. He was there when they died."

Raoul swore silently. What a nightmare for the kid. He had no idea what to say.

Peter looked at him. "You really think I'll get big enough to play football in high school?"

"I really do. In fact, let's go practice some drills right now."

Peter's sad face slowly transformed into a smile. "Yeah?"

"Come on. It'll be fun."

The boys all stood and grabbed their trays. After dumping them on the counter by the kitchen, they ran for the door leading outside. Peter walked more slowly than the rest.

Raoul caught up with him. "I'm sorry about your folks," he said. "I never knew my dad. I lost my mom when I was a little older than you. It's hard."

Peter nodded without speaking.

Raoul wanted to give him a hug, but he knew there was a firm "no touching" policy at the school. Not knowing what else to do, he vowed to pay attention to the kid whenever he was around, then asked, "Want to learn how to throw farther than everyone else?"

"You can teach me that?" Peter asked eagerly.

"You bet."

"All right!" The boy laughed and ran toward his friends.

Maybe, for today, it was enough.

"You should have been more clear about the food," Pia said as she scooped kung pao chicken onto her plate, then licked her finger where a little sauce had dribbled.

Raoul sat across from her at the small table in his kitchen. "Because then you would have jumped right on the pregnancy-buddy wagon?"

"Absolutely. I know it's not sophisticated or elegant, but offer me a snack and I'm practically your slave."

"Good to know."

Humor danced in his dark eyes. Humor that made her want to smile. Of course looking at his face, or any other part of him, made her want to do other things, too. Like ask him to get naked. Or let her get naked. Or touch her. Although she really appreciated the theory of "one last fling," making love with Raoul had left her hungry for more.

Even if he hadn't been very explicit on the temporary nature of their relationship, she couldn't have asked for a replay. Not with the embryos hanging on by a thread...or whatever it was they hung on by. Maybe in a few weeks, when the doctor said everything was normal, she could consider doing the wild thing. But until then, she was only thinking pure and maternal thoughts.

"This may be my last Chinese for the duration," she said, scooping up a mouthful of fried rice on her fork. "I've been reading one of those pregnancy books and I have to watch my salt intake. I also have to give up alcohol, caffeine, over-the-counter medicines and in six or seven months, my ankles. Babies are really demanding."

He grinned. "Don't they also say it's worth it?"

"Sure, but that's a whole lot easier to write than live. And that's for later. Right now I'm living in month one of being pregnant. Assuming I am."

"Any symptoms?"

"Just the voices."

He grinned.

She picked up an egg roll. "Nothing, really. They say some women can tell the second they conceive, but I guess I'm not that sensitive. Probably a good thing. I have a feeling I'm going to make myself crazy worrying as it is."

She glanced around at the modest house. The kitchen had been updated with new appliances and countertops, but nothing about the space especially screamed "famous sport celebrity abode."

"What was your place like in Dallas?" she asked.

"Big."

"Two bedrooms? Five?"

"Three stories and some rooms I never saw." He shrugged. "It was more an investment property."

She tried to remember what else she'd read about him. "Did you move to Los Angeles a while ago?"

He nodded. "About a year after I got married. When we split up, I moved back to Dallas but never settled. Then I retired and here I am."

She wondered about the ex-Mrs. Moreno but wasn't sure she was comfortable asking questions. From what she could see, Raoul was annoyingly close to perfect. Why would any woman let him go?

Maybe it hadn't been her choice. Maybe he'd dumped her.

"Are you going to buy a house in town?" she asked.

"I've been looking around," he admitted. "There's no hurry. This place works fine."

"You're renting from Josh, right?"

Raoul grinned. "He seems to own a lot of the town."

"He's into real estate. He had to do something with all his winnings." She tilted her head. "Is it tough for the two of you to share the spotlight? I mean with your large egos and all."

He raised an eyebrow. "You've seen my ego—you tell me."

"Very funny. I guess if anyone would have the problem, it would be Josh. He's been the favorite son for years. But I don't think he's the type to care if you get more of the attention."

"You like Josh." Raoul didn't seem to be asking a question.

"Sure. I've known him most of my life. He was a few years ahead of me in high school. Very crush-worthy."

"Did the two of you ever…"

She looked at him, pretending confusion. "Did we ever?"

"Get involved. Date."

"Oh," she said with mock understanding. "Did I ever see his ego?"

Raoul stared at her without speaking. She wanted to believe his interest was an important clue into how he felt about her. That even as they sat there, he was realizing he was wildly in-fatuated with her and seconds away from falling in love.

Or maybe not. Did she really need a guy in her life right now? Weren't three potential children enough?

"We never dated," she said. "I've never seen his ego." She grinned. "Although his butt *is* on a screensaver, so I've seen that." She lowered her voice. "Yours is better."

"It's not a competition," he grumbled.

But he had been asking, she thought, amused. Raoul was such a guy.

She sipped her water, studying him. His dark hair fell across his forehead.

"You need a haircut," she told him.

"No, thanks. It sounds too complicated, what with the war-ring hairdressers and all."

"I'll take you. Show you off."

"Thanks." He leaned toward her. "Have you told anyone about the embryos?"

"Marsha knows. She may or may not have told Charity. I'm waiting. I guess until it's sure. I just didn't want a lot of people speculating until there was something to speculate about. It seems wrong. This is Crystal's moment, not mine."

"You're the one who's going to be pregnant."

"I'll be peeing on a stick in a few days," she said. "I'm think-ing that will be a wake-up call."

"I want to be there."

"Okay, although that's lovely, we're really not that close."

He shook his head. "In the house, not in the room."

She wasn't sure about peeing on command, especially with someone waiting to know the results, but she supposed she could run water or make him hum loudly.

"Okay."

"Good."

He handed her the last egg roll. The overhead light caught the thin scar on his cheek.

"What happened?" she asked, pointing to the scar. "Let me guess. You were helping an old lady across the street."

"Would you feel better if I told you I got it in a bar fight?"

"Yes, but I'd think you were lying."

"How about if I ran into a fence during practice."

And impaled his cheek? She shuddered at the thought. "Maybe the bar fight makes a better story."

"Whatever makes you happy."

After dinner, he insisted on walking her home.

It was already dark and the night was cool. Pia pulled her sweater around her and crossed her arms over her chest. "We'll have snow by November," she said.

"Do you like winter?"

"Most of the time. We don't get a ton of snow, which is nice. The resort is only a few miles up the mountain, but even a couple thousand feet can make a big difference. They usually get several feet. At least I don't have to worry about shoveling a driveway. I can walk everywhere."

He put his arm around her and drew her against him. "If you have any shoveling needs, just let me know."

"More pregnancy-buddy duties?"

"Absolutely."

"You should put out a brochure, so I can know what to expect."

"I'll do that."

He felt warm, she thought as she leaned into him. Safe. All the things a pregnant woman could want in a man. Or a non-pregnant woman.

Once again she thought about the woman he'd been married to before and wanted to ask what had happened. But she wouldn't. For reasons she couldn't explain, Raoul wanted to take care of her for a little while. For someone who had been on her own since she was seventeen, having someone to lean on felt good. Especially now, she thought, pressing her hand to her belly.

They reached her apartment building. He held open the front door, then followed her up the stairs. When they reached her door, he turned and faced her.

"You going to be okay by yourself?" he asked.

"I've been living here for years. I can handle it."

"If you need anything, call me."

"I don't want to interrupt your hot date."

He adjusted the front of her sweater. "You're my hot date."

Words to make her heart beat faster, she thought, knowing giving in to emotional temptation would be a really bad thing.

"Raoul…"

Before she could say anything else, he pressed his mouth to hers.

The kiss was soft and tender, more caring than passionate. He didn't try to deepen it or even touch her anywhere else. Yet the feel of his lips against hers was devastating. Not from wanting in a sexual way, but because the gentleness ignited a longing she rarely allowed herself to experience. The kiss made her dream about what it would be like to fall in love, to risk her heart, to believe she could have someone to care about. Someone who wouldn't leave.

Unexpected tears burned in her eyes. She pulled back, dug her keys out of her pocket and opened the door.

"Thanks for dinner," she said, doing her best to keep her tone light. "Especially for the last egg roll."

"All part of the full-service plan. You'll let me know when you're going to pee on the stick?"

Despite the emptiness inside of her, she laughed. "No one's ever asked me that before, so I have to say yes."

"Good. Night, Pia."

"Good night."

She waited until he started down the stairs, then she closed the door, locked it and leaned back against the sturdy surface.

"Don't go there," she whispered into the quiet room. "Don't believe in him. You know what will happen if you do."

What always happened. He would leave. She had a feeling that telling herself she was used to being on her own wouldn't make dealing without him any easier to take.

CHAPTER TEN

"IT WAS THE weirdest thing," Pia said as she and Montana sat in Pia's office, going over details for the bachelor auction. Technically now an auction/talent show.

"I don't understand," Montana said, frowning slightly. "Isn't the auction enough?"

"Apparently not. Nearly thirty women will be getting up onstage and performing in one way or another. They have a three-minute limit." Pia told her about the woman who bragged about a lack of cavities. "I grew up here. When did the women in town get so distressed about the lack of men?"

"Some women want to be in a relationship."

"I agree, but not like this." Pia looked at her friend. "Have you noticed all the extra men in town?"

Montana nodded. "Three guys in a car whistled at me yesterday. It was strange. But kind of nice."

Pia winced. "Tell me you're not going to be there, meeting the bus."

Montana laughed. "I can barely hold down a job, let alone find and keep a man."

"Tell me about it," Pia grumbled. "I've never had a guy stay. And I can't figure out why. Is it me? Do I give off the leave-me vibe? Is there something fundamentally wrong with me?"

"No. You're great. Smart, funny."

"Well, so are you."

Montana wrinkled her nose. "No, I'm scattered. I feel like it's been harder for me to grow up than for everyone else. Maybe that's why I haven't found the one."

"I don't have an excuse," Pia told her. Not that it would matter now, what with the implantation and all.

Without meaning to, she found herself thinking about Raoul. She appreciated the pregnancy-buddy support, but she was going to have a serious talk with him about the kissing. They couldn't keep doing it. She was finding it confusing. Not the kissing itself—that was easy. But the wanting that followed. She was fine wanting sex. But wanting more...that was the real danger.

"I want to find where I belong," Montana said, then sighed. "Don't laugh, but I have an interview for a job."

"Why would I laugh at that?"

"Okay—not laugh exactly. I'm really excited, but just, I'm nervous."

Pia patted Montana's arm. "As long as it's not starring in porn, I'm good with it."

Montana's mouth twisted. "Well, crap."

Pia stared at her. "Oh, God. You're seriously going to be in a porn movie?"

Montana laughed. "I'm kidding."

"Very funny. What is it?"

"There's this guy named Max. He lives outside of town and he trains therapy dogs. They're the ones who go into hospitals and nursing homes. Being around them makes people feel better. He also trains dogs for a reading program. They've done studies and kids who have trouble reading do a lot better reading to a dog rather than a person. I guess they feel they're not being judged. Anyway, he's looking for someone to help him run the kennel and help with the training and take the dogs to their various programs."

Montana drew in a breath. "There's a lot to learn. When I

spoke to Max, he said I would have to take a couple of classes online and get certified as a dog trainer. While I was doing that, I would work in the kennel and get to know the dogs. He's giving me a four-month trial period. If that goes well, he'll start me actually working with the therapy dogs. I have an interview in a couple of days."

Pia was still reeling from the porn joke. "You sound excited."

"I am. I like the idea of working with the dogs and helping people. I want to make a difference, but I still don't know if this job is the right one. Dakota and Nevada both just knew what they wanted to do with their lives. I'm an identical triplet. Shouldn't I be like them?"

"You have to follow your own path and figure out what's right for you. It sounds like you might have found it."

"I hope so. I'm tired of messing up."

"Montana, don't beat yourself up. When have you messed up?"

Her friend shrugged. "I just turned down a full-time job with benefits. Who does that?"

"Someone who's thinking long term."

"I want to be good at something. Look at you. You're great at your job."

"I organize festivals. That's hardly saving the world."

"You're an integral part of the community. What you do marks the passage of time and makes memories. Parents look forward to bringing their kids to their first Fall Festival or the Saturday of Giving. People plan their travel schedules to come here for their favorites. What you do changes the way people live."

Pia stared at her. "Wow. I should ask for a raise."

Montana laughed. "I'm serious."

"So am I." She'd always loved her work, but it had never seemed all that important. Montana's words made her rethink that concept. "I'd always focused on the fact that I bring tourists to town, which means more money for all the local businesses."

"It's not just about money."

"You're right. Which is why you shouldn't feel bad about turning down the full-time library job. You have to think about what's really important to you."

"I want to make a difference," Montana said firmly. "I've watched some videos about the service dogs. They're wonderful. I could be a part of that."

"Then I hope you get the job."

"Me, too. It would be nice to find where I belong. I want to be more than my family name."

"Don't discount being a Hendrix," Pia told her. "You're already part of something wonderful."

"I know, but they're just family."

Pia thought about her relatively solitary life. How she'd been on her own for so long, with no one to depend on. Now she was going to be responsible for three new lives. At least that was the hope.

"Family can be the most important thing of all," she said, thinking it was sad that Keith and Crystal had only had each other, and now the babies would only have her.

Montana rolled her eyes. "Now you sound like my mother."

"Denise is wonderful, so thanks for the compliment."

"You're welcome."

"I DON'T NEED MY HAIR CUT," Raoul told Pia as they walked down the street.

"You sound whiny," she told him. "I expect a fairly high level of maturity from my pregnancy buddy. Don't let me down."

"When did you get bossy?"

"I always have been," she said with a laugh. "I thought you would have noticed."

The day was cool. Pia had pulled on a bright red coat over her jeans and sweater. Her boots made her a little taller, which meant she was the perfect height for kissing, he thought absently.

He liked kissing Pia. He'd liked doing more, but under the circumstances, that wasn't on the table. She might be pregnant, and neither of them would do anything to hurt the babies. Not that she'd shown any interest in getting back in his bed. Although given what had happened the last time they'd been together, he doubted either of them would say no.

Still, he had a higher purpose here: taking care of Pia as she took care of Crystal's embryos.

"It's a simple rule," Pia told him. "You alternate between the sisters. Today we're seeing Bella. Next time you'll go to Julia's shop."

"I still think getting my hair cut out of town solves the problem."

"Coward."

"Football taught me when to drop back and let my guys cover me."

She paused by the glass door of the salon. "It doesn't matter if you go out of town, Raoul. They'll still be mad at you. Haven't you figured it out? There's no way to win this fight, so why not get a front-row seat and enjoy the show?"

"There's a show?"

She smiled. "Actually, you're the show."

She walked inside. He hesitated for a second, then followed her into the salon.

It was midday, midweek and still nearly every station was full. As he entered the well-lit, modern space, every single person—aka woman—turned to stare at him.

A middle-aged woman with dark hair and beautiful brown eyes studied him appraisingly. "Pia, what have you brought me?"

Pia linked her arm through Raoul's. "Bella, you can borrow him, but you can't keep him. This is Raoul Moreno. Raoul, please meet Bella Gionni."

Bella moved toward him, her hand extended. "My pleasure," she purred. "So strong, so handsome. Josh is my favorite. After all, I've known him since he was a boy, but you... You come very close."

Raoul shifted uncomfortably, then shook hands with the woman. "Ah, thanks."

"You're welcome. I'm ready for you."

He leaned toward Pia. "You're not leaving, are you?"

"No. I'm here to protect you."

"Good."

He was aware of every woman in the place watching him. He was used to attention, but it usually wasn't so blatant.

Bella seated him in a chair and wrapped a plastic cape around him. Then she stood behind him, her hands on his shoulders, and met his gaze in the mirror.

"What would you like?"

"Just a trim," Pia said, her eyes sparkling with amusement. "This is his first haircut in town."

Bella smiled. "And you came to me."

"Where else would we go?" Pia asked.

"Exactly." Bella reached for a spray bottle and dampened his hair, then combed through it. "Are the two of you together?"

"No," Pia said quickly.

"Yes," Raoul insisted just as fast.

Bella raised her eyebrows. "You should probably get that part figured out."

Pia looked at him. "We're not dating."

"We're together."

"Okay, but not in that way. Just because we've..." She stopped and glanced around, as if aware of everyone listening.

He'd been talking about him being her pregnancy buddy, but he realized she'd been thinking about their night together.

"Men," she muttered, as she stalked off and started talking to one of the other hairdressers.

Bella combed and cut efficiently, her hands moving confidently. "So you like our Pia, do you?"

"Very much."

Bella's expression sharpened. "As a friend or more?"

"We're friends."

"Then you're a fool."

He held in a grin. He'd always enjoyed women who spoke their minds. "Why?"

"Pia is worth ten of whatever women you've been dating. She's a good girl. Smart, caring, beautiful."

He turned his head so he could see Pia in the mirror. She'd shrugged out of her coat and he could see the way her sweater clung to her curves. She laughed at something he couldn't hear, but the sound of her amusement made him smile.

She was all Bella said and more. She had heart and character. No one knew about the embryos. She could have walked away from them, had them donated to science or simply thrown away. But none of the options had occurred to her. There weren't a lot of people he admired, but she was one of them.

"What happened to her was sad," Bella continued. "Losing her father that way, then having her mother run to Florida. There was Pia, in her senior year of high school, and she lost everything. She had to go into foster care."

"I'd heard," he murmured, wondering what kind of mother simply abandoned her kid without a second thought. The grief and loss could have drawn them closer together. Instead Pia had had to deal with all the crap on her own.

He found himself wanting to fix the problem—even though it had happened over a decade ago. Still, the need was there, to do something. To act.

"She's had boyfriends, you know," Bella announced.

"I'm sure she has."

"They never stay. Poor girl. I don't know what goes wrong, but they leave."

Not a conversation he wanted to be having with Bella, he thought. His gaze once again returned to Pia. She'd had a difficult road and her life was about to get three times more complicated. Who was going to take care of her? Who would be there when she needed help?

He knew she had friends and they would help. The town would pull through. Fool's Gold seemed like that kind of place. But on a day-to-day basis, Pia would be on her own.

He wondered if she'd thought that part through. If she knew what she was getting into. She turned and met his gaze in the mirror, then smiled. He winked at her and she returned her attention to her conversation.

He'd been in love twice in his life. He and his first girlfriend had grown apart, and Caro had betrayed every part of their marriage vows. He wasn't looking to feel that way ever again. Not getting involved was safer. But there was still the reality of wanting a family—needing that connection. He couldn't have one without the other. Or so he'd always believed.

"I CAN HEAR YOU," Pia yelled through the closed bathroom door.

"I'm just sitting. There's nothing to hear."

Even so, she was sure there were noises. Or maybe the problem was there weren't. Talk about pressure, she thought as she stood and pulled up her bikini panties and jeans. Is this what it was like to be a guy? Pure performance anxiety?

She opened the bathroom door.

"I can't do this with you in the room," she said, then held up a hand. "Don't bother saying you're not in the room. It's practically the same thing."

Raoul shook his head as he got to his feet and turned to face her. Laughter brightened his dark eyes. "Can't stand the heat, huh?" he teased.

"The heat isn't the problem."

"Have you tried turning on the faucet? The sound of running water might help."

"I'm not going to stand here having a conversation with you about my inability to pee."

"You already are."

She rolled her eyes, then pointed at the front door. "Go stand in the hall until I'm done."

"I've had my tongue in your mouth."

"So not the point."

"We can have sex, but I can't be in the next room while you go to the bathroom?"

"Exactly."

"Fine." He crossed the room and let himself out. Then he stuck his head back in. "What should I tell the neighbors if they ask why I'm loitering?"

"Don't make me kill you."

He laughed and shut the door behind him.

"Men," she muttered, then returned to the bathroom and pulled down her pants.

After sitting on the toilet, she turned on the faucet and reached for the plastic stick from the pregnancy test. Everything was fine, she told herself. She peed several times a day. It didn't require a lot of thought or effort. It was natural. Easy.

But at that moment, it felt far from easy. It felt impossible. She turned off the water, tried humming, shifting, breathing more slowly. Her bladder stubbornly refused to empty.

Never again, she told herself. Pregnancy was too hard. When she finally managed to pee on the stick, she was going to get ice cream. The fact that it was chilly outside didn't matter. She wanted a hot fudge sundae with whipped...

"Oh, no!"

When she'd finally stopped paying attention, her body had responded. She did her thing with the stick, set it on a tissue, then got up, flushed and pulled up her pants. After washing her hands, she walked out to get Raoul.

"Finally," he said when she opened the door. "Success?"

"I have peed."

"I'm so proud."

"Be nice or I'll make you touch it."

She went back into the bathroom and carefully carried out

the stick on the tissue and set it on a paper towel on the kitchen counter.

"How long?"

"Just a few minutes."

They stared at the little screen, which showed an hourglass. She could hear the faint ticking of a clock and feel the rapid thudding of her heart. According to the test, the result would announce her condition. Pregnant or not pregnant. As simple as that.

She didn't allow herself to speculate. Part of her was afraid that she'd lost Crystal's babies—that they hadn't been able to hang on. But another part of her was terrified they had.

Raoul put his arm around her. She leaned into him and hung on.

The screen changed and she saw a single word.

Pregnant.

There was no misunderstanding that.

Her body went cold, then seemed to heat from the inside. Her stomach flopped over, making her wonder if she was going to throw up. Reality loomed, like a really big storm, but she couldn't take it all in. Pregnant. She was pregnant.

"You did it!" Raoul crowed, then grabbed her around the waist and spun her in the center of the room. "You're going to be a mom."

He sounded delighted. She felt like she was going to pass out, although that could have been from the world blurring around her.

A mom? Her? "I can't," she whispered.

He set her down. "Sure you can. This is great, Pia. The embryos implanted. This is great news."

Intellectually, she could agree. This is what Crystal wanted. But in her gut, she was deathly afraid of screwing up.

"I have to sit down," she said, making her way over to a kitchen chair and dropping onto it. She closed her eyes and focused on breathing.

Pregnant. Right now there were babies growing inside of her. Babies who would be born and become actual children, then real people. Babies who would depend on her and expect her to take care of them.

Raoul pulled up a chair and sat across from her. He took her hand in his. "What's wrong?"

"I don't think I can do this. I can't have children. I don't know how."

"Don't they do all the hard work themselves?"

"The forming and growing, maybe, but then what? They're going to have expectations. I'm not prepared for this."

He leaned toward her. "You have eight and a half months and I'll help."

"You're going to be my pregnancy buddy." She pulled her hand free and stood. "Don't get me wrong—I appreciate the support. But I'm less concerned about being pregnant than what comes after. I'm going to have to buy stuff. I haven't got a clue what. There must be a list somewhere, right? On the Internet?"

He rose. "I'm sure there is."

"And I'll need to move. This place is too small. I'll need a house." She made okay money, but it wasn't a fortune. Could she afford a house? "And there's college. I should start saving, but I don't know what to invest in. I don't understand the stock market."

He moved close and put his hands on her shoulders. "One thing at a time," he told her. "Relax. Breathe. I can help with all this. We'll find you a great place, and I can get you the best investment advice available. It's going to be okay, Pia. I promise."

She nodded, because that was the expected thing to do. And sure, he would help and she would appreciate it. But when the babies were born, his work was done. He would walk away and she would be left on her own. With triplets.

"THIS IS FUN," Jenny said as she ran the wand over Pia's belly. "I don't usually do ultrasounds this early." She kept her gaze on the monitor. "You know we won't be able to see anything specific. Just whether the embryos have implanted."

"I know," Pia whispered, hanging on to Raoul's hand with all her strength. Under normal circumstances she would worry about hurting him, but he was a tough football player. She was sure he could take it.

Besides, he'd offered to come with her to the doctor's office. If any part of this freaked him out, he would have to deal with it himself.

She'd had less than forty-eight hours to get used to the idea of being pregnant. So far the information hadn't become any more real. She alternated between shock and panic. Neither was especially comfortable.

She'd tried a little reading from the pregnancy books she'd bought, but that only made things worse. Knowing the statistical odds of getting hemorrhoids by the end of term wasn't exactly the sort of information she was looking for.

"Okay," Jenny said cheerfully. "Let me get the doctor."

Pia waited until the tech left, then turned to Raoul. "Did we know she was going to do that? Is it okay she's getting Dr. Galloway?"

He bent over her, smoothing her hair back with his free hand. "It's fine. She said she would be getting the doctor before she started. This is all routine, Pia. You're doing great."

Did all mothers-to-be feel such a numbing sense of responsibility? Because whatever happened wasn't just about her—it was also about Crystal and Keith.

"I want them to be all right. The babies. I hate being scared all the time."

"You need to relax. Keep breathing."

She did her best. Fortunately, Dr. Galloway returned quickly and stood by the monitor as Jenny moved the wand.

"There they are," the doctor said, pointing at the screen. "We have three implantations." The older woman smiled. "Good for you, Pia. They're all in place."

Pia stared at the screen, trying to see what they were point-ing at. It all looked blurry to her, but she didn't care. It was enough to know that for now, everything was going the way it was supposed to.

Although, honestly, the thought of triplets was enough to send anyone over the edge. Two months ago, she'd had a cat who didn't like her. Now she was carrying triplets.

Dr. Galloway wiped off her stomach. "Go ahead and get dressed, Pia. We'll meet in my office and discuss what hap-pens next."

Pia nodded.

Raoul helped her to sit up, then waited as she got to her feet. "I'm right here," he told her.

She nodded because speaking seemed impossible.

After dressing, she went out into the hall. Raoul was waiting. He took her hand in his and led the way to the doctor's office.

She went in first, trying to smile at Dr. Galloway.

"You've begun the journey," the other woman told her. "I'm so proud of you, Pia. Not many people would do what you're doing."

Probably because they were sane, she thought as she took a seat. Raoul settled next to her.

"What's next?" he asked.

"Many things," Dr. Galloway said, pulling out papers and brochures. "A multiple birth brings much joy but also a few chal-lenges. We know early and can make the preparations. Pia, you need to focus on good food and good sleep. You're healthy and I don't foresee any problems, but we will take a few precautions."

She passed over the papers. "I want to see you in a month. I'll be monitoring you more closely than if you were carry-ing only one baby. Between now and then, do the reading I've highlighted. You can call the office with any questions. Every-thing will be fine."

Pia thought about pointing out there was no way the doctor could actually know that, but why state the obvious? She and

Raoul said their goodbyes and somehow made it to the parking lot. She knew, because suddenly they were standing by his sleek, red car. She stared at him across the low roof and saw he looked as stunned as she felt.

"So it's not just me," she said. "That makes me feel better."

"I was faking it," he admitted, then swore. "Triplets. Did you see them on the screen?"

"No, but I wasn't looking too hard. I'm already weirded out by the whole thing."

"They're real," he said slowly. "The babies were just an idea before, but they're going to be born. You're having triplets."

She nodded, wishing people would stop saying that. She didn't need the pressure. Then she looked more closely at him. There was something odd in his eyes. A tightness.

He was going to tell her he couldn't do it, she thought sadly. That this was more than he'd signed on for. Not that she blamed him. She was living in stunned disbelief, as well. But for her, there was no going back. The babies were in her body, doing their thing.

Even though a part of her wanted to beg him not to abandon her, she knew that wasn't fair. He'd already been more than generous. The right thing, the honorable thing, was to release him. Sort of a "Go with God" moment.

"It's okay," she told him. "I understand. I'm going into a place that makes me uncomfortable. I can't begin to imagine what you're feeling. You've been great and I thank you for everything. Please don't feel obligated to do anything more."

He frowned. "What are you talking about?"

"I'm giving you an out. You don't have to be my pregnancy buddy anymore."

"Why would you do that?"

"You look like you want to bolt. I get that."

He walked around the car and stood in front of her. Despite her heels, the man still loomed over her. He was close enough that she had to tilt her head to meet his gaze.

"I'm not running," he said. "But you're right about one thing. I don't want to be your pregnancy buddy anymore."

She hoped her disappointment didn't show. She refused to think about going through the pregnancy by herself. Once she got home, she would have a big hissy fit, followed by a breakdown. But for now, she would stay in control. "I understand."

He took her hand again. He seemed to do that a lot. The problem was she liked it—too much. And now she was going to lose the hand-holding and pretty much everything else when it came to him.

"No," he said. "You don't. Pia, I want more. I want to marry you."

CHAPTER ELEVEN

RAOUL HADN'T PLANNED to propose, but he wasn't completely surprised by what he'd said. He'd been thinking about her a lot lately, about the babies she carried and their future. He admired her and respected her. Despite her fear and worry, she'd plowed ahead, taking each next logical step. His desire to help was something he'd learned from Hawk—to step in and make a difference.

He also hadn't been able to get Keith out of his mind. The man had died fighting for his country. He would have assumed that Crystal would go ahead and have their children. He would have believed his family would go on. Thanks to Pia—it would. But it wasn't right that she do all this alone.

Pia stared at him, her eyes wide, her mouth open. She tried to speak, swallowed, then said, "Excuse me? What?"

"I want to marry you."

She shook her head slightly, as if not sure of her hearing. She looked stunned and a little dizzy. He wondered if he should get her into the car so she could sit. She solved the problem by opening the door herself and slumping into the seat.

He went around to the other side and got in, then he angled toward her.

"I mean it, Pia. Marry me."

"Why?"

A reasonable question, he thought. "I admire what you're doing. Most people would have run in the opposite direction, but you didn't. And don't say you had doubts and questions. If you didn't you wouldn't be competent to have the children."

He leaned toward her. "I've seen a lot of different kind of people in my life. Those who give and those who take. Those who think about others and those who think about themselves. I've told you about my coach and how he changed everything for me. Nicole opened her home and her heart to me. They taught me what's important. I want to do what they did—make a difference to someone."

Her expression of shock changed to something that looked a lot like annoyance. "Thanks, but I'm not interested in being your charity case of the week."

"No, that's not what I mean."

"It's what you're saying."

He reached for her hands, but she snatched them back. "Don't."

She was pissed. Damn. He'd screwed up. "Pia, I'm saying this wrong. I want to take care of you. That's all. I want to be there for you and the babies. I want to be a part of your lives."

"If you're so hell-bent on being a husband and father, go marry someone else and have your own kids."

"I tried that," he admitted. "And failed."

"One divorce," she muttered. "Big deal. It happens to more than half of marriages. So what? Try again."

"That's what I want to do. With you."

They were words Pia had never thought she would hear. A proposal of marriage. Only everything about the situation was wrong. Okay—not the man. He was pretty amazing, but she didn't want him proposing like this. Out of some weird sense of obligation to a former mentor. She wasn't interested in being anyone's merit-badge project.

"You can't fix whatever's wrong with you by marrying me," she told him. "Go get therapy."

She'd thought the words would annoy him, but he simply smiled at her.

"Do you really think that's what I'm doing?"

"Yes. You don't love me. We haven't even dated." There'd been that single, amazing night, but that wasn't enough to build a relationship on.

She supposed on some level she should be flattered he was offering to help, but instead she felt cheated. Even though she'd never had a relationship get to the "I love you, please marry me" stage, she'd always dreamed one day it would happen. That the man of her dreams would propose.

But it was supposed to be a romantic event—a magical time. Not a mercy offer made in a medical parking lot.

"Pia, I like you a lot," he said, sounding annoyingly earnest. "I respect and admire you. You're smart, funny, charming and you lead with your heart. You've given up your life to have your friend's children. How many people would do that?"

The switch in subject startled her. "Crystal left me her embryos. What was I supposed to do? Ignore them?"

"That's my point. You couldn't. You had to take care of your friend, even after she was gone. I might not have known Crystal, but I did know her husband. I can't explain it, but I know that I owe him. These are his kids, too. I want to take care of you. Of them."

The Keith part made sense, she thought. But marriage? "You barely know me." Although she had to admit his assessment of her character had been very flattering.

"I know enough. Is it that you don't know me? Ask me anything. What do you want to know?"

She felt as if she'd stepped into an alternate universe. "I don't know enough to figure out what to ask."

"Then I'll tell you." This time when he reached for her hand, she let him. "You know about parts of my past. I told you I had a serious girlfriend in high school. I was crazy about her. I never even looked at another girl while I was with her. I never cheated. Once we broke up, I had my wild times, but after Hawk got me on the right track, I calmed down. I dated a lot of women, but one at a time. When Caro and I started dating, that was it. I was all in."

He shifted in his seat, as if trying to get closer to her. As if his words weren't enough to convince her and that he would use the magnetism of his presence to tip the scale in his favor.

"When I commit, I give a hundred percent. It doesn't matter if it's football or marriage or my business. I'll be there for you."

She felt overwhelmed. Everything was happening too fast. Worse—she was tempted. Hearing that a guy was "all in" was a leap-without-bothering-to-look-first moment if there ever was one.

It wasn't love. She understood that. Raoul wanted a family without the trauma of giving his heart. He wanted to help her and Keith, and in return he got all the trappings of family without a whole lot of risk.

"I have my flaws," he continued. "I can be impatient. I'm not a morning person and can push back to try to get my way. But I can be reasoned with." He touched her cheek with his free hand. "I'd never hurt you."

She had a feeling he meant what he said. But no one could promise not to hurt another. It didn't work that way.

"Raoul, you're being really nice, but this isn't going to happen."

"Why not?"

"Marriage? It's a huge step and we barely know each other."

"I want you."

As much as she wanted to bask in the words, she couldn't. "No, you want a cause."

"So you get to be someone who loves your friend, but I'm just a guy doing a good deed? You're not the biological mother to these babies, but you're giving up your life to take care of them.

Why can't I want to do the same? That's what I'm offering. You need support and a partner. I want a wife and kids. I want to be their dad. Permanently. Yes, getting married is a practical solution for both of us, but that doesn't make it any less real."

She stared into his eyes, wishing she could see down to his heart. Did he mean it?

"Define real," she said softly.

"The whole thing. A ring, a judge, a piece of paper. We'll live together, raise the kids together. I'd like it if you'd take my name, but I'll pretend it's okay if you don't. We'll be listed as the parents on the birth certificates. We'll buy a house, make love, argue, make up, raise kids, get a dog and grow old together. I'm not talking temporary, Pia. I'm offering you everything I have. I'll be a husband to you and a full-time father to those kids. And if you decide to leave me, you can take me to the cleaners in court."

He was saying all the right things, but more than that, he seemed to believe them. Which made her want to believe him.

She would admit to being tempted. On a practical level, having someone to depend on while raising triplets would be amazing. Raoul had already shown he was responsible and supportive. On a personal level, she *did* like him—probably more than she should. The thought of sharing a bed with him for the next fifty years was kind of exciting.

He wasn't offering her love. At least he was honest about it. She'd always expected to fall madly in love at some point, but it hadn't happened yet. And once she had kids, what were the odds? Was a practical marriage based on mutual need such a bad thing?

"What about kids of your own?" she asked.

"I'm hoping you'll agree in a couple of years. Wouldn't you like a baby of your own, too?"

She nodded slowly. That, too, had been part of her fantasy. And Raoul offered an enticing gene pool.

"I meant what I said," he told her. "I'm all in, Pia. I'll be there for you, no matter what. I'll be your husband and partner in every way possible. I give you my word. You'll be able to count on me until the day I die."

She knew enough to recognize he was the kind of man whose word meant something. He was offering her all he had—except his heart. She believed he would take care of her and after all she'd been through, that was nearly impossible to resist. Compared with security, love came in a very distant second.

But this wasn't just about her. "It's one thing to marry me without being in love," she said. "But the babies are different. You can't be any different with them because they're not biologically yours."

"I know. They have my word, too. Marry me, Pia. Say yes."

She looked into his dark eyes and knew that he would be with her every step of the way. That for reasons she couldn't explain, this man wanted to take on her and three unborn children that were no relation to him.

The thought of not having to do everything herself, of knowing there was someone else who would have her back, was tempting. The fact that the guy in question was Raoul made it irresistible.

"Yes," she whispered.

He stared at her. "Yes? You're accepting?"

She nodded, once again feeling slightly faint. Maybe it wasn't the pregnancy, she thought as he pulled her into his arms. Maybe it was him.

Then his mouth claimed hers and she couldn't think at all. She could only feel the warmth and affection and even a slight hint of passion.

"You won't regret this," he told her. "I'm going to buy you the biggest house, the biggest diamond ring. I'll take care of everything."

She drew back slightly and eyed him. "You're not going to become some freakish, controlling guy, are you?"

He grinned. "No. Are you objecting to the diamond or the house?"

"It was the 'I'll take care of everything' part that threw me."

"How about I'll take care of everything after running it by you?"

"That works."

"Good."

He kissed her again, then straightened in his seat and grabbed his seat belt. She did the same. He started the car and they drove out of the parking lot.

Pia stared at the familiar road and told herself it was okay. That the fluttering sensation in her stomach was anticipation, not frenzied dread. Marrying Raoul was a good thing. It's not as if she would ever get tired of looking at him, and despite the fame and fortune, he was a nice guy. In marriage, nice mattered.

This would work, she told herself. In fact, she was downright lucky. It was the right thing to do for the babies. As for her dream of falling in love and being swept away by a handsome prince...given everything going on in her life, this was as close to the fantasy as she was going to get.

AFTER DROPPING PIA OFF at her office, Raoul returned to his house. He walked through the two-bedroom place and knew there was no way it was going to work for a family of five. He'd been thinking about buying something permanent for some time now, but there hadn't been a rush. That had all changed. Now he had a family to provide for.

The thought would have brought some guys to their knees, but Raoul was excited by the prospect. He was ready to be married again, ready to be a father. If things had gone the way they were supposed to with Caro, he would already have at least one kid.

Sure, his arrangement with Pia wasn't traditional, but little about his life had been. He was a street kid who'd been blessed with the ability to think on his feet and throw a football a hundred yards. Now he was getting lucky again. Besides, Hawk and Nicole would be thrilled to be honorary grandparents to the triplets. Hawk would be proud of Raoul for doing the right thing.

He left his rental and headed downtown. On the way, he passed a jewelry store. Jenel's Gems was located in a small square of exclusive shops. He'd probably passed it a dozen times and hadn't noticed. Now he changed direction and went inside.

The interior was all glass and light. Sleek and sophisticated, it was the kind of place that made you feel as if everything you bought was special.

A tall, pretty blonde walked over to him. "Hi. Can I help you?"

The last time he'd gotten engaged, he'd designed the ring himself. He'd had very specific ideas and had spent two days picking out the diamond. He'd had this idea that the ring had to represent who he was and what he wanted his marriage to Caro to be. The ring was to have been a statement.

Talk about a crash-and-burn, he thought to himself.

"Are you good at keeping secrets?" he asked.

The woman smiled. "I sell engagement rings. I have to be."

"Good. Do you know Pia O'Brian?"

Surprise and pleasure flickered in the woman's blue eyes. "Yes, of course. I like her very much."

"Me, too. I want a ring for her. Something that suits her taste. Something she'll love."

"I see. And may I ask what this ring is for?"

"She's agreed to marry me."

The woman tilted her head and smiled. "Then you're a very lucky man."

"I think so."

"I have a ring," she began. "The design is unique but classic. Let me go get it."

She disappeared into the back for a few minutes, then returned with three rings on a lavender velvet display tray.

"This is the engagement ring," she said, holding out a diamond ring. "The center stone is two carats. It's surrounded by a bead-set diamond border." She turned it upright. "See how the stone is set up to catch the light, but the border not only protects it, it makes it less likely to catch on anything. Like a sweater."

Or hurt a baby, he thought.

The woman turned the diamond ring again, to show the pro-file. "These are channel-set square diamonds on the side. As you can see, I have two matching bands of the square diamonds. They would slide in on either side, completing the look."

"They're the wedding bands?"

She nodded. "They can be worn alone, if Pia prefers."

He picked up the ring. It glittered in the overhead lights. There was something right about it. Something that told him Pia would like it.

"Let me show you a few other things," the woman said. "For comparison."

They went through the cases. He asked to see a couple of things, then shook his head. "The first one," he told her. "That's it."

"I think so, too. Are you going to faint when I tell you the price?"

"No."

"It's a high-quality diamond and a custom setting."

"That's okay."

Fifteen minutes later, he had all three rings in boxes tucked into his jacket pocket. He'd refused the shopping bag, not want-ing anyone in town to see him carrying it. He was starting to get a handle on Fool's Gold. He knew how word would spread.

Now that he had a ring, it was time to go see a man about a house.

PIA STOOD IN front of her dry-erase and corkboard calendar, checking the events against her master list. Some of the festi-vals only required minimal prep work, but others took weeks of planning. If decorations were required, they had to be pulled out of storage and installed. The city maintenance workers appreciated plenty of lead time, and she knew better than to annoy the muscle portion of her operation.

With Halloween coming soon she would need to get the decorative flags changed and put out the scarecrows and hay bales, which reminded her that she needed to order fresh hay. The stuff they'd used last year had looked a little ragged.

She crossed to her desk and had started to pick up her phone when her office door burst open and Liz Sutton and Montana surged into the room.

"I can't believe it!" Montana shrieked. "We sat right here talking about my boring life when you had news like that? How could you keep it to yourself? I may never forgive you."

Pia might have been worried except she had no idea what her friend was talking about, and the fact that Montana and Liz were both grinning like fools meant that it wasn't bad news.

Liz reached her first and hugged her. "Congratulations. He seems really sweet. And hunky, which is always a nice plus. I know I get a little shiver every time I see Ethan. Especially when he's naked."

Montana winced. "Hello, that's my brother we're talking about. Don't share details."

"Sorry," Liz said with a laugh, then turned back to Pia. "Well?"

"Well, what?"

Montana and Liz grabbed each other's arms and actually jumped up and down. It was a little bit scary, Pia thought, taking a step back.

"You're marrying Raoul!" they shrieked together.

"I'm going to forgive you for not telling me if you promise to spill all the details," Montana said. "Start at the beginning and talk slow. You said hi and he said?"

Oh, no. Pia sank into her chair and groaned. This wasn't good at all. It had been a matter of—she checked her watch—four hours. How could word already be spreading?

The truth was she'd barely accepted that he'd proposed to her, let alone the fact that she'd accepted. The impossible situation had left her too confused to do much more than pretend it hadn't happened. It had been the only way to get work done.

"Pia?" Liz asked, her smile fading. "Are you all right?"

"I'm fine. Just confused. How did you hear?"

Montana and Liz exchanged glances.

"Raoul went to see Josh," Liz said. "Ethan was there and heard the whole thing. Raoul said he wanted to buy a bigger house. One with a lot of bedrooms. Josh wanted to know why and Raoul said the two of you were getting married but not to tell anyone. Josh and Ethan swore they wouldn't, then Ethan called me."

Pia winced. It wasn't his fault—he probably thought the information was safe with his close friends. He wasn't a small-town guy and would have no idea how this sort of news fed on itself. In a matter of hours, it would be everywhere.

"I ran into Montana on my way over here and told her," Liz continued. "But you don't look very happy. What's wrong?"

They each pulled up a chair and sat close, looking concerned. Pia wanted to bolt, but these women were her friends. If she couldn't explain the situation to them, how could she possibly go through with it? Not that she was having second thoughts—she wasn't. It was just that everything was complicated.

She drew in a breath. "Crystal left me her embryos," she began, then explained how she'd made the decision to have the babies.

"At first Raoul offered to be my pregnancy buddy," she continued. "He said he would help out while I carried the babies."

"That's so sweet," Montana said with a sigh.

But Liz was more like Pia—less of an overt romantic. Her gaze narrowed. "Why?"

"That was my question." She hesitated. "It turns out he knew Keith. Raoul went over to Iraq with some football guys and Keith was part of their escort team. They became friends. Keith told him about Fool's Gold and Crystal. Raoul was there when he died."

"I didn't know any of this," Montana said, her eyes wide. "Is that why he came here?"

Pia nodded. "Normally he wouldn't have paid extra attention to our invitation to the pro-am golf tournament, but he recognized the name of the town and wanted to check it out. He liked what he saw and decided to move here."

"Did he talk to Crystal?" Liz asked.

"No. He didn't know what to say. So he didn't know she was dying or about the embryos until I found out she'd left them to me and had a bit of a breakdown in front of him. Everything sort of spiraled from there."

"And now he wants to marry you," Montana said with a sigh. "It's so romantic."

It was more practical than romantic, but why state the obvious?

Pia shrugged. "He really wants to be a part of things. And I sort of liked the idea of not being so alone."

"You're not alone," Montana told her. "You have us."

"I know and that's great." She hesitated.

Liz got it right away. "But having friends with lives isn't the same as having someone who is always there for you. When I was pregnant with Tyler, I was scared and confused. You're having triplets."

Pia nodded. "I try not to think about the actual number. Anyway, Raoul's been with me as I made every decision. He's been a rock. Today, after the ultrasound confirmed all three embryos have implanted, he asked me to marry him."

"You're having Crystal's babies," Liz said, her eyes filling with tears. "That's such a blessing for both of you. She would be thrilled."

Pia was still in the confused camp, but she smiled anyway. "I'm committed now."

"Babies," Montana said. "And a proposal. Was it wonderful? Did he get down on one knee?"

Pia hesitated. "Montana, we're not in love. Raoul wants to marry me and be a part of the babies' lives. He wants to be their father. When I asked him why, he pointed out that I'm not their biological mother and no one is questioning my commitment. I'm willing to have them for a friend, because it's the right thing to do. He wants to be their father, and me to be his wife, because of Keith and because it's the right thing to do."

Just saying the words was tough. Believing them would take some time.

"I wasn't sure whether to say yes at first," she admitted. "But he can be really convincing. We like and respect each other. He's a good man and I trust him. I haven't been able to say that about a guy before."

Liz hugged her. "I have a good feeling about this," she said. "Arranged marriages have worked for generations."

"But you're not in love," Montana said, looking crushed. "Don't you want to be in love?"

"Sometimes you have to be practical," Liz told her. "Love can grow."

Pia hadn't thought of that. She wasn't sure if she could make herself that vulnerable—especially with so much at stake. It would hurt too much if he didn't return her feelings and, worse, it could make their arrangement awkward.

"Maybe he'll fall madly in love with you," Montana told her.

"I don't think so," Pia said firmly. "To date, all the men in my life have resisted the process…and me. Men who claim to want to be with me tend to leave. I'd rather have the truth up front. Raoul's been honest and I appreciate that."

"I guess." Montana didn't sound convinced. "It's just not romantic, you know?"

"Romance can be painful," Pia reminded her.

Liz sat back down. "So there's no love allowed?"

"We haven't discussed the rules," Pia admitted. "But it's understood."

"Hmm. You'll need to be careful, then. The heart is a tricky beast."

"Trust me. I have big plans to stay emotionally whole." She hesitated. "Could you two please not say anything about why we're getting married? It's okay to tell Charity, but no one else."

"Of course we won't talk," Liz promised. "You don't need that kind of speculation right now. But brace yourself. Everybody is going to find out about you and Raoul, not to mention the pregnancy. You're going to be a star."

"I can handle it." Pia had been the center of attention in town once before and it had been awful. Now the reasons were different and she was sure everything would be fine.

Raoul had given his word and she chose to believe him. He would stay with her and the babies. Maybe they weren't crazy in love, but that was okay. There were a lot of different ways to make a happy family and they would find theirs.

CHAPTER TWELVE

PIA AVOIDED GOING to the grocery store as long as she could. If there was one place in Fool's Gold where she was likely to run into people wanting to talk about her upcoming marriage, it was somewhere between produce and the frozen-food aisle. But she'd used up the last of her milk that morning and there was absolutely nothing in her freezer, so it was time to grit her teeth and get through it.

Thinking that the store would be quieter midday rather than after work, she used her lunch hour to go there. The trip there was stressful enough with lots of men she didn't recognize strolling through town. Some guy had even pulled out a grocery cart and handed it to her as she entered the store. Talk about strange.

She got through cleaning supplies, the meat counter and was halfway to the dairy case when Denise Hendrix spotted her.

"Pia!" the woman cried, abandoning her own cart and rushing over. "I heard. I'm so happy."

Pia braced herself for a warm, enveloping hug. Denise was the matriarch of the Hendrix family. An attractive woman in her early fifties, she'd lost her husband about ten years before. She was an active member of the community and the mother of six, including her daughters who were identical triplets.

They embraced, then Denise stepped back.

"Look at you, having Crystal's babies. That's such a blessing."

"Thanks. I'm still in denial, with a slight bend toward panic."

"Of course you are, but you're doing it anyway. I'm so proud of you." She smiled. "I am available anytime for advice or conversation or to talk you down from the panic. A multiple birth is completely manageable. You just need to plan."

"I've heard that." Planning was important, Pia thought. Just as soon as the idea of having three babies at once became real to her, she would start. "I appreciate the offer to talk. I'm sure I'll have a lot of questions. I just don't know what they are right now."

"Don't worry. I'm not going anywhere. Let me know when you're ready." Denise raised her eyebrows. "I also heard that more congratulations are in order." Her gaze dropped to Pia's bare left hand. "Have you set a date?"

"Not yet." She tucked her hand behind her back. She was still slightly stunned to find herself engaged.

"I imagine you'll want a small, quiet wedding. You're not going to have the energy to plan anything large. Unless you want to wait until after the babies are born. Then you could go all out."

Marriage was one thing, Pia thought, feeling slightly uneasy. But a wedding? She hadn't put those pieces together. "I, um. We haven't decided which way we're going," she admitted. "Everything happened so fast."

"I knew you'd find someone wonderful," Denise told her. "You've always been such a lovely girl. After all you've been through with your parents." She cleared her throat. "There's no need to talk about that. Anyway, you've found your happy ending. From all I've heard, Raoul is very special. And handsome. He's giving Josh a run for his money."

Pia laughed. "I don't think there's a competition."

"Then you haven't had your hair done at Julia's place lately.

There was a very heated discussion about the two of them just last week."

Pia thought about the talk at the city council meeting—the argument about who had the better butt. "We need more to think about in this town."

"There are those men coming to town," Denise said. "There's a subject. Have you noticed they're everywhere? Just yesterday two men whistled at me." She sounded both outraged and faintly pleased.

"I have no idea what we're going to do with them."

"I thought there were already several events planned."

"A few, but what are they going to do the rest of the time? Troll the streets, looking for easy conquests?"

Denise laughed. "I'm old enough to be your mother, so it's not right that I'm the one to point out that no one says 'easy conquests' anymore."

"Okay, you're right, but still."

Denise still looked amused. "I'm sorry you're not excited about the influx of men, but that's because you've already found someone wonderful. I wonder if any of the men will be older."

Pia had been caught up in the fact that everyone assumed she and Raoul had fallen madly in love and wondering if they should say anything. But she found herself distracted by Denise's last comment.

"You're interested in a man?" Pia asked.

"Interested is too strong a word," Denise said with a shrug. "I'm...curious. Ralph has been gone a long time. My kids are old enough to deal with me dating. I like my life, but sometimes I think it would be nice to have someone else around."

"Way to go," Pia told her. "I think that's great. I have no idea about the ages of the men arriving, but I can let you know if I see any good ones." She grinned. "What about someone younger?"

Denise sniffed. "I'm not a cougar."

"You could be."

Denise was pretty, with her short dark hair and bright eyes. She had a body that someone fifteen years younger would envy.

"I'd prefer someone around my age," the other woman said. "Then there's less I have to explain. Do you really think anyone who wasn't there could understand the thrill of hearing 'Rhinestone Cowboy' on the radio?"

"Probably not," Pia admitted. "Point taken. We'll find you a nice man who remembers the seventies."

Denise looked worried. "You're not taking me on as a project, are you?"

"No. And I won't mention anything to your daughters. I'll let you tell them you're on the prowl."

Denise laughed and held up her hands. "No prowl. I'm thinking. There's a difference. Enough about me. Remember, I'm here if you have any questions. Also, when you get ready to register for your shower gifts, we should talk. Some things you really will need three of, but others you won't."

"Okay."

Shower gifts? As in baby shower? Pia wasn't prepared for that. Of course, as she'd already figured out, there was moving and getting married to contend with, as well. Compared with that, a baby shower should be easy.

"All right, my dear," Denise said, hugging her again. "I'm delighted. You deserve every happiness."

"Thanks."

Denise waved and pushed her cart toward the front of the store. Pia completed her own shopping, then took everything home and put it away. When she left her apartment again, she headed for Raoul's office, rather than her own.

Ten minutes later, she found him alone in the big, empty space.

"You really need to get some more furniture," she told him as she walked to his desk, her heels clicking on the cement floor. "Maybe a few employees."

"I have Dakota. She's at lunch." He rose and smiled at her. "This is a nice surprise."

"We need to talk."

He settled on the corner of his desk. "Should I be worried?"

"No. Nothing's wrong." She drew in a breath. "You do realize that word is spreading. Everyone in town is going to know we're getting married."

"I figured that out. Josh violated the guy code."

"Did you tell him not to mention the engagement?"

"Yes, but it didn't do any good."

"This isn't like Dallas or Seattle. Everybody knows everyone else's business."

He stood and pulled her close. "Is that a problem?"

"It's not something that can be changed."

"I meant are you upset people know we're getting married?"

Standing there, feeling the heat of his body against hers, wrapped in his strong arms, it was tough to be upset about anything.

"I'm not upset, I just thought we'd have more time to get used to it ourselves."

He touched her cheek with his fingers. "Meaning people are coming up to you and saying stuff." She nodded.

"Want to change your mind?" he asked.

"No."

"Good. Me, either." He lowered his head and brushed his mouth against hers. "I meant what I said, Pia. I'm all in."

Until he said those words again, she hadn't realized there was a knot in her chest. It loosened and suddenly it was easier to breathe.

"Thanks," she whispered. "Me, too."

"Good."

He kissed her again, lingering this time, making her body heat up from the inside.

"Want to come over for dinner?" he asked. "I'll cook."

"You know how?"

He shrugged. "I'll barbecue. Fire good."

She laughed. "It's cold outside."

"It's in the forties at night. I'll survive the time it takes me to grill a couple of steaks." He pressed his mouth against her ear. "There's this new thing called a jacket. I have one."

"You're so cutting-edge."

"Tell me about it." He straightened. "Was that a yes?"

"I'll be there."

"Great. I'm heading up to the school now, but when I'm done there, I'll go get steaks and some salads. Does six work?"

"Sure."

He kissed her one more time before she left and headed back to her own office. As she walked, she felt a faint tingle on her lips—the lingering effect of his mouth on hers. The man could sure get to her.

She liked him. Considering they were getting married, that was a good thing. But Liz was right—she had to be careful. Liking him too much would leave her vulnerable. She'd already been hurt enough in her life. She didn't need to go looking for trouble. Most of the time, it seemed to find her without any help.

RAOUL ARRIVED AT the camp just as the kids were let out for afternoon recess. It was cool but clear, with blue skies visible between the breaks in the trees. He found himself in the middle of a rush of children wanting to make the most of their twenty minutes of playtime.

"Hey, Raoul," Peter called as he ran past. "Come play."

He'd seen the boy a few times since they'd had lunch together. Peter was smart, friendly and interested in sports. There hadn't been a hint of any kind of abuse. Maybe Raoul had imagined Peter flinching that first day during the fire. Or maybe the fire itself had made the boy nervous.

He followed the kids onto the playground. The noise level grew as the play began. There were shrieks and calls, along with plenty of laughter.

Looking around, he was pleased at what the camp had become. This was right, he thought as several girls tried to coax him into turning one end of a jump rope. Finally he agreed.

They lined up to be the next one to jump.

"Faster," a little girl with curly hair demanded. "I jump really good."

He and the teacher holding the other end obliged, spinning the rope more quickly. The girl kept up easily, laughing as she jumped.

Out of the corner of his eye, he saw several boys on the jungle gym. A flash of red caught his attention. He turned and saw Peter climb to the top. In a moment that was like something out of the movies, Raoul saw what was going to happen, even as he knew he was too far away to stop it.

Peter started to lower himself down. His hand slipped. Raoul took off running, the boy grabbed for the bar, slipped again, screamed and tumbled to the ground. Despite all the noise around him, Raoul would have sworn he heard the thunk of the fall. Peter landed on his arm, and Raoul knew before he reached him that it was going to be bad.

"Stay still," he instructed as he reached the kid's side.

Peter looked more stunned than hurt. He started to get up, then his face went pale and he gasped. Raoul saw the awkward angle of Peter's forearm.

The boy's face screwed up. "It hurts," he said and began to cry.

"I know. It's your arm. Do you hurt anywhere else?"

Peter shook his head. Tears spilled down his cheeks.

He helped the boy shift his arm against his chest. Peter screamed once, then continued crying. Raoul gathered him up in his arms and stood.

A bunch of students had gathered around. Teachers came running.

"He's broken his arm," Raoul said as he walked. "I don't know if he's hurt anywhere else. I'm taking him to the hospital. It'll be faster than waiting for an ambulance. Call the hospital and let them know we're coming. Call the police and see if they can meet me at the bottom of the mountain to escort us to the hospital, then find his foster parents."

Peter weighed practically nothing, Raoul thought, hurrying out to the parking lot. One of the teachers had come with them and fished his keys out of his jacket pocket. She opened the door. He crouched down and carefully slid the boy onto the seat.

Mrs. Miller appeared on his left. "I'm coming, too. I'll drive my own car and follow you down." She bent down and smoothed her hand over Peter's face. "You're going to be fine. We'll take care of you."

The boy continued to cry.

Raoul fastened the boy's seat belt. Mrs. Miller stepped back and he closed the door.

"You know where the hospital is?" she asked as Raoul hurried to the driver's side.

"Yes."

"I'll meet you there."

NEARLY TWO HOURS LATER, Raoul sat in the emergency waiting room. Peter had been seen almost at once. X-rays showed a clean break that should heal quickly. He was off getting a cast on, while Mrs. Miller waited to talk to the social worker who had been called. So far Peter's foster parents hadn't shown up.

"Mr. Moreno?"

He looked up and a saw a tall, blonde nurse with a chart. "Yes," he said as he rose.

"Hi. I'm Heidi. Peter's going to be just fine. They're finishing up now. I wondered if I could talk to you for a minute."

"Sure."

He followed her into an empty examination room.

"How do you know Peter?" she asked.

"Through the school. He goes to the one that burned down,

so all the kids are up at my camp. I've played ball with him and his friends a few times. Why?"

She pressed her lips together. "He's very thin for his age. We have some concerns about the food he's getting. His bones aren't as dense as we would like. From what Mrs. Miller told us about the playground, he shouldn't have broken a bone in that fall. Do you know if he gets enough to eat?"

He shook his head, ignoring the rage that bubbled inside of him. He had no patience for people who didn't take care of the kids entrusted to them. He'd been through plenty of that himself as he'd been growing up.

"Are you going to do any tests?" he asked.

"We need to talk to his parents about that."

"Foster parents," he corrected. "He lost his parents a while ago."

"I don't like the sound of that," Heidi said. "Now I know why Mrs. Miller wanted us to call social services. I'll talk to the caseworker when she gets here and ask her to follow up."

Raoul looked at her. "Are there any signs of physical abuse?"

"We didn't see any. Do you suspect that something's going on?"

"I was there during the fire. Peter was one of the last kids to leave. When I went to help him out of the room, he pulled away. It could have just been one of those things, but…"

"Maybe." Heidi didn't sound convinced. "I'll mention that, as well. It doesn't hurt to be cautious." She made some notes. "Thanks for the information."

He and Heidi walked out of the room. He saw Mrs. Miller hurrying toward him.

"Can you come to Peter's room," the teacher asked as she approached. "He's not doing well."

"What's wrong?" Heidi asked. "He was fine a few minutes ago."

"The cast is on and they've given him something for the pain," the older woman said. "It's not his arm." She lowered her voice. "Apparently the last time he was in the hospital was after that horrible car accident that killed his parents. He keeps talking about them and asking for you." She looked at Raoul. "I think seeing you would make him feel better."

"Sure."

"You go ahead," Heidi told them. "I'm going to check on the caseworker and see when we can expect her."

As Peter was due to be released in an hour or so, he hadn't been given a room on one of the regular hospital floors. Raoul followed Mrs. Miller through the maze of hallways that made up the E.R. Peter sat up on a bed, looking small and pale. The cast went from his wrist to his elbow and was Dallas Cowboy blue. But the kid looked anything but okay as he covered his face with his free hand and tears ran down his cheeks.

"Hey, buddy," Raoul said as he walked into the room. "What's going on?"

"I want to go h-home," the boy cried.

"We're getting ahold of your foster parents," Raoul told him.

"N-not them. I want my mom and dad."

Raoul swore silently. This was a problem that couldn't be fixed. He looked at Mrs. Miller, who was obviously fighting tears of her own, then back at the boy.

Raoul moved to the bed and pulled the boy into his arms. Then he carried him to the chair in the corner and sat down, holding Peter close.

The kid clung to him, wrapping his uninjured arm around Raoul's neck and crying into his shoulder.

He was so damn skinny, Raoul thought. All bones and angles, too light for a kid his age. He held Peter, rubbing his back, not saying anything. After a few minutes, the crying softened and the kid seemed to go to sleep.

"I feel so bad for him," Mrs. Miller whispered. "I've called all the numbers his foster parents left and there's no answer. Mr. Folio's employer said the man was out of town for a few days. But if that's true, who's looking after Peter?"

Raoul didn't have any answers. He knew the situation with the boy wasn't all that unusual. That being underage and alone in the world was never a good thing. There were excellent foster parents out there, but plenty of them were only in it for the money.

An older woman entered. She looked worn and tired, with her gray hair pulled back and glasses hanging from a chain around her neck.

"I'm Cathy Dawson," she said, then saw Peter and lowered her voice. "Is he all right?"

"The break was clean and, according to the doctors, he should heal quickly," Mrs. Miller said. "I can't get ahold of his foster parents, however."

The social worker frowned, then put on her glasses and read the papers in her hand. "I see there is also some concern about his physical well-being. He might not be getting enough to eat." She sighed. "All right. Give me a few minutes."

Just then Peter stirred and sat up. He blinked at Raoul, then turned.

"Hi, Mrs. Dawson," he said, then yawned.

"Hello yourself. It looks like you fell."

Peter nodded. "I broke my arm." He held up the cast, then glanced at Raoul. "It's Dallas Cowboys blue."

"I noticed that," Raoul said. "Are you going to let me sign your cast?"

"Uh-huh." The boy smiled shyly.

"Good."

Mrs. Dawson pulled up the other chair and sat across from them. "Peter, where have you been staying for the past few days?"

"With the lady next door." He gave the name.

"How long have your foster parents been gone?"

Peter shrugged. "A while."

Mrs. Dawson's expression stayed friendly. "Since the weekend?"

Peter wrinkled his nose. "Before that, I think."

"I see. Do you know when they'll be back?"

He shook his head, then cradled his arm against his chest. "Are they gonna be mad because I got hurt?"

"Of course not," she said firmly. "They'll be happy you're all right. We all are." She paused. "You know what I think?"

"What?" Peter asked suspiciously.

"I think you probably need a little ice cream. I know they have some down in the cafeteria. If you don't mind, I'm going to get you some."

Relief showed in Peter's expression. He grinned. "I don't mind."

"That's very nice of you. But you know, it's a big hospital. Would you mind if Mr. Moreno showed me the way?"

"Okay."

Raoul wasn't sure what the social worker was up to, but he stood and put Peter back on the bed. "I might have some silver-star stickers at my office," he said. "I'll check tomorrow and if I do, we can put some on your cast."

The boy grinned.

Mrs. Miller moved toward him. "I'll wait for you here," she said.

Raoul followed Mrs. Dawson into the hallway.

"The cafeteria is that way," she said, pointing.

"So you don't need my help finding it."

"I wanted a chance to talk to you. I assume you have people in town who know you?"

"Yes," he said cautiously.

"Good. That will help us push through the paperwork. I know a sympathetic judge. If you'll give me two or three people to use as character references, we can get this done in an hour or so."

"Get what done?"

Mrs. Dawson stopped and stared at him. "Having Peter stay with you until his foster parents return and we can figure out if it's safe for him to go back with them, of course."

PIA ARRIVED AT RAOUL'S place at seven. There'd been so much to carry, she'd had to drive. Now she grabbed two shopping bags and headed toward the front door. He had it open before she made it to the small porch.

"What's all that?" he asked.

"Dinner for many days to come. There's more in the car."

"More what?"

Poor man, she thought, handing him the bags. "Food. Word got out about you taking in Peter. People didn't know when you'd get home, so they brought it to me."

He was still standing there looking confused when she went back to her car for the second load. She collected the last three bags, shut her car door with her hip, then returned to the house.

"I don't understand," Raoul said, following her to the kitchen.

"Pia!"

She turned and saw Peter running toward her. He had a cast on his skinny forearm and had already changed into race-car pajamas.

"Hey, you," she said, putting her bags on the kitchen table. "What happened?"

"I fell." He held out his cast. "See."

"Very impressive. Does it hurt?"

"No. I have drops."

Some kind of pain medicine, she would guess. "Cool. Have you had dinner?"

Peter shook his head. "Just ice cream."

Pia raised her eyebrows.

"Don't look at me," Raoul told her. "It was Mrs. Dawson's idea."

"A likely story," Pia teased, then shrugged out of her coat and hung it on the back of a chair. "So, what are we in the mood for? There are lots of choices."

She moved to the counter and started taking casserole dishes out of the various bags. "Lasagna, always a favorite. Seven-layer tamale pie." She read each item as she set it down. "Chicken-

and-noodle casserole, a vegetable bake." She wrinkled her nose at Peter. "Probably not that one, huh?"

He laughed. "I like lasagna."

"Me, too." She glanced at Raoul. "Would you set the oven to three-fifty? It's not frozen, so it won't take long to heat up."

He stood there, staring at her. "I don't understand."

She faced him. "When people heard that Peter would be staying with you for a few days, they brought food to help out. So you don't have to cook dinner every night."

"How did they hear?"

"Someone told them. Have you learned nothing about small-town living?"

She turned on the oven, then walked to the fridge. "Tell me the freezer's empty, because you have food for days."

He nodded, still looking shell-shocked.

"Why don't you go help Peter wash his hands? You know the cast can't get wet, right?"

"Yes."

"Good. I'll get things together in here. I'll leave two dinners in the refrigerator for the next couple of nights. Oh, and there are stickers in that white bag. For your cast."

"Cool!" Peter reached into the bag and pulled out the sheet of stickers. "Can we put them on now?"

Raoul looked at her. She laughed. "Go ahead. Dinner will be ready in about thirty minutes."

They left the kitchen. A few minutes later, Raoul was back.

"I'm sorry," he told her.

"For what?"

"We were supposed to have dinner together tonight."

"We are."

"Not like this," he said. "I don't know exactly how it happened. One second the social worker was talking, the next I had a kid."

She patted her stomach. "I know the feeling."

"You're not mad?"

"Why would I be? Peter's all alone, he's hurt and no one knows where his foster parents are. You stepped up. Honestly, it makes you even nicer."

"You hate nice."

"I'm making an exception."

"Okay. Thanks."

He disappeared down the hall.

She stared after him, telling herself that just because he was a great guy didn't mean it was safe to open her heart to him.

BY THE TIME they finished dinner and got Peter settled in Raoul's spare bedroom, it was after nine. Pia curled up on the sofa, telling herself that she had to get it together and head home. Despite not having many symptoms of her pregnancy to date, she was a little more tired than usual. Raoul sat at the other end of the couch, angled toward her.

"Thanks for everything," he said.

"I just showed up with other people's effort. There's nothing to thank me for."

"Poor kid." Raoul sipped his beer. "Talk about a hell of a situation."

"They really don't know where his foster parents are?"

"That's what Mrs. Dawson said. I hope they investigate them when they finally get back. Peter hasn't said anything bad about them, but there are a few red flags."

He'd already told her about the possibility that the kid wasn't getting enough to eat. There was no excuse for neglect, she thought. But that didn't stop it from happening.

He set down the bottle. "I had other plans for the evening," he told her.

For a second she thought he meant sex. Her body reacted with an internal happy dance, and various parts of her went on alert.

He pulled open a small drawer from the underside of the coffee table and withdrew a small, square lavender jewelry box.

She recognized the color and the design on the box. Jenel's Gems was known for elegant, upscale, one-of-a-kind designs.

Her throat went dry and she had an odd and unexpected sense of shyness. The wanting faded as confusion took its place.

"I don't understand," she said.

"We're getting married," he reminded her. "I believe an engagement ring is traditional."

"Yes, but…" Theirs wasn't a traditional engagement. "I wasn't expecting anything. You don't have to do this."

"I want to."

He eased toward her and took her left hand in his. "Pia, thank you for agreeing to marry me. We're going to make this work. I'll be there for you, no matter what."

His words made her ache. They were exactly what she'd always wanted to hear…almost.

"I'll be there for you, too," she whispered.

He smiled, then opened the box.

If she hadn't been sitting, she would have fallen. The ring was incredible. Beautiful and sparkling, and large enough to make her nervous.

"The two diamond bands are wedding bands," he said. "If you don't like them, we can get something else."

"They're wonderful. Everything is stunning, but it's too much." She looked at him. "I would have been fine with a simple gold band."

"Are you saying you're not a diamond kind of girl?"

She returned her attention to the ring. "I haven't been."

"Then we need to change that."

He drew out the engagement ring, then slid it on her finger. The fit was perfect. She stared down at the diamonds glinting on her finger.

"Thank you," she told him.

"You're welcome."

He wrapped both arms around her and held her against him. She closed her eyes and told herself everything would be fine.

That she was making the right decision. Love would have been nice, but wasn't it better to sacrifice that silly dream in order to make sure Crystal's babies would be taken care of their whole lives? Isn't that what her friend would have wanted?

CHAPTER THIRTEEN

RAOUL SPENT A sleepless night. Not that Peter was a problem, but because he kept getting up to check on the kid. But the boy never stirred.

They both woke up to Raoul's alarm, then had a busy morning of getting ready. The plastic sleeve the hospital had provided protected the cast while Peter showered. The kid had managed to dress himself, except for tying his shoes, and had shown up at the kitchen table hair damp, face smiling, eyes eager.

"What's for breakfast?" he asked.

"Waffles."

Those green eyes got bigger. "You know how to make waffles?"

Raoul showed him the waffle maker he'd bought a few months ago after wandering through a big-box store and seeing a demonstration.

"That is so cool!" Peter told him.

He scrambled out of his seat and hurried around to watch as Raoul finished mixing the batter.

"Here's the cup we use," Raoul said, pointing to the plastic container with a big pour spout. "Go ahead and fill it to the line there."

"I can do it?"

"Sure."

Peter's break was in his left forearm, and he was right-handed.

The boy carefully dipped the cup into the batter and scooped up the right amount. Raoul raised the lid on the waffle maker.

"Go ahead and pour it in the center. It's already hot so it will spread out on its own."

Peter did as instructed, then watched as the batter oozed out along the grid. "It's not filling in all the way."

"I know, but this is the fun part."

Raoul closed the waffle maker, locked the two handles together, then spun it until it was upside down.

"Whoa!" Peter stared. "That's the best."

"Want to do the second one?"

"Sure."

Raoul watched him, pleased the boy seemed rested and not in any pain. He was easy to be with. Bright and curious. When he thought about the fact that his foster parents might not be taking good care of him, he wanted to find them—or at least the dad—and beat the shit out of him.

Not an option, he reminded himself. He would trust the system to work this out. But just in case, he would talk to Dakota about what steps he could take to make sure Peter was in a safe environment.

But when he got to his office, after dropping Peter off at camp, Dakota wasn't there. She'd left early the day before. He checked the machine to see if she'd called in sick, but there wasn't any message.

By ten, he was worried and wondering whom to talk to. Just when he picked up the phone to call Pia, Dakota walked in.

She looked like hell. Her face was pale, her eyes red and swollen. There was an air of grief and loss about her, as if something important to her had been taken away from her. He was on his feet the second he saw her.

"What happened?" he demanded.

She shook her head. "Nothing."

"It's not nothing. Were you in an accident? Did someone hurt you?"

If she'd had a boyfriend, he would assume he'd beaten her or slept with her best friend. But as far as he knew, Dakota wasn't dating.

"I'm fine," she said, her mouth trembling as she spoke. "You have to believe me."

"Then you need to be more convincing."

She forced a smile that was more ghoulish than happy. "How's that?"

"Frightening."

She sighed. "I'm fine. I know I look bad. I'm not hurt, I'm not sick." She swallowed. "Everything is how it's always been."

"Dakota, get real. Something happened."

"No, it didn't." Tears filled her eyes. "It didn't." The tears spilled down her cheeks.

Instinctively, he walked toward her, but she shook her head and backed away.

"I'm sorry," she whispered. "I can't do this. I can't be here today. I need a day or two. Sick days, vacation days, whatever you want."

He felt helpless and confused. "Take whatever time you need. Can I call someone? One of your sisters? Your mom?"

"No. No one. I'm fine. I have to go."

With that she grabbed her purse and practically ran out of the office. Raoul stared after her, not sure what he was supposed to do now. Let her go? Follow her? Call a friend?

She wasn't physically hurt—he could figure out that much. So what had happened? Had she heard bad news? But if there'd been a disaster in the family, he would have heard about it. News traveled fast in Fool's Gold.

He would give her time, he decided. If she wasn't back at work in a couple of days, he would go talk to her. If she wouldn't talk to him, he would insist she talk to someone else.

PIA STUDIED THE signs and did her best not to shudder. Bad enough that busloads of men were pouring into town. Worse that there was going to be a bachelor auction.

It was embarrassing. Not for her specifically, but for the town.

"I just don't like this," she said.

Montana grinned. "That's because you already have a good guy in your life."

"Even if I didn't, this would scare me. Who are these guys? What do they want?"

"If you have to ask the question, then Raoul is doing something very, very wrong."

Pia turned away from her friend and did her best not to blush. "I'm newly pregnant. We're not...you know."

"I guess it would be weird to have sex knowing that someone else's embryos are growing inside of you."

Pia winced. "Thank you for spelling that out so clearly."

"Am I wrong?"

"No, but still."

Montana grinned. "So, did you ever...you know? Before the pregnancy?"

Pia thought about that amazing night. "Once," she admitted, then waited to be struck by lightning for the lie. "Actually it was one evening, but several times."

"Impressive. A man with stamina."

"It is an appealing characteristic." Although she was sure there would come a time when it was safe for them to do the wild thing while she was pregnant, she had a feeling she was going to have to wait until after the babies were born to have a repeat performance of that one, magical night.

"He did set the standard really high," she added, "and we should talk about something else. How's your sex life?"

"Nonexistent."

"Then you should check out the new guys."

"No, thanks." Montana stapled the cardboard handles onto the auction paddles. "I'm focusing on my career right now."

"You got the job?"

Montana grinned. "I did and I love it. The dogs are so great. Well-trained and friendly. Max is the best, too. He's really patient. I'm doing lots of reading and I've started my online class. I'm going to Sacramento in a few weeks for an intense three-week training seminar. Max is even paying for that, if you can believe it."

"You like Max," Pia said, pleased to see her friend so happy.

"Of course. He's so nice and he knows everything about dogs and..." Montana wrinkled her nose. "Um, no. Don't even go there."

"Office romances are very stylish."

"It's not like that. He's in his fifties and even if he wasn't, I admire him. I don't want a romantic relationship with him. We're friends."

"If you say so."

"I do." She nudged Pia. "It's already happening. You're engaged and now you want everyone else paired up."

"I don't. I just want my friends to be happy and if—" She paused as she saw Montana's eyes practically bug out of her head. "What?"

"The ring. It's incredible."

Pia resisted the urge to tuck her hand behind her back. She loved her engagement ring, but she was having a little trouble getting used to it. And not apologizing for it. The stones were stunning and the whole thing was so bright, it was practically a light source.

"Raoul picked it out," she murmured.

"Does he have a brother?"

Something she should know, but didn't. "I can ask."

Montana grabbed her hand and stared at the ring. "I love it more than life."

"Thanks."

"Make you a little nervous?"

"Some. Nothing about the situation feels real to me. Not the engagement or even being pregnant." She lowered her voice. "I've peed on a stick and had an ultrasound. I'm really, really pregnant. So why don't I feel different?"

"You've gone through a lot in a very short period of time. You'll get there."

"I hope." Although Pia was starting to have her doubts. Maybe there was something wrong with her. "What if I can't bond with the babies when they're born? What if I can't love them?"

"You won't have a choice. You're going to be a great mom, Pia. Stop doubting yourself."

Pia put down the signs. "I want to believe you, but I can't. Both my parents left me. So has every guy I've ever cared about. I want to think it will be different with Raoul and the babies, but I'm not sure."

"Raoul's not going anywhere. He's a good guy."

He was a guy who was marrying her to get a readymade family. Not because he was crazy in love with her.

"Besides," Montana continued. "You never know how things are going to work out. My parents loved each other every day of their marriage. When my dad died, we were all scared Mom wasn't going to make it. But he wasn't the only love of her life."

Pia hadn't heard that. "What do you mean?"

Montana grinned. "She has a tattoo on her hip. It says Max."

"Your Max?"

"No. He's new to the area. The tattoo is old. Over the years, Dakota, Nevada and I have tried to find out who he is, and Mom isn't saying a word. My point is, love happens. You're going to do great with the babies and I'm guessing Raoul is going to fall madly in love with you. You'll see."

RAOUL PARKED IN front of the large house. "I know it's old," he told Pia, "but I had Ethan go over the whole thing and it's sound. The floor plan is great. Plenty of bedrooms, a large kitchen, which needs to be gutted, but then you could have everything you wanted. There's a big yard out back, some great trees for climbing. It's the perfect family home."

He waited anxiously while Pia glanced at the three-story house with round eyes. It was in one of the older neighborhoods in town—an affluent section built in the 1920s. The second he'd seen the house, he'd known it was exactly what he'd been looking for.

"There are eight bedrooms, including three on the third story. The second story has a decent-size master, but I thought we could tear down the wall between it and the smallest bedroom to expand it. Upgrade the bathroom, make the closet bigger."

She turned to him, her expression unreadable. "Because you have a lot of shoes?"

"I know you do. It's a chick thing."

"I guess it is."

She didn't seem that excited about the house. "Are you okay?" he asked. "Don't you like the place?"

"It has potential," she said, opening the car door. "We should go inside."

He followed her, wondering what was going on with the women in his life. Dakota had returned to work the next day, but she still wasn't herself. He'd asked what was wrong several times and she kept insisting everything was fine. Too bad she was a lousy liar. And now Pia was acting strangely.

He followed her up to the front porch. It was as wide as the house and several feet deep.

"Are you mad because I went looking at houses without you?" he asked.

"No. You said you were going to. It's fine."

He thought about mentioning he'd brought Peter with him the previous day and the kid had loved the house, but he wasn't sure it would help.

"I know I've been busy," he said as he fished the key out of his jacket pocket. "Having Peter around. His foster parents are due back in a couple of days. Mrs. Dawson has been investigating them and can't find any kind of trouble, so he'll be going back to them."

She turned to him and pressed her hand against his chest. "Raoul, I'm not mad because you're taking care of a little boy who's hurt. I think it's wonderful and amazing. In fact, I'd love to come to dinner with the two of you, before Peter has to leave. I'm not mad about the house. I'm not mad about anything."

"You swear?"

"Yes."

She raised herself on tiptoe. He bent down and kissed her.

The feel of her mouth against his, her body so close, made him want to pull her against him and take advantage of the empty house. One night with Pia hadn't been enough. But until he talked to her doctor about when it was okay to seduce Pia back into his bed, he wasn't going to do anything to put the babies in danger.

"Tonight?" he asked, knowing they were talking about dinner but wishing it were something else. "Sure."

He opened the front door and led the way inside.

They stepped into a large two-story foyer. The formal living room was to the left, the dining room to the right. There was a study, an eat-in kitchen and a family room, all on this level.

"Let's start at the top," he said, pointing to the stairs.

"Okay."

He led the way. At the top floor, he pointed out the three bedrooms. There were several large linen closets off the hall.

"If we give up this closet," he said, pointing, "we can have a Jack-and-Jill bath. Now with three kids, it could still be a problem, so I talked to Ethan about turning this other one into a half bath. Just a toilet and sink."

"Uh-huh."

He showed her the three bedrooms. They were all about the same size, with sloped ceilings and bay windows with window seats.

"Great for reading," he said.

"Especially on rainy days. You'd need a bunch of cushions, though, and maybe some blankets."

He watched her cautiously. She was saying all the right things, but something was wrong. He felt it in his gut.

She led the way to the second floor. The master bedroom was in the back. He showed her the small bedroom that could be made part of the master suite, the hall bath that was huge and the excess of storage.

"It's nice," she said. "Lots of light and space. I really like the craftsman details."

They went to the main floor. He told her everything he wanted to do in the kitchen. Then he led the way to the study.

"This room is great," he told her. "I don't usually like paneling, but the combination of wood and windows really works. There are plenty of bookshelves."

He waited for her to walk in, but instead of looking at the room, she took a step to the side and tucked her hands behind her back.

"Pia?"

She seemed lost in thought. "You're going through a real estate agent, right? Josh doesn't own this house."

"He recommended someone. His houses are all smaller. With three kids coming, I knew we'd need something bigger."

She looked at him. "Did the agent say anything about the family who lived here before?"

"No." His gut clenched. "Did you know them?"

She nodded. "My family owned this house."

She'd lived here? Talk about being an idiot, he thought. "Why didn't you say something? Why did you let me give you a tour?"

"I wanted to know what it would be like to be back in the house. I wanted to know..." She stared at the study. "My father committed suicide in there. I'm the one who found the body."

PIA WAS PLEASED SHE could say the words without flinching. It was almost as if she were telling a story about someone else.

Perhaps enough time had passed that the past didn't have any power over her, although she had her doubts.

She turned her back on the study and walked into the living room. This space was safer, she thought. Fewer memories.

"I had the whole third floor to myself," she told Raoul. "I slept in one room and had another set up with couches and a TV. My friends all came here because I had the cool parents who didn't care what we did. We could stay up all night, talk on the phone, even steal liquor from the cabinet in my dad's study. Whatever the hot thing was, I had it. Everyone envied me. They thought I was lucky."

He didn't speak, he just stood next to her, listening. She looked out the window because it was easier than seeing the pity in his eyes.

"It took me a while to figure out neither of them ever cared about me. I was just another way to show status. We only cared about how things looked, not how they were. I grew up selfish and mean. Having more clothes than I could ever wear didn't make up for having parents who never loved me. I resented the other kids who were smarter, or had a great family."

Involuntarily, she looked at him. Thankfully, there was no emotion in his expression.

"I was mean," she said flatly. "I tormented everyone who wasn't in my circle of friends. I made fun of them, spread rumors about them, told lies. And because of who my parents were, everyone believed me." She tried to smile and failed. "You would have hated me."

"I doubt that."

"You would have. And I would have deserved it." She was sure of it. "When I was sixteen, my father was charged with embezzling from his company. The news only got worse. He hadn't paid taxes or bills. I don't know where the money went. Maybe we spent it all. By the beginning of my senior year, it became clear that he was going to be charged with some serious crimes. Rather than face the felony charges, he put a gun to his head and pulled the trigger."

Raoul reached out to her, but she stepped back. He couldn't touch her—not now. If he did, she wouldn't be able to get through the story.

"I heard the noise and came running. I burst into his study." She paused, willing herself to say the words, but not actually remembering what it had been like. "It's not the same as the movies. It's not that clean. There was blood everywhere."

She swallowed. "I called 9-1-1 and then I don't remember very much. My mom left for Florida and I went into foster care. Everything was different. I didn't have this house or half my things. And all those kids I'd tortured got their revenge. They made my life a living hell."

She turned to look out the window again. "I don't blame them. I deserved it."

"What about your mom? Did you want to go with her?"

She nodded. "She wouldn't let me. She said she needed time. There was no discussion about what I might need. She told me it was important for me to graduate with all my friends, and when I tried to tell her I didn't have friends anymore she wouldn't listen."

She folded her arms across her chest. "I don't know what happened to the house. If it was sold or repossessed or what. I finished school. My grades had never been better, probably because I didn't have any distractions. I was voted off the cheerleading team, my boyfriend dumped me. I applied for a part-time job with the city, which is how I got involved with what I do now. My mother didn't come back for my high school graduation and she made it clear I wouldn't be welcome in Florida. I haven't seen her since."

She felt him moving toward her and even though she wanted to duck away, she didn't have the energy. She was unable to move, even as his strong arms came around her and held her tight.

"I'm sorry," he murmured, his breath whispering across the side of her face. "I'm so sorry."

"I'm fine."

He turned her so they were facing each other and stared into her eyes. "You know what? You really are. You went through hell and survived."

She shrugged out of his embrace. "Don't be nice."

"Why not?"

"Because then I might believe you."

He studied her for a long time. She felt naked and vulnerable. Alone. Broken.

Then he pulled her close again and held on so tight it was hard to breathe. She should have wanted to pull away, but it felt good. Too good.

"You can believe in me," he told her. "I'm going to marry you, Pia. Nothing bad will ever happen to you again."

She closed her eyes and let herself lean into him. "You can't promise that."

"I know, but I'll do my best." He released her just enough to cup her face in his hands, then he kissed her. "No one is ever going to leave you again."

His words made her eyes burn.

He cleared his throat. "Given what happened this time, you should probably pick the next house."

Despite everything she laughed. "You think?"

He kissed her again. "Are you going to be okay?"

She nodded. From the safety of his arms, she had a feeling everything was going to be just fine.

CHAPTER FOURTEEN

THE BACHELOR AUCTION and talent show were being held in the Fool's Gold Convention Center, a grand term for a cement-and-block-wall structure that had been planned as a big-box store. Twenty years ago some local contractor—long since out of business—had subscribed to the philosophy of "if you build it, they will come." He'd built it and no one had shown up to rent the space. The city had bought the building and used it for various events.

The advantage was plenty of open space that could be broken up into nearly any size room. About ten years ago, the interior had been updated with a huge industrial kitchen and lots of bathrooms. Pia had taken over about half the building for the night. The place wasn't exactly elegant, but it was functional and free, which was important, given her meager budget.

A stage had been assembled at one end, and several city workers were setting up chairs. Off to the side the banner proclaiming Fool's Gold's Bachelor Auction had yet to be hung and she did her best to avoid looking at it. Talk about a hideous event. The talent show was only going to make things worse. No doubt all the media attending would go out of their way to make the town look like a refuge for men-starved women of a certain age.

Because her days weren't already crammed with plenty to

do, Raoul had called that morning and informed her his former coach was visiting. Pia knew how much Hawk had meant to him. No doubt he was looking forward to the visit. Pia, on the other hand, was having a case of nerves brought on by meeting the emotional equivalent of the in-laws. Hawk was bringing his wife, Nicole.

She had no idea if Raoul was going to tell them the truth about the engagement, and honestly she couldn't decide which she wanted. Faking being in love in front of the two people who cared about Raoul most seemed like a challenge. But if they knew what was really happening, wouldn't they try to talk him out of it? And as freakish as the idea of marrying for reasons of practicality might be, Pia had found herself depending on the fact that Raoul was going to be there for her.

Dakota crossed the cement floor of the convention center, her arms filled with an overflowing box of auction paddles. "Do you really think we're going to need this many?"

Pia nodded. "Oh, yes. We're having quite the turnout. It's not just ladies from Fool's Gold who will be attending. We're pulling them in from the whole county."

"Lucky us."

Montana followed her sister. She had a box full of programs for the talent show. "Did you look at these?" she asked. "There's a woman who's dancing with her dog."

Pia led them to the table against the wall. "I saw her audition. It's not as scary as it sounds. They both do ballet."

The sisters stared at her.

Dakota set down her box. "On what planet isn't that scary?"

"At least they're not dancing together."

"Okay," Montana said slowly, lowering her box to the table. "Tell me it's not a poodle."

Pia pressed her lips together. "Sorry. It's a big one, if that helps."

"It doesn't."

They all laughed, although Dakota's amusement seemed a

little forced. Montana must have noticed that as well, because she turned to her sister.

"Are you okay? You don't seem perky."

"I'm perky."

"Want to take a vote?" Montana asked.

Dakota shrugged. "I'm thinking about some stuff in my life. Reevaluating. I feel as if I've been drifting."

That was news to Pia. "Drifting how?"

Montana sank into a folding chair. "Oh, God. If you getting your PhD and helping children is drifting, what does that make me? An earthworm?"

"It's not about what I do," Dakota said. "Getting the work done isn't the point. You have so much passion for your life. I feel like I'm going through the motions. I'm not sure what's important to me. I'm not dating, but it doesn't really bother me. I want to wake up excited about my life." She shrugged. "I have some thinking to do."

Pia had to agree with Montana. Dakota was one of the most together women she knew. It was kind of scary to think someone she'd always thought of as borderline perfect had issues. If Dakota had trouble figuring things out, what hope did the rest of them have?

Montana crossed to her sister and hugged her. "I want you to be happy."

"I *am* happy."

Montana shook her head. "You're not."

Dakota smiled. "Okay. Then I will be. How's that?"

"Better," Montana said. "I love you."

"I love you, too."

Pia felt her throat get a little tight as she watched the sisters hug each other. She'd always wondered what it would be like to grow up with a sibling. While she would never know, Crystal's babies would have that experience.

She lightly touched her stomach. "You're always going to have each other," she whispered. "Won't that be great?"

Before the moment could spiral into a hugging, tearful vat of emotion, two other women approached. Pia recognized one as a head nurse from the hospital. The other was a lawyer in town. Both were in their fifties, with the lawyer slightly closer to sixty than her friend.

Bea, the lawyer, stopped in front of Pia. "About this auction," she began without a greeting. "Have you vetted the men? Done background checks? Will they have papers?"

Pia had worked with Bea before and was used to her abrupt style. "They're coming to a dinner-dance, not immigrating into the country. What kind of papers are you looking for?"

"How do we know they're safe?"

Pia sighed. "Buyer beware."

Bea's friend, Nina, smiled at Pia. "Will there be a preview? Can we look them over before we bid? Is there a list of what they will or won't do?"

Crap, crap, crap. "We're sponsoring the auction, ladies. We're talking dinner and dancing, not anything else."

Bea snorted. "She thinks you're looking for sex, Nina."

Nina, a petite brunette, flushed. "Oh, no. Not that. I was wondering if I could ask the guy to clean out my gutters. There's a lot of leaves up there and I hate getting on a ladder."

Gutters? From the corner of her eye, Pia saw Dakota and Montana trying not to laugh.

"You win a night that includes dinner and dancing," Pia repeated, telling herself it was important to be patient. "The woman pays. Proceeds from the auction itself go to the city for various charity projects."

"Who needs a man for dancing?" Bea muttered. "I'm too old to care about that."

Nina tilted her head. "I don't know. A night of dancing sounds kind of nice."

"There are plenty of young women who'll be in competition with you, Nina. Bidding against you."

Nina grinned. "Yes, but being of a certain age has advantages. We have more money."

Bea didn't look amused. "Perhaps you should use some of that precious money of yours to hire someone to clean out your gutters."

"You're always so crabby," Nina complained, then turned back to Pia. "Thanks for the information. I guess I'm going to have to find another way to get the gutters cleaned."

"Pick up the phone book," Bea muttered. "I know you can spell."

The two women walked away.

"I thought the auction was going to be boring," Montana admitted when Bea and Nina were out of earshot. "But now I can't wait to be here."

"Are you going to bid?" Dakota asked.

"No, but I'm bringing popcorn. Talk about a show."

Pia sank into a chair and rubbed her temples. "I don't get paid enough to do this."

"Probably not," Dakota said cheerfully, "but at least it's never boring."

"Right now, boring sounds really, really good."

RAOUL WALKED ONTO the playground at the mountain school only to find himself surrounded by kids.

"Come play with us."

"No, me."

"Can you help me throw harder?"

"We want to jump rope. Will you hold the rope?"

Raoul felt like the leader of a very short tribe. He raised his hands in the air. "I'm here to check on my main man. Then we'll talk about playing."

There were a few grumbles, but the kids fell back, allowing him to walk over to Peter and his friends. The boy grinned when he saw Raoul and launched himself at him. Raoul caught him easily.

"How are you doing?" he asked the boy. "All settled?"

Peter had returned to his foster home the previous afternoon. Mrs. Dawson had done a thorough investigation and while she admitted the Folios weren't her favorite family, she couldn't remove a child based on a feeling. There had to be something closer to proof.

The boy hung on to Raoul. "It's okay. They're being really nice. Don says he's going to sue the school 'cause of my fall. But I don't know who Sue is."

Raoul put down the boy and made a mental note to talk to Don about his plan. If he thought he could get some easy money out of the school district and keep it for himself, he was about to have a change in attitude.

"I've been practicing throwing," Peter continued happily.

"Just throwing, right? No catching."

The kid sighed. "I know. Not until my arm is better."

"If you want to play football, you need to be strong all over. That means letting your arm heal."

"Will I be as big as you?"

"I don't know." Raoul didn't have any details about Peter's real parents. He wondered if he could ask around and get some information. "Want to show me what you can do?"

"Uh-huh."

Peter ran over to the box of balls. Several other boys spotted what he was doing and followed. Raoul quickly organized them into groups and had them throwing back and forth to each other, like in a training camp.

"Good," he said, walking behind them, watching them throw. "Billy, straighten that arm. Your strength is in your shoulder, not your wrist. Nice, Trevor. Great follow-through."

He felt someone tug on his jacket and looked down to see a girl in glasses and pigtails staring up at him.

"Can I throw, too?" she asked.

The boy closest shook his head. "No girls. Go away."

The girl ignored him. "I want to learn."

"Girls play, too," Raoul said, leading her to the end of the line. He motioned for Jackson to throw him a ball, then get in position to catch. "Why don't you show me what you can do."

The girl took the ball, pushed up her glasses, then threw the baseball with enough power to make a pop when it hit the glove. Jackson winced.

Raoul grinned. "You've got quite an arm there, young lady."

"I want to be able to hit my big brother in the head and knock him out. He's always teasing me."

"Okay. I'm happy to help you with your throwing, but you have to promise never to aim at your brother's head. The way you throw, you could hurt him really bad."

Her eyes widened. "He says I'm a weak, whiny girl."

"Probably because you're better than him."

She beamed. "I never thought about that."

Dakota walked up. "Creating dissension between the sexes at such a young age?"

"I'm not that young."

She laughed. "You know what I meant."

"I do." He studied her, seeing that she looked rested and a lot less sad. "You're feeling better."

"I am.

"Good. Want to talk about what happened?"

"No."

The bell rang, indicating that it was time to head back into class. The kids threw the balls and gloves into the box and raced past them. Peter looked back and waved.

"You did good with him," Dakota said.

"He made it easy."

"You hold yourself back from most of the kids, but with him, you're different."

They walked toward the main building. He wasn't surprised she'd figured out the truth about him.

"Old habit," he said.

"I'm sure there are a lot of reasons," she said. "The fame,

for one thing. You can't know who's interested in you for you or because they want something."

"Less of an issue now."

"Possibly. Plus I would guess there are just too many kids to help individually. You can't be in more than one place at once. So you created the camp to help as many kids as you can. It has the added benefit of allowing you to keep your distance."

"You really feel the need to use your psychology degree, don't you?"

"Sometimes. It can be very flashy at parties."

He knew she was right about all of it. He did hold himself back. He'd been burned plenty of times in college and during his first few years in the NFL. Finally he'd learned the lesson that helping from a distance was a whole lot easier.

Since things had gone bad with Caro, it was also smarter. Her betrayal had shaken him on many levels. She'd made him question his ability to read someone.

"You don't have to do anything at all," Dakota said. "It's not required."

"Sure it is. I was taught that if life gives you advantages, you give back."

"Your former coach?"

"Uh-huh. If I wasn't doing something, he'd come down here and kick my ass."

She smiled. "Cheap talk. You didn't buy this camp for him. You bought it because you wanted to."

He shrugged. "Hawk can be the voice in my head, telling me what to do."

"My mom is that for me. I think it's a good thing."

"Psychologically sound?" he asked.

She laughed. "Definitely. I think it's important to stay on the side of sanity."

"You're the professional." He held open the door to the main building.

"How's Pia doing?" she asked.

"Good. Why?"

"Aren't Hawk and his wife coming to visit for a couple of days?"

"Sure."

"Technically they don't qualify as family, but emotionally, these are the in-laws. Don't you think that's going to make her nervous?"

He hadn't thought of it that way. "There's nothing for her to worry about. They'll like her."

Dakota's expression turned pitying. "You've been married before. Do you really think that's what she's sitting around thinking?"

His face fell. "Oh. Right. I should probably go talk to her, huh?"

Dakota patted his arm. "Don't take it personally. You can't help it, just being a man and all."

PIA TOLD HERSELF that pacing counted as exercise and exercise was healthy. It's not as if her body knew she was wearing a path in Raoul's carpet rather than striding through the park or doing time on a treadmill. Life was about reframing, she told herself.

"Would you relax?" Raoul walked into the living room and crossed to her. After putting his hands on her shoulders, he leaned in and kissed her. "They're going to love you."

"Do you have proof? Because proof would be nice."

"They'll love you," he repeated.

"Saying something over and over again doesn't make it happen. No matter how many times I tell you I'm a giraffe, you're not going to believe me."

He eyed her. "Have you had coffee today?"

"No. This isn't me hyped on caffeine. I'm doing this all myself."

"You should try breathing."

As if that would help. "What if I don't want to meet them?" she asked. "I'm sure they're very nice people, but this all seems so unnecessary. I'll be taking up your visiting time. Why don't you meet them by yourself and tell me about it. You can take pictures. It'll be like I was there."

"I'd rather you *were* there."

"Think of the babies. All this stress can't be good for them. I think I need to throw up."

"Relax," he said softly, right before he kissed her.

It was a good kiss, too, damn him. One that lingered and made her feel all melty inside.

"That's cheating," she said when he straightened.

"I prefer to think of it as getting the job done."

"It's still cheating."

He stared into her eyes. "I'm going to marry you, Pia. Hawk and Nicole are my family, so they'll be part of your life, as well. Why put off the inevitable?"

"Because putting it off makes me feel better." She heard the sound of a car pulling into the driveway. Her stomach twisted. "I think they're here."

He took her hand and led her to the front door, then stepped outside.

A large four-door BMW pulled up. Pia wasn't sure there was a name or number, mostly because she couldn't tell one fancy car from the other. Okay, it was green, but that was the best she could do.

As she thought seriously about throwing up, she watched a tall, good-looking man step out. Based on what she knew about Hawk, he had to be in his late forties, but he looked a lot younger. Then his wife got out of the car. She was a beautiful, elegant blonde. Despite the jeans and button-down shirt, she looked sophisticated—like the kind of woman who always knew what to say.

Pia held in a whimper.

"You made it," Raoul said as he stepped off the porch. He walked to Hawk and the two men hugged. Nicole joined them.

Raoul kissed her cheek. She held on to him for several seconds before letting go and stepping back.

"Small-town life agrees with you," she said. "You look good."

"Always," Raoul said with a laugh. "Come meet Pia."

She'd agonized about what to wear, wanting to make a good impression without trying too hard. There was also the pregnancy to consider. Despite having puffy and bloated moments, she wasn't really showing. In the end, she'd settled on a tunic-length forest green top over black jeans. As a tour of the town was on the agenda, she'd put on flats.

"Hello," she said, holding out her hand first to Hawk. "Nice to meet you."

"Didn't you warn her?" Hawk asked as he ignored the outstretched hand. Instead he grabbed her around her waist and pulled her into a bear hug. "Welcome to the family, Pia." He swung her around a full 360 degrees before setting her on the ground.

"Thanks," she managed while doing her best to regain her footing.

"You'll scare the poor girl," Nicole said, stepping close and hugging Pia more gently. "He's just a big lug of a man. You'll have to forgive him."

"Of course," Pia said, feeling a little disoriented. She'd been worried about Raoul's family judging her and being standoffish. Apparently that wasn't going to be a problem.

Nicole linked arms with her and they walked inside. "I understand you and Raoul are looking for a house. That's so fun. Hawk and I have been in our place forever now. And as much as I love my children, I am, I confess, delighted to be away from them for a few days."

"Raoul said you drove down from Seattle."

"Yes, we're going to Los Angeles."

"Road trip," Hawk said, coming in with Raoul. "One of my former students is playing for USC. We're going to catch a game, then drive home."

"I said let's fly," Nicole told Pia, her tone weary but her eyes bright with amusement. "We could have stopped in Sacramento and rented a car to come here. But no…"

She released Pia's arm. Hawk came up behind Nicole and slipped his arms around her waist. "Are you saying you haven't enjoyed being in a hotel room with me for the past two nights?"

"Hawk! The children."

Pia wanted to point out that she was twenty-eight and that Raoul was a few years older than her, but she didn't. In a way it was kind of nice to have someone a little older than her worrying about her. It had been a lot of years since that had happened.

Hawk kissed his wife. "Nicole, I hate to break it to you, but they've already had sex. They know what it is."

Pia hoped she wasn't blushing.

Raoul caught her eye and grinned. "See what I have to deal with?" Everyone laughed.

They settled on the sofa and chairs in the living room and talked. Nicole brought Raoul up to date on what her kids were doing. Hawk and Raoul talked football. Pia mostly listened. After about half an hour, Raoul stood.

"Let's do a tour of town. Then we can have lunch."

"Want us to drive?" Hawk asked.

Raoul shook his head. "We'll walk. There's not that much to see."

As they walked down the sidewalk, Pia noticed that Nicole kept pace with her while Hawk and Raoul seemed to be getting ahead of them. She recognized the separation of the sexes for what it was.

"Why don't you two meet us at the restaurant in an hour," Nicole called. "Go talk about sports. I get enough of that at home." The older woman smiled. "We can entertain ourselves until then."

Pia forced a smile and told herself that Nicole seemed really nice. Everything was going to be fine.

They strolled down by the park, toward the lake. Pia pointed out Morgan's Books, the store with the fabulous fudge and the entrance to her office. She noticed there were a lot more men out and about than usual, but she didn't want to bring that up. Telling Nicole about Fool's Gold's sudden influx of men would probably scare her.

They chatted about the weather, reality TV and how it would be a good thing if cropped pants never came back in style.

Nicole pointed to the Starbucks. "Come on. I'd kill for a latte."

When they had their drinks—a mocha for Nicole and an herbal tea for Pia—they settled at a table by the window. Pia did her best not to acknowledge the men watching them.

"Raoul mentioned you're in charge of the festivals in town," Nicole said. "Thanks for taking time off work to meet us."

"I wanted to," Pia said, telling herself that now that she'd met Nicole, it wasn't exactly a lie. "You're his family."

"He's been important to us for a long time." She glanced out the window and sighed. "I love it here. What a great place to grow up."

"We do have less rain than Seattle."

"I think the Amazon jungle has less rain than Seattle," Nicole joked. "I was worried about Raoul after his divorce. He couldn't figure out what to do with himself. I thought he'd come back home, but this is better. He needs to make his own way. Hawk was lucky. When he left the NFL, he knew he wanted to coach high school football. Not everyone is so clear."

"You know about the camp Raoul bought?" Pia asked.

"Uh-huh. It sounds great. And now there's a school up there?"

Pia explained about the fire. "It's probably going to take a couple of years for the regular school to be repaired. They're hoping to get the money quickly and get started, but who knows. Without the camp, the kids would have been shoved into already crowded schools."

"Raoul is hero material," Nicole said with a smile. "He gets that from Hawk."

From what she'd heard, the couple had been together for a long time, yet they were still obviously in love. Pia felt a twinge of envy. Loving someone that long, being loved…it had to feel very safe and yet exciting at the same time. For a second she allowed herself to imagine what it would be like to experience that herself. To have love grow stronger every year.

Longing filled her, a physical ache that made it difficult to breathe. She wasn't going to get that with Raoul. Theirs was a practical arrangement. Perhaps, with time, they would grow to love each other, but it wouldn't be the same, she thought sadly. The history of a courtship would never be there. The "falling in love" that made everything seem right in the world.

Nicole leaned over and touched Pia's left hand. "Beautiful ring."

"Thank you." She pressed her lips together, telling herself *not* to say she hadn't been expecting a ring at all—let alone one this amazing.

"We're happy Raoul's found someone."

The statement made Pia nervous. She couldn't tell if Nicole knew why they were getting married. Though she was willing to stay quiet on the whys of the engagement, she wasn't willing to lie about the pregnancy.

"Did Raoul tell you I was pregnant?" Pia asked.

Nicole raised her eyebrows, then laughed. "No, he didn't. How wonderful. Raoul's finally having a child. Excellent."

She felt as if she'd just stepped into something sticky. "Maybe I shouldn't have said anything."

Nicole laughed. "Much like pregnancy itself, there's no do-over. Sorry. Besides, I'm really happy. For what it's worth, I was pregnant when Hawk and I got married."

"Yes, but it was probably his baby."

To give her credit, Nicole barely blinked. She picked up her mocha, took a sip and said, "Why don't you start from the beginning?"

CHAPTER FIFTEEN

PIA EXPLAINED ABOUT Crystal and Keith and the embryos. "I'm still not sure why she left them to me, but she did and they're implanted and I'm pregnant."

"Triplets," Nicole said. "I'm a twin and I had twins, so I know what that's like. You're going to have three. That's a lot of diapers."

"I try not to think about it," Pia admitted. Or feedings, or getting them all to sleep at the same time. In fact, she was pretty much in denial.

"What did Raoul say when you told him what you wanted to do?" Nicole asked.

She was assuming they'd been dating, Pia thought. That the embryos had added an extra dimension to an already ongoing relationship.

"He offered to be my pregnancy buddy," she said, determined to stick to the truth as much as possible.

"That sounds like him." Nicole studied her. "You could have walked away from them."

"No," Pia said firmly. "I would never abandon them." She knew what that felt like.

"What about giving them to someone else?"

Pia shook her head. "Crystal left them to me. I may never

know why, but I'll do the best I can with her children. She was my friend."

Nicole reached out and squeezed her hand. "You're nothing like Caro, are you?"

"I don't know much about her. What was she like?"

Nicole released her hand and leaned back in her chair. "Beautiful. Smart. She's a news anchor."

Pia already hated her. "Great."

Nicole laughed. "Please don't tell Raoul, but that was my reaction when I met her. She says all the right things, but I always had the feeling she would rather have been anywhere but with us. I want to say I'm sorry about their divorce, but honestly I was relieved. I'm so glad he found you."

"Me, too," Pia said. Maybe theirs wasn't the fantasy love every little girl dreamed of, but it was stable and solid and for her, that was going to be enough.

RAOUL AND HAWK made their way to Jo's Bar.

"Brace yourself," Raoul said as he pulled open the door. "It's not what you think."

Hawk stepped inside, then came to a stop as he stared at the big-screen TVs. Three were on the network soaps and the fourth was on a home shopping channel.

"What the hell?"

"Don't ask," Raoul told him, then glanced toward the bar. "Jo, could you send over two beers?"

"Sure. Going into your man cave?"

"As fast as we can." He pointed to the doorway off to the side. "Through there. You'll feel better."

The smaller room had a couple of pool tables, a couple of TVs tuned to sports and was a masculine dark blue color. A relief from the pink and lime green Jo had recently painted the main room. For once it was relatively crowded with men, most of whom Raoul didn't recognize.

Jo delivered the beers and left them with a bowl of pretzels.

"Interesting place," Hawk said, then took a sip of his beer. "You like it here."

Raoul nodded.

"Are you happy?" his former coach asked.

"Not a real masculine question," Raoul joked.

"I've been married nearly all my adult life," Hawk told him. "I can barely hang on to any masculinity. Just don't tell anyone I talk about my feelings."

"I won't say a word." Raoul rested his forearms on the table and looked at his mentor. "I'm happy. I didn't know what to expect when I moved here, but it's turning out even better than I thought."

"You have the camp."

Raoul explained how it was being used as a school. "It'll be a while until they're able to move back into their old building. We'll still have camp in the summer, when the local kids are out of school, but we've had to put our winter plans on hold."

"You okay with that?"

"I would have liked to get started with the math and science programs sooner rather than later, but they needed a place to have school. I'm not going to put three hundred kids out on the street because I have an ego problem."

Hawk slapped him on the shoulder. "I like hearing that. It means I did a good job raising you."

"It couldn't be my sterling character?"

"Not likely."

They laughed and clinked bottles.

"Pia seems nice," Hawk said.

"She is. She was born and raised here. I told you she runs all the festivals in town. It's a lot of coordinating, working with different people. When the school needed an emergency fundraiser and supply drive, she got it done in a couple of days." He glanced at his friend. "She's pregnant."

Hawk raised his eyebrows. "You okay with that?"

"Yeah. I'm happy." He hesitated. "The babies aren't mine."

Hawk picked up his beer bottle but didn't drink. "Okay," he said slowly. "Tell me about it."

Raoul explained about Crystal and the embryos.

"That's a lot to take on," Hawk said when he'd finished. "Responsibility, time, money. They're not going to be yours."

Raoul didn't fall for it. "They'll be mine. I'll be there when they're born and see them through their whole lives. How could they not be mine?"

Hawk didn't look convinced. "You doing this because of Caro? Are you secretly figuring it won't be as big a problem because they're not your biological children? You're wrong—they'll be yours in every sense of the word. You won't be able to hold back with them."

"I don't want to hold back."

"You sure about that?"

It was a question Raoul had wrestled with since finding out about Pia's plans for the embryos. He'd meant it when he'd promised to be there for her, to be a real father to those children.

"I want to be their father. I want to be involved with them, the way you were there for me. You might have come into my life when I was in high school, but that doesn't mean you didn't shape everything about me. I can do this. I want to do this."

Hawk took a long drink of his beer. "Kids aren't easy under the best of circumstances. Triplets. That's a load and a half."

Raoul grinned. "It's probably three loads."

"Smart-ass." Hawk shook his head. "You sure about this? Once you commit, there's no turning back."

"I'm sure." It was what he wanted.

"Make sure you get married for the right reasons."

Raoul could do the translation. Hawk wanted him to be sure he was marrying Pia because he loved her and couldn't live without her. Not because it was the right thing to do.

It was the only secret he would keep from his friend. The truth was, not loving Pia was part of the appeal. He'd been in love once, had married Caro and had paid the price. Never again, he'd promised himself, and he meant it.

"Pia's the one," he said, sidestepping the issue.

"Then I'm happy for you."

Raoul couldn't tell if Hawk believed him or was simply going along with things. In the end, he supposed it didn't matter. Whatever the outcome, Hawk would be there for him, just like he would be there for the babies Pia carried.

PIA LOOKED UP from her desk to find Charity Jones-Golden standing in the doorway.

"You're busy," her friend said.

"I have the auction tonight, followed by the dinner-dance in a week. Busy doesn't cover it. Hysterical is closer. In fact, I think hysterical is pretty accurate."

"So you probably don't have time to go shopping."

Pia perked up. "I certainly do. In fact a little retail therapy is exactly what I need. On the way back, I'll grab a sandwich to eat at my desk and call it lunch."

Charity smiled. "Really? You'd do that for me?"

"Mostly I'm doing it for myself, but you can pretend it's about you if it makes you feel better." Pia saved her computer program, then closed it, grabbed her purse and stood. "What are we shopping for? Jewelry? Furniture? A vacation in the south of France?"

"Maternity clothes."

Pia plopped down on her seat, her gaze settling on her friend's growing tummy. "Tell me you're kidding."

"I need to buy some things, and you're way better at the stylish thing than I am. I want to look good as I approach my whale days. Or as good as I can. 'Help me, Obi Wan. You're my only hope.'"

"Oh, please. Don't try *Star Wars* on me. I'm too young to remember anything but the remastered versions, and so are you."

Charity continued to stare at her, all wide-eyed and pleading.

"Fine," Pia grumbled, standing again. "I'll help you buy your stupid maternity clothes."

"The point of bringing you along is so they're not stupid. Besides, you might want to get a few things for yourself. It took me a while to pop out of my regular clothes, but I'm not carrying triplets."

"Thanks for mentioning that."

"Anytime."

Pia followed her into the hallway, then locked the door. As they made their way down the stairs, she had to admit that Charity was right...sort of. Lately it had seemed her pants were getting snug, and she would swear her breasts had gone up a full cup size. She was starting to spill out of her bras. In the few weeks between now and looking like a woman who had swallowed a beach ball, she could probably make some great money posing for breast-enhancement ads.

"How are you feeling?" Charity asked. "Any morning sickness?"

"I'm fine as long as I stick to crackers for the first hour. Then I can pretty much eat what I want. Of course, based on the list of things I should be eating, all those fruits and vegetables, the protein and dairy, there's not much room left for empty calories." She sighed. "I miss empty calories."

"Me, too. And coffee. I would kill for a glass of wine." She glanced at Pia. "Do you think it's wrong to bring a saucy little Merlot into the recovery room?"

"I think they'd frown on it. Plus, won't you be breastfeeding?"

They reached the street and turned left. There was an exclusive maternity boutique right next to Jenel's Gems.

"Breastfeeding is in the plan," Charity admitted. "Are you?"

"I haven't gotten that far," Pia admitted. "I'm one breast short, to begin with, so I'm not sure how it would work. I'm not really doing a lot of reading yet. I have time."

"Of course you do. It's nice that you're not totally obsessed with your pregnancy. The first two months, I couldn't stop reading about it, or talking about it. I became one of those horrible, self-absorbed friends who only cared about herself."

"I remember," Pia said, her voice teasing.

Charity gave her a mock glare. "A true friend wouldn't mention my slip in judgment."

"A true friend would have given you a good slap if it had continued much longer."

Charity laughed.

Pia joined in but was pleased when the conversation changed topic. In truth, the reason she hadn't started doing a lot of reading about her pregnancy had nothing to do with being calm and everything to do with the fact that she still didn't feel connected to the babies growing inside of her. They were an intellectual exercise, not an emotional bond. She knew she was pregnant, but those were just words.

In time things would get better, she told herself. From finding out about the embryos to implantation had only been a matter of a few weeks. It made sense that she would need time to catch up emotionally. At least that was the plan.

"Josh keeps saying we have to register." Charity grimaced. "I've gone online where they have those lists of what is 'essential,' and it's enough to freak me out. They talk about things I've never heard of. And some other stuff that's really weird. Do you know there's a device that keeps baby wipes warm? You drop in a container of wipes and it keeps them toasty. The reviews say not to get it because then the kids scream when you're away from home and have to use a cold baby wipe."

Pia felt the first hint of fear. "I have to make a decision about baby wipes? Can't I just buy what's on sale?"

"Sure, but then do you heat them? It's incredible. I swear, if you took along everything that they said, you wouldn't need a baby bag so much as a camel. And you'll have three times that amount."

Pia felt a little light-headed. "We should talk about something else," she murmured.

"And the diapers. Do you know how many diapers babies go through in an average week?"

"No," she whispered.

"Eighty to a hundred."

Charity kept talking, but Pia was too busy doing the math. With triplets, she could be looking at two hundred and forty to three hundred diapers in a week. If she used disposable ones, wouldn't she be personally responsible for any overflow in the Fool's Gold landfill?

Three hundred diapers? How many were in a box? Could she fit that many in her car? Was Raoul going to have to buy a semi to bring in supplies?

"That's pretty." Charity had stopped in front of the window of the maternity store. A pregnant mannequin wore a sophisticated burgundy pantsuit, with a fly-away-style jacket. The fabric was a high-quality knit that skimmed the body and held its shape but would probably wash like a dream.

"The color would be great for you," Pia said. "With your light hair."

"I wonder if the set comes with a skirt. Or I could get a black skirt and a patterned top. That would give me a lot of work outfits." She glanced at Pia. "Or am I being too matchy-matchy?"

"You're doing just fine. Let's go in and see what they have."

The store was larger than it looked from the outside. There was plenty of light, lots of mirrors and racks of clothes set up by type. In the back, an archway led into a massive separate store that sold everything baby. Pia caught sight of a stroller and crib before carefully averting her eyes. She was here to shop for her friend, not freak herself out. Later, when she could sit down, she would think about all the equipment babies apparently required and try not to hyperventilate. And maybe she would take Denise Hendrix up on her offer to explain what exactly the mother of a triplet needed three of and what she could avoid buying in bulk.

"Hi, ladies," a salesclerk called. "How are you doing?"

"Great," Charity said. "I'm browsing first."

"Let me know if I can help."

Pia wandered toward the dress racks. Maybe dresses would be easier, as they would give her more breathing room—so to speak. But as it got colder, she preferred pants or nice jeans. Plus, did she really want to deal with maternity tights or nylons?

She crossed over to the jeans and grimaced when she saw a very unattractive elastic kind of band thing stuck in front. Was that what she had to look forward to?

"Look at this," Charity said, pointing to a mannequin. "It's a tummy sleeve." She leaned in and read the sign. "Oh, this is great. It helps with transition. When you're too big for your regular pants but maternity ones are too big for you. It covers the open zipper." She grinned. "I wish I'd thought of that. You should get one."

What Pia should get is out of the store. She wasn't ready for any of this. Not yet. She was barely pregnant and she still hadn't accepted she was having one baby, let alone three.

She watched Charity collect several items of clothing, then waited while her friend tried them on.

"You look adorable in everything," Pia told her.

It was the truth. Charity genuinely glowed. She was pleasantly rounded, blissfully happy and excited about being a mother. Pia felt like a crabby fraud.

"You don't want to pick out anything?" Charity asked as she paid for her clothing.

Pia shook her head. "I'm not ready."

"I would guess with triplets, you're going to have to get ready soon. Is this where I ask you to come with me next door to look at furniture and you refuse?"

"I'll look."

Maybe poking around in a baby store would help. If nothing

else, she could look for a book on multiple births. The books she had at home only had a chapter or two on multiples.

They walked through to the baby store. There were cribs and changing tables, mobiles and teddy bear lamps.

"Come see," Charity told her, pointing to the left. "There's a bedroom set I really love. But it's pretty girly and if we have a boy, I'm not sure it's appropriate."

Pia followed her friend to a display done in pale wood. The small nightstand, crib, dresser and changing table were all carved with fairies and angels, the edges scalloped. Pink-and-gold drawer pulls sparkled with a touch of glitter.

"Too girly doesn't describe it," Pia said with a grin. "I think it's great, but you need to make sure you're having a girl before you get this."

"It's too over the top for a boy?"

"It will give Josh a heart attack, and that's the last thing you want."

"I know." Charity sighed. "I had planned not to know the sex of the baby until the birth. I thought that would be fun. I've always been such a planner. This seemed like the ultimate in letting go."

"Then you're going to have to let go on the furniture selection," Pia told her. "This is a whole new dimension of girly."

"You're right," Charity said, sounding reluctant. "What are you going to do?"

Pia turned to her. "About what?"

"Knowing the gender of the babies."

"I haven't really thought about it."

"From what I know about IVF, you're going to have fraternal rather than identical triplets," Charity said. "Three embryos mean they fertilized three different eggs. That could make things interesting. Does Raoul want to know?"

They hadn't talked about it, Pia realized. In fact they hadn't talked much about the babies at all. She didn't know anything about his thoughts on children, except he wanted them. What were his hopes and dreams for these babies? Did he spank or prefer time-outs? Would he want to know if they were having boys or girls?

She put her hand on the dresser to steady herself. There was more. They hadn't talked about financials or their goals for their lives. She didn't know what religion he was, if he opened his presents Christmas Eve or Christmas morning. They hadn't even discussed which way to load a dishwasher.

How could she have agreed to marry someone she didn't know at all? Shouldn't they have a plan to get to know each other? Of course, she was the same person who had blithely had her friend's babies implanted into her body without considering the future.

She was going to be the mother of three children. She was going to have to raise them for the next eighteen years. Longer if housing prices kept going up. She could barely take care of herself. There was the whole humiliating relationship failure with Jake, the cat.

"I can't do this," she said.

"What's wrong?" Crystal asked, sounding concerned.

Pia had to get out of there. She couldn't breathe, couldn't think.

She glanced at her watch. "I have to go. I have..." Her mind went blank, then rebooted and provided her with the perfect excuse. "I have a city council meeting tomorrow. I need to get back to work and prepare."

"Me, too," Crystal told her. "We're talking about the budget, which is a serious drag. Neither of us can have caffeine. How are we supposed to stay awake?"

Pia was amazed. She must still look and sound normal, when on the inside, she was seconds from a meltdown.

Somehow she made it back to her office. But instead of preparing for the meeting, she stood in her tiny bathroom, her arms braced against the sink.

The obvious question was what had she been thinking. But

she knew the answer to that. She hadn't been. She'd been reacting to the loss of a dear friend. And now that she was pregnant,
was she doing her very best to be informed? Had she made even
one change in her life to support the babies?

Okay, sure she'd given up alcohol and caffeine and she was
taking the vitamins and eating lots of fruits and vegetables. But
was that enough? She hadn't known how many diapers a baby
needed a day. She didn't want to look at furniture or maternity
clothes. If Crystal really knew what she was like, she would be
horrified to know her future children would be in Pia's custody.
Because for the first time ever, the babies were finally real to
her and she was terrified.

THE ENTIRE TOWN turned out for the auction. Pia stared at the
huge crowd and found that being the object of so much male
attention was kind of good for her emotionally fragile state.

Since arriving at the convention center, she'd been ogled,
had her butt pinched twice and asked out more times than she
could count.

There had to be at least three hundred guys milling around
the open space and twice that many women. The concession
stands were doing a brisk business, which meant plenty of income for the city. All good.

"Hey, pretty lady."

Pia glanced up from her clipboard and saw a tall, slightly
grizzled older man smiling at her. He was missing a couple of
teeth and needed a shave.

"You gonna bid on me tonight?" he asked, wiggling his eyebrows.

"Would that I could," she said with a heavy sigh. "But I'm
pregnant."

His gaze dropped to her belly and he took a couple of steps
back. "I'm not interested in no kids."

"I hear that a lot."

The man turned and nearly ran in the opposite direction. Montana hurried up to her.

"This is great. I can't wait for the talent show. Some guy just felt me up. I should probably be mad, but it's so strange, it's almost funny."

"Give it an hour," Pia told her. "It'll get annoying. I'm telling every guy who talks to me that I'm pregnant. It's very effective."

Dakota joined them. She had a soda in one hand and popcorn in the other. "The lady with the dancing dog is first up in the talent show. I can't wait."

Pia laughed. "This is a serious event, you two. Act accordingly."

"It's a woman dancing with her poodle," Dakota said with a laugh. "I do love this town."

Pia glanced around at the crowd filling the convention center. Despite the craziness, she loved it, too.

THE NEXT AFTERNOON, Pia managed to sit through the city council meeting without dozing off. Given her wild night at the auction, that was a serious accomplishment.

The performances had gone off on time, the bachelor auction had been nearly orderly. The more attractive men who claimed to have jobs had gone for the most money, and nothing really embarrassing had happened, which meant the media coverage should be relatively benign.

One crisis endured, forty-seven others waiting in the wings, she thought. At least the activities of last night had kept her from dwelling on her inadequacies as a potential mother.

She was trying and that should count, she told herself. As she got more pregnant, she would bond more with the babies. She promised herself she would read more and figure out what she was supposed to do next.

"We're hoping revenue from the influx of tourists helps," the city treasurer was saying.

"By tourists she means men," Mayor Marsha said with a

heavy sigh. "Pia, the auction went very smoothly last night. Thank you for that."

"You're welcome. I don't have the money totals yet, but we made a lot. We're taking costs out of the auction proceeds, and then all the profits go directly to the city."

"I suppose if we have to be in the middle of this circus, we might as well benefit in some way," Marsha said. "What's next?"

Talk turned to budgeting. At one point, Charity tried to stifle a yawn, then caught Pia's gaze and grinned.

Pia nodded in agreement. Not exactly a topic to keep one up in anticipation. She shifted in her seat, feeling a faint cramping in her stomach. At first she didn't think anything about it. She listened to the latest information on the cause of the fire at the school and the projections for repair costs.

The cramps increased. She frowned as she tried to remember if her period was due. Usually she noted that on her calendar so she could be prepared with...

Dread swept through her. She wasn't going to get her period. She was pregnant. She shouldn't be cramping. Not like this.

"Oh, God," she breathed, terrified to move, not sure what to do.

Everyone turned to look at her. Another cramp hit her. This one was horrifyingly worse.

Then she felt it. A rush of something liquid. Involuntarily she stood and looked down. Blood pooled in the seat.

Pia began to scream.

CHAPTER SIXTEEN

PIA GULPED FOR AIR. Even as she gasped, she choked on a sob. Despite the nurse's insistence that she had to calm down, she couldn't stop crying.

The nurse held on to Pia's hand. "Honey, is there someone I can call? Do you want me to get your mom?"

The irony of the question only made Pia cry harder. Marsha would have phoned Raoul already, and he would get here as quickly as he could. There was no one else.

"I'm fine," Pia managed.

"You've got to quiet down. This isn't good for you or the babies."

Babies. Because there were two left. At least that's what the ultrasound had shown. Only one had been lost.

Pia did her best to slow her breathing. Getting upset only made things worse. She knew that, but she couldn't seem to control herself. Not when she knew she was to blame.

"Where is she?" a male voice asked from the hallway. "Pia O'Brian. She's my fiancée."

"Raoul!"

The nurse left her side and hurried to the open door. "In here."

Raoul rushed in and raced to her side. "Pia." He bent over

her and took her hand in his, then kissed her forehead. "Are you all right?"

The worry and concern had her crying again. But instead of backing away, he leaned close and wrapped his arms around her.

She cried and cried until she felt empty inside. Until there was no way to find relief.

"I lost one of the babies," she said, the words hoarse in her swollen throat.

"I know." He smoothed her hair. "It's okay."

"It's not. It's not okay. I'm the reason. It's my fault." She felt her eyes fill again. Grabbing his hand with both of hers, she stared into his eyes. "It's my fault. I did this. They were never real to me. I didn't want to tell you, but they weren't. I knew in my head I was pregnant, but I didn't feel it. I wasn't maternal. The baby knew. It knew and now it's gone."

"Pia, no. That's not what happens."

"It is. I did it. I was out with Charity yesterday. She wanted to look at maternity clothes and I didn't. I didn't want to think about how big I'm going to get, or what's going to happen to my body. Then I freaked out about the furniture. I didn't even know how many diapers a baby uses in a week."

The tears flowed again, trickling down her cheeks. "Crystal trusted me. She trusted me and one of her babies is gone and I can't fix it. I can't make it better. I loved her and she believed in me and look what I've done."

Raoul shook his head. He looked uncomfortable and helpless. "Sometimes babies don't make it."

She raised her bed a little, so she could see him more easily. "There's more. I'm the reason." She swallowed, knowing she had to tell him the truth, even if it meant he would walk away from her forever.

Maybe that would be for the best, she thought, feeling sick to her stomach. Then when the babies were born, he could have child protective services take them from her so she wouldn't damage them further.

"I got pregnant when I was in college."

Raoul didn't want to hear anything more. He knew where the story was going, what she was going to say. Anger grew. He pulled his hand back.

Pia was talking. He forced himself to listen, to pretend he wasn't judging.

"I knew he wouldn't marry me, and I started…" She gasped for breath. "I started wishing the baby would go away. That's what I thought in my head. How everything would be better if it just went away."

She closed her eyes. The tears continued to flow, but they no longer touched him.

"Then it did," she whispered.

"It didn't go away," he said harshly. "You did something."

She nodded. "I know. The baby knew or sensed and then it was gone. Dr. Galloway said I can't take responsibility. That not every baby starts out right and when they don't, nature takes care of things. That's the medical explanation. The baby wasn't right. But it wasn't the baby, it was me."

He stared at her, confused by what she was saying. "You didn't have an abortion?"

"What?" Her eyes opened. "No. Of course not. I was figuring I'd give the baby up for adoption. I even had a few brochures. But it was gone, just like today. That's what I kept thinking. That I was being punished for not wanting that first baby. So I don't get to have these."

His anger and sense of betrayal faded as if they'd never been. Shame replaced them—for thinking the worst of Pia. She was nothing like Caro. He already knew that.

He returned to the bed, grateful she hadn't noticed his retreat, and pulled her close again.

"I'm sorry," he said, apologizing for his mistake.

"You didn't do anything."

He would tell her later, he thought. When she was better.

"Neither did you," he told her. "You're not being punished."

"You can't know that."

He looked into her eyes. "Yes, I can."

"I lost one of Crystal's babies."

"No," he said quietly, for the first time understanding exactly what had happened. "We lost one of ours."

Twins, he thought sadly. Twins, not triplets.

Her eyes widened. More tears came. "You're right," she said on a sob. "Oh, God. Make it come back."

A prayer that would never be answered, he thought sadly as he held her.

They hung on to each other for a long time. When she seemed to have calmed down a little, he sat next to her on the bed and stroked her face.

"I look terrible," she said. "Puffy and swollen and miserable."

"You're beautiful."

"You're either a liar or you need your eyes checked."

He gave her a smile, then let it fade. After kissing her mouth, he said, "Don't for one minute think it's your fault. It's not. It can't be. Blame comes with a deliberate action."

He paused, then decided it was time. "You know that I was married before. Caro was a former beauty queen turned local news anchor. We met at a charity function in Dallas."

Pia leaned back against her pillows. "Is it okay to hate her?"

"Sure."

"Good. Because I do."

At one time he had hated her more. But time had healed him. He would never understand, but he'd ceased wanting her punished.

"We were the perfect couple," he continued. "Shortly after we got engaged, she was offered a job with a national affiliate in Los Angeles. Her career was important to her, so we moved to L.A. and during the season, I commuted."

"That sounds very civilized."

"It was. We talked about starting a family. We both wanted kids. One day I got a call that Caro was in the hospital. I came as fast as I could. I didn't understand what was wrong and she didn't want them to tell me."

He could remember everything about that moment. Standing in the hallway, staring at a doctor who wouldn't tell him what was wrong with his wife.

"I don't understand," Pia said. "The doctor wouldn't tell you?"

"Not without her permission. I went into her room. She was pale. There were a couple of IVs and blood. I remember seeing the blood dripping into her."

That had scared him the most. The thought that she might die.

He looked at Pia. "She'd had an abortion that afternoon and something had gone wrong. She'd been bleeding internally. She had surgery and was fine. That's what she said. 'I'm fine.'"

He shook his head. "I didn't even know she was pregnant. She hadn't told me. She said she wanted kids one day but not right then. Not when her career was going so well." He turned away. "If she hadn't ended up in the hospital, I never would have known. She made the decision without me. While I believe a woman has a right to choose, this was different. We were married. We were trying to have a kid—actively trying to get pregnant right then so I could be with her when it was born during the off-season. But it was all a lie."

Pia's breath caught. She couldn't believe what she was hearing. That Raoul's wife had betrayed him, betrayed *them* that way. It was one thing to put off having kids, or to discuss an unexpected pregnancy, but to pretend to be trying for a baby, then abort it when it happened was inexcusable.

"I'm sorry," she whispered. "I know that's a stupid thing to say, but I'm sorry."

He turned back to her. She saw the hurt in his eyes and the loss.

"I'm sorry, too."

They stared at each other, sharing their pain. Despite their practical arrangement, she'd never felt closer to him. More connected.

There was a short knock on the door. They both turned and saw Dr. Galloway walk in.

"Pia, my dear," she said. "I'm so sorry."

"Me, too."

The doctor shook hands with Raoul, then moved to her side. "From what we can tell, the other two babies are hanging on just fine. They're growing and look healthy."

"You're saying don't give up hope."

The older woman patted her shoulder. "I'm saying don't beat yourself up about this. I want you to try to relax. You'll stay here tonight and we'll do another ultrasound in the morning. I expect everything will be fine and you'll go home. There's no reason for us to believe you'll have any other problems, but we'll take precautions, just to be sure."

Pia nodded.

"I'm going to have the kitchen send up some dinner. I want you to eat. Do you promise?"

"Yes."

"I'm staying," Raoul said firmly. "I'll make sure she eats."

"I suspect you will," the doctor said cheerfully. "All right, Pia. Get some rest. I'll see you in the morning."

"Thank you."

"You're welcome." Dr. Galloway's mouth straightened. "No blaming yourself for this, hear me?"

"I'll try."

When the doctor left, Raoul moved to her side again.

"We'll get through this," he promised.

"I know."

Having him here helped, she thought, relaxing back against the pillows. He was someone she could depend on, and right now that seemed like the best thing of all.

PIA STRETCHED OUT on the sofa and tried to get comfortable. It wasn't that she was hurting, she just felt weird inside. Unsettled. Afraid. Unworthy. Not exactly emotions designed to make her day restful.

She'd come home from the hospital that morning. It had taken a while to convince Raoul that it was perfectly safe to leave her for a few hours. Actually, it hadn't been her words that had done the trick—instead it had been the steady stream of visitors, showing up with flowers, cards, food and baby gifts for the remaining twins. When he'd figured out she was unlikely to be alone for more than a few minutes at a time, he'd agreed to head out to check in at his office.

Now she breathed a sigh of relief at the silence and hoped it would be hours until she next heard a knock on the door. It was a whole lot easier to feel sorry for herself and guilty when she was alone.

The second ultrasound had shown the two remaining babies were doing very well. They seemed unaffected by what had happened to their sibling. One of her visitors—Nina, the nurse from the hospital—had brought over a chicken casserole and had explained about vanishing twins. That it wasn't uncommon to lose one baby during gestation.

Pia appreciated the attempts to make her feel better, but right now she felt mired in guilt and depression. It was possible that in time she would feel better, but she couldn't imagine that ever happening.

There was a knock on her front door.

"Come in," she called, hoping she sounded at least slightly enthusiastic.

Denise Hendrix pushed open the door and walked into Pia's living room.

"Hi," she said, smiling gently. "How are you feeling?"

Pia shrugged. "Okay, I guess. Sad."

"Sure you are. You're going to be for a while." Denise held up the grocery bag she had. "Ice cream. Nearly every Ben & Jerry's flavor. Think of it as your dairy. I'll go put it in the freezer."

She returned in a few minutes. Instead of sitting in the chair opposite the sofa where Pia lay, Denise sat on the coffee table and leaned close.

"You look miserable," she said flatly. "Like you lost your best friend."

"Or killed her baby," Pia murmured, then shook her head. "Sorry. I didn't mean to say it out loud."

"You didn't kill Crystal's baby."

"It feels like it. They weren't real to me, Denise. I was going through the motions."

"So? Why isn't that enough? You're growing children inside of you, not providing a spiritual education. Right now your only job is to take care of yourself and them to the best of your ability." She sighed. "I raised six kids. Do you think I was fully present every second of every day? Do you think I liked it when the boys were fighting and the girls had colic? That I didn't wish myself away to some tropical island with nothing more than a quiet room to sleep in and a good book to read?"

Pia blinked at her. "But you're a great mom."

"Thank you. I loved my kids and tried my best, but I wasn't perfect. No one is. And if the babies you had implanted aren't real to you, so what? You'll get there. It's not as if you've violated the universal pregnancy time line. This is a huge change in your life, Pia. You've given up so many things to honor your friend's request. I liked Crystal a lot, but I have to tell you, there's a part of me that thinks she had no right to do this to you."

Pia felt her eyes widen. "What are you talking about?"

"You don't just leave someone embryos without talking to them first. It's wrong. She should have talked to you, made sure this was what you wanted, too. She was asking a hell of a lot, and she didn't give you the chance to say no."

Pia hadn't thought about it that way. "I could have walked away."

"Walking away was a possibility, yes, but not for you. That's not who you are. We all see it in how you are with this town. You get the details right, you do the work. And anyone who knows you personally, knows that you've been hurt by the people who were supposed to protect you. And that you would never do that to anyone else. You don't need to worry about connecting with the babies you're carrying. It will happen. The reason you're sad is you've lost one of your children, as well. If this was just about Crystal, you'd only feel guilty."

Pia turned the other woman's words over in her mind. "You're right," she said slowly. "If I didn't care, I guess I'd secretly be relieved. Two babies is going to be a lot easier than three. But I can't get away from the sense of loss. And letting Crystal down."

"This isn't about your emotions. An embryo could have been lost at any point in the process. It's a miracle all three of them got this far. Do you know how unlikely it was for you to get pregnant at all? You've done great."

"Thanks."

Somehow Denise had cut to the heart of the problem. In a way, exposing the issue to the light made Pia feel better.

"I worry that I won't do a good job," she admitted. "I'm not ready to buy maternity clothes or look at baby furniture."

"Most women get married, then plan having a baby. This was thrust upon you without warning. You need time to catch up. As for maternity clothes, trust me, it won't be long until you don't have a choice." She smiled. "The baby-furniture issue will take care of itself. Pretty soon you'll have freakish hormones coursing through your body. You'll be biologically compelled to nest. But until that happens, don't sweat it. You're being too hard on yourself."

"I'll try to do better."

"I hope so. You're going to be a great mother. You already are. If you need anything, you know we'll all be there for you. This whole town loves you."

The two women hugged. As Denise straightened, Pia heard footsteps on the stairs. Seconds later, Raoul entered the apartment.

He'd brought a small duffel with him. More clothes, she thought.

"Denise," he said. "Thanks for stopping by."

"I had to see our girl. She's doing better."

Raoul glanced at her anxiously. "I hope so." He hesitated, then said, "I'm trying to convince her to move in with me, at least temporarily. My house is all one level."

Pia rolled her eyes. "I'm fine."

"You can't take the stairs."

There was a difference between can't and don't want to, Pia thought. Although she was supposed to take it easy for the next few days, after that, there weren't any restrictions. Which might be medically sound, but emotionally, the thought of taking stairs made her beyond nervous.

Denise glanced between them. "Pia, it might be a good idea. You'd be more relaxed if you didn't have to worry about stairs. It's only for a week or so, then you can move back." She raised her eyebrows. "Although I'm not sure how long you're going to want to climb those three flights as your pregnancy progresses."

Raoul looked both pleading and smug. "See."

It might be the practical solution, but Pia didn't like it. Moving in with Raoul said something about their relationship. Or maybe it simply made things more real. Not that she'd been able to ignore the very large engagement ring on her left hand.

"I'll think about it," she promised. It was the best she could do.

Denise hugged her again. As she was bent over, she whispered, "He's very handsome and doting. There are worse traits in a man."

"I know. Thanks for coming by and talking to me."

Denise kissed her forehead. "Anytime." She straightened. "Take care of her. She's precious to all of us."

"I will," Raoul told her, then walked her to the door.

They spoke for a few seconds. Pia couldn't hear what they were saying, which was probably the point. She leaned back against the sofa and closed her eyes. Despite being exhausted, she couldn't seem to fall asleep. Every time she tried, she flashed back to the sight of the blood on the chair and felt the same terror flooding her. Not exactly a sequence designed to get her to nod off.

Instead she thought about what Denise had told her. Denise's observation that it was amazing that the babies had gotten this far was the most help. Maybe it was okay that she hadn't totally absorbed the idea of being pregnant. Maybe all that would change with time.

She opened her eyes and saw Raoul close the door. He glanced back at her.

"Why don't you try to rest," he suggested.

She nodded because it was easier than admitting she couldn't sleep. She closed her eyes and tried to think about nothing at all. That seemed safest.

But she found herself remembering his story about his first wife. How Caro had betrayed him. There was no excuse for what she'd done. Pia couldn't imagine lying to the one person you were supposed to love more than anyone. Not like that. If she hadn't wanted to have children, she should have told him and gone on the Pill or something.

But the most difficult part of what he'd told her had been the realization that he'd loved Caro. The truth had been in the way he'd spoken about her, in the emotion in his eyes. He'd met her, dated her, fallen in love with her and proposed. Just like it was supposed to be.

She wasn't going to get that. She wasn't going to have the kind of love Hawk and Nicole shared, or that Denise had had with her late husband. There might be respect and a growing affection, there might be a shared goal of raising the twins and perhaps having more children, but there wasn't a heart-pounding, hair-raising, oh-my-God kind of falling in love.

The knowledge hurt more than she would have expected. It made her want to curl up and give in to tears. Some for what she'd lost, but also for the realization of how much she'd wanted that in her life. She'd wanted her happy ending.

With Raoul.

She sat up straight and opened her eyes. After checking to make sure he wasn't in the room, she turned the thought over in her mind. With Raoul? As in… What? She was falling for him?

A dangerous place to go, she told herself. It was insane to fall for a guy who'd made it clear he didn't want his heart to get involved.

She reminded herself she'd always been practical. This was completely the wrong time to be thinking with her heart.

"My HANDS STILL SMELL FUNNY," Peter said with a laugh, holding one up for her to inspect. "And I washed 'em like five times."

"Garlic's tricky that way," Pia told him, enjoying having the boy to talk to. It was difficult to stay depressed in the presence of a happy ten-year-old.

"Raoul said a bad word when he dropped the spaghetti in the boiling water," Peter said in a whisper. "It was funny."

"I'm sure it was."

Despite her misgivings about moving in with Raoul, practicality and her fear of stairs had won. He'd packed up her stuff and carried her down two flights of stairs—a testament to his workout commitment. Now she was settled in his guest room.

He'd called Peter's foster parents and asked if the boy could join them for dinner. Pia appreciated having someone else there that first night. It made her feel less weird about being in Raoul's house.

He appeared in the doorway, a dish towel over his shoulder. "I drain the meat before putting in the sauce, right?"

"Yes. But don't put the grease down the drain."

"Cooking is complicated."

She laughed. "I told you not to start with making spaghetti. You could have heated up one of the casseroles. That would have been easier."

"But I love a good challenge."

"Typical man."

He chuckled and left.

Peter sat down next to her on the sofa. "Raoul said you were sick and you have to be careful." He held out his arm which now sported a green cast. "Is it like my arm?"

"A little like that. You still have to be careful about not getting it wet, right?"

"Uh-huh."

"But it will get better."

"Like you?" Peter asked, leaning against her.

She put her arm around him. "Like me," she said, and hoped she was telling the truth.

CHAPTER SEVENTEEN

LIZ STRETCHED OUT on the other sofa in Raoul's living room. "Seriously," she said. "You have to be bored."

"I'm getting there," Pia admitted. This was day four and her last day of resting. "I keep thinking about everything that has to be done and how behind I'm going to be."

Liz winced. "Yes, well, about that. Montana organized a work party."

Pia straightened. "Do not tell me she let people into my office."

"Okay, I won't."

"Are you kidding? They were touching my files?"

Liz laughed. "It's not like they were feeling up your underwear drawer. It's just files."

Pia groaned. "They're my files. I have a system. What if they messed it up?"

"What if they were just trying to help because they care about you?"

"Helping is nice," Pia said. "But not if it makes more work for me."

"Someone needs her attitude adjusted. You should be grateful we all care about you. This town takes care of its own."

Pia narrowed her gaze. "You weren't so happy with all the

meddling when you first moved back to town. If I remember correctly, you wanted to leave and never come back."

"That was different."

"Why?"

"It was happening to me."

Pia relaxed back on the sofa and laughed. "Typical. We're all so self-absorbed."

"Speak for yourself." Liz's humor faded. "How are you doing?"

"No. I'm tired of talking about myself. How are you doing? How is life with three kids and a fiancé?"

"You forgot the puppy," Liz said. "Ethan's bright idea, although I get the blame. I allowed a vote. Of course everyone wanted the puppy but me and now in addition to everything else, I'm potty training a very energetic Labradoodle named— wait for it—Newman."

Pia giggled. "Newman?"

"Can you believe it?"

At the beginning of summer, Liz had discovered she had two nieces she hadn't known about. The oldest, a fourteen-year-old, had contacted her through Liz's Web site, admitting their father was in prison and their stepmother had taken off, leaving them on their own. Liz had packed up her son and her computer and driven to Fool's Gold to rescue the girls.

The difficult situation had been complicated by the fact that Ethan, the oldest of the Hendrix children, had been the father of Liz's ten-year-old son. Through a series of miscommunications, Liz thought he knew about Tyler, but he hadn't been told. After a very rocky few months, they'd realized they were still madly in love. Now Ethan was building them a house, they were engaged and Liz had custody of her two nieces. And Newman.

"Don't you have to go on a book tour soon?" Pia asked.

Liz was a bestselling mystery author.

"Next week," Liz said with a sigh. "Denise is moving in for the duration. I've warned her it's not going to be the big party she's expecting. The good news is Newman is about ninety percent on knowing where to pee."

"Meaning not in the house?"

"Exactly. I finally have a chore list for the kids that seems workable, and everyone is doing their own laundry. It means that Tyler sometimes has pink socks, but he's learning to deal with that." Liz shook her head. "I'm normally gone about three weeks, but under the circumstances my publisher very graciously agreed that ten days was better. Honestly, I'm looking forward to being alone in a hotel room. No loud music or TV, no fighting over the Wii control, no yells asking what time is dinner."

"No Ethan."

"That's the downside, but I'll survive. Actually, he's a big help with the kids. The girls adore him. He's helping Abby with her pitching. There's a softball team in middle school and she wants to get on it."

"You've settled in to living here. For a while I didn't think that was going to happen."

"Me, either," Liz admitted. "It was tough at first, because of my past, but eventually the town and I made peace with each other."

Pia studied her friend. She considered it a sign of her good character that she didn't mind that Liz was beautiful, with shiny red hair and a perfect body.

"You look happy," Pia said.

"I am. I know you don't want to talk about it, but how are you doing?"

"Better. I'm sleeping. I'm desperately bored, which is probably a good sign. Now that I know people are mucking around in my office, I'm even more anxious to get back." She lightly touched her stomach. "It's hard not to be scared about the two little ones still in there."

"Not surprising. When's your next doctor's visit?"

"In a couple of days. I want her to tell me everything is going to be all right, and I know she can't make that promise."

"She can get close," Liz told her.

"I hope so. Right now I feel as if everything I do puts the babies at risk. Once they're born, I'll be able to relax."

Liz raised her eyebrows. "Sorry to disillusion you, but no. In some ways it will be better, but in others, it will be worse. Every stage brings new joys and new traumas. It's amazing that any of us ever have kids, given all that can go wrong."

"The need to procreate burns hot and bright."

"Apparently. In the end, it's worth it though. You'll love those babies in a way you've never loved before. It's magical and you'll be so grateful to have them."

"I look forward to that," Pia admitted. "Losing one has brought me closer to the others. I'm thinking of them as tiny, little people inside of me. I want to see what they're going to look like and hold them and keep them safe."

"Look at you. A few weeks ago, you didn't know why Crystal had left the embryos to you. Are you still asking yourself that question?"

"Less than I was."

"So we're both happy," Liz said. "Which is the way it's supposed to be. Have you and Raoul set a date for the wedding?"

"No." Despite his proposal and the very impressive ring she wore, she couldn't imagine getting married. Visualizing the ceremony was beyond her. "One crisis at a time."

"Ethan and I are thinking of doing something quiet over the Christmas holidays. Just friends and family. I told him the pressure is on, because I'm not marrying him until the house is finished. There's no way I'm starting my married life in the house where I grew up."

Pia understood. Liz had never known her father, and her mother had been distant and an alcoholic. Men had come and gone with a frequency that had led many people to believe that Liz's mother was in it more for the money than the relationship. Liz had been emotionally and physically neglected, and sometimes there had been unexplained bruises.

"So Ethan is a motivated guy," Pia teased. "That's very smart of you."

"It's more desperation than intelligence. I keep telling myself that the house is great. It's all fixed up and there aren't any ghosts, but I'm looking forward to moving out."

Pia leaned back against the sofa. "When did you realize you'd fallen back in love with him?"

"It was more finding out I'd never stopped loving him. That was a shock," Liz admitted. "Time and distance had done nothing to kill my feelings. I guess it's sometimes like that. People can love for a lifetime. Why?"

"Just curious." She held up a hand. "Don't read more than that into the conversation."

"You're not falling for Raoul?" Liz asked cautiously.

"I don't think so." Pia told herself it wasn't a lie—she hadn't decided yet.

"If you are, maybe it's not a bad thing."

"Why do you say that?"

"Because you're you and he'd be a fool not to love you back."

Pia sighed. "If only," she whispered.

DR. GALLOWAY HELPED Pia into a sitting position, then settled on her stool.

"You're fine," the doctor told her. "Everything looks just as it's supposed to. Both babies are growing very well. Developmentally, they are on target. Your blood work is good, you're healthy."

Pia allowed herself to relax a little. "So they're going to be fine?"

"Sometimes babies don't make it, Pia, and we can't know why. Nature has her own way of solving problems. Although they check the embryos before implantation, science is not perfect. But there is no reason to think you'll have a difficult time from here on. Have you resumed your regular life?"

"Except for stairs. They scare me."

"They are exercise and exercise is good. I'm not saying this is the time to take up a new sport, but do what you did before. Walk, talk, laugh, take the stairs."

Pia drew in a deep breath. "All right. I will."

"Good. Keep stress to a minimum, as much as you can. Get plenty of rest and enjoy that handsome man of yours." Dr. Galloway's expression turned stern. "Are you having sex with him?"

"What?" Pia felt herself blush. "No. Of course not."

"Probably best for the first few days, but now, it's fine."

Pia couldn't imagine ever doing that again. "Even with the babies in there?"

"It's not like they know what's happening. Nor can they see what you're doing. For them, it's a gentle ride and when Mom has an orgasm, then it's even more fun."

Babies and sex didn't go together in Pia's mind. Besides, she was confused about her feelings for Raoul. Making love at this point would only complicate an already difficult situation.

"I'll think about it," she said.

"I want more than thinking," the doctor told her with a grin. "I want doing." She rose. "Be happy, Pia. All is well."

"Thank you."

She waited until Dr. Galloway left before standing and reaching for her clothes.

The babies were okay. That was the main thing. Knowing that, she would try to relax. To, as Dr. Galloway had said, live her life.

One month down and only eight to go, she thought, wishing there was a way to hurry along the pregnancy. Or maybe not, she told herself, remembering the eighty-to-a-hundred-diapers-a-week statistic. Maybe it was better to let things happen in their own time.

"IT'S MY JOB," PIA SAID, wondering if she hit Raoul with something really, really hard, she could make him understand. Or knock him unconscious, which would allow her to do her job. At this point, either worked for her.

"You can't spend the day on your feet."

"I won't. I have chairs set up all over the park, and several people who are going to make sure I sit." Despite Dr. Galloway's all clear, she wasn't willing to take any risks. "I'll be fine."

He moved close and wrapped his arms around her waist. "I worry about you."

"I worry about me, too, but I have a job that I love and I need to get to it."

He held her a second longer, his dark eyes gazing into hers.

In truth, she didn't want to move just yet. She loved being in his arms, feeling his body against hers. There was something so right about them being together. But there was a time and place for the mushy stuff, and this wasn't it.

She stepped back. "I have to get going."

"I'll see you tonight."

"Yes, you will."

She grabbed her purse and left. On the way to the park, she found herself thinking about Raoul instead of the impending event. Not a good thing. Thinking about him was dangerous to her heart. Work was safe.

She walked the few blocks to the park and found the setup had been completed in the early hours of the morning. Booths lined the walkway and vendors were already putting out their goods. The smell of barbecue mingled with the sweet scent of melting caramel.

The Fall Festival was one of her favorites. Sure the days were getting shorter and the first snow was right around the corner, but she loved the changing colors, the promised quiet of winter, the scent of a wood fire.

Each festival had its own personality. This one was going to be a little different because of all the men in town. She'd added extra games to keep them happy and a second beer vendor. To counteract the latter, there were also extra police on patrol.

A heavyset man in a Fool's Gold safety vest walked up to her. "Pia, we're five portable toilets short. The guy's lost."

"Not for long," Pia said. "Have someone get his cell number, then call him and talk him in. We need the extra bathrooms."

An electrician needed to be dispatched to fix a faulty outlet, the shift in the wind meant smoke from the meat smoker was choking the jewelry vendors and someone had forgotten to put up the no-parking cones to reserve spots for the fire truck.

Pia handled each crisis quickly and easily, as she had for years. She turned to take a quick tour, only to find Denise Hendrix walking toward her, a folding chair under one arm.

"I have the first shift," Denise said cheerfully. "It is now eight-thirty. You are to sit until nine."

"But I have to go check on the setup."

"No, you don't. And you're not going to." Denise batted her eyelashes. "Don't make me use my bad-mom voice, because you won't like it."

"Yes, ma'am," Pia said meekly and sank onto the chair.

Denise saw Montana and waved her over.

"Hi, Mom," Montana said, then grinned at Pia. "I have the eleven-thirty-to-twelve shift and then I'm on again this afternoon. Bossing you around is fun."

"Gee, thanks." She was being forced to sit for thirty minutes of every hour. "Can you go talk to the vendors and make sure they have everything they need? Also, there's water for them in the back of Jo's pickup. Find her and make sure it's put somewhere the vendors can find. And if you see a guy driving around with portable toilets on the back of a truck, let me know."

Montana stared at her. "You expect me to do all that?"

Pia flashed her clipboard. "That's not even all of page one."

"Jeez, I wouldn't want your job," Montana grumbled. "Mom, if you see Nevada, tell her to come help me."

"Of course, dear."

Montana left.

"Impressive," Denise told Pia. "You're resting *and* getting your work done."

"I'm an expert multitasker."

Denise stared after her daughter. "Montana seems excited about her new job."

"She does. I admire her—she gives her all to whatever she does."

"I know she's worried about finding the right kind of work. Not that she won't but that it's taking too long. I keep telling her that everyone finds his or her own path in his or her own time, but she won't listen. One of the thrills of being a mother." Denise smiled. "Wait until your little ones are teenagers."

"At this point I simply want them to be bigger than a rice grain."

"That will happen, too."

The sound of a large truck caused them both to turn. Denise shaded her eyes with her hand, then turned to Pia.

"That's interesting. Were you expecting elephants?"

RAOUL WALKED WITH PETER through the crowded park. Fool's Gold was holding yet another of its many festivals. Knowing Pia was going to be working, he'd arranged to take Peter for the afternoon. The Folios didn't seem to mind him spending time with the kid, which was good. While the couple seemed pleasant enough, Raoul was still concerned about their caretaking abilities.

He and Peter had already checked on Pia, who was being confined to a lawn chair until the top of the hour. She swore she wasn't the least bit tired and that she'd never had so many assistants or done so little work at any festival.

"Want to get ice cream?" he asked, pointing to a stand.

"Sure!"

Peter led the way. They both got two scoops, then went over to a bench.

"This is so cool," Peter said between licks. "I like how there are different festivals at different times of the year. It's really fun. My parents used to bring me all the time."

"You grew up in Fool's Gold?"

"Sort of. My dad worked at one of the wineries and we lived out of town. But I went to school here." His smile faded. "After they died, I was in a group home for a while. I didn't like that. It was really hard because the other kids made fun of me when I cried."

Raoul felt his pain. "It's okay to feel stuff and be sad."

"Boys don't cry."

"Plenty of boys cry." Raoul hesitated, knowing there was a fine line between saying what was healthy and the reality of being tortured by peers. "Losing your parents is a big deal."

"I know." Peter licked his cone. "I still miss them."

"That's good. You loved them. You're supposed to miss people you love."

"Mrs. Dawson says they're watching me from heaven, but I don't know if that's true."

"Every time you remember them, you know how much they loved you. That's what's important."

Peter took a few more licks, then held up his cast. "I get this off in a couple of weeks. The doctor says I'm healing really fast."

The advantage of youth, Raoul thought, remembering feeling like roadkill the morning after his last few games. There was nothing like being trampled by a few three-hundred-pound guys to make a man feel humble.

"Wait until you see your arm," Raoul told him. "It's going to look weird from being in the cast."

"Cool! I wish I could see it now." He raised his arm and turned it back and forth, as if trying to see inside the cast. Then he turned to Raoul. "You know there's a school carnival next week, right? We're gonna have games and stuff. It won't be as big as this, but it will still be fun."

While the boy went on about the different events at the

school, Raoul was aware of three women standing on the path a few feet away. He'd never seen them before, so he guessed they were tourists, in town for the festival, or possibly the influx of men. They were in their midthirties, talking to each other and pointing at him. The tall brunette raised her camera and took a picture.

When they realized he'd noticed them, the smaller blonde waved and walked over.

"You're Raoul Moreno, aren't you?" she said, her voice high and excited. "I recognized you right away. Oh my God! I can't believe it. You are just as good-looking in person. This is really exciting. We came here when we heard about all the men. There was an auction and everything. Too bad you weren't in it. You would have gotten a lot of money."

Her friends joined her.

Raoul tossed his ice cream and rose. Normally this sort of thing didn't bother him, but it had been months since anyone had approached him as a fan. Living in Fool's Gold where everyone treated him normally had spoiled him for the real world. Right now he wanted to spend the day with Peter—not deal with three women who probably weren't going to be satisfied with a picture.

"Is that your son?" the taller blonde asked.

"He doesn't have children," the brunette said scornfully. "Are you in one of those charity programs? Is he disadvantaged? Look at his poor broken arm."

Raoul stepped between the women and Peter. "That's enough. Take your pictures and then move on."

The petite blonde stepped closer. "This is a free country. We don't have to do anything. We can spend the whole day just following you around."

"I don't think so."

The firm words came from behind him. He turned and saw Bella Gionni walking up. With her were Denise Hendrix and a few women he didn't recognize. They looked serious.

"Morning, ladies," Denise said pleasantly. "How can we help you?"

"You can't," the brunette said. "This is a private conversation."

"You can say anything in front of us." Bella moved between him and Peter. She put her hand on the boy's shoulder, then slipped her arm around his. "We're close."

Her friends took up places around him and Peter.

The younger women looked at each other and frowned.

"What's going on?" the taller blonde asked.

"You're welcome to say hello to Raoul and even take his picture, but that's as far as it goes. You don't follow him or disturb him in any way. Nor do you get to talk to Peter." She smiled at the boy. "Girls," she said in a mock whisper.

He was wide-eyed, more interested than scared. "I know," he whispered back.

Raoul was as startled by the rescue as by the potential stalkers. While he appreciated the concern, his pride didn't welcome the idea of being protected by a half dozen women in their forties and fifties.

Not that he was willing to take them on either. Ego be damned—for now he was keeping his mouth shut.

The three women turned their attention to him. "Are you serious? You're going to let them tell us what to do?"

He gave them his best grin. The one he wore in all his publicity pictures. "Absolutely."

"This town is stupid," the petite blonde said. "We should leave. I don't know why we thought we could have a good time here."

"Us, either," Bella told her. "Drive safe, ladies."

The brunette flipped her off.

Bella only smiled. "Looks like you need a manicure, missy. Chipped polish is so cheap. Just like you."

The three stomped off.

Raoul watched them go, then looked at his posse. "Thank you."

"You're welcome," Bella told him. "I'm sure you could have dealt with them yourself, but why waste time on trash?"

"If I was ten years older," he began.

Bella patted his shoulder. "Sorry, but no. If you were ten years older, I'd wear you out and then you'd die of a heart attack. So let's not go there."

Denise moved up to him and kissed his cheek. "Admit it. You're secretly humiliated."

"Some."

"Then our work here is complete." She glanced at Peter. "Do you mind if I borrow this handsome young man? There are bumper cars set up across the park and I do love a good bumper car. My kids are all too old. I'll return him right after that."

"Sure. If it's okay with you, Peter."

"Sure."

Peter took Denise's outstretched hand and went off, still licking his ice cream. Raoul thanked the other women, then waited until they'd left before making his way to where Pia held court from her lawn chair.

"Talk to the peanut guy," she was saying. "He always packs up early. Like he's going to beat the traffic. Tell him if he does that this time, he's not coming back. Remind him I can get fifty peanut vendors to replace him with just a phone call."

She smiled at Raoul. "Hi. Where's Peter?"

"Riding bumper cars with Denise." He sank down on the grass next to her chair. "I was just rescued by middle-aged women."

"What are you talking about?"

He told her about the women who had stopped by and how Bella, Denise and their friends had taken care of the situation.

"That's sweet," she said, amusement dancing in her eyes. "The big bad football player rescued by older women."

He winced. "This isn't good. I'm capable of taking care of myself. But I just stood there and let them do all the talking."

"Did you think they would allow it to happen any other way? You're one of us now. We take care of our own. It's just like the food everyone brought over after I lost the baby."

"It's nothing like that."

"Don't freak. It's adorable."

He wasn't amused. "You can't tell my friends."

"What will you give me if I don't?"

"Anything."

She laughed.

He enjoyed the sound, and looking at her. She was lovely, with her large eyes and laughing mouth. Her tumbling curls bright in the sun. She was the perfect combination of attitude and kindness.

It wasn't just her, he thought, glancing around at the crowd enjoying the Fall Festival. It was the town. He'd lived in a lot of different places and while he'd always enjoyed the cities, he'd never felt connected to the community. Not like here. A few people recognized him, but the most they wanted was an autograph.

While he wasn't happy that he'd been rescued by a bunch of women, he knew the significance went beyond their gender and age. It was that they'd seen the problem and acted. They'd stepped in—as if he were their responsibility. He'd moved to Fool's Gold to find a place to settle, and what he'd found instead was home.

CHAPTER EIGHTEEN

NORMALLY, AFTER A daylong event, like the Fall Festival, Pia would be exhausted. But as she'd spent exactly half her day just sitting, she felt rested and ready to party at the town's dinner-dance. Well, in a very quiet, protect-the-babies kind of way.

She finished applying mascara and leaned back to check her makeup in the mirror. She'd taken Dr. Galloway's advice about stairs and taken the two flights to come back to her place to get ready. All her clothes were here, along with her serious makeup. Raoul was going to pick her up and take her to the dance, then back to his place.

She fluffed her hair, then tightened her robe around her waist. The big question was what to wear.

Sometime in the last day or so, she'd gotten a case of serious bloat. Her pants were tight and no matter how much lemon water she drank, she couldn't get her belly to go down. There were a couple of dresses she knew wouldn't fit. But she had one that had an empire waist. The style was forgiving and—

She stopped in the doorway to her bedroom. Her mind replayed her last thoughts, then she started to laugh. She wasn't bloated, she realized. She was pregnant. Talk about an idiot.

She touched her stomach. "I'm hoping you two weren't thinking your mom would be a rocket scientist, because that's simply not going to happen. Pregnant. You'd think I would have grasped that by now."

She crossed to the full-length mirror on the back of her closet door, then opened her robe. When she turned sideways, she saw the rounding she'd thought was too much water.

"How are you two doing?" she asked, lightly touching her stomach. "Everything okay? I'm fine. Still sad, but recovering. It's going to be okay. I want you to know that. I'm going to take really good care of you both. I promise."

There wasn't an answer, which was probably good. Voices from inside her body would scare the crap out of her. But she felt a sense of peace—a knowing. The rightness of what she'd done settled on her. She was having Crystal's babies. More important, these were also *her* babies. They might not have her DNA, but they were growing inside of her. She was nurturing them with every beat of her heart. When they were born, she would be their mother in every sense of the word.

"It's going to be great," she whispered.

She went into her closet and pulled out the black dress. The bodice was lightweight velvet, with a deep vee. The skirt began just under her breasts. That fabric was lighter, more flowy, ending just above her knee.

She'd already rubbed a shimmering body lotion on her bare legs. Now she hung the robe on a hook and reached for the dress. After slipping it on, she secured the side zipper. She stepped in front of the mirror to see if it worked.

"Oh my."

While she'd had breasts since she was about thirteen, they'd never looked like this, she thought, staring at the cleavage filling the vee of the dress.

"At least now I know what I'd look like if I got implants."

Fortunately the dress had a short jacket. She pulled that on and saw it hid virtually nothing. Raoul was simply going to have to endure.

She'd chosen a medium-heel black sandal. She'd barely slipped them on when she heard a knock at the front door.

"Come in," she called as she walked to the living room.

The door opened and Raoul stepped inside.

She'd never seen him in a suit before. The dark, tailored fabric fit him perfectly, skimming over impossibly broad shoulders. He was elegant and handsome and hers.

The latter admission was as difficult to believe as the pregnancy had been. Were they really going to get married?

His gaze swept over her, starting at her shoes and working his way up. When he reached her chest, she saw him tense. He crossed the room in two strides, cupped her face in his hands and kissed her with a passion that had her trembling in her heels.

His mouth moved against her, claiming, enticing, promising. Heat poured through her.

Without thinking, she grabbed his hands and lowered them to her chest. He pushed aside her jacket and cupped her eagerly, finding her already tight nipples and rubbing them.

Fire shot through her. She was wet and ready in seconds. She shrugged out of her jacket and fumbled with her zipper. He undid it for her, then pushed down her dress to her waist. Then her bra was gone and his mouth was on her breasts.

The feel of his lips and tongue, the stroking and sucking, nearly brought her to the brink. Her breath came in sharp pants. Need threatened to drown her. She hung on to him to keep standing.

He moved one hand between her legs, slipping under her panties and finding her center with one sure stroke. He rubbed that place hard, as if aware how close she already was. Around and around, his mouth still on her breasts, her hands on his shoulders, her legs shaking so hard she wasn't sure she could stay standing.

She came without warning. One second she was riding the wave, the next she was shivering and convulsing, rubbing herself against his fingers, gasping out his name. The contractions faded and the world righted itself.

She straightened, as did he. They stared at each other. Then his mouth curved in a very satisfied male smile.

"You look good," he said. "Did I get a chance to mention that?"

She was still dealing with aftershock. Where had that orgasm come from? Fifteen minutes ago—five minutes ago—she would have sworn she wouldn't have a single sexual thought ever again. Or at least not until after the babies were born.

She paused to take stock of her body. Except for the lingering sense of well-being, she felt fine.

She smiled at him. "You didn't."

His gaze lowered to her bare breasts. "Those are new."

"You like?"

"The other ones are great, but these will be fun, too."

She stepped out of her shoes. "Your turn."

He hesitated. "We probably shouldn't."

She could see his erection straining against the fabric of his pants. "Dr. Galloway said it was fine. That the babies can't see anything."

She reached for his belt. "How about we get you almost all the way there and you finish inside me? Everybody wins."

Wanting and concern battled. "I don't want to put you or them in danger."

"Me, either."

She unzipped his pants and withdrew him. He was hard and thick and when she ran her hand down the length of him, his breath hissed between clenched teeth.

He moved closer and kissed her. She gripped him in her hand, moving up and down in a steady rhythm. As they kissed deeply, she moved faster. He touched her breasts, using his fingers to lightly toy with her nipples. Arousal began again inside of her. She felt the need building.

"Raoul," she breathed.

He must have heard the desperation in her voice because he dropped one hand to her thigh, then moved it between her legs and found her center.

The sure touch pushed her closer. She felt him tense.

She quickly pushed down her panties. He pulled them the rest of the way off and drew her to the sofa.

"Now," she said and guided him inside of her.

He thrust in slowly, carefully. She felt the restraint in his hard muscles. She grabbed his hips to pull him in. He withdrew and she whimpered. Another thrust. He slipped a hand between them and found that magical spot again. It only took a second for her to feel the shuddering beginning again, deep inside.

She breathed his name and lost herself in her release. He pushed in again and shuddered.

They clung to each other, breathing hard.

When she could speak, she asked, "Was that okay?"

He kissed her lightly. "It was great. There's something to be said for going slow. How do you feel?"

She knew he wasn't asking about her afterglow. "Good. Really good." There was no way to explain it to him, but she had a sense of certainty. A knowledge that everything was going to be all right from now on.

She glanced at the kitchen clock and gasped. "We're going to be late. We have to hurry."

"Yes, ma'am."

He stepped back and was dressed in a matter of seconds. It took Pia a little longer, but they were out the door in less than five minutes.

At the bottom of the stairs, he pulled her close and kissed her again. She let herself feel the warmth of his embrace, the safety she found in his arms and knew that somewhere along the way, she'd gone and fallen in love with him.

THE DINNER-DANCE WAS held at the convention center. Tables had been set up in the center, with the dance floor up by the stage. A local DJ would provide the music during dinner before the live band arrived at eight. Dancing went on until midnight. There was a cash bar, plenty of tacky decorations and balloons floating on the ceiling.

"Impressive," Raoul said as they walked in.

She laughed. "You're mocking our efforts."

"I would never do that. It's charming."

"Small-town America at its best."

They wove their way through the crowd, stopping to talk to people they knew. Pia was aware of all the unfamiliar men in the crowd. It was odd to have so many male strangers around. During festivals, most of their visitors were families.

Dakota greeted them.

"You look beautiful," she told Pia. "Positively glowing."

Pia did her best not to blush. She had a feeling that any glow came from making love with Raoul rather than the pregnancy, but there was no need for anyone to know.

Raoul must have been thinking the same thing because his hand tightened on hers.

"Thanks," Pia said. "You look great, too."

Dakota turned, showing off her blue dress. "I'm dateless, so I'm only here for the dinner. Then I'm heading home to my small, spinster life."

Raoul looked around the room. "There are plenty of single guys. Go find one."

She wrinkled her nose. "Not this week. I'm not in the mood. Nevada and Montana are coming over and we're having a chick-flick marathon. They're both staying the night." She raised her eyebrows. "Besides, compared with you, they're just not that interesting."

"Oh, please." Raoul didn't look the least bit impressed.

Pia laughed. "If I see anyone special, I'll send him your way."

"Please don't."

They parted and continued to their table. Pia spotted a tall, thin man talking to Mayor Marsha. He was gesturing wildly, talking quickly, although it was impossible to catch any part of the conversation over the other talking in the room.

"Let's go see what that's about," she said, pointing.

They walked between tables and reached Marsha just as the man moved off. The mayor gave Pia and Raoul hugs, then sighed.

"I'm getting too old for this job," she said. "Do you recognize that man?" She pointed at the guy she'd been talking to.

"No," Pia said.

Raoul shook his head.

"I didn't recognize him, either," Marsha said. "Which insulted him deeply. Apparently he's some Hollywood-producer type."

"As in movies?" Pia asked.

"As in reality television. According to him, we're hot right now."

"Lucky us," Pia muttered.

"That's what I said. He wants to do a show about the bachelors coming to Fool's Gold. He's going to get me the details in the next day or so."

A reality show? "Is that something we want in town?" Pia asked.

"No, but I'm not sure how to keep him out. If he's not blocking traffic or otherwise getting in the way of everyday life, there's not much I can do. California has very supportive laws when it comes to filming."

"Want me to beat him up for you?" Raoul offered.

Marsha smiled. "Aren't you sweet? Let me think about it. At this point I'm more inclined to have a glass of wine and not deal with any of this until tomorrow." She smiled at them. "You two have a good time."

"We will," Raoul said.

"A reality show," Pia said as they found their table and sat down. "That's kind of icky."

"It should bring in revenue."

"And weird people." She leaned against him. "Like Marsha said, a worry for tomorrow."

He wrapped his arms around her. "Did I tell you how beautiful you look?"

"About three times, but it never gets old."

"You're stunning."

"Thank you. You're pretty hunky yourself."

AFTER DINNER, the dancing began. Pia excused herself to use the restroom. Along with her puffy tummy came the need to pee forty-seven times a day. Charity joined her along the way.

"How's it going?" her friend asked.

"Good. I feel much better."

"Nice to hear."

Pia turned to her. "I wasn't ready before, but I think I am now. Want to try the shopping thing again?"

Charity smiled. "I'd love to. I still have to make that all-important baby-wipe-heater decision. We can have an intense conversation about it over hot chocolate and cookies to gain our strength, then face the maternity clothes and baby store, ready to conquer."

"It's a date."

They reached the restroom, only to find the usual line.

"I knew we needed more women's restrooms when we remodeled," Pia grumbled. "But did Ethan listen?"

"Complain to Liz," Charity told her. "She'll punish him."

An older woman walked out of the restroom, then stopped by Pia. "How are you feeling, dear?"

"Fine."

"I was so sorry to hear about your loss. I miscarried two before having my Betsy. She was a blessing. I know it's sad but you have to trust that happier days are ahead."

"Thank you," Pia said.

The woman in front of them turned around. "I lost a baby,

too. At four months. It was horrible, but you go on. It's hard, but moving forward helps with the healing."

A white-haired lady using a cane to walk stopped by Pia and patted her arm. "Just make sure you're taking care of that stud of yours in the bedroom. If God hadn't meant for us to have sex while we're pregnant, he wouldn't have made it so much fun. My George, God rest his soul, and I went at it until two weeks before I gave birth. All six times. As soon as the doctor gave us the all clear, we were at it again." She winked. "One time a little sooner than we should have."

Pia felt her mouth drop open. She consciously closed it, then swallowed.

"Yes, ma'am. Thank you for the information."

"You're a good girl, Pia. Have lots of sex. It helps."

The woman teetered off, leaning heavily on her cane.

Beside Pia, Charity burst out laughing. "I can't decide which is worse. Her calling Raoul a stud or the intimate details of her marriage."

"I know which is worse," Pia muttered. "I'm just trying not to think about it."

After using the restroom, she returned to the table. Raoul stood.

"What's wrong?" he asked, sounding worried.

"Nothing."

"You look…" He frowned. "Shocked."

"Old ladies are telling me how important it is to have regular sex with you."

He grinned. "Did I ever tell you how much I love this town?"

THEY ARRIVED BACK at Raoul's place a little after ten. The long day had caught up with Pia and she felt exhausted. Raoul guided her into the house, then put his arms around her and leaned his forehead against hers.

"I want us to share a bed tonight," he said, then smiled. "I'm not going to try to have my way with you. I just want to know you're okay."

He'd never asked her that before, she thought, both tempted and frightened by the invitation. In theory, they would be married soon, and after that, they would share a bedroom like every other couple. It wasn't that big a deal. There was no reason the idea should make her uneasy.

"Sure," she said, ignoring the warning voice in her head. "That would be nice. You're not a blanket hog, are you?"

"You can have all the blanket you want."

A lovely invitation, but in truth she was interested in a whole lot more than a blanket. She wanted him. All of him. Not just a practical invitation to a marriage that made logical sense. She wanted his heart and soul. She wanted to be the most important part of his life and the best part of his day. She wanted him to love her.

Afraid he would sense what she was thinking, she stepped back. "I'm going to go get ready for bed."

By the time she'd taken off her makeup and changed into a nightgown, she'd nearly convinced herself that everything was going to be fine. That she was over-reacting. Sleeping with Raoul shouldn't be that big a deal. It was probably better that they get used to each other one night at a time. She could think of this as a practice run.

But when she walked out of the bathroom and found him already in bed, her heart seemed to stumble a little. Although they'd shared a bed the first night they'd made love, somehow this was more intimate.

She shrugged out of her robe, then got into bed.

"Tired?" he asked.

"Exhausted."

"Back sleeper or side sleeper?"

"Side."

"Go ahead and get comfortable," he said, then turned off the bedside light.

She felt self-conscious as she turned on her side, away from him. He moved up behind her, putting his arm around her. His thighs nestled the backs of her legs, his chest pressed against her spine. He wrapped his arm around her waist, holding on as if he would never let go.

"Good night," he murmured.

"Night."

Pia found herself getting more awake by the second. She wasn't used to sleeping with anyone, and everything about being so close to him felt strange. And scary. She knew in her heart she could get to like this. That it wouldn't take much for her to want him nearby all the time. And then what? Did she spend the rest of her life loving a man who wouldn't love her back? Did she get lost in her kids' lives so as not to notice that her marriage was only a shell of what she wanted?

His steady breathing told her that he'd fallen asleep. She wasn't sure how long she lay there, fighting tears and a crushing sadness that told her the engagement was a mistake.

RAOUL READ THE grant proposal he'd received. A grad student had come up with an idea to link high school math and science programs to specific industries. The industries as a whole would underwrite the cost of the special math or science classes with the idea that most of the students would want to study that field and after college would come back to work for the sponsoring companies. The student wanted to study feasibility and approach different industries. The grant amount was modest enough.

Raoul made some notes in the margin of the proposal. He would call a couple of friends in aerospace, one of the suggested fields, and get their thoughts on the idea.

The door to the large office opened and Pia walked in.

He rose and smiled at her, pleased she'd stopped by. The last few days had been better than he could have anticipated. He liked having Pia around. They got along well. She made him laugh and always had an interesting world view.

Now, however, she looked serious and concerned.

He walked toward her. "Is everything all right?" he asked. "The babies?"

"We're fine." She drew in a breath. "I know why Crystal left me her embryos."

While he hadn't questioned the reason, he knew she'd had several concerns. "Tell me."

"She believed in me. She knew she could trust me to care for her children, to raise them as my own. The only person who had doubts was me. I couldn't believe in myself. I didn't think I was capable. So I took the easy way out."

She squared her shoulders. "I've moved out, Raoul. I did that this morning, after you left. Liz helped me. I'm back in my apartment."

"I don't understand. Why would you do that?"

Leaving him? She couldn't. He wanted her there—maybe even needed her in his life.

Her gaze flickered, then grew steady again. She pulled the engagement ring off her left hand and held it out to him. "I'm not going to marry you."

He stared at the ring, watching how it twinkled in the overhead lights.

She couldn't mean it, he told himself. She needed him. They needed each other.

"We're going to be a family. I'm helping you with the babies. What's changed?" They'd made plans. They were going to raise the children together. Have a kid of their own. He thought it was what they both wanted.

"I appreciate the offer," she told him. "You're a really great guy." She paused for a second. "But it's not enough. I don't want a practical solution to a difficult problem. I want what Hawk and Nicole have. I want to be in love and be loved in return. I want a passionate, loving, messy marriage, practical or not. I want it all."

What Hawk and Nicole had came around once every thousand years, he thought bitterly. He'd tried to find it with Caro and had been shot down. She wanted it all. Meaning she wanted him baring it all for her, handing over his heart. And then what? There weren't any promises, no guarantees.

She wanted more than he was willing to give.

Her mouth curved into a sad smile. "I can see by your face that you're not exactly excited about my news. I'm not surprised. I was hopeful, of course."

"We don't need that," he told her. "We can make it work the other way. We don't have to be in love to be happy."

"Too late," she said lightly. "I already am in love with you. And I won't be with someone who doesn't feel the same way about me."

She loved him? Impossible. Was she trying to trap him?

Even as he thought the words, he wondered if they were true. After all, he'd been the one to propose, not Pia. He'd been the one pushing for them to be a family. He wanted to be a part of the babies' lives. She'd never come to him.

But no matter how logical it all sounded, he couldn't believe it. Or maybe he wouldn't. Either way, he wasn't taking the next step. He'd already done it once. He refused to be betrayed a second time.

"What happens now?" he asked stiffly, feeling as if he'd been sucker punched but not wanting that to show.

"We go on like we did before. People knew about the engagement, so you'll have to answer a few questions. Don't worry. I'm going to make it clear this was my decision. You won't get run out of town."

She held out the ring again, but he didn't take it. She walked around him and set it in the center of the desk.

"You're playing it safe," she said quietly.

He turned to face her. She stared down at the ring, then returned her attention to him.

"You're looking for an easy solution to a difficult problem," she repeated. "You can't play at being a family, Raoul. Life isn't that tidy. If you want to be happy, you're going to have to give it all—risk it all. Life demands that from us. You think if you're logical enough you can make sure no one ever hurts you again. But the only thing that makes life worthwhile is loving other people and being loved by them."

She sighed. "For what it's worth, I didn't mean to fall for you. It just happened. If you change your mind, if you want to take a chance, I'd love to be that girl."

Then she turned and walked away, leaving him alone in an empty office. Everything he'd wanted was gone, and all he had to show for it was the engagement ring he'd bought for the woman he'd just lost.

CHAPTER NINETEEN

PIA TOLD HERSELF there was no reason to believe she was going to throw up. That the churning in her stomach would eventually go away. At least she wasn't crying. It was one thing to walk through Fool's Gold nauseous—at least no one could tell. But sobbing hysterically might get a question or two.

She reached city hall and went inside. She automatically greeted everyone she passed, smiling and waving, as if everything was fine. Only a few more feet, she told herself as she rounded the corner and saw Charity's office. The door stood open, so she knew her friend was at least in the building.

Luck was on her side. Charity sat behind her desk, staring intently at her computer. She looked up as Pia entered.

"Thank goodness. I'm going crazy with—" Charity stood, her pregnancy obvious in her brightly colored knit shirt. "What's wrong?"

Pia sucked in a breath and twisted her hands together. "I told Raoul I couldn't marry him. That while I appreciated the offer, I can't be in a practical marriage with someone I've fallen in love with."

She paused, waiting for Charity to burst out laughing. After all, what did Pia expect? That he would fall at her feet and beg her to let him love her back?

Instead Charity walked around the desk and hugged Pia. "Good for you."

Pia held herself stiffly. "What? Good for me? I've just walked away from a guy worth millions who wanted to marry me and take care of me for the rest of my life."

"You love him."

"So?"

"You're convinced he doesn't love you. Therefore you made the right decision."

Pia sank into the chair and covered her face with her hands. Reality crashed all around her, leaving her breathless and shaking. "What was I thinking? I can't do this on my own—be the single mother of twins. How will I pay for it? When will I sleep? I don't know anything about infants or children."

Charity pulled up another chair and sat across from her. "You'll be fine. You can do this. You were planning to do it before Raoul proposed."

"I was an idiot."

"No, you were exactly the same person you are now. Capable and loving. Pia, if you can organize the four thousand festivals we have every year and get a fundraiser up and running in three days, you can certainly handle having a couple of kids."

Pia lowered her hands to her lap. "You think?"

"I know. You'll be amazing. Besides, you might technically be a single mother, but you're not going to be alone. You have your friends and you have this town. We all love you and we'll be there for you."

"But Raoul would have given me everything."

"Not his heart."

Pia felt her chest tighten. "No. Not his heart."

"So this is better."

"How can you be sure?" Pia desperately wanted to know she hadn't made the wrong decision.

"You convinced me," Charity said kindly. "When you said no."

PIA HAD SPENT the rest of the day buried in work. Maybe it wasn't the most mature way to handle heartbreak, but it sure cleared out her in-box. Now tired and ready to have some serious pity-party time, she walked home. As she entered her building, she heard a lot of people talking. The higher she climbed, the louder the noise got. She stepped out onto the landing to find most of her friends waiting for her.

Their arms were filled with packages and grocery bags. Liz spotted her first.

"Here she is."

Everyone turned.

"Pia!" Montana hurried over. "Are you okay?"

From the various looks of concern, Pia realized that word had spread. Not just about the broken engagement, but about their practical but ultimately unworkable relationship.

All three triplets were there, along with Charity and Liz. Marsha held a basket filled with what looked like baby stuff. Denise Hendrix, several women from city hall, along with Bella and Julia Gionni, the feuding hairdressers.

Everyone crowded into her small apartment, pulling in chairs from the kitchen or settling on the floor.

"Jo wanted to be here," Nevada told her, "but she has to work. She sends her love."

Pia quickly realized no one expected her to provide anything for the impromptu party. There were plastic cups and paper plates, all kinds of food, from Chinese dumplings to taquitos. Wine was opened, along with sparkling water for Pia. She was settled in the center of the sofa, handed food and drink and surrounded with love.

"How are you doing?" Charity asked anxiously.

"Better now," Pia admitted. "It's been a tough day, but I know I did the right thing."

"I don't know. Marrying a guy worth millions seems like a smart decision, too," Bella muttered.

Everyone laughed. Julia rolled her eyes at her sister and stayed on her side of the room.

"You did the right thing," Montana assured her. "You have to marry for love. You deserve that. The proposal, the begging."

"You need the begging," Denise assured her. "Trust me. Courtship is the best time in a relationship for a woman. Marriage is the best time in a relationship for a man. Who gets their best time longer? So you need to make it last. Besides, you deserve someone who adores you, Pia."

There were several nods of agreement.

"Do you want us to call him names?" Dakota asked helpfully. "Or have him beat up?" She frowned. "That might take two guys, but we can arrange it."

Pia felt her eyes burning. She blinked away tears. "He hasn't done anything wrong. Don't forget, he wanted to take care of me. That's a good thing. I'm not mad. I'm the one who changed the rules, not him."

Julia shook her head. "It's been a long time since I've seen a man beat up. I was hoping to watch."

"There's something wrong with you," Bella snapped.

Denise raised one hand. "Ladies, it's a testament to your love for Pia that you're both here. Let's not forget our purpose."

The sisters grumbled at each other.

Charity, who sat next to Pia, leaned close. "I never did hear why they aren't speaking. What's the story?"

"No one knows. It's a big secret."

Charity grinned. "I thought Fool's Gold didn't have any."

"There are a few."

"We have many gifts," Montana said, taking charge of the piles. "Most of this you can open later, but you should see this one now."

She handed Pia a large white envelope. Pia set her plate of food on the coffee table and opened it. Inside were dozens of pieces of paper. Each one was from someone different. Most offered hours of babysitting or company after the babies were born. There were consultations for baby room decorating, the promise of a weekly massage from now until birth, coupons for free diaper service for the first three months and a sheet where the women in town had signed up to deliver dinners for the first six weeks she was home with the babies. Three flyers showed houses for rent.

This time she was unable to stop the tears. They spilled down her cheeks before she could brush them away.

"I don't know what to say," she admitted. "This is wonderful."

"We all love you," Denise told her. "And we want you to know that we'll be there for you. No matter what."

It might not be the romantic proposal she'd dreamed about, but it was damned close. These women and this town were going to take care of her. Pia allowed herself to accept the love offered and let it heal her shattered heart. Then she touched her belly and silently told her growing children that no matter what, they were going to be just fine.

RAOUL SAT AT THE BAR, ignoring the reality show playing on the big TVs around him. Jo's Bar was quiet tonight, for which he was grateful. He'd tried staying home but he'd been unable to stand the solitude. While he wanted to be out, a crowd would have been too much. There were times when a man needed a little space to get drunk, and this was one of those nights.

He'd started on his second beer when Josh slipped onto the seat next to him.

"Hey," he said. "Jo called and said you looked like you needed a friend."

Raoul glanced at the bartender, who gave him a level look as if daring him to challenge her.

"She's wrong," he said flatly.

"Doesn't matter to me," Josh told him. "Charity's out. There's some girl thing going on at Pia's. They're making her feel better, which I guess makes you the ass who broke her heart."

Raoul sipped his beer and kept his gaze on the TV screen. A dozen or so people were bent over sewing machines. What the hell? A show about sewing?

Josh turned toward him. "Did you hear me?"

"I didn't break her heart. I asked her to marry me. I offered to spend my life with her, to take care of her and the kids. I'm not the bad guy."

Josh took the beer Jo offered and drank some. "So why are you here and why is she back at her place drowning in Ben & Jerry's ice cream?"

"She wouldn't be practical."

"An impractical woman. There's a stunner."

He turned to Josh and saw the raised eyebrow. "You don't understand. We had a deal. I didn't change it. I didn't change anything. I care about her."

"But?"

"It wasn't enough." Raoul drained his glass and pushed it toward the front of the bar. Jo turned her back on him. Typical, he thought grimly. "I wanted to take care of her."

"Did it ever occur to you that Pia can get all that without you? Right now my wife and several of her friends are reminding her that she's not alone. Except for the sex, which I doubt was very good, she's covered."

Raoul continued to stare at the TV screen. "You know I could take you."

"In your dreams."

He thought about taking Josh on, of showing the other man how unprepared he was. But there wasn't any point. Beating up Josh wouldn't make the hole inside of him go away.

The bottom line was he missed Pia. She wanted the impossible and he couldn't give it to her, but he still wanted her in his life. They could have been good together.

"The problem you have," Josh said conversationally, "is that she was never alone. It took her a while to remember that, but once she did, you became a lot less interesting."

Raoul turned and glared at him. "Do you think that's why she left? She loves me, you hothead."

Josh's expression turned satisfied. "I'd wondered if you'd caught that. You're right. She loves you. Like most women, she's not willing to settle. She wants it all. That's what women specialize in—demanding every scrap of humanity we have. Our hearts, our souls and our balls. You can fight it, my friend, but I've learned it's a whole lot smarter to hand it all over quietly. They're going to win in the end and if you resist, you only end up having to beg more." He took another drink. "Unless you don't love her."

I don't.

Raoul started to say the words but couldn't. He knew that was the real problem. If he could convince himself that he'd only been doing a good thing, something noble and important, the rejection was easier. That's how this whole problem had started. It should have been easy to forget her.

But it wasn't and that bothered him. Because it meant there was a possibility that Pia was more than a project, more than a way to get what he wanted without having to risk anything.

Without saying goodbye, he tossed a twenty on the bar and left. Once outside, he sucked in the cold night air, then started walking. But instead of heading to his rental, he crossed the street and went by Pia's apartment building.

Most of the units were dark, except for one on the top floor. A window was partially open and he heard the sound of voices and laughter drifting down to him.

She wasn't alone. While the information wasn't news, the proof of it made him feel better. He didn't want her to be by herself. He didn't want her to suffer. He'd really been trying to take care of her. Maybe he'd gone about it in an unconventional way, but he wasn't the bad guy in this.

And neither was she.

He stood there for a long time before turning around and heading to his own place. The echo of the laughter stayed with him, making him feel more alone than he ever had before. He missed her. Even if he couldn't be with her, surely he could talk to her. Explain.

Explain what? That his way was better? The truth was Pia deserved more, and that's what ate him up inside. She'd been right to walk away from him, to demand more. He respected her, admired her, wanted her...

But for the rest of it—she needed more than he had left to give.

THE SCHOOL CARNIVAL WAS LOUD, a crowded funfest with plenty of kids and parents in attendance. Raoul had gone to support all the kids he'd made friends with and found himself dodging dads who wanted autographs or to talk sports.

"Ah, the price of fame," Dakota said, coming up behind him as he explained that no, he hadn't had his head up his ass during that third-quarter play at his last Super Bowl.

He glanced at her gratefully. "Excuse me," he told the group of men and grabbed her arm. "I need to talk to Dakota about some business."

"Using me as a getaway?" she asked.

"Whatever works." He led her out of the crowd, toward the main building. "The mothers are either snubbing me or telling me I'm a jerk, and the fathers all want to talk about specific plays during games I barely remember. There's no elaborate planning in the middle of a football game. You have to react to what's happening. If you aren't prepared to trust your gut and go with what you feel is right, you'll never win."

He paused as she stared at him with rapt attention.

"Oh, please," she breathed. "Tell me more. Don't leave out any details."

"Funny," he muttered, then drew his eyebrows together. "Hey, you're speaking to me. Aren't you supposed to ignore me?"

"I work for you."

"I thought you'd be pissed about Pia." Everyone else was.

As she'd promised, Pia had spread the word that she'd been the one to break up with him. The problem was not enough people believed her. Or they assumed he'd done something so awful she'd been forced to end things with him.

"You didn't change the rules," Dakota said easily. "She did."

He stared at her, waiting for the "but."

"Not that you weren't an idiot," she continued. "If you're not willing to risk your heart for someone like her, you're completely cowardly and stupid. If you can't see you're already in love with her, then you're just dumb."

So much for having someone on his side. "Tell me what you really think," he said.

She patted his arm. "You'll figure it out. I have faith."

He liked her theory, but she didn't have all the information. She didn't understand the past he was fighting.

"Did that guy really want to know if you had your head up your ass?" she asked.

"Those were his exact words."

She laughed. "I want to say it must be refreshing to have people talk to you like you're a regular guy and not a sports celebrity, but I'm thinking right now you'd enjoy a little reverence."

"It wouldn't hurt. Want to stick around and be my wingman?"

"Not really. You'll be fine. Chin up and all that. They're people, too."

"Are you paid by the cliché?" he asked drily.

She smiled and walked off.

Alone in blissful quiet for a few seconds, he thought about what she'd said. About him being stupid for not risking his heart for someone like Pia.

As much as he wanted to give Pia all that she wanted, it wasn't as if there was a switch inside that he could simply turn on and off. He wasn't willing to take the chance again. Period. There was nothing anyone could say or do to change his mind. If that meant losing Pia permanently, then so be it.

He turned to return to the carnival, only to see Peter heading toward him. A short, beefy man trailed behind.

"Hi!" Peter waved his left arm. "Look. My cast is off. And you're right—my arm looks really weird. All scaly and skinny. The doctor says I'm doing really good, though."

"I'm glad to hear it," Raoul said, then held out his fist to start their elaborate greeting. The one Peter and Pia had come up with.

The downside of small-town living, he realized. There wasn't going to be anywhere to escape.

"My foster dad wants to meet you," Peter said in a low voice when they'd finished. "I hope that's okay."

"Sure."

Raoul walked over and shook hands with the other man. Don Folio eyed him from under thick, dark eyebrows.

"You've been spending a lot of time with Peter," he said.

"He's a great kid. Very special."

There was something about the man Raoul didn't like.

"We appreciate your taking care of him when we were out of town."

"It wasn't a problem." Raoul smiled at Peter, who grinned back.

Don dug a dollar out of his pocket and handed it to Peter. "Raoul and I need to talk, kid. Go play a game or something."

Peter hesitated, then nodded and hurried toward the arcade. Don faced Raoul.

"I can see you have a soft spot for the boy."

"Sure. I like spending time with him."

Don raised his eyebrows. "How much do you like spending time with him?" he asked.

Raoul felt a flicker of alarm over the oily nature of the question, but he wanted to see where Don was going with this. "If I could have more personal time with Peter, that would be ideal," he said slowly.

Don nodded energetically. "I'm a man of the world and I

get these kind of things. But the foster care system, they have some rules."

Raoul ignored the burst of fury that flared up inside of him. He kept his expression neutral, his body language open.

"The way I see it," Don continued, "there are options. You want the kid and I don't care if you have him. Only it's going to cost you."

Out of the corner of his eye, Raoul saw Mrs. Miller approaching. Casually, he stepped to the right to block her path.

"You're saying I can have Peter for a price?" he said just loud enough for the other woman to hear.

She froze, her face going white. He risked a single glance. She nodded, as if to say she was going to stay back and keep listening.

"Sure. And I don't care what you do with him. To each his own."

"You have a price in mind?"

"Fifty thousand. In cash." Don held up his hand. "I'm not interested in bargaining on the price. This is a onetime offer. If you don't want him, I can find someone else who does."

Raoul pretended to consider the offer. "You have a way of clearing this through social services?"

"Sure. I go to Mrs. Dawson and say Peter would be happier with you. You had him before and he never said what happened. The kid knows how to keep a secret, I guess. Boys aren't my thing, but I'm an understanding kind of guy."

Raoul wanted nothing more than to put his fist in the man's face. It would give him pleasure to grind Don Folio into the dirt.

He didn't know how this man had gotten ahold of Peter in the first place, but it was going to stop now. Today.

Don handed over a business card. "My cell's on the back. You have twenty-four hours."

Raoul nodded, and the other man walked off. When he was gone, Mrs. Miller hurried up to him. "It's disgusting."

Raoul closed his hands into fists. "He has to be stopped."

She pulled out her cell phone and scrolled through the contacts. "I'm calling Mrs. Dawson right now."

The social worker arrived in less than thirty minutes. Less than ten minutes after that, Police Chief Barns was threatening a very nervous-looking Don Folio. Raoul didn't think they could charge the guy with much—money hadn't actually changed hands—but he wasn't likely to ever take in a foster kid again. At least that was something.

Peter came running toward him.

"I heard," the boy said, grinning and slightly out of breath. "I'm not going to be with them anymore. You're going to take me."

Raoul stared at the kid, then held up both his hands. "Peter, I think you misunderstood. You'll be safely away from the Folios and another family will be found for you."

Peter's expression froze. The happiness faded from his eyes and tears appeared. He went pale and his mouth trembled. "But I want to go with you. I stayed with you before. You're my friend."

Raoul ignored the sense of being kicked in the gut. "We *are* friends. We'll still be friends and I'll see you at school. But I'm not a foster parent."

"You were before," he insisted, the last word coming out on a sob. "You took care of me."

Mrs. Dawson hurried toward them. "Peter, we need to go."

Peter lunged for Raoul. For a second, he thought the kid was going to hit him, but instead Peter wrapped his arms around Raoul and hung on as if he would never let go.

"You have to take care of me," he cried. "You have to."

Mrs. Dawson shook her head apologetically. "Come on, Peter. I have to get you to the group home. It's only for a few weeks until we find something else."

Raoul stood there, not moving. Although the boy wasn't doing anything, he still felt his heart being ripped out all the same. People were stopping to stare.

Just when he thought he was going to have to forcibly push

the kid away, Peter let go. Mrs. Dawson led him away, and neither of them bothered to look back.

MONDAY MORNING, Raoul arrived at work at his usual time. Seconds later, Dakota walked in, slammed her purse down on his desk and put her hands on her hips.

"I can't decide if I should quit or back my car over you," she announced.

He stared at her. "What are you pissed about now?"

"What you did to Peter."

Raoul didn't want to talk about that. He hadn't slept all night and he still felt as if he'd been hit in the gut. "He's safe now," Raoul said flatly. "I talked to Mrs. Dawson this morning and from what the psychologists can tell, he wasn't abused by anyone. Folio's threats about giving the kid to someone else were designed to make me hurry. He's not part of a big child-stealing ring. He's just an asshole."

She glared at him. "And that's all you see?"

"What else is there?" He knew he sounded defensive, but it was all he had.

"Peter's crushed," she snapped. "You swept in and saved him. Do you think he doesn't know what you did? You've been there for him all this time. You took him home when he broke his arm. You've been his friend."

She spoke as if he'd been burning the kid with a cigarette.

"All that stuff is great," he yelled. "So what's your problem?"

She jabbed him in the chest with her index finger. "You led that poor kid on, you jerk. You let him believe that you cared about him and when they took his foster dad away, he thought he'd be going home with you."

"You think I don't know that? It was a mistake. All of it." Getting involved in the first place. He knew better. He did his best work from a distance.

"It wasn't a mistake." She spoke more calmly now. "Don't you remember what that was like? Packing everything you owned into a trash bag because you didn't have a suitcase and moving on? Do you remember how scary it was to find yourself in a new place, to not know the rules? Now it's happening again. And you've made that reality worse. You let him believe in you, trust you, and it all turned out to be a lie."

Raoul wanted to protest that he'd never promised the boy anything. That he'd been there in a crisis, but that was all it was. Nothing more.

Only Peter wouldn't have seen it that way, he thought grimly. He would have expected Raoul to rescue him again.

She shook her head. "I didn't blame you for the Pia thing, but I'm starting to see a pattern here. You play at making a difference, at being the good guy, but none of it is real. You're too afraid to give what really matters. You're all flash and no substance."

She turned away, then spun back to him. "Do us all a favor. Stay away from 'causes.' You've already done enough damage here."

CHAPTER TWENTY

RAOUL'S DAY OF hell only went downhill from there. Dakota left him alone with his guilt. He wanted to do something, hit something—mostly himself. Nearly as bad, he honestly didn't know if she'd stalked off because she was mad or if she'd quit.

He paced back and forth in the large empty space he'd rented, trying to find an answer. But it all came back to the same thing. He'd let Peter believe in him, and then he'd let him down.

About an hour later, when he was still trying to come up with a plan, Mayor Marsha Tilson walked into his office. Normally, she was someone he enjoyed talking to. But there was something about the way she moved so purposefully that made him aware he might not like what she was going to say.

"I've heard what happened with Peter," she said, getting right to the point. "I must say, I wish things had turned out differently, Mr. Moreno."

Looking at her, seeing the disappointment in her eyes, was nearly the toughest thing he'd ever done, but he would be damned if he'd allow anyone to make him flinch.

"I do, too."

"Do you?" she asked. "When you first arrived we were all impressed by your financial generosity," she continued, her blue eyes dark with disillusionment. "Your reputation elsewhere was that of a man who cared about others. One who gave back to the community. So when you indicated you wanted to move here, we welcomed you as one of our own."

She pressed her lips together. "I don't know all the details about what happened with Pia, but I do know that she is a loving, giving young woman. To see her unhappy pains me. It pains us all."

His body tensed. He squared his shoulders. "I didn't hurt Pia. We had a deal. She changed her mind."

"If she's not hurt, then why was she crying over you?"

Pia crying? She'd been so sure when she'd left. How could she be wounded?

The mayor drew in a breath. "I'm sure you have some measure of guilt for all this, but fear not. It will pass. Peter will be taken care of, and Pia, too, because that's what we do here. We protect our own." She put her hand on his arm. "I want to believe you're a good man trying to be a better one. But from what I can see, you're getting in your own way when things get personal." She stared into his eyes. "For your own sake, and for Pia and Peter, maybe it's time to risk more than your money."

With that, she turned and left. Raoul watched her go, feeling the slice of every honest word. He had never been what Hawk had raised him to be. It *was* all on the surface.

He crossed to the window and stared out at the town.

He'd wanted to settle here, to make a difference. He'd thought he would grow old here. But that wasn't going to happen. He didn't belong. No one would say it to his face, but it was true. He deserved to be run out with pitchforks and torches.

He swore, not knowing which was worse—that he'd lost Pia, or that he'd broken the heart of a little boy who'd been foolish enough to believe in him.

He continued to stand by the window, waiting for the day to pass. He needed it to be dark so he could slink home without being seen and figure out what he was supposed to do next.

"APPARENTLY MARSHA GAVE him one of her famous talks," Charity said, as she and Pia sat at the Fox and Hound having lunch. "She wouldn't give me details, but I'm sure she got inside his head and messed with him."

Pia felt awful. Not only was she still hurting from missing Raoul, she felt terrible about Peter's situation. While she agreed that Raoul had given the boy the impression he would be there for him, she knew the man she loved would never deliberately hurt anyone. It seemed there were no winners in this situation.

"Did she say how he looked?"

"No." Charity studied her. "You really do love him, don't you?"

"You sound surprised."

"I thought this would disillusion you."

"No. He has a good heart and he's a good guy. None of this is easy for him."

She thought about his past, how Caro had betrayed him. How he was afraid to trust.

"Everyone needs to give him a break," she said firmly.

Charity hesitated. "Marsha thinks he might be leaving town."

Pia's breath caught. "Leaving? Why? He's settled here. He has the camp, which is what brought him here. There are plans for special classes and intensive learning. He would never give that up." The camp represented his future.

She looked at her friend. "There's no way he would make the decision on his own. What happened? Did Marsha run him out of town?"

"No, but she made it clear she was disappointed. How will he handle that?"

"I don't know," Pia admitted. Would he leave? If he didn't feel comfortable in town, he might. She hated the thought of Fool's Gold without him.

"I'm sorry," Charity told her.

"Me, too," Pia said. "I want him here. I want him to stay. While I'm at it, I want him to love me back."

"You don't get to decide any of that," her friend reminded her.

If only things could be different, Pia thought sadly. But they weren't.

RAOUL'S PLAN TO wait until dark lasted about an hour. He paced in his office, tried working, then had to fight the need to throw the damn computer across the room.

He was furious and ashamed and disappointed—all with himself.

He'd come here with big ideas for finding the right place, the right way to give back. Being like Hawk, changing lives, had driven him. Everything about Fool's Gold had appealed to him. The friendly small town had made him feel welcome. Then what had he done? Blown it.

Years ago, in college, he'd screwed up big-time. Hawk had been the one to get him back on track. Since then, Raoul had managed to find his way on his own. Until now.

He couldn't figure out where it had all gone wrong. With Pia, he supposed it had been when he'd offered to marry her so he could have everything he wanted without putting any part of himself on the line. He'd taken the easy, safe way out, and it had all gone to hell.

He should have known he couldn't have it all for free. That was like making a deal with the devil. If it looked too good to be true, it was.

As for Peter, he'd simply stepped in it with the kid. His motivations had all been aboveboard, but somewhere along the way, he'd forgotten he was dealing with a ten-year-old boy's heart. He'd befriended Peter, wanting only to save the kid. Instead he'd hurt him again.

Unable to stand the confines of his office, he stalked to the door and opened it. He half expected an angry mob with pitchforks waiting for him, but the town looked as it always had. The turning leaves fluttered in a light breeze. The sky was blue, the sun a little lower in the horizon than it had been a month ago. Winter was coming.

He'd wanted to see the town in snow, to experience the changing seasons. He'd wanted to ski at the resort, to lie with Pia by a fire, to watch her grow heavy with their two babies. It didn't take much effort to add Peter to the mix. He could see the boy playing by the fire, or laughing as he and Raoul played video games.

As he stepped out into the afternoon, he realized the solution was obvious and simple. He could have them both, if he was willing to hand over all he was. What had Josh said? Heart, soul and balls. Without Pia, he had no use for them anyway. As for Peter, the kid probably deserved better, but Raoul hoped he was willing to accept what was offered.

He half expected the heavens to open and angels to sing. He got it. He really got it. After all this time and running to avoid the only thing he wanted, he understood the point.

It wasn't about giving money or loaning a camp to a school. It was about giving all he had, all he was. It was about risking his heart.

Pia, he thought frantically. He had to get to Pia.

He turned toward her office, only to nearly run into a half dozen middle-aged women. They were staring at him purposefully, which wasn't a good thing.

"Hi," the one in front said. "I'm Denise Hendrix. Dakota's mother? We met at the Fall Festival."

He held in a groan. "Yes. Nice to see you again." He nodded at the other women. "Ladies."

The other women stared at him without responding. He noticed Bella in the crowd, but she didn't look as happy as she had the day she'd also helped rescue him from the overaggressive tourists.

"We need to talk to you," Denise told him.

"This isn't a good time for me."

"Do we look like we're getting any younger?" the oldest in

the group snapped. "You'll listen, young man, and you'll listen good. We have ways of making your life a living hell. Do you really want to test us on that?"

Like any good sportsman, he knew when he'd met a superior opponent. "No, ma'am."

"I didn't think so." She sniffed. "Go on, Denise."

"We've been talking," Dakota's mother told him. "We looked you up on the Internet. I don't know what went wrong with your first wife, but she wasn't anyone we would trust."

The other women nodded in agreement.

"You've been single a few years now, so you're obviously over her. You came here to settle down, which shows you're intelligent. You seem like a nice enough man."

Obviously these women hadn't been talking to Mayor Marsha, he thought grimly.

"But you're stuck."

Bella pushed through the other women and moved in front of him. "Pia loves you, so we want her to have you."

Denise patted her friend's arm. "Bella, I think we need to be more delicate. Raoul might not know he's in love with Pia. We might have to explain things."

"He gets it," another woman said. "How could he not? She's wonderful. If he doesn't love her, he doesn't deserve her."

"I agree," someone else said. "But I've said it before. If we wait for the man we deserve, we'll never get married."

"At least he's handsome."

"And rich."

"He has nice, thick hair," Bella told them.

"And a great butt."

The last comment was Raoul's tipping point. "Ladies," he said loudly. "I appreciate the intervention. I know Pia will be grateful when she hears of your very vocal support." Humiliated, he thought while smiling for the first time in hours, but grateful.

"However, this is between me and Pia. Now if you'll excuse me, I need to go talk to her."

Denise grabbed his arm in a surprisingly strong grip. "Not so fast. What are you going to say?"

He stared at them all. While he could easily tell them it wasn't their business, he hadn't changed his mind about settling here. Fool's Gold was going to be his home for a very long time, and these women were his neighbors.

"The truth," he said simply. "That I'm desperately in love with her and I'm begging her to give me a second chance."

Several of the women sighed.

Denise gave him a shove. "Don't just stand there," she said. "Go find her."

He took off at a jog, trying to figure out where to go first. It was midafternoon. He would start with her office and spread out from there.

He took the stairs two at a time and burst onto the landing. Her door stood partially open. He hurried toward it, aware of voices down by the first-floor entrance. Ignoring them, he pushed open Pia's door and found her alone in her small office.

She looked much as she had the first time he'd seen her. Pretty with curly brown hair and bright, hazel eyes that showed every emotion. The difference was now he knew that she was kind and loving, funny and smart. That she was rational and compassionate, even when panicked, that she gave with her whole heart and that he could search the world and never find anyone even close to her.

She looked up, startled. "Raoul. Are you okay? I heard about Marsha's visit and I want to tell you I had nothing to do with that."

"I know."

"She's upset, but no one wants you to leave town."

"Good, because I'm not going."

"Really? Well, that's great. I mean of course you can live

where you want. This is a free country. Sometimes small towns have an inflated sense of themselves."

He moved around the desk and drew her to her feet. Her gaze flickered, as if she was afraid to stare directly at him.

"Pia?"

"Yes."

"Look at me."

She sighed, then did as he requested.

He knew her face. He'd seen it hundreds of times. But he would never get tired of seeing her and touching her. Only her, he thought. He would take the chance with her, because he didn't have a choice. Without her, he was only half-alive.

"I offered you a marriage of convenience," he began. "Because I wasn't willing to get involved again. My first marriage ended badly. I'd made a mistake and I didn't know where I'd gone wrong. Rather than figure that out, I decided to never take the chance again."

Her fingers were warm against his. He felt her faint trembling. While he wanted to reassure her, he knew he had to tell her the truth, first.

"What Caro did was wrong, but I don't believe she meant to betray me. Her career mattered more than anything else. I'd known that, but I didn't think through what that meant. I wanted a wife and a family. She said the right words, and I took them at face value because it gave me what was important to me. I think she knew I wouldn't like hearing that she wanted to wait to start a family."

He brought one of Pia's hands to his mouth and kissed her palm.

"I moved here, thinking it would be easy," he continued.

"Foolish man."

"Tell me about it. It wasn't easy, but it was where I belonged. This is home. But it's an empty, cold place without you." He stared into her eyes. "I love you, Pia O'Brian. I was too stubborn and scared to admit it until now, but I love you. Please marry me. Not because it's convenient, but because we can't imagine life without each other."

Hope brightened her face. Her lips curved into a smile.

Everything inside of him relaxed. She still cared. They could be together. Except...

"But it won't just be us," he told her. "You, me and the twins. There's also Peter. I can't leave him in the group home. I want to talk to Mrs. Dawson about adopting him."

She bit her lower lip. "And if I say no to that?"

He tensed again, feeling the fist hit his gut. "We're a package deal."

Everything he'd ever wanted and needed hung on what she would say next. He wanted to tell her that he would take care of her forever. That he would always love her and their children. But he couldn't bribe her into accepting. They both had to follow their hearts.

"Right answer," she whispered. "And yes."

Happiness exploded inside of him. He hauled her against him and kissed her with all the love and passion he had. Behind them he heard something that sounded like both cheering and sniffing. After a few seconds, he raised his head and glanced over his shoulder.

The women he'd met on the street all stood there, joined by the mayor and Mrs. Dawson.

"I'm so happy," the social worker said, dabbing at her eyes. "You were cleared as an emergency foster parent when Peter went to stay with you the first time. You can go get him now."

The other women nodded. Marsha smiled. "I knew you had it in you."

"You didn't say that earlier."

"It wouldn't have helped."

Note to self, he thought, kissing Pia again. Do *not* get on the mayor's bad side.

Pia wrapped her arms around Raoul's neck and leaned against him. She'd hoped, prayed and done her best to believe it would all work out, but she'd also been scared. Scared that she would spend the rest of her life loving a man who wouldn't love her back. It was nice to be wrong.

He kissed her again. Her insides started that melty thing, which was also very nice.

"We've got a lot to do," he said, his forehead resting against hers. "Approve the house plans, get married, start birthing classes."

She laughed. "Don't worry. I'm really good at details. Right now there's only one thing that matters."

He nodded. "Peter."

"Yes. He should be home from school by now. Let's go tell him the good news."

Raoul hesitated. "You're sure about this? We'll have three kids."

"I'm sure."

There were other considerations. Like the fact that being a mom to newborn twins and Peter probably meant she was going to need an assistant to help her with all the festivals. And that until their new house was built, things were going to be a little crowded in the rental. And that they should get married right away so she could move in with Raoul and Peter. But those were for later. Now they were off to make a little boy's dreams come true.

PETER SAT ON the narrow bed he'd been assigned. This was the same group home he'd been in before, but the kids were different. Not so mean. No one teased him about crying himself to sleep every night.

He tried really hard not to be scared all the time. He told himself he was bigger now. He didn't need anyone. He was strong. Except when he thought like that, his chest hurt and his throat got tight and then he started crying.

He knew what would happen next. He would be sent to a foster home where he wouldn't know the rules and the other kids would stare at him. He would try to do everything right, but he wouldn't and then he'd get yelled at and maybe hit. And he would be alone.

From downstairs, he heard voices. Adults talking. For the first couple of days he'd waited for Raoul to come. To say he'd made a mistake, that he'd changed his mind. That he wanted Peter with him forever.

He'd thought...he'd hoped...

He shook his head. He'd been wrong. No one was coming for him. Not ever.

"Peter?"

He heard Mrs. Goodwin call his name.

"Peter, would you please come downstairs?"

Peter stood and wiped his face so no one would know he'd been crying. He moved to the landing, his head down, his shoulders hunched.

He took one step, then another. When he glanced up, he saw Raoul and Pia standing in the living room, watching him.

Without meaning to, he came to a stop and stared at them. They both looked kind of funny. Not mad, exactly but... Scared, he thought at last. Only adults didn't get scared, did they?

Raoul walked to the bottom of the stairs and looked up at him.

"I'm sorry," Raoul said. "For making you come here. I messed up."

Peter shrugged. "Whatever." He knew people were supposed to apologize, but he didn't know why. Saying you were sorry didn't change anything.

"No. Not whatever," Raoul said, his gaze intent. "All I could think about was getting you away from the Folios. But there was a next step. You didn't just need to be away from them, you needed to find your way to a real home."

He cleared his throat. "Pia and I are getting married. We wanted to know if you'd like to come live with us." Raoul paused. "No, that's not right. We want to adopt you, Peter. If you'll have us as your family."

Peter's whole body felt hot and cold at the same time. The words were like magic, making everything okay again. Okay for the first time in forever. Tears filled his eyes, then he was coming down the stairs so fast, he was practically flying. He launched himself at Raoul.

Raoul caught him and held him so tight it was hard to breathe, but that was okay. Peter was crying, then Pia was there, hugging them both. She was saying something about babies and puppies and his own room.

Peter didn't understand it all and he knew it didn't matter. All he cared about was that he'd finally found a place to belong. A family with people who loved him. Raoul's strong arms held him. Pia kissed his cheek and smoothed away his tears.

For the first time since the car accident, he looked up at the ceiling and knew his parents really were watching him from heaven.

"You can stop being sad now," he whispered. "I'm going to be okay."

* * * * *

Only Mine

CHAPTER ONE

"WHAT'S IT GOING to take to get you to cooperate? Money?
Threats? Either works for me."

Dakota Hendrix looked up from her laptop to find a very tall,
stern-looking man standing over her. "Excuse me?"

"You heard me. What's it going to take?"

She'd been warned there would be plenty of crazies hanging
around, but she hadn't actually believed it. Apparently she'd
been wrong.

"You have a lot of attitude for someone wearing a plaid flannel shirt," she said, standing so she was at least something close
to eye-level with the guy. If he hadn't been so obviously annoyed, she would have thought he was pretty decent-looking,
with dark hair and piercing blue eyes.

He glanced down at himself, then back at her. "What does
my shirt have to do with anything?"

"It's plaid."

"So?"

"It's hard to be intimidated by a man wearing plaid. I'm just
saying. And flannel is a friendly fabric. A little down-home for
most people. Now if you were in all black, with a leather jacket,
I'd be a lot more nervous."

His expression tightened, as did a muscle in his jaw. His gaze sharpened, and she had a feeling that if he were just a little less civilized, he would throw something.

"Having a bad day?" she asked cheerfully.

"Something like that." He spoke between clenched teeth.

"Want to talk about it?"

"I believe that's how I started this conversation."

"No. You started by threatening me." She smiled. "At the risk of sending your annoyance level from an eight to a ten, sometimes being nice is more effective. At least it is with me." She held out her hand. "Hi. I'm Dakota Hendrix."

The man looked as if he would rather rip off her head than be polite, but after a couple of deep breaths, he shook hands with her and muttered, "Finn Andersson."

"Nice to meet you, Mr. Andersson."

"Finn."

"Finn," she repeated, being more perky than usual, simply because she thought it would bug him. "How can I help you?"

"I want to get my brothers off the show."

"Hence the threats."

He frowned. "Hence? Who says that?"

"It's a perfectly good word."

"Not where I come from."

She glanced down at the worn work boots he wore, then back to his shirt. "I'm almost afraid to ask where that is."

"South Salmon, Alaska."

"You're a long way from home."

"Worse, I'm in California."

"Hey, you're in my hometown. I'll thank you to be polite."

He rubbed the bridge of his nose. "Fine. Whatever. You win. Can you help me with my brothers or not?"

"It depends. What's the problem?"

She motioned to the seat across from her small desk. Finn hesitated for a second, then folded his long body into a seated position. She took her chair and waited.

"They're here," he said at last, as if that explained everything.

"Here instead of back in South Salmon?"

"Here instead of finishing their last semester of college. They're twins. They go to UA. University of Alaska," he added.

"But if they're on the show, then they're over eighteen," she said gently, feeling his pain, but knowing there was very little she could do about it.

"Meaning I don't have any legal authority?" he asked, sounding both resigned and bitter. "Tell me about it." He leaned toward her, his gaze intense. "I need your help. Like I said, they're one semester from graduating, and they walked away from that to come here."

Dakota had grown up in the town of Fool's Gold and had chosen to return after she'd finished her schooling, so she didn't understand why anyone wouldn't want to live in town. But she would guess Finn was a lot more worried about his brothers' future than their location.

He stood. "Why am I even talking to you? You're one of those Hollywood types. You're probably happy they've given up everything to be on your stupid show."

She rose as well, then shook her head. "First of all, it's not my stupid show. I'm with the town, not the production company. Second, if you'll give me a moment to think instead of instantly getting angry, maybe I can come up with something that will help. If you're like this with your brothers, I'm not surprised they want to get a couple thousand miles away from you."

Given the little she knew about Finn from their thirty-second relationship, she half expected him to snarl at her, then disappear. Instead he surprised her by grinning.

The curve of his lips, the flash of teeth, wasn't anything unique, but it hit her in the stomach all the same. She felt as if all the air had rushed out of her lungs and she couldn't breathe. Seconds later, she managed to recover and told herself it was a momentary blip on her otherwise emotionally smooth radar. Nothing more than an anomaly. Like a sunspot.

"That's what *they* said," he admitted, returning to his seat with a sigh. "That they'd hoped being at college would be far enough away, but it wasn't." The grin faded. "Damn, this is hard."

She sat down and rested her hands on the table between them. "What do your parents say about all this?"

"I'm their parents."

"Oh." She swallowed, not sure what tragedy had brought that about. She would guess Finn was all of thirty, maybe thirty-two. "How long ago...?"

"Eight years."

"You've been raising your brothers since they were what? Twelve?"

"They were thirteen, but yes."

"Congratulations. You've done a good job."

The smile faded as he scowled at her. "How would you know that?"

"They made it into college, were successful enough to get to their final semester and now they're emotionally tough enough to stand up to you."

The scowl turned into a sneer. "Let me guess. You're one of those people who calls rain 'liquid sunshine.' If I'd done my job with my brothers, they would still be in college, instead of here, trying to get on some idiotic reality show."

There was that, Dakota thought. From Finn's perspective, nothing about this was good.

He shook his head. "I can't figure out where I went wrong. All I wanted was to get them through college. Three more months. They only needed to stay in school three more months. But could they do that? No. They even sent me an email, telling me where they were—like I'd be happy for them."

She reached for the files on her desk. "What are their names?"

"Sasha and Stephen." His expression cleared. "Is there something you can do to help?"

"I don't know. As I said, I'm here representing the town. The producers came to us with the reality show idea. Believe me,

Fool's Gold wasn't looking for this kind of publicity. We wanted to say no, but were concerned they would go ahead and do it anyway. This way, we're involved and hope to have some kind of control over the outcome."

She glanced at him and smiled. "Or at least the illusion of control."

"Trust me. It's not all it's cracked up to be."

"I'm getting that. All the potential contestants were vetted thoroughly, background checks on everyone. We insisted on that."

"Trying to avoid the truly insane?"

"Yes, and criminals. Reality television puts a lot of pressure on people."

"How did the TV people hear about Fool's Gold if the town wasn't courting them?" he asked.

"It was just plain bad luck. A year ago a grad student writing her thesis on human geography discovered we had a chronic man shortage in town. The hows and whys became a chapter in her project. In an effort to bring attention to her work, she shopped her thesis around various media outlets, where the part about Fool's Gold was picked up."

He frowned. "I think I remember hearing about that. Didn't you get busloads of guys coming in from all over?"

"Unfortunately. Most of the reports made us sound like a town of desperate spinsters, which isn't true at all. A few weeks later, Hollywood came calling in the form of the reality show."

She flipped through the stack of applications of those who had made it to final selection. When she saw Sasha Andersson's picture, she winced. "Identical twins?" she asked.

"Yes, why?"

She pulled out Sasha's application and passed it to Finn. "He's adorable." The head shot showed a happy, smiling, younger version of Finn. "If he has a personality more exciting than that of a shoe, he's going to get on the show. What's not to like? Plus, if there are two of them…" She set down the folder. "Let me put it another way. If you were the producer, would you want them on the show?"

Finn dropped the paper. The woman—Dakota—had a point. His brothers were charming, funny and young enough to believe they were immortal. Irresistible to someone looking to pull in ratings.

"I'm not going to let them ruin their lives," he said flatly.

"The show is ten weeks of filming. College will still be there." Her voice was gentle and hinted at compassion. Her dark gaze was steady. She was pretty enough—had he been looking for that kind of thing. All he cared about right now was getting his brothers back to college.

"You think they'll want to go back after all this?" he demanded.

"I don't know. Have you asked them?"

"No." To date he'd only lectured and issued orders—both of which his brothers had ignored.

"Did they say why they wanted to be on this show?"

"Not specifically," he admitted. But he had a theory or two about their thinking. They wanted to be out of Alaska and away from him. Plus, Sasha had been dreaming of fame for a long time.

"Have they done this sort of thing before? Run off against your wishes, given up on school?"

"No. That's what I don't get. They're so close to being finished. Why couldn't they suck it up for one more semester?" It was the responsible thing to do.

Until now, Sasha and Stephen hadn't given him much grief. There'd been the usual driving too fast, a few parties with friends and plenty of girls. He'd sweated bullets waiting to hear one of his brothers had gotten a girl pregnant. But so far that hadn't happened. Maybe his thousands of lectures about using birth control had gotten through. So them wanting to leave college for a reality show had stunned him. He'd always figured they would at least finish school.

"They sound like great kids," Dakota said. "Maybe you should trust them."

"Maybe I should tie them up and throw them in the back of a plane headed for Alaska."

"You wouldn't like jail."

"They'd have to catch me first." He stood again. "Thanks for your time."

"I'm sorry I can't help."

"Me, too."

She rose and circled the table so she was standing in front of him. "To repeat a cliché, if you love something, set it free."

He stared into her dark eyes. They were an interesting contrast to her wavy blond hair. "If it comes back, it was meant to?" He managed a smile. "No, thanks. I fall into the 'if it doesn't, hunt it down and shoot it' category."

"Should I warn your brothers?"

"They already know."

"Sometimes you have to let people mess up."

"This is too important," he told her. "It's their future."

"The key word being *theirs,* not yours. Whatever happens here isn't unrecoverable."

"You don't know that."

She looked as if she wanted to argue more. She wasn't a yeller, and he appreciated that. Her points were well thought out. But there was no way she could change his mind on this. Come hell or high water, he was getting his brothers out of Fool's Gold and back to college, where they belonged.

"Thanks for your time," he told her.

"You're welcome. I hope the three of you can come to terms." One corner of her mouth twitched. "Please remember we have a very efficient police force in town. Chief Barns doesn't take kindly to people breaking the law."

"I appreciate the warning."

Finn walked out of the small trailer. Filming or shooting or whatever they called it was due to start in two days. Which gave him less than forty-eight hours to come up with a plan to either convince his brothers to return to Alaska on their own or physically force them to do what he wanted.

"I OWE YOU," Marsha Tilson said over lunch.

Dakota picked up a French fry. "Yes, you do. I'm a highly trained professional."

"Something Geoff doesn't appreciate?" Marsha, the town's sixty-something mayor, asked, her blue eyes sparkling with amusement.

"He does not. I have a Ph.D.," Dakota muttered. "I should make him call me doctor."

"From what I know of Geoff, I'm not sure that would help."

Dakota bit into her fry. She hated to admit it, but Mayor Marsha had a point. Geoff was the producer of the reality show that had invaded the town—*True Love or Fool's Gold.* After randomly sorting twenty people into couples, the pairs would be sent on romantic dates, which would be filmed, edited and then shown on television with a one-week delay. America would vote off the couple least likely to make it.

At the end, the last couple standing would receive $250,000 to share and a free wedding, if they were really in love.

From what Dakota could tell, Geoff didn't care about anything except getting good ratings. The fact that the town didn't want the show around hadn't bothered him at all. In the end, the mayor had agreed to cooperate on the condition that there be someone on his staff who was looking out for the interests of the good citizens of Fool's Gold.

All that made sense to Dakota, though she still didn't know why *she'd* gotten the job. She wasn't a public relations specialist or even a city employee. She was a psychologist who specialized in childhood development. Unfortunately, her boss had offered her services, even agreeing to pay her salary while she worked with the production company. Dakota still wasn't speaking to him.

She would have turned down the assignment, except Mayor Marsha had pleaded. Dakota had grown up here. When the Mayor needed a favor, the good citizens agreed. Until the production company had shown up, Dakota would have sworn she would happily do anything for her town. And, as she'd told Finn a couple of hours before, it was only for ten weeks. She could survive nearly anything that long.

"Have the contestants been picked?" Marsha asked.

"Yes, but they're keeping it a secret until the big announcement."

"Anyone we need to worry about?"

"I don't think so. I've looked over the files and everyone seems fairly normal." She thought about Finn. "We do have a family member who isn't happy." She explained about the twenty-one-year-old twins. "If they're half as good-looking in person as they are in their pictures, they're going to be on the show."

"Do you think their brother will make trouble?"

"No. If the boys were still underage, I would worry that he would try to ground them. As it is, he can only worry and threaten."

Marsha nodded sympathetically. Dakota knew the mayor's only daughter had been something of a wild child, then had gotten pregnant and run away. It couldn't be easy, raising a child. Or in Finn's case, two brothers. Not that she knew about being a mother.

"We can help," Marsha said. "Look out for the boys. Let me know if, or maybe when, they're chosen for the show. We don't have to like that Geoff brought us this mess, but we can make sure to keep it contained."

"I'm sure the twins' brother will appreciate that," she murmured, suspecting Finn might be grateful but wouldn't have much expectation for the town helping.

"You're doing a good thing," Marsha told her. "Keeping an eye on the show."

"You didn't give me much of a choice."

The mayor smiled. "That's the secret to my success. I box people into a corner and force them to agree."

"You're very good at it." Dakota sipped her diet soda. "The worst part is I actually like reality TV. Or I did until I met Geoff. I wish he'd do something illegal so Chief Barns would arrest him."

"We can always hope." Marsha sighed. "You've given up a lot, Dakota. I do want to thank you for taking on the show and protecting the town."

Dakota shifted in her seat. "I haven't done all that. I'm on set and making sure they don't plan anything truly insane."

"I feel better knowing you're around."

She was good, Dakota thought, eyeing the older woman. Years of experience. Marsha was the longest-serving mayor in the state. Over thirty years. She thought of all the money the town had saved on letterhead. It never had to change.

While this was far from Dakota's dream job, working for Geoff had the potential to be interesting. She knew nothing about making a television show, and she told herself she would enjoy the opportunity to learn about the business. At least it was a distraction. Something she wanted these days—anything to avoid feeling so…broken.

She reminded herself not to go there. Not everything could be fixed, and the sooner she accepted that, the better. She could still make a good life for herself. Acceptance would be the first step in moving on. She was a trained professional, after all. A psychologist who understood how the human mind worked.

But knowing and believing were two different things. Right now it seemed as if she would never feel whole.

"THIS IS GOING TO BE GREAT," Sasha Andersson said as he leaned against the battered headboard. He glanced down at the copy of *Variety* he'd bought from the old guy at the bookstore. Someday, he would be making thousands, or even millions, and he would subscribe and have it delivered to his phone, as the real stars did. Until then, he bought a copy every few days, to keep costs down.

Stephen, his twin brother, lay across the other bed in the small motel room they shared. A worn *Car and Driver* sat open on the floor. Stephen dangled his head and shoulders off the mattress as he flipped through an issue he'd probably read fifty times.

"Did you hear me?" Sasha asked impatiently.

Stephen looked up, his dark hair falling over his eyes. "What?"

"The show. It's going to be great."

Stephen shrugged. "If we get picked."

Sasha tossed the paper to the foot of the bed and grinned. "Hey. It's us. How could they resist?"

"I heard there were over five hundred applicants."

"They narrowed that number down to sixty and we're going to make the final cut, too. Come on. We're twins. TV audiences love that. We should make it seem like we don't get along. Fight and stuff. Then we'll get more camera time."

Stephen shifted on the bed, then rolled onto his back. "I don't want more camera time."

A fact that was both irritating and true, Sasha thought grimly. Stephen wasn't interested in the business.

"Then why are you here?"

Stephen drew in a deep breath. "It beats being back home."

Something they agreed on. Home was a tiny town of eighty people. South Salmon, Alaska. In the summer, they were flooded with tourists wanting to see the "real" Alaska. For nearly five months, every waking moment was spent working impossible hours, struggling to keep up with the crowds, to get the job done and get paid before moving on to the next job. In winter, there was darkness, snow and crushing boredom.

The other residents of South Salmon claimed to love everything about their lives. Despite being direct descendants of Russian, Swedish and Irish immigrants who had settled in Alaska nearly a hundred years before, Sasha and Stephen wanted to be anywhere but there. Something their older brother, Finn, had never understood.

"This is my chance," Sasha said firmly. "My shot. I'm going to do whatever it takes to get noticed."

Without even closing his eyes, he could see himself being interviewed on *Entertainment Tonight,* talking about the blockbuster movie he was starring in. In his mind, he'd walked a million red carpets, celebrated at Hollywood parties, had women show up naked in his hotel room, begging him to sleep with them. Which he graciously agreed to do, he thought with a grin. Because that's the kind of guy he was.

For the past eight years, he'd wanted to be on TV and in movies. But the industry never made it to South Salmon, and Finn had always dismissed his dreams as something he would outgrow.

Finally old enough to be able to do what he wanted without his brother's permission, Sasha had been waiting for the right opportunity. A casting notice for *True Love or Fool's Gold* had been it. The only surprise had been when Stephen had wanted to come with him on the interview.

"When I get to Hollywood," he began, playing a familiar game, "I'm going to buy a house in the hills. Or at the beach."

"Malibu," Stephen said, rolling onto his back. "Girls in bikinis."

"Right. Malibu. And I'll meet with producers and go to parties and make millions." He glanced at his brother. "What are you going to do?"

Stephen was quiet for a long time. "I don't know," he said at last. "Not go to Hollywood."

"You'd like it."

Stephen shook his head. "No. I want something different. I want…"

He didn't complete the sentence, but then he didn't have to.

Sasha already knew. He and his twin might not share the same dreams, but they still knew everything about each other. Stephen wanted to find a place to belong, whatever the hell that meant.

"It's Finn's fault you're not excited about this," Sasha grumbled.

Stephen looked at him and grinned. "You mean because he's so hell-bent on us finishing college and having a good life? What a jerk."

Sasha chuckled. "Yeah. Where does he get off demanding we're successful?" His humor faded. "Except it's not about us. It's about him. He just wants to say he's done a good job."

Sasha knew it was more than that, but he wasn't willing to admit it. Not out loud, anyway.

"Don't worry about him," Stephen said, reaching for the magazine. "He's a couple thousand miles away."

"Right," Sasha said. "Why let him ruin our good time? We're going to be on TV."

"Finn will never watch the show."

True enough. Finn didn't do anything for fun. Not anymore. He used to be wild—before...

Before their parents had died. That's how all the Andersson boys measured time. Events were either before or after the death of their parents. But their brother had changed after the accident. Today Finn wouldn't know a good time if it bit him on the ass.

"Just because Finn knows where we are doesn't mean he's going to come after us," Sasha said. "He knows when he's beat."

Someone knocked on the door.

Since Sasha was closer, he stood and leaned over far enough to reach the knob. The door eased open. Finn stood there, looking as mad as he had the time the twins had trapped a skunk and left it in his bedroom.

"Hello, boys," he said, stepping inside. "Let's talk."

CHAPTER TWO

FINN TOLD HIMSELF that yelling wasn't going to accomplish anything. His brothers were technically adults, although it wouldn't be hard to make a case that, over eighteen or not, they were idiots.

He stepped into the tiny motel room, crammed with two full-size beds, a dresser, battered television and the door to an equally small bathroom.

"Nice," he said, glancing around. "I like what you've done with the place."

Sasha rolled his eyes as he sank back on his bed. "What are you doing here?"

"Coming after you."

The twins exchanged a look of surprise.

Finn shook his head. "Did you really think an email telling me you'd left college to come here was enough? That I would simply say, 'No problem. Have fun. Who cares if you abandon college in your last semester?'"

"We said we were fine," Sasha reminded him.

"Yes, you did and I do appreciate it."

As there weren't all that many motels in Fool's Gold, locating the twins had been relatively easy. Finn knew that money would be tight, which had eliminated all the nice places. The motel manager had recognized them immediately and hadn't minded giving Finn their room number.

Stephen watched him warily but didn't speak. He'd always been the quieter of the twins. Despite the fact that they looked nearly exactly alike, they had different personalities. Sasha was outgoing, impulsive and easily distracted. Stephen was more silent and usually considered his actions. Finn could understand Sasha taking off for California, but Stephen?

Stay calm, he reminded himself. Having a conversation would get him further than shouting. But when he opened his mouth, he found himself yelling from the very first word.

"What the hell were you thinking?" he demanded, slamming the door shut behind him and planting both hands on his hips. "You had one semester left of college. Just one. You could have finished your classes and graduated. Then you would each have had a degree. Something no one could take away from you. But did you think of that? Of course not. Instead you took off, quitting before you were finished. And for what? Some chance to be in a ridiculous show?"

The twins looked at each other. Sasha sat up and sucked in a breath. "The show isn't ridiculous. Not to us."

"Because you're both professionals? You know what you're doing?" He glared at them both. "I want to lock you in this damn room until you figure out how stupid you're being."

Stephen nodded slowly. "That would be why we didn't tell you until after we were here, Finn. We didn't want to hurt you or scare you, but you're holding on too tight."

Words Finn didn't want to hear. "Why couldn't you finish college? That's all I wanted. Just to get you through college."

"Would it really end there?" Sasha asked him, coming to his feet. "You said that before. That all we had to do was finish high school and you'd get off our butts. But you didn't. There you were, pushing for college, staying on us about our grades, our classes."

Finn felt his temper rising. "How is that wrong? Is it bad that I want you to have a good life?"

"You want us to have your life," Sasha said, glaring at him. "We appreciate all you've done. We care about you, but we can't do what you want anymore."

"You're twenty-one. You're kids."

"We're not," Stephen said, sitting up. "You keep saying that."

"Maybe my attitude has something to do with your actions."

"Or maybe it's just you," Stephen told him. "You've never trusted us. Never given us a chance to prove what we could do on our own."

Finn wanted to put his fist through a wall. "Maybe because I knew you'd pull something like this. What were you thinking?"

"We need to make our own decisions," Stephen said stubbornly.

"Not when they're this bad."

Finn could feel control of the conversation slipping from him. The sensation got worse when the twins exchanged a look. One that said they were communicating silently, in a way he'd never understood.

"You can't make us go back," Stephen said quietly. "We're staying. We're going to get on the show."

"And then what?" Finn asked, dropping his hands to his sides.

"I'm going to Hollywood to be on television and in the movies," Sasha told him.

Hardly news, Finn thought. Sasha had been starstruck for years.

"What about you?" Finn asked Stephen. "Want to become a spokesmodel?"

"No."

"Then come home."

"We're not going back," Stephen told him, sounding strangely determined and mature. "Let it go, Finn. You've done all you needed to. We're ready to be on our own."

They weren't. That's what killed Finn. They were too young,

too determined to screw up. If he wasn't nearby, how could he keep them safe? He would do anything to protect them. Briefly he wondered if he could physically wrestle them into submission. But then what? He couldn't keep them tied up for the entire trip back. The thought of kidnapping wasn't pleasant, and he had a vague notion that he would be flirting with felony charges the second he crossed state lines.

Besides, getting them back to Alaska wouldn't accomplish anything if they weren't willing to stay and finish school.

"Can't you do this in June?" he asked. "After you graduate?"

The twins shook their heads.

"We don't want to hurt you," Stephen told him. "We really do appreciate all you've done. It's time to let go. We're going to be fine."

Like hell they were. They were kids playing at being adults. They thought they knew it all. They thought the world was fair and life was easy. All he wanted was to protect them from themselves. Why did that have to be so hard?

There had to be another way, he thought as he stalked out of the small motel room and slammed the door behind him. Someone he could reason with. Or, at the very least, threaten.

"GEOFF SPIELBERG, NO RELATION," the long-haired, scruffy-looking man said as Finn approached. "You're from the city, right? About the extra power. Lights are like ex-wives. They'll suck you dry if you let them. We need the power."

Finn studied the skinny guy in front of him. Geoff "with a G" was barely thirty, wore a T-shirt that should have been tossed two years ago and jeans with enough rips to make a stripper nervous. Not exactly Finn's mental image of a television executive.

They stood in the middle of the town square, surrounded by cords and cables. Lights had been set up on stands and strung up on trees. Small trailers lined the street. Two trucks carried enough Porta-Potties for a state fair, and tables and chairs were set up by a tent with a buffet line.

"You're producing the show?" he asked.

"Yes. What does that have to do with my power? Can I get it today? I need it today."

"I'm not from the city."

Geoff groaned. "Then go away and stop bothering me."

Even as he spoke, the producer was heading toward a trailer parked on the street, his attention on the smart-phone in his hand.

Finn kept pace with him. "I want to talk about my brothers. They're trying to get on the show."

"We've made our casting decisions. Everything will be announced tomorrow. I'm sure your brothers are great and if they don't make it on this show, they'll find another." He sounded bored, as if he'd said those same words a thousand times.

"I don't want them on the show," Finn said.

Geoff looked up from his phone. "What? Everybody wants to be on TV."

"Not me. And not them."

"Then why did they audition?"

"They want to be on the show," he clarified. "I don't want them to be."

Geoff's expression shifted to disinterest again. "Are they over eighteen?"

"Yes."

"Then it's not my problem. Sorry." He reached for the handle of the trailer door.

Finn got there first and blocked his way.

"I don't want them on the show," he repeated.

Geoff sighed audibly. "What are their names?"

Finn told him.

Geoff flipped through files on his phone, then shook his head. "You're kidding, right? The twins? They're going to make it. The only way they'd be better for our ratings is if they were girls with big boobs. Viewers are gonna love them."

Not a surprise, Finn thought. Disappointing, but not a surprise. "Tell me what I can do to change your mind. I'll pay you."

Geoff laughed. "Not enough. Look, I'm sorry you're not happy, but you'll get over it. Besides, they could be famous. Wouldn't that be fun?"

"They should be back in school."

Geoff's attention had been captured by his phone again. "Uh-huh," he murmured as he scrolled through an email. "Right. You can make an appointment with my secretary."

"Or I could convince you right here. You like walking, Geoff? Want to keep being able to do that?"

Geoff barely glanced at him. "I'm sure you could take me. But my lawyers are a whole lot tougher than your muscles. You won't like jail."

"You won't like a hospital bed."

Geoff looked at him then. "Are you serious?"

"Do I look serious? We're talking about my brothers. I'm not going to let them screw up their lives now because of your show."

Finn didn't enjoy making threats, but nothing was more important than making sure Sasha and Stephen finished their degrees. He would do what he had to. If that meant physically crushing Geoff, then he would do it.

Geoff shoved his phone in his pocket. "Look, I appreciate your position, but you have to see mine. They're already on the show. I have nearly forty people working for me here, and I have a contract with every one of them. I'm responsible to them and to my boss. This is a lot of money."

"I don't care about the money."

"You wouldn't, mountain man," Geoff grumbled. "They're adults. They can do what they want. You can't stop them from doing this. Say I kick them off the show. Then what? They head to L.A.? At least while they're here, you know where they are and what they're doing, right?"

Finn didn't like the logic, but he appreciated it. "Maybe."

Geoff nodded several times. "You see what I'm saying. Better they're here, where you can keep an eye on them."

"I don't live here."

"Where do you live?"

"Alaska."

Geoff's nose wrinkled, as if he'd just smelled dog excrement. "You fish or something?"

"I fly planes."

The scruffy producer brightened immediately. "Planes that hold people? Real planes?"

"As opposed to those that are remote controlled? Yes."

"Sweet. I need a pilot. We're already planning a trip to Vegas and we're flying commercial to keep costs down. But there are other places, maybe Tahoe and Frisco. If I rented a plane, you could fly it, right?"

"Maybe."

"It would give you a reason to stick around and watch your kids."

"Brothers."

"Whatever. You'll be part of the production staff." Geoff placed his hand on his chest. "I have family. I know what it's like to care about someone."

Finn doubted Geoff cared about anything or any one but Geoff. "I would be there while you were filming?"

"As long as you didn't get in the way or cause trouble. Sure. We've got some chick from the city hanging around already." He shrugged. "Denny, Darlene. Something."

"Dakota," Finn said dryly.

"Right. Her. Stick with her. She's gotta make sure we don't hurt her precious town." Geoff rolled his eyes. "I swear, my next gig is going to be filming in the wilderness. Bears don't have demands, you know? That's a whole lot easier than this. So what do you say?"

What Finn wanted to say was no. He didn't want to hang around while they filmed their reality show. He wanted his brothers back in college, and he wanted to return to South Salmon and get on with his life.

Standing between him and that was the fact that his brothers weren't going to go home until this was over. His choices were to agree or walk away. If he walked away, how could he make sure Geoff and everyone else didn't screw them?

"I'll stay," he said. "Fly you where you need to go."

"Good. Talk to that Dakota chick. She'll take care of you."

Finn wondered how she would feel about him hanging around.

"Maybe the twins will be voted off early," Geoff said, opening the trailer door and stepping inside.

"My luck's not that good."

DAKOTA WALKED TO her mother's house. The morning was still cool, with a bright blue sky and the mountains to the east. Spring had come right on time, so all the trees were thick with leaves, and daffodils, crocuses and tulips lined nearly every walkway. Although it was before ten, there were plenty of people out on the sidewalks, residents as well as tourists. Fool's Gold was the kind of place where it was easier to walk to where you were going. The sidewalks were wide, and pedestrians always had the right of way.

She turned onto the street where she'd grown up. Her parents had bought the place shortly after they'd married. All six of their children had grown up here. Dakota had shared a room with her two sisters, the three of them preferring to live in the one bedroom through high school, even after their older brothers had moved out.

The windows had been replaced a couple of years ago, the roof a few years before that. The paint color was cream instead of green, the trees taller, but little else had changed. Even with all six kids out on their own, Denise still kept the house.

She walked around to the backyard. Her mother had said she would be spending much of the week working on the garden.

Sure enough, when she opened the gate, she found Denise Hendrix kneeling on a thick, yellow pad, digging vigorously. There were tattered remains of unworthy plants scattered on the grass by the flower beds. Her mother wore jeans, a Tinkerbell hoodie over a pink T-shirt and a big straw hat.

"Hi, Mom."

Denise looked up and smiled. "Hi, honey. Was I expecting you?"

"No. I just stopped by."

"Good." Her mom stood and stretched. "I don't get it. I cleaned up the garden last fall. Why do I have to clean it again in the spring? What exactly are my plants doing all winter? How can everything get so messy, so quickly?"

Dakota crossed to her mother and hugged her, then kissed her cheek. "You're talking to the wrong person. I don't do the garden thing."

"None of you do. I obviously failed as a parent." She sighed theatrically.

Denise had been a young bride to Ralph Hendrix. Theirs had been a case of love at first sight, followed by a very quick wedding. She'd had three boys in five years, followed by triplet girls. Dakota remembered a crowded house with plenty of laughter. They'd always been close, drawn more so by the death of their father nearly eleven years before.

Ralph's unexpected passing had crushed Denise but not destroyed her. She'd pulled herself together—most likely for the sake of her children—and gone on with her life. She was pretty, vibrant and could pass for a woman in her early forties.

Now she led the way through the backdoor, into the kitchen. It had been remodeled a few years ago, but no matter how it looked, the bright open space was always the center of the home. Denise was nothing if not traditional.

"Maybe you should get a gardener," Dakota said as she collected two glasses from the cupboard.

While her mother pulled out a pitcher of iced tea, Dakota

filled the glasses with ice cubes, then checked the cookie jar. The smell of fresh chocolate chip cookies drifted to her. She tucked the ceramic ladybug container under one arm and made her way to the kitchen table.

"I would never trust a gardener," Denise said, sitting across from her daughter. "I should plow the whole thing under and pour cement. That would be easy."

"You've never been into easy. You love your flowers."

"Most days." She poured iced tea. "How's the show going?"

"They announce the contestants tomorrow."

Humor brightened her mother's dark eyes. "Will we see you on the list?"

"Hardly. I wouldn't have anything to do with them if Mayor Marsha hadn't guilted me into agreeing."

"We all have a civic responsibility."

"I know. That's why I'm doing the right thing. Couldn't you have raised us not to care about others? That would have been better for me."

"It's ten weeks, Dakota. You'll live."

"Maybe, but I won't like it."

Her mother's mouth twitched. "Ah, that maturity that always makes me so proud."

The teasing was good, Dakota thought. Things were about to get a lot more serious.

She'd put off this conversation for several months now, but knew it was time to come clean. It wasn't that she wanted to keep things a secret, it's that she knew the truth would hurt her mother. And Denise had already been through enough.

Dakota took a cookie and put it on a napkin in front of her but didn't taste it. "Mom, I have to tell you something."

Nothing about Denise's expression changed, yet Dakota felt her stiffen. "What?"

"I'm not sick or dying or going to be arrested."

Dakota drew in a breath. She studied the placement of the

chocolate chips, the rough edges of the cookie, because it was easier than looking at the one person who loved her best.

"You know at Christmas I talked about wanting to adopt?"

Her mother sighed. "Yes, and while I think it's wonderful, it's a little premature. How do you know you won't find a wonderful man and get married and want to have kids the old-fashioned way?"

Material they'd been over a dozen times before, Dakota thought, knowing she only had herself to blame. Regardless of her mother's opinion, she'd gone ahead with the paperwork and had already been vetted by the agency she'd chosen.

"You know my period has always been difficult for me," she began. While her sisters sailed through "that time of the month," Dakota had suffered from a lot of pain.

"Yes. We went to the doctor a few times about it."

Their family doctor had always said everything was fine. He'd been wrong.

"Last fall things seemed to get worse. I went to my gynecologist and she did some testing." Dakota finally raised her gaze and looked at her mother. "I have a form of polycystic ovarian syndrome and pelvic endometriosis."

"What? I know what endometriosis is, but the other?" Her mother sounded worried.

Dakota smiled. "Don't panic. It's not all that scary or contagious. PCOS is a hormone imbalance. I'm handling it by keeping my weight down and exercising. I take a few hormones. On its own it can make getting pregnant really difficult."

Denise frowned. "All right," she said slowly. "And the pelvic endometriosis? That means what? Cysts or growths?"

"Something like that. Dr. Galloway was surprised I had both, but it can happen. She cleaned things up so I don't have the pain anymore."

Her mother leaned toward her. "What are you saying? Did you have an operation? Were you in the hospital?"

"No. It was a simple outpatient thing. I was fine."

"Why didn't you tell me?"

"Because that was the least of it."

Dakota swallowed. She'd been so careful not to let anyone know. She hadn't wanted to have to listen to sympathy, to hear people say it would be fine when she'd known it wouldn't be. She'd been in a place where words would only make things worse.

But weeks, then months, had passed and the old cliché about time healing all wounds was nearly true. She wasn't healed, but she could finally say the truth aloud. She should know—she'd been practicing in her small rented house for days now.

She forced herself to look into her mother's concerned, dark eyes. "The PCOS is under control. I'm going to live a long, healthy life. Either condition makes it more difficult to get pregnant. Having both of them means it's pretty unlikely I can get pregnant the old-fashioned way, as you said. Dr. Galloway says it's about a one-in-one-hundred shot."

Denise's mouth trembled and tears pooled in her eyes. "No," she whispered. "Oh, honey, no."

Dakota had half expected recriminations. A cry of "Why didn't you tell me?" Instead her mother stood, then pulled her to her feet and held on as if she would never let go.

The warmth of the familiar embrace touched Dakota's cold, dark places. Those buried so deep, she hadn't even known they were there.

"I'm sorry," her mother told her, kissing her cheek. "You said you found out last fall?"

Dakota nodded.

"Your sisters mentioned something had upset you. We thought it was a man, but it was this, wasn't it?

Dakota nodded again. She'd gone into work after finding out what was wrong and had started sobbing in front of her boss. While she'd never told him the cause, her grief hadn't exactly been subtle.

"I shouldn't be surprised you kept it to yourself," her mother told her. "You were always the one to think things through before talking to anyone."

They sat back at the table.

"I wish I could fix this," Denise admitted. "I wish I'd done more when you first had these problems as a teenager. I feel so guilty."

"Don't," Dakota told her. "It's just one of those things."

Denise drew in a breath. Dakota could see the determination returning to her mother's eyes.

"Regardless," Denise said firmly, "you're healthy and strong and you'll get through this. As you said, there are things that can be done. When you get married, you and your husband can decide what you want to do." She paused. "This is why you're adopting. You want to be sure you have children."

"Yes. When I found all this out, I felt broken inside."

"You're not broken."

"I know that in my head, but in my heart I'm not so sure. What if I never get married?"

"You will."

"Mom, I'm twenty-eight years old. I've never been in love. Isn't that weird?"

"You've been busy. You had your doctorate before you were twenty-five. That took tremendous effort."

"I know, but..." She'd always *wanted* a man in her life. She just couldn't seem to find him. At this point, she wasn't even searching for Mr. Right. A reasonably decent guy who didn't run screaming into the night at the sight of her would be pretty darned fabulous.

"I don't want to wait anymore. I'm perfectly capable of being a single mom. It's not like I'll be alone—not in this town, or with my family."

"No, you wouldn't be alone, but having children will make it difficult to find the right man."

"If I meet someone who can't accept all of me, including an adopted child, then he's not the guy for me."

Denise smiled. "I raised such wonderful children."

Dakota laughed. "Because it's all about you."

"Sometimes." She leaned forward. "All right, adoption it is. Have you started looking? Can I help?"

Emotions swelled inside of Dakota—the most powerful was gratitude. No matter what, she could always depend on her mom.

"I couldn't go through it without you. Adopting as a single parent isn't easy. I researched international adoptions and applied with an agency that works exclusively in Kazakhstan."

"I don't even know where that is."

"Kazakhstan is the ninth largest country in the world and the largest country that is completely landlocked." Dakota shrugged. "I did research."

"I can tell."

"Russia is to the north, China to the southeast. The agency was very open and encouraging about the adoption. I filled out the paperwork and prepared to wait."

Her mother's mouth dropped open. "You're getting a child."

Dakota winced. "No. In late January, after I'd finished the paperwork and had the home and background checks, they called and said they had a little boy for me. But the next day they called back and said there's been a mistake. He was going to another family. A couple."

She drew in a breath to keep from crying. At some point the body should just run out of tears, but she had enough personal experience to know that didn't happen.

"I'm not clear if it was an honest mistake or if they prefer couples and that's why I didn't get him. I'm still on the waiting list and the director of the agency swears it's going to happen."

Her mother leaned back in her chair. "I can't believe you've been through all this on your own."

"I couldn't talk about it," Dakota said quickly. "Not with anyone. At first I felt too frail to discuss it at all. Then I was afraid I'd jinx the adoption. It wasn't you, Mom."

"How could it be?" Denise asked. "I'm practically perfect. But still."

For the second time, Dakota laughed. It felt good to find humor in life again. She'd had a few months where nothing had been happy or right.

Dakota touched her arm. "I'm dealing. Most days it's okay. Sometimes it's hard to get out of bed. Maybe if I'd been in a relationship, I wouldn't have felt so unlovable."

"You're not unlovable. You're beautiful and smart and fun to be with. Any man would be lucky to have you."

"That's what I tell myself. Apparently the entire gender is blind and stupid."

"They are. You'll find someone."

"I'm not so sure. I can't blame my lack of love life on the man shortage here. Not entirely. I didn't date when I was away at college, either." She shrugged. "I haven't told anyone, Mom. I'll talk to Nevada and Montana in a few days. If you wouldn't mind, I thought you could tell my brothers after that." Denise would explain what had happened in simple terms, and it would be a whole lot less embarrassing than coming from her.

Her mother nodded. Once her sisters knew, they would want to rally, but there wasn't anything to do. Her body was different. Most of the time she was okay with that.

"You're still on the list to get a baby from Kazakhstan?" her mother asked.

"Yes. Eventually I should get a call. I'm staying positive."

"That's important. I know you don't love working on the reality show, but it's a nice distraction."

"It's beyond crazy. What were they thinking? Mayor Marsha is terrified something bad is going to happen. You know how she loves the town."

"We all do," Denise said absently. She frowned slightly. "Just because you haven't fallen in love yet doesn't mean you're not going to. Loving someone and being loved is a gift. Relax and it will happen."

Dakota hoped she was right. She leaned toward her mother. "You got really lucky with dad. Maybe it's a genetic thing, like being a good singer."

Her mother grinned. "Meaning I should start dating again? Oh, please. I'm too old."

"Hardly."

"It's an interesting idea, but not for today." She rose and walked toward the refrigerator. "Now, what can I fix you to eat? A BLT? I think I have some frozen quiche, too."

Dakota thought about pointing out that this wasn't a problem that could be fixed by food. Not that her mother would listen. Denise was nothing, if not traditional.

"A BLT would be nice," she said, knowing it wasn't the sandwich that would make her feel better, but the love that went into it.

DAKOTA WAS MEETING her sisters at Jo's Bar. She arrived a little early—mostly because her house had gotten too quiet, with only her thoughts to keep her company.

She crossed to the bar, prepared to order a lemondrop martini, only to realize that Finn Andersson was standing in the center of the room, looking more than a little confused.

Poor guy, she thought as she walked toward him. Jo's Bar wasn't the usual kind of hangout where a man went at the end of a difficult day.

Until very recently, most of the businesses in Fool's Gold were owned by and catered to women. Including everyone's favorite bar.

Jo was a pretty woman in her thirties. She'd moved to town a few years ago, bought the bar and converted it into the kind of place where women felt comfortable. The lighting was flattering, the bar stools had backs and hooks for hanging purses, and the big-screen TVs were tuned to *Project Runway* and pretty much anything on HGTV. Music always played. Tonight it was '80s rock.

The men had their place—it was a small room in back with a pool table. But without preparation, Jo's Bar could be shocking to the average male.

"It's okay," Dakota said, coming up behind Finn and leading him to the bar. "You'll get used to it."

He shook his head as if trying to clear his vision. "Are those walls pink?"

"Mauve," she told him. "A very flattering color."

"It's a bar." He looked around. "I thought it was a bar."

"We do things a little differently here in Fool's Gold," she told him. "This is a bar that mainly caters to women. Although men are always welcome. Come on. Have a seat. I'll buy you a drink."

"Is it going to have an umbrella in it?"

She laughed. "Jo doesn't believe in putting umbrellas in drinks."

"I guess that's something."

He followed her to the bar and took a seat. The padded stool seemed a bit small for his large frame, but he didn't complain.

"This is the craziest place I've ever been," he admitted, glancing at her.

"We're unique. You heard about the man shortage, right?"

"The very piece of information that brought my brothers to town."

"A lot of jobs traditionally held by men are held by women here. Nearly all the firefighters, most of the police, the police chief and, of course, the mayor."

"Interesting."

Jo walked over. "What'll you have?"

The words were right, Dakota thought, telling herself not to blush, but Jo's look of speculation promised many questions to come.

"I'm meeting my sisters," Dakota said quickly. "I rescued Finn. It's his first time in."

"We generally serve your kind in the back," Jo told him. "But because you're with Dakota, you can stay here."

Finn frowned. "You're kidding, right?"

Jo grinned. "Not the brightest bulb. Too bad." She turned to Dakota. "Your usual?"

"Please."

Jo strolled away.

Finn glanced at Dakota. "She's not going to serve me?"

"She's bringing you a beer."

"What if I don't want a beer?"

"Do you?"

"Sure, but…" He shook his head again.

Dakota held in a laugh. "You'll get used to it, don't worry. Jo's a sweetie. She just likes messing with people."

"You mean men. She likes messing with men."

"Everyone needs a hobby. So how are things? Have you convinced your brothers to leave?"

His expression tightened. "No. They're determined. Solidarity in numbers and all that."

"I'm sorry things aren't working out, but I'm not surprised. You're right about the solidarity thing. I'm a triplet and my sisters and I always protected each other." She thought about the conversation she was going to have with them later. "We still do."

"Identical triplets?"

"Uh-huh. It was fun when we were younger. Now it's less thrilling to be mistaken for someone else. We try to look as different as possible." She tilted her head. "Now that I think about it, looking different has gotten easier as we've gotten older and started developing our own style." She glanced down at the blue sweater she'd pulled over jeans. "Assuming we have something close to style."

Jo appeared with her lemondrop and a beer. She set down the drinks, winked at Finn, then walked away.

"I'm going to ignore her," Finn muttered.

"Probably for the best." Dakota took a sip of her drink. "What happens now? If your brothers are staying, are you going back to Alaska?"

"No. I talked to Geoff." He took a drink of his beer. "I threatened him, he threatened me back."

"And you're taking a house together on the shore?"

"Not exactly. He said Sasha and Stephen were both going to be on the show, so I volunteered to work as his pilot. Flying contestants around, that sort of thing. I'm staying."

Dakota told herself that having a tall, handsome, caring man in town was a meaningless bit of info. That any pleasure she took in sitting next to him, having a drink, was just her natural joy in spending time with a fellow human. She wasn't impressed by the strong line of his jaw, the crinkles by his eyes when he smiled or the way he filled out his plaid shirt.

"You're a pilot?"

He nodded absently. "I have a cargo company back in South Salmon." He picked up his beer. "I'd rather knock both of them senseless and drag them back home," he said. "But I'm doing my best to show restraint."

"Think of this as a growing experience," she said.

"I'd rather not."

She smiled. "Poor you. Do you have a place to stay for a few weeks?" The words replayed in her mind. "I, ah, mean that if you want something other than a hotel room, I can recommend a couple of furnished rentals, or…" She swallowed and held on to her drink.

Finn turned to her, the stool shifting until he faced her. His dark eyes started on her face, dropped a little lower, before returning to lock with her gaze.

There was something intense about all that attention. Something that made her previous rocklike stomach give a little wiggle. Nothing overt. Just the slightest quivery shift.

"I have a place," he said, his voice low and a little gravelly. "Thanks."

"You're welcome. I, ah, do think your brothers could be on the show for a while."

"That's what I'm afraid of." He leaned toward her. "I have a life back in Alaska. The plane cargo business comes with a partner. Bill is going to explode when I tell him I have to stay." He ran one hand through his dark hair. "It's early spring. In about six weeks, we'll start our busy season. I need to be back by then. They should have come to their senses by then, right?"

She wanted to give him hope, but knew it would be silly to lie. "I don't know. It depends on how much they're enjoying themselves. They could get voted off early."

"And then head for L.A." He grimaced. "That's what Geoff said. At least here, I can keep my eye on them. Kids. Giant pain in the ass. You have any?"

"No." She sipped her drink, searching for a shift in topic. "It's just the three of you?"

"Yeah. Our parents were killed in a plane crash."

"I'm sorry."

"It was a long time ago. For years it was just us, you know? My brothers were great when they were young. There were a few scrapes, but they tried to be responsible. What the hell happened?"

She stared into his dark eyes. "Don't take it personally. You've done a great job with them."

"Obviously not."

She touched his arm, feeling heat through the soft cotton of his shirt. *Note to self,* she thought. It had been a very long time since she'd had a man in her bed. She would have to do something to fix that.

He was staring at her. It took her a second to remember she'd been making a point.

"Um, this is just a blip in their lives. You see it as huge, but I don't think it will be. They're testing boundaries, testing themselves, but you'll be here if they need help." She carefully removed her hand, then waited for the sense of heat and strength to fade.

It didn't.

"They won't ask for help," he grumbled, obviously not the least bit affected by her. Which was very annoying.

"Maybe they will. Besides, you should take pride in the fact that they're comfortable enough with themselves and their lives to risk disappointing you. They're not worried about losing your love and support."

The glower from that morning returned. "You're way too happy a person. You know that, right?"

She laughed. "I'm actually pretty normal on the happy scale. I think you're jaded."

"You got that right." He drained his beer, then tossed a couple of bills on the bar. "Thanks for listening."

"You're welcome."

He stood. "I guess I'll see you at the show or on the set."

"I'll be there."

Their eyes locked. For a second, she thought he might lean in and kiss her. Her mouth was more than ready to take him for a test drive. But he didn't. Instead he gave her a slight smile and headed out.

She stared after him, her gaze dropping to his very nice butt and lingering. They knew how to grow 'em in South Salmon, she thought, raising her glass toward the north. At least she thought it was north.

She told herself that finding Finn attractive was a good thing. As far as she could tell, she hadn't had a single sexual thought since last fall, when her gynecologist had told her about her inability to have children. If she was stirring, so to speak, then it must mean she was healing. Healing was good.

Having Finn kiss her would have been better, but at this point, she would take whatever she could get.

CHAPTER THREE

"WHO'S THE GUY?" Montana asked as she walked up to Dakota. "He's cute."

"His brothers will probably be on the show and he's not happy. He wants them to finish college."

Montana raised her eyebrows. "Good looking *and* responsible. Is there a wife?"

"Not that I know of."

Montana grinned. "Better and better."

Jo waved at her and pointed to a table that had opened up in the corner. Unlike regular bars, Jo's was more crowded midweek when it was easier for women to get away. Come weekends, the place went more "date night," and that wasn't as appealing to the regulars.

Dakota grabbed her drink and followed her sister to the empty table. Montana had been letting her hair grow out. It came more than halfway down her back, a cascade of different shades of blond. Last year it had been brown—the blond looked better.

All three sisters had their mother's coloring with blond hair and dark brown eyes. Denise said it was the result of her surfing childhood—a humorous claim considering she'd been born and raised in Fool's Gold and the town was over two hundred miles from the nearest ocean.

Dakota settled across from Montana. "How's it going?" she asked.

"Good. Max is keeping me busy. Some guy from the government came by earlier in the week. I'm not sure which agency he works with, mostly because he didn't tell us. He'd heard about the work Max does and wanted to test some of our dogs for their ability to differentiate scent."

Last fall Montana had left her position at the library and gone to work for a man who trained therapy dogs. She'd attended several seminars, had learned to train the dogs and seemed to be loving everything about her new job.

Dakota sipped her lemondrop as a Madonna song played in the background. "Why?"

Montana leaned toward her and lowered her voice. "I think they would be trained to sniff out explosives. The guy wasn't very clear. He knew Max from before, which makes me curious about his past. Not that I'm asking. I know Max likes me and all but I swear sometimes when he looks at me, he's wondering if I even have half a brain."

Dakota laughed. "You're being too hard on yourself."

"I don't think so."

Nevada walked up to the table. Although she was the same height and weight as her sisters, she managed to look completely different. Maybe it was the short hair or the jeans and long-sleeved shirts she favored. While Montana had always been on the girly end of the spectrum, Nevada preferred the tomboy look.

"Hi," she said as she sat down across from Dakota. "How's it going?"

"You should have been here earlier," Montana said with a grin. "Dakota was with a guy."

Nevada had raised her arm to wave at Jo. She froze in place

and turned her brown eyes toward her sister. "Seriously? Anyone interesting?"

"I'm not sure if he's interesting, but he's yummy," Montana said.

Dakota knew there was no point in fighting the inevitable. Even so, she tried. "It's not what you think."

Nevada dropped her arm and grinned. "You don't know what I'm thinking."

"I can guess." Dakota sighed. "His name is Finn and his brothers are here to appear on the reality show." She briefly outlined the problem—at least the one from Finn's point of view.

"You should offer to comfort him in his hour of need," Montana told her. "A hug that lingers. A soft kiss with a whisper of need. Soul-stirring touches that…" She looked at her sisters. "What?"

Nevada glanced at Dakota. "I think she's slipped over the edge."

"I think she needs a man," Dakota told her, then looked at Montana. "Soul-stirring touches? Seriously?"

Montana dropped her head to her hands. "I need to spend some quality time with a naked man. It's been too long." She straightened, then smiled. "Or I could get drunk."

"Whatever works," Nevada muttered, accepting the tall vodka tonic Jo handed her. "Montana's slipping over the edge."

"It happens to the best of us," Jo said cheerfully, passing Montana a rum and Diet Coke.

As Jo left, the front door opened and Charity and Liz walked in. Charity was the city planner, married to cyclist Josh Golden, while Liz had married the triplet's brother, Ethan. Both women saw the sisters and headed over.

"How are things?" Charity asked as they approached.

"Good," Dakota said, eyeing her friend. "You look amazing. Fiona is what—three months old? You'd never know you just had a baby."

"Thanks. I've been walking a lot. Fiona is sleeping longer, so that helps."

Liz shook her head. "I remember those baby nights. Thank goodness mine are older."

"Wait until they start wanting to drive," Nevada told her.

"I refuse to think about that."

"Want to join us?" Montana asked.

Liz hesitated. "Charity's been reading my work-in-progress and wants to discuss a couple of things. Next time?"

"Sure," Dakota told them.

Liz wrote a successful detective series that had, until recently, featured victims who looked surprisingly like their brother Ethan. Now that he and Liz were together, Dakota had a feeling the next dead body would be completely different.

The two women walked to another table.

"How's work?" Nevada asked Montana.

"Good. I'm training a couple of new puppies. I talked to Max about the reading program I've been researching. I have an appointment with a couple of school board members to talk about a trial program."

Montana had discovered several studies that explained that kids who were bad readers improved more quickly when they read to dogs instead of people. Something about dogs being all support and no judgment, Dakota thought. When her sister had approached her about the studies, Dakota had done a little research and found even more supportive literature.

"I love the idea of going into schools and helping kids," Montana said wistfully. "Max says we're going to have to expect to do it for free in the beginning. Once we show results, the schools will hire us." She wrinkled her nose. "Honestly, most of what we do is for free. I can't figure out where he gets his money. Someone is paying my salary and to take care of the dogs. Even if he owns the land and the kennel is paid for, there's still upkeep."

"He hasn't said where the support comes from?" Nevada asked.

Montana shook her head.

"You could ask him," Dakota told her.

Montana rolled her eyes and picked up her drink. "That's not going to happen."

Montana wasn't big on confrontation, Dakota thought. She turned to Nevada. "How are things with you?"

"Good. The same." Her sister shrugged. "I'm in a rut."

"How can you say that?" Montana asked. "You have a great job, you've always known what you want to do."

"I know. I'm not saying I want to stop being an engineer and take up pole dancing, but sometimes..." She sighed. "I don't know. I think my life needs to be shaken up a little."

Dakota smiled. "We could always set Mom up on a date. That would be a distraction."

Both her sisters stared at her.

"Mom date?" Montana asked, her eyes wide. "Has she said anything?"

"Not seriously, but she's vibrant and attractive. Why wouldn't she date?"

"It would be weird," Montana said.

"Or uncomfortable." Nevada picked up her drink. "She would probably find a guy in fifteen seconds. I can't remember the last time I was on a date."

"That's what I thought, too," Dakota admitted. "But don't you think one of us should be successful at the dating thing?"

"You don't see the humiliation of that person being our mother?" Nevada asked.

Dakota grinned. "There is that."

Montana shook her head. "No. She can't. What about Dad?"

Dakota studied her. "It's been over ten years since he died. Doesn't she deserve a life?"

"Don't get all logical and therapist-y on me. I'm very comfortable not being the mature one."

"Then you shouldn't worry. We were just joking about it." As a way to release tension, Dakota thought sadly. As a distraction from the truth about her inability to have children.

"She didn't sign up for the show, did she?" Nevada asked. "Not that I wouldn't support her if she did."

"No, she didn't."

"Thank God." Nevada leaned back in her chair. "Speaking of the show, when do they announce the contestants?"

"Tomorrow. They've already made their casting decisions, but they're not telling anyone in advance. I think they're broadcasting live or something. I'm trying to stay out of it as much as I can."

"Will Finn be there?" Montana asked.

"Nearly every day."

Montana raised her eyebrows. "That will keep things interesting."

"I'm sure I don't know what you mean," Dakota said lightly. "He's a nice man, nothing more."

Nevada grinned. "You expect us to believe that?"

"Yes, and if you don't, I expect you to pretend."

AURELIA DID HER best to tune out the rant as she carefully put dishes into the dishwasher. The tirade was a familiar one. That Aurelia was a terrible daughter, selfish and cruel, who cared about no one but herself. That her mother had cared for her for years so it wasn't wrong to expect a little support and comfort in her old age.

"I'll be gone soon," her mother declared. "I'm sure you're counting the days until I'm dead."

Aurelia turned slowly to face the woman who had raised her on a secretary's salary. "Mama, you know that's not true."

"So I'm a liar?" her mother demanded. "Is that what you tell people?" Her mother's face crumpled. "I've only ever loved you. You're the most important person in my life. My only child. And this is the thanks I get?"

As always, Aurelia couldn't quite follow the train of the argument. She was clear on the fact that she'd messed up—she always messed up. No matter what she did, she was a constant disappointment. Much like her father, who had abandoned both his wife and daughter.

Aurelia didn't know if her mother had been a professional victim before he'd left, but she'd certainly taken on star status in the "poor me" department after.

"Look at you," her mother continued, pointing to Aurelia's long, straight hair. "You're a mess. You think this is how to find a man? They don't even see you. This is Fool's Gold. There aren't that many men. You have to try harder to get one here."

Harsh words that were true, Aurelia thought. She moved through the world in a bubble. Doing her job, going out to lunch with her work friends, invisible to every man, including the president of the company. She'd worked for his firm for nearly two years, and he still had trouble remembering her name.

"I want grandchildren," her mother declared. "I ask for so little, but do you give them to me?"

"I'm trying, Mama."

"Not hard enough. You're with businessmen all day long. Smile at them. Flirt a little. Do you even know how? Dress better. You could lose a little weight, too. I didn't put you through college so you could be alone your whole life."

Aurelia closed the dishwasher and then wiped down the counter. Technically her mother hadn't paid for college at all. Aurelia had received a couple of small scholarships, a few grants and had worked to pay the rest. However, she had lived at home for free, so that was support. Her mother was right—she *should* be more grateful.

"You'll be thirty soon," her mother went on. "Thirty. So old. When I was that age, you were five and your father had been gone four years. Did I have time to be young? No. I had responsibilities. I had to work two jobs. Did I complain? Never. You lacked for nothing."

"You were good to me, Mama," she said dutifully. "You still are."

"Of course I am. I'm your mother. You need to take care of me."

Which was what had happened a few years ago. Aurelia had graduated, gotten her first job and moved out. A year or so later, her mother had mentioned money was a little short and asked her to help her out. A few dollars here and there had become the reality of nearly supporting her mother.

While her accounting job paid well, paying rent on two places, not to mention utilities and groceries, didn't leave very much left over.

Other parents seemed proud of their children's successes. Not her mother. She complained that Aurelia took horrible care of her. In this household, being a child meant a never-ending debt that only grew with time.

Aurelia stared out the kitchen window at the backyard beyond. Instead of a neat garden, she saw a giant balance sheet covered in red. Near-physical proof that she was trapped forever.

It wasn't supposed to have been like this, she thought sadly. She'd always had dreams of finding someone special, of falling in love. She just wanted to belong without having to feel there was always a payment to be made.

An impossible fantasy, she reminded herself. She wasn't especially pretty or interesting. She was an accountant who actually loved her work. She didn't go to clubs or bars, and should a man ever speak to her, she wouldn't have a clue what to say back.

"If you get picked for that show," her mother warned, "don't embarrass me by saying or doing something stupid. Be on your best behavior."

"I'll try."

"Try!" Her mother, a small woman with penetrating dark eyes, threw her arms in the air. "It's always *try* with you. Never *do*. You try and then fail."

Not exactly a pep talk designed to make her feel better, Aurelia thought, walking through the kitchen to the small living room. She hadn't wanted to audition for the reality show being filmed in town, but her mother had bullied her until she'd agreed. Now she could only hope she wasn't chosen.

She'd even tried to get out of it by saying that she had to work, but when she'd mentioned the application to her boss, it had been one of the few times he'd seemed interested in her. He'd told her she could take off time during the day whenever she needed as long as she got her work done later.

"I need to get home," she said. "I'll see you in a couple of days."

"Your own apartment," her mother said with a scowl. "So selfish. You should move back here. Think of the money you'd save. But no. It all has to go for your pleasure, while I have nothing."

Aurelia thought about pointing to the check she'd left on the table by the door. The one that would cover the rent and utilities for the month. Her mother was still working, earning what she'd always earned. So where was her money going? Perhaps for things like the new car in the garage and the stylish clothes she favored.

Aurelia shook her head. There was no point in going there. After all, once she gave her mother the money, it wasn't her business how it was spent. A gift was to be given freely.

Although the checks never felt like a gift. They were much more a guilt payment.

She grabbed her purse, told her mother goodbye and stepped out onto the small porch. Her own apartment was only a few blocks away and she'd walked.

"I'll see you soon," she called over her shoulder.

"You should move back," her mother yelled.

Aurelia kept walking. She might not be able to stand up to her mother, but she was determined that she would never live with her again. She didn't care if she had to work five jobs or sell her own blood. Moving back would be the end of anything close to a life.

As she walked along the tree-lined streets, she wondered where she'd gone wrong. When had she decided it was okay for her mother to treat her so badly, and how was she supposed to figure out how to stand up for herself without allowing a lifetime of guilt to get in her way?

FINN HAD NEVER been on a movie set, so he couldn't speak to what happened there, but from what he could tell, television was all about the lighting.

So far the crew had spent nearly an hour adjusting lights and big reflectors in a newly built soundstage on the edge of town. Rows of chairs had been set up for the audience that was due to arrive, and there had been at least three sound checks on microphones and the canned music, but it was the lights that seemed to have everyone frantic.

He kept out of the way, watching from a far corner. Nothing about the situation interested him. He would rather be back in South Salmon, getting ready to ferry shipments north of the Arctic Circle. Unfortunately, his regular life wasn't much of an option. Not until he could drag his brothers with him.

A few people walked toward stage. He thought he recognized the tall man wearing a suit and what looked like an inch of makeup. The host, Finn thought, wondering what was the least bit appealing about being on TV. Sure, the pay was good, but at the end of the day, what had anyone really accomplished?

The host guy and Geoff had a long conversation with plenty of arm waving. A few minutes later, all the would-be contestants were led on stage. The curtain had a logo of the cable company on it—the stylized letters meaningless to Finn. He rarely watched network television, much less cable.

He saw a few people well over forty, a lot of good-looking kids in their twenties, a few ordinary types who were seriously out of place and the twins.

It was all he could do not to stomp onto the stage, grab one under each arm and head for the airport. Only a couple of things stopped him. First, the fact that it was unlikely he could actually wrestle either of his brothers into submission. They were as tall as him, and while he had more muscle and experience in a fight, he cared about them too much to really hurt them. Second, he had a feeling someone with the production company would call the police and the situation would go downhill from there.

"You're looking fierce about something," Dakota said, coming up and standing next to him. "Plotting to kidnap them?"

Finn was impressed by her mind-reading skills. "Want to be an accomplice?"

"I make it a rule to avoid situations that end with me going to jail. I know that makes me less fun at a party, but I can live with that."

He glanced at her and saw her brown eyes were bright with laughter.

"You're not taking my pain seriously enough," he told her.

"Your pain is in your head. You know your brothers are capable of making their own decisions."

"If we exclude their present situation."

"I don't agree with that." She turned to the stage. "Everyone deserves to follow his or her dream."

"They'd do better to finish college and settle down," he grumbled.

"Did you?"

He studied his brothers. "Sure. I'm the poster boy for responsible."

"Because you had to be. What were you like before your parents died and you were left with two thirteen-year-olds? Something tells me you were a lot wilder than they've ever been."

She was right, damn it. He shifted. "I can't remember."

"Do you expect me to believe that?"

"I might have been slightly less responsible."

"Slightly?"

He'd been crazy, he thought, refusing to admit it to her. He'd loved parties and women and defying every law of physics in his airplane. He'd gone beyond testing boundaries—he'd been reckless.

"That was different," he said. "We didn't know what could happen."

"Meaning they do and should act accordingly? They're twenty-one. Give them a break."

"If they go back to college, I'll give them a break."

"Silly, silly man." Her gaze was both amused and slightly pitying.

Under normal circumstances, that probably would have annoyed him, but he found he liked spending time with Dakota. Even when she disagreed with him, he liked hearing what she had to say.

He was aware of her standing close to him in the dark shadows of the back of the soundstage. They would see everything, and no one knew they were there. For a second, he wondered what he would have thought of her under other circumstances. If he weren't here because of his brothers. If he didn't have to worry about their welfare. If he was just a guy intrigued by an attractive woman with a killer smile.

But these circumstances didn't allow for distraction. He'd promised himself that once he got his brothers through college, it would be *his* turn to follow *his* dream. After eight years of taking care of them, he'd earned it. He didn't want to spend the rest of his life flying cargo. But that thought was for later—after he'd gotten his brothers out of this mess and knew that they were safe.

On stage, Geoff shooed everyone out of view. The potential contestants were gathered together.

Dakota glanced at her watch. "Show time," she murmured.

From what he'd been able to figure out, there would be a combination of live scenes and taped segments of the various potential contestants. Whatever it took to drag out the show, he thought grimly. He stared at his brothers, willing them to suddenly come to their senses. Neither of them noticed him.

The big lights went on, someone called "We're live in five, four, three..." Cameras were moved silently, then the host began.

He welcomed the viewers, explained the premise of the show and started introducing the potential cast. Dakota reached for Finn's hand and drew him through the darkness to the other side, where they had a better view of a wide-screen television.

She released his fingers and leaned toward him. "That's the feed going out," she murmured, her voice soft, her breath tickling his ear.

He inhaled a feminine scent—something floral and clean. Heat from her body seemed to slip across his arm, making him aware of her curves. For a second he considered pulling her deeper into the darkness and paying attention to her mouth instead of the screen.

Don't go there, he told himself. *Big mistake.* He had to remember what was important, and right now that was the twins.

On stage, the host began calling names. Finn found himself stiffening. The first couple was older. Late '50s early '60s. He ignored them. A blond guy got paired up with a dark-haired, busty Amazon. At least that was something, he thought. The girl looked like she could take Sasha and Stephen together.

"I promised you some fun contestants," the host said with a smile. "Here's where it gets interesting." He motioned for Sasha and Stephen to join him on stage.

"Twins," he said with a grin. "Can you believe it? Sasha and Stephen."

Finn watched his brothers carefully. They looked at ease on the stage. They smiled at the camera, chatted with the host. They looked like they belonged.

"Now which one of you is which?" the host asked.

Sasha, wearing jeans and a blue pullover, the same damn color as his eyes, grinned. "I'm the better-looking one. So I must be Sasha."

Stephen gave his brother a shove. "I'm better-looking. We could take a vote."

The host laughed. "You boys are going to do just fine. Now let's find out if you made it on the show."

Finn felt his fingers curl into fists. Tension swept through his body. If only, he thought. But he knew what was going to happen. It had been inevitable from the day his brothers had left South Salmon.

The host looked at the card in his hand. He turned it over and showed it to the camera. Sasha's name was clearly visible. The audience, mostly bused in for the show, although a few locals had shown up, applauded. The host drew another card from his suit pocket. The girls waiting just behind him leaned toward the camera. A couple seemed ready to grab Sasha and run for the hills. A sentiment Finn could understand, although his reasons were different.

"Are you ready?" he asked Sasha.

Sasha grinned for the camera. "I can't wait to meet her."

"Then let's get the two of you together." The host turned the second card toward the camera. "Lani, come meet Sasha."

A petite, dark-haired, beautiful young woman stepped toward Sasha. Her eyes were large, her smile welcoming. She moved with an easy grace that had every man in the room watching her. Even Finn noticed her beauty.

Sasha's expression was comical as his eyes bugged out, and he leaned so far forward, he nearly lost his footing. He and Lani moved toward each other.

"Hi," she said softly. "Nice to meet you."

"Ah, nice to meet you, too."

They stared at each other. If Finn didn't know better, he would swear he was witnessing love at first sight. But he did know better. Or rather he knew his brother. Sasha would never let a girl stand between him and what he wanted.

"They look good together," Dakota said. "Or should I not point that out? Are you dealing okay?"

"I'll survive, if that's what you're asking."

"Not that you'll like it?"

He glanced at her. "What's to like?"

"You're not really a go-with-the-flow kind of guy, are you?"

"What gave me away?"

"Something tells me we're going to be seeing a lot more of those two," the host said cheerily.

Finn had yet to meet the man. He didn't know his name, but he knew he didn't like him. He couldn't imagine having to listen to him for ten or twelve weeks, or however the hell long the show lasted. Although disliking the host was the least of his problems right now.

Sasha and Lani linked hands and stepped to the side of the stage. The host put his arm around Stephen. "Guess you're next. Nervous?"

"More excited than nervous," Stephen said.

The host nodded to the girls waiting behind them. "Got a favorite?"

Stephen smiled. Unlike his brother, he didn't feel the need to charm the world. He'd always been serious. More studious. He had a sincerity the girls had always liked. If Sasha was the flash, then Stephen was the substance.

"Do I have to pick just one?" his brother asked.

The host chuckled. "You need to leave some for the rest of the contestants. How about if I pick one for you?"

Steven turned back to the camera. "Whichever one you pick is fine with me."

The host called for quiet. Finn wanted to point out that no one was talking but knew his comments wouldn't be appreciated. Once again the host removed a card from his suit pocket and held it up for the camera.

"Aurelia."

The camera panned across the girls, then paused as one of them stepped forward. Finn frowned. It wasn't that the girl was unattractive, or even badly dressed. She was just…different from the other girls. Less polished, less sophisticated. Plain.

She wore a navy dress that fell past her knees, low-heeled shoes and no makeup. Her long hair fell in her face, making it hard to see her eyes, not that she looked up as she approached. When she finally stepped next to Stephen and glanced at him, her expression was more one of horror than anticipation.

Finn studied her for a second, then frowned. "Wait a minute. How old is she?"

"Aurelia?" Dakota shrugged. "Twenty-nine or thirty. She was a year or two ahead of us in school."

He swore. "There's no way this is happening. I'm going to crush Geoff. I'm going to leave him bleeding and broken on the side of the road."

"What's wrong?"

He spun toward Dakota and glared at her. "Can't you see it? She's what? Nearly ten years older than Stephen. There is no way in hell I'm going to stand by while my brother is devoured by some cougar."

The corners of Dakota's mouth twitched. "Seriously? You think Aurelia is a cougar?"

"What else would she be? Look at her."

"I am," Dakota said. "*You* look at her. She's mousy. She was always like that in high school. I don't know her whole story but I'm pretty sure I remember she has an awful mother. Aurelia never got to do anything. She wasn't allowed to go to school dances or football games. It's kind of sad. You don't have to worry—she's not the type to trap him by getting pregnant or something."

"Cry me a river. I don't care about her past, I care about her being with my brother." He froze. "Pregnant?" He swore. "She can't get pregnant."

Dakota winced. "I shouldn't have said that. Stop worrying. She's no danger to Stephen. Come on, Finn, she's a nice girl. Isn't that what you want for your brother? A nice girl?"

"Sure I want a nice girl, but I want a nice girl who's his age."

Dakota grinned. "It may seem like a big age difference now, but when he's forty-two she'll only be fifty."

"You're not making me feel better. I don't think you're even trying."

Finn was done talking. Bad enough that his brothers had come to Fool's Gold to be on the stupid show. Maybe he could learn to live with that, but he was not going to stand here and let his brother be set up for a fall.

But before he could stomp down to the front of the stage and disrupt the live broadcast, Dakota stepped in front of him.

"Don't go up there," she said firmly, staring into his eyes. "You'll regret it, but more important, the boys will be humiliated on live television. They'll never forgive you. Right now you're an annoying older brother who wants to keep them safe. That's a livable condition. I'm serious, Finn."

He could see the truth in her eyes, and as much as he didn't want to believe her, he knew he had to. But the thought of leaving his brother alone with that woman…

"He doesn't have any money."

"Aurelia isn't after his money."

"How do you know that?"

"She has a great job. She's an accountant. From what I've heard, she does amazing work. There's a waiting list to be one of her clients." Dakota grabbed his arm again and stared into his eyes. "Finn, I know you're worried. Maybe you have reason to be. It would have been great if your brothers had stayed in college like you wanted them to. But they didn't. Please don't make this worse by going out there and acting like an idiot."

"I know you're trying to help," he said, realizing he sounded frustrated.

"Look at it this way. If she is as boring as I think she is, they'll get voted off early."

"If she's not, he'll be in trouble."

She dropped her hands to her sides. "You'll be here to make sure nothing bad happens."

"Assuming he'll listen."

He glanced toward the stage. Aurelia stood next to Stephen. If her body language was anything to go by, crossed arms, averted gaze, posture so stiff it was as if she were made of steel, she really wasn't happy about the situation. Maybe he would get lucky and they wouldn't last a date. He was due for some luck.

"You're quite the tough guy," Dakota told him. "Is that an Alaska thing?"

"Maybe." He took a deep breath and looked into her dark eyes. "Thank you for talking me off the ledge."

"I'm a paid professional, it's my job."

"You're good at it."

"Thank you."

He continued to stare into her eyes, mostly because he liked it. She was easy to be around. And his body couldn't help but be aware of the smoothness of her skin, the shape of her mouth.

"I need to get going," she said. "Can I trust you to stay here on your own?"

"Sure."

"Have a little faith," she said, stepping back. "It's going to be okay."

She couldn't know that, he thought. But for today, he was going to believe her.

He waited until she had left before walking out of the sound studio. After pulling his cell phone out of his pocket, he dialed the number for his office in Alaska.

"South Salmon Cargo," a familiar voice said.

"Hey, Bill, it's me."

"Where the hell are you, Finn?"

"Still in California." Finn shifted the phone to his other ear. "Looks like I'm going to be stuck here for a while. They both got on the show."

A couple of thousand miles away, Bill sighed. "We're going

to get busy soon. I can't do this by myself. If you can't get back here soon, we're going to have to freelance a couple of extra pilots."

"I know," Finn said heavily. "Go ahead and start looking. If you find somebody good, hire him. I'll be back as soon as I can."

"I need faster than soon," his partner told him.

"I'll do my best."

The business mattered, he thought as he ended the call. But his brothers would always be more important. He was stuck here until he finished the job he'd come to do.

CHAPTER FOUR

THE AIRPORT AT the north end of Fool's Gold was typical for its size. There were two runways and no tower. Pilots were responsible for staying out of each other's way. Finn was used to flying under those conditions. It was the same in South Salmon but with a lot worse weather.

He got out of his rented car and walked to the main office of Fool's Gold Aviation. He'd been told this was the best place to find out about renting a plane. He was also going to talk to the owner about picking up some extra work. There was no way he could stay in town for any length of time without doing something more productive than flying show contestants a couple of times a week.

He knocked on the open door and stepped into the two-room office. There were a couple of battered desks, a coffeepot on a rickety table by the window and a view of the main runway. An older woman sat at the larger of the desks.

When he entered, she looked up. "Can I help you?"

"I'm looking for Hamilton." He'd been given a single name and little else.

The woman, a pretty redhead in her fifties, sighed. "He's out with his planes. I swear, if he could sleep with them, he would." She pointed to the west. "That way."

Finn nodded his thanks and went around the building. He saw an older man bent low over the right tire of a Cessna Stationair.

Finn was familiar with the plane. It had a 310 fuel-injected horsepower engine and could cruise for nearly seven hours. The rear double doors made it easy to load cargo.

Hamilton looked up as Finn approached. "Thought I felt the tire go when I landed last night," he said, straightening. "Seems fine now."

He walked toward Finn and held out his hand. Hamilton had to be in his seventies, with wild white hair and a permanently lined face.

"Finn Andersson," Finn told him, shaking hands.

"You a pilot?"

"On a good day." Finn told him about his cargo business up in Alaska.

"That's wild flying," Hamilton said. "We don't get weather like that here. We're below twenty-five hundred feet, so we miss the worst of the snow and wind. There's some fog, but nothing like what you deal with. What brings you to Fool's Gold?"

"My brothers," Finn admitted and told Hamilton about the twins and their involvement with the show.

"They're going to use me to fly people around. I guess to save money."

"I don't care who rents my planes as long as they know what they're doing. Sounds like you do."

Finn knew the old man would need more than his word, but confirming credentials would be easy. "I'm stuck here for a few more weeks and wondered if you needed a pilot. I can fly cargo or people."

Hamilton grinned. "I do have some extra business. I hate to turn it away, but I've only got one set of hands and can only take on one flight at a time." He sighed. "There's plenty to be done. Rich people like to fly back and forth to town. Makes 'em feel special. The restaurant at the lodge is all fancylike and I fly in their fish. I have contracts with a few delivery companies, that kind of thing. Just tell me when you want to work and I can keep you busy."

"I'd appreciate that," Finn told him, relieved to know he wouldn't have to spend his day sitting around and watching his brothers.

"Let's go back to my office and see what's on the schedule. I guess I'll need to make it official and check on your license. We can go for a flight when we're done with the paperwork, if you have time."

"I have time," Finn told him.

"Good."

Back in the building, they went into Hamilton's office. It was smaller than the front room, but tidy. There were pictures of old planes covering the walls.

"How long have you been here?" Finn asked.

"Since I was a kid. Learned to fly before I could drive, that's for sure. Never wanted to do anything else. My wife keeps bugging me to move to Florida, but I don't know. Maybe soon." He glanced at Finn. "The business is for sale, if you're interested."

"I have a business," Finn told him. "Although you could do a lot here." Not just charter and deliveries, he thought. Air tours could be lucrative. And there was that idea of his about teaching flying.

Dreams for another day, he reminded himself. When he knew for sure his brothers were grown-up enough that nothing bad would ever happen to them.

"If you change your mind, let me know," Hamilton told him.

"You'll be the first."

IN HER REGULAR LIFE, Dakota spent her days working up curricula for math and science programs. In theory, a year or two from now, students from around the country would be able to come to Fool's Gold and spend a month immersed in a math or science program. Dakota and Raoul worked hard to solicit donations from corporate and private benefactors. It was work that excited her. It was work that made a difference. But was she doing that important work now? No. Instead, she'd spent the past hour on the phone with various hotels in San Diego, negotiating room rates so reality show contestants could have a dream date.

The door to her makeshift office opened and Finn stepped inside. She hadn't seen him in a couple of days, not since the contestants had been announced. She half expected to read an article in the local paper saying that two twenty-something twins had gone missing. But so far, Finn seemed to be holding it all together.

"Am I interrupting?" he asked.

"Yes, and I'm desperately grateful." She tossed the papers she'd been holding. "Do you know I have a doctorate? I can make people call me doctor. I don't, but I could. Do you know what I'm doing with that degree right now?"

He took the seat across from her desk. "Not loving your job?"

"Not today," she said with a sigh. "I tell myself I'm doing the right thing. I tell myself I'm helping the town."

"Let me guess. It's not working."

"I'm getting very close to wanting to bang my head against the wall. That's never a good sign. As a health care professional, I'm very aware of that."

She leaned back in her chair and studied him. Finn looked good. Hardly a surprise. When had the man looked bad? He was solid. Dependable. His concern about his brothers proved that. She supposed her next line of thought should be that he was nice. Instead she found herself acknowledging that he was every woman's definition of a hot, sexy guy.

"Can I help?" he asked.

"I wish." She sighed. "Let's talk about something else. Nearly any topic would be more cheerful." She pointed to the papers on her desk. "I see Geoff kept his word. You're the pilot of choice for several of the dates. What you're doing for your brothers—"

she smiled "—let's just say, parents across America will be so proud."

"That's one way of looking at it," he said. "I'd rather not have to be here at all." He looked at her. "Present company excluded."

"Thanks. Are you still going to come between Stephen and Aurelia?"

Finn shrugged. "Once I figure out how. They haven't been on a date yet, and both my brothers are avoiding me."

"Are you surprised?"

"No. If I were them, I'd be avoiding me, too." He shook his head. "Why couldn't they rebel in Alaska?"

"Missing home?" she asked.

He swung his gaze back to her and shrugged. "Some. This is very different."

"The landscape or the people?"

"Both," he admitted. "Compared to where I come from, Fool's Gold is the big city. Back in South Salmon, there's still snow piled ten-feet deep. But the days are getting longer and warmer. Bill—that's my business partner—and I should be gearing up for the busy season. Instead Bill's doing it himself." Finn sank lower in the seat. "We're going to have to hire a couple of temporary pilots."

"That can't be good," she said.

"It's a pain in the ass."

"You blame your brothers."

He raised one dark eyebrow. "Any reason I shouldn't?"

"Technically, you don't have to be here."

"Yes, I do." He glanced out the window. "If I wasn't worried about my brothers and work, being here wouldn't be so bad."

She smiled. "Are you saying you like Fool's Gold?"

"The people are friendly enough." He straightened. "I went out to the airport and talked to a guy there about renting planes for the show. I'm going to work with him while I'm here."

"Flying cargo?"

He nodded.

"I didn't know we flew cargo in and out of Fool's Gold."

"You'd be surprised what comes in by air. Even here. He also has charters. Taking people to remote places."

"Do you do that in South Salmon?"

"Some, although Bill and I focus mostly on cargo. I've thought about expanding, or even starting a new company. Bill wants to avoid dealing with passengers. It may be hard to believe, but I'm more of a people person." He grinned.

She reacted with a burst of heat to her belly and the knowledge that he'd made her toes curl. Thankfully, the latter was something he couldn't see.

"You're willing to take on the tourists?" she asked, trying to speak without having to clear her throat.

"They can be fun. I've also thought about opening a flying school. There's freedom up there, but you can't be stupid about it. My dad used to say the only time he knew I wasn't taking crazy chances was when I was flying." He chuckled. "Of course, he was wrong about that. Still, it teaches responsibility."

"Sounds like a calling."

"In some ways it is." He gazed at her. "You've been nice to me. I know you don't have to be, and I appreciate your counsel."

Nice? Great. She wanted him to think she was sexy and irresistible. Someone he couldn't wait to get in his bed. Wouldn't you just know it—the first man to get her attention in nearly a year thought she was nice.

"I do what I can," she said lightly. "If there are any particular goods or services you need in town, just let me know."

His dark gaze settled on her face. His mouth curved into one of those smiles designed to make a woman do just about anything. "I've been looking for a place to have dinner," he said. "Somewhere quiet. Somewhere a man can have a conversation with a beautiful woman."

If she'd been standing, she would have been in danger of tumbling over in shock. Was Finn asking her out to dinner? Or was he talking about someone else? It was pretty presumptuous of her to assume she was the beautiful woman in question. If he had said reasonably attractive, that she could have bought into.

"Well, I…" She paused, not sure what to say.

Finn shook his head. "I'm obviously out of practice. I was trying to ask you out to dinner, Dakota."

"Oh." Now was her turn to smile. "I'd like that." Then before she could stop herself, she added, "What if I cook? I mean, you could come to my place. I don't do gourmet or anything, but I know a couple of good recipes."

"Sounds perfect," he told her. "Just tell me when and I'll be there."

"How about tomorrow?"

"Works for me."

They settled on a time and she gave him her address. When he left, Dakota found herself smiling just a little more broadly as she picked up the phone to call another hotel in San Diego.

AURELIA STOOD IN front of Geoff's desk and did her best to look confident, rather than horrified. Despite his jeans and worn T-shirt, a Hollywood producer intimidated her. Not a huge surprise, she thought. Most people intimidated her. The only place Aurelia felt confident was at work. In her office, with her computer and her numbers, she ruled her world. Everywhere else, it was all she could do not to apologize for simply breathing.

"There's been a mistake," she said, forcing herself to stare at him rather than at the ground. "I really appreciate being picked for the show. I didn't expect to be. It's just…"

How to say it? How to explain the truth without confessing her deepest, darkest secrets?

"I'm not a cougar," she said, speaking very quickly. "I'm actually allergic to cats. I'm not a man magnet." She could feel herself blushing. The man magnet statement was ridiculous. Geoff could tell what she was and wasn't simply by looking at her.

The producer glanced up from the laptop on his desk and

frowned, as if he hadn't known she was in the room. "Who are you?"

"Aurelia. I'm paired with Stephen. He's one of the twins. They're twenty-one." She twisted her fingers together, not sure how she was going to make him understand. "Maybe there was a mistake. Or we could make a change. What if I was with someone older? Maybe a widower with a disadvantaged kid. I could do that."

Geoff returned his attention back to his laptop. "Not gonna happen. We need ratings. There are no ratings with a widower and some kid. Cougars are hot right now. It'll be fun."

She could tell he'd already lost interest in the conversation. Normally, she would simply accept whatever the circumstance was and go with it. But this time she couldn't. This time she had to fight.

She squared her shoulders and stared at the man who held her destiny in his indifferent hands. "No," she said firmly. "I'm not a cougar. Look at me." When he didn't glance up from his computer screen, she repeated the instruction. "Look at me!"

Reluctantly, Geoff raised his gaze from his screen. "I don't have time for this," he began.

"You're going to make time," Aurelia told him. "I'm only on this show because my mother insisted. She makes my life a living hell, and you don't get to do that to me, too. Sure I want to meet someone. Sure I want to get married and have children. I want a normal life. But I'm never going to have that with her around, dragging me down. I thought maybe, just maybe, if I did this, I could catch a break."

She felt her eyes starting to burn with tears and did her best to blink them back. "And look what happened. You put me with a *child!*"

When she'd finished, she expected Geoff to tell her to get out and return his attention to his computer. Instead he leaned back in his chair, folded his hands behind his head and studied her.

She felt his slow gaze start at her mousy brown hair and move down to her knees, which was about all that was visible, what with her standing in front of his desk.

She'd come straight from work, so she was dressed in one of her conservative navy suits. They were a uniform of sorts. She had five, along with two black suits and one in pale gray for when it was really hot in the summer.

On the same rack in her closet were an assortment of blouses. On the carpet below were a row of sensible, low-heeled pumps. Hers was not a wardrobe any cougar would be caught dead in.

Geoff dropped his hands to the desk. "You're right—you're not a cougar. But sex sells and a woman on the prowl is interesting to viewers."

"Not when that woman is me. I've never prowled."

His mouth turned up slightly. "You never know. People might feel sorry for you."

She held in a wince. How nice. The pity vote.

"I can't do this."

Geoff shook his head. "I hate to be a pain in your ass, Aurelia, but here's the thing. You're with Stephen or you're out."

While the words weren't a surprise, she had been hoping for a miracle. Apparently the universe was fresh out. Or busy with someone else.

"I have to do this," she said earnestly. Contestants were paid twenty thousand dollars. It wasn't a huge amount, but it was enough. When added to the small amount she'd managed to save, she would finally be able to buy a condo. She would own her own home.

The dream was better with a husband and child, but right now she was willing to take what she could get.

"Then do it," he told her. "If you need to be on the show to get your mother to back off, you have to take the chance. Go through with it. What's the worst that could happen?'"

The humiliating possibilities were endless, but that wasn't the point. Geoff was right. If she believed the show was her way out, then she had to be willing to do the show.

"For what it's worth," Geoff said, "Stephen isn't a bad guy."

"Can I get that in writing?"

He laughed. "No way. Now get out of here."

Aurelia felt a little better as she stepped out of Geoff's office. She *could* do this, she told herself. She could be strong. She might even be able to fake being a...

Her proud, brisk exit walk came to a halt when she slammed into someone tall and broad.

"Oh, sorry," she said, then found herself looking up and up until she fell into the dark blue gaze of Stephen Andersson.

She'd only seen him one other time—during the initial filming, taping, whatever they call it, of the show. During those brief minutes, she'd barely glanced at him. All she'd been able to think about was her humiliation. The reality that he was absolutely the last man she could ever imagine dating. Okay, Gerard Butler would have been worse, but only marginally.

"You really think it's going to be that bad?" he asked. "Being with me?"

The question was horrible enough, but worse was the realization that he had heard at least part of her conversation with Geoff. She felt herself flush.

"It's not you," she said quickly. "It's me. I'm sure you're a great guy."

"Don't say nice," he warned her. "That only makes it worse."

"Okay, then," she said slowly. "I'm sure you're not nice. Is that better?"

He surprised her by smiling. A casual but friendly smile. One that made her forget how to breathe.

"Not by much." He took her elbow and led her into an empty meeting room. "So what's the deal? Why don't you want to be on the show with me?"

It was hard to think with his fingers curled around her elbow like that. In her world, men didn't touch her. They barely knew she was alive.

He was standing too close. How was she supposed to think

with him taking up all the air in the room? While this would be a good time to self-edit, the truth bubbled up before she could stop it.

"Look at you," she said. "You're this gorgeous guy. You could have anyone. You should be hitting on coeds. You're not anyone who would be interested in someone like me. Even ignoring the age difference, I'm not your type. Do you know what I do in my regular life? I'm an accountant. Look up boring in the dictionary and you'll find some version of me."

Knowing that if she didn't get some small measure of self-control soon, she was going to make an even deeper hole to fall into, Aurelia pulled her arm free and stepped back.

Instead of looking horrified, Stephen appeared amused. Humor brightened his eyes, and one corner of his mouth twitched slightly.

"That's quite a list," he told her. "Where should I start?"

"No," she said with a sigh. "I understand this is my fault. I should never have signed up to do the show. I didn't really want to, it's just…" She twisted her hands together. "At the risk of being a cliché, my mother made me do it. She's always on me about stuff. And the money. I thought…maybe, if there was someone else, it would be easier to stand up to her." She groaned. "That makes me sound so pathetic."

"Hey, I get it. I know what it's like when someone in your family thinks they can run your life. Not wanting to do what they say doesn't mean you don't love them."

Aurelia wasn't sure what she felt for her mother. Love, of course, but sometimes the love felt more dutiful than sincere. Which made her a horrible person, she knew.

"My brother flew here from Alaska to yell at me about leaving college," Stephen said. "That's how much he doesn't want me to do this."

"What's wrong with you doing the show?" She did the math in her head, then looked at him. "You're really close to graduating, aren't you?"

Stephen, all six plus feet of hunky guy, shifted uncomfortably. "I was in my last semester."

"Before graduating?" she asked, her voice a slight shriek. "You left school for this?"

"Now you sound like my brother."

"Maybe he has a point."

"I couldn't do it anymore. I had to get away."

She shook her head. "You get how idiotic that is, right?"

The smile returned. "Maybe, but I'm still not going back."

"I feel the need to take your brother's side in this."

"But you're not going to, are you?" Stephen shoved his hands into his front pockets. "Because if I leave, you don't do the show."

Something she hadn't thought about. "Why are you here? I mean really, why are you here? I can't believe school was that difficult."

"It wasn't hard, if that's what you mean." He sighed. "Our folks died about eight years ago. There was Sasha and Finn and me, and no one else. We were close before, but losing them changed everything. It was hard."

Aurelia had a feeling the word *hard* didn't begin to describe what they'd gone through. "At least it brought you together," she said, thinking that the loss of her father hadn't brought her and her mother together.

"Finn won't let go. He's holding on too tight. Sasha found the audition in the paper. He's the one who wants to be on TV. I just want to be anywhere but South Salmon." He stared into her eyes. "It seems to me, we could help each other. I get your mom off your back and you protect me from Finn."

"I'm not sure you need protecting."

"Everyone needs protecting now and then."

There was something about the way he said the words. A vulnerability that only made him more appealing. Maybe Stephen wasn't as scary as she had first thought. But scary or not, she was taking a big risk. So much could go wrong.

"I won't let anything bad happen to you," he said quietly.

His words stunned her. It was as if he could read her mind. No one had ever done that before, probably because no one had ever taken the time to get to know her.

"You can't know that," she said, wanting to believe him, but afraid to try.

"Sure, I can. Why don't we try being here for each other?"

A tempting offer, she thought.

She stared into his eyes, searching for the truth. As she looked, she realized the answer wasn't to be found in Stephen. It was in herself. Either she gathered the courage to take the next logical step, or she was trapped forever.

"Let's do it," she said and promised herself there would be no regrets.

DAKOTA STARED AT the raw chicken in the pan, not sure if she should put it in now or wait until Finn arrived. What had she been thinking, inviting him over to dinner? In truth, he'd sort of invited himself, but still. Their evening was clearly a date, which should have been good but wasn't because now she was rattled. Worse, her thighs had been quivering all day.

Before she could decide about the chicken, the doorbell rang. She hurried toward the door, only to run back into the kitchen, pull open the oven and set the pan inside. Dinner would be ready in forty minutes. They would have to figure out a way to fill the time until then.

She sucked in a breath, squared her shoulders and opened the front door.

"Hi," she said.

It was good she spoke quickly, before she could really see him. Once she took in the long, lean body, the handsome face, the cotton shirt that wasn't plaid, she found herself feeling the tiniest bit disoriented.

"Hi, yourself," Finn said with a smile, as he handed her a bottle of red wine. "I hope this is okay." He pointed at the wine.

"I stopped at a store in town to pick it up. The guy made several recommendations. I'm not much of a wine guy. I wouldn't mind learning about it. You probably know something about wine, what with all the wineries around here."

As his words swirled around her, she realized he was talking too quickly. Was it possible Finn was nervous, too? The thought made her feel a whole lot more comfortable about the evening.

"I know nothing about wine," she said, holding up the bottle. "Except that I usually like it. Come on in."

He followed her into the kitchen. She only had to search two drawers before finding the corkscrew. Finn took the bottle from her and made quick work of the cork. She set glasses on the counter and he poured. After they toasted each other, she led the way back into her living room.

The house was small—two bedrooms—and a rental. Intelligent thinking and her slightly feminist sensibilities had told her to buy a house. After all, she was a professional who could take care of herself. But she was enough of a traditionalist to want to buy her first house with the man she loved. Hence, the rental.

Finn sat on the overstuffed chair her brother Ethan had talked her into buying. At the time, she'd thought it was too big for the room. Now, seeing Finn in it, she knew her brother had been right.

"This is nice," Finn said, glancing around the room.

"Thank you."

They stared at each other, then looked away. Dakota felt disaster looming. She knew she wasn't much of a dater, and, based on what Finn had told her, he didn't date much, either. This could be bad.

"I hope you're okay not eating meat," she said quickly. "I'm a vegetarian."

He looked slightly trapped, but nodded bravely and said, "Vegetarian is fine."

"Oh, great. So you like tofu. A lot of guys refuse to eat it."

He swallowed visibly. "Tofu?"

"Uh-huh. It's one of my favorite casseroles. Tofu, a special sauce mostly based on green vegetables. Soy ice cream for dessert."

"Sounds delicious."

She could see the panic in his eyes and couldn't help laughing softly. "I'm kidding. I made chicken."

His gaze narrowed. "Seriously? That's your idea of fun? Torturing me?"

"Everyone needs a hobby."

He leaned back in his chair and studied her. "You're not predictable, are you?"

"I try not to be. Besides, you're easy."

"It was the sauce made with green vegetables that pushed me over the edge."

"Not the soy ice cream?"

"I figured I'd leave early."

"Coward."

They smiled at each other. She felt the bad tension bleed away and a nice, new boy-girl tension take its place.

"You grew up with brothers, didn't you?" he asked.

"How can you tell?"

"You're not worried about my ego."

"Interesting observation," she said, then sipped her wine. "I hadn't thought about that, but you're right. I have three older brothers."

He raised his eyebrows. "Six kids?"

"Yes. I think my mom really wanted a girl. Instead she got three for the price of one."

"That had to have been a shock."

"I'm sure it was. Apparently having triplets is really hard on the woman's body. She was in the hospital after we were born. For a while, the doctors were concerned she wasn't going to make it. My dad had to have been freaked out, and my brothers were really young and missing their mom. Complicating everything was the fact that it was Christmas. To distract them, he told them they could name us, but that all three of them had to agree on the names."

She paused and wrinkled her nose. "Which is why we're Dakota, Nevada and Montana."

"Very patriotic."

She laughed. "When I used to get frustrated at their choice, my mom would point out that it could have been a lot worse. Apparently Oceania was in the running."

"Sounds like a fun family."

"It is." She shifted on the sofa. "What was it like for you? Before you lost your family?"

"Good. Fun. We were close." He shrugged. "My brothers are a lot younger than me, which influenced the relationship."

"You must have been devastated when your parents died."

He nodded. "I was. I didn't know how I was going to do it. Raise the boys and not screw up."

"Be proud of what you've accomplished. I don't think I could have done it. We lost my dad ten years ago. My sisters and I were just out of high school, ready to start college. My brothers were either in college or done. There was nothing for me to do but get through the mourning. And it was hard every day. I can't imagine having to deal with the emotional loss and raise two younger brothers."

Finn looked uncomfortable with the praise. "I did what had to be done. Some days I think I did okay. Others, like when I'm in my hotel room here in Fool's Gold, I think I screwed up completely."

"You didn't. What they're doing now has nothing to do with you."

He looked at her. "I want to believe you."

"Then you should."

"You're bossy. Has anyone ever told you that?"

"Are you kidding? With three brothers? I have a crown. I'm the queen of bossy."

Finn laughed. The warm sound filled the room and made her

smile. They continued talking until, in the kitchen, the timer dinged.

"Come on," she said, rising to her feet. "Our tofu surprise awaits."

FINN ENJOYED HIS DINNER. Not just the chicken and mashed potatoes, which were the best he'd had in months. Maybe years. But also the conversation. Dakota told funny stories about growing up in Fool's Gold. He knew what small towns were like, but South Salmon made Fool's Gold look like New York City. Where he lived, people tended to keep to themselves. Sure, you could count on a neighbor to help, but everyone minded their own business. From what Dakota said, Fool's Gold was the town that meddled.

"If you'd come here under other circumstances," she said, "I'm sure you would've liked it a lot more."

"I like Fool's Gold just fine," he told her.

"This is always going to be the place your brothers ran off to."

"Look at it this way," he said. "When Sasha moves to L.A., I'll hate it there, instead."

"That's not very comforting."

They smiled at each other across the table. He liked how the light played on her hair, bringing out the various shades of blond. When she laughed, her eyes crinkled in a way that made him want to laugh, too. Dakota was easy to talk to. He'd forgotten how nice it could be to enjoy a woman's company for an evening.

"How come your boss is so understanding?" he asked. "You said you had another job. What's he doing while you're working with the show?"

Dakota wrinkled her nose. "Not missing me," she grumbled. "Raoul is busy playing house with his new wife. Do you follow football?"

"Some. Why?"

"My boss is Raoul Moreno."

"The Dallas Cowboys quarterback?"

"That's him. When he retired, he wanted to settle down and found his way here. There was an old abandoned camp up in the mountains. He bought it and refurbished it. He hired me to coordinate the various programs. He had this whole idea to use it year-round. In the winter we were going to offer math and science programs. Intensive learning for middle-school-age kids. Get them all interested in the possibilities."

Sounded like a good idea, he thought. "What happened?"

"One of the local elementary schools burned down. It was a freak thing with the furnace. Raoul offered the camp to the school district. That was last September. Until the new school is built and the kids move back, the camp is full. Our big plans are on hold. Which is one of the main reasons he didn't mind me helping out with the reality show."

She leaned toward him. "The other reason is, he recently got married. Pia, his wife, is pregnant with twins. She's due in a couple of months, and that's keeping him busy."

"What are you going to do between the end of the show and when the school is done using the camp?" he asked.

"Raoul wants me to keep working for him. There's plenty to do. We have to apply for grants, find corporate sponsors, come up with a curriculum."

"All of which you'd rather be doing," he said.

She smiled. "Absolutely."

"Is leaving an option? Do you ever think about living anywhere else?"

"I've lived other places. Got my undergraduate degree at UCLA, my masters and Ph.D. at Berkeley. But Fool's Gold is home. It's where I belong. Do you think about leaving South Salmon?"

At one time he had. When he'd been Sasha and Stephen's age he'd dreamed of seeing the world. But then his parents had died and he'd had two brothers to raise. There hadn't been time for dreams.

"I have a business there," he said. "Leaving is impractical."

"And you're a practical guy?"

"I've learned to be," he admitted.

"You said you were wild before." Her gaze locked with his. "Would I have liked you?"

"I would've liked you."

He felt the awareness crackling between them. Everything about Dakota appealed to him. Sure, she was pretty, but it was more than that. He liked listening to her. He liked her opinions and how she looked at the world. Maybe part of him liked that she was as firmly connected to Fool's Gold as he was to South Salmon. They couldn't make a mistake because it couldn't go anywhere.

Wanting stirred. It had been a long time since he'd had the time or energy to be interested in a woman. Given how concerned he was about his brothers, it was extraordinary he was interested now. Which begged the question—what did he do next?

"I have dessert," Dakota said, coming to her feet. "And it's not soy-based. Interested?"

He stood as well, then came around the table. He supposed he should ask. After all, this wasn't just about him. Dakota was a rational, thoughtful woman. She would appreciate getting all the details out of the way first, assuming she was interested at all. But instead of asking, he moved closer. He cupped her face in his hands, leaned in and kissed her.

CHAPTER FIVE

DAKOTA HAD EXPECTED something along the lines of, "What flavor of ice cream do you have?" She hadn't expected Finn to kiss her.

His hands were warm on her face, which was nice enough. But what really got her attention was the feel of his mouth on hers. His lips were soft enough to tempt her and firm enough to allow her to relax. He kissed her gently, but deliberately enough to let her know that he really meant it. He kissed like he was hungry and she was an unexpected buffet.

His lips teased hers, moving lightly, as if searching for the best place to land. It'd been a long time since a man had kissed her. A long time since she'd wanted one to. Last fall, before she discovered she was broken inside, she would have said she wanted to be in a relationship. After, everything had changed. Now she wasn't sure. But with Finn, it didn't matter. He wasn't staying and anything between them wasn't permanent.

A very freeing concept.

He dropped his hands to her waist and drew her against him. She wrapped her arms around him and leaned in to the embrace. Her head tilted, he moved closer. He tasted of the wine they'd had with dinner. He smelled clean and masculine. As she moved her hands from his shoulders to his arms, she felt the strength of him.

The kiss continued. Skin on skin, warm. Appealing. Then something changed. Maybe it was the way he shifted his hands to her back and spanned the length of her spine. Maybe it was her thighs brushing his. Maybe it was the placement of the moon in the sky. Or maybe it was finally time for something good to happen to her.

Regardless of the reason, one second she was enjoying a perfectly respectable kiss from a very charming man. The next, fire swept through her body. It was as unexpected as it was intense. Heat was everywhere. Heat and hunger and the kind of wanting that stole a woman's will and left her prepared to beg.

Instead of holding on to him, she found herself clinging. The need to get closer grew until it overwhelmed her. She parted her lips, hoping to deepen the kiss. Thankfully, he read her mind. His tongue swept inside, brushing against hers.

It was heaven. Every stroke made her insides clench, her legs shake. She kissed him back, enjoying the growing sense of arousal. She wanted to be swept away, to be reminded of exactly what her body could do.

She'd been numb for so long, she realized. Disconnected from everything but the pain. She'd blocked off nearly all emotions, going through the motions so well, she'd even fooled herself.

He kissed her more deeply. She closed her lips around his tongue and sucked gently. He tensed in her embrace, as if holding back.

He was going to stop. But he couldn't. She needed this. He had to...

Only he didn't have to do anything. This wasn't her, she told herself firmly. She didn't attack guys in her kitchen—or anywhere else. The polite course of action seemed to be to step back.

Oh, but she wanted him. Her breasts ached. Her nipples were so sensitive, the feel of her bra was nearly agony. Between her legs, she was swollen and hungry. She wanted his big hands to touch her everywhere. She wanted to see him naked and hard in her bed. She wanted to be filled over and over until she found her release and with it, maybe a little healing.

It took every ounce of self-control, but somehow she managed to drop her hands to her sides and put some room between them. She was aware of her frantic breathing and hoped she didn't look too desperate. Sexual confidence was attractive. Desperation tended to send a man running.

Finn's eyes were dark with passion, which was nice. She was tempted to glance down to see if there was physical proof of his feelings, but she couldn't figure out how to do it without being obvious. Still, there was every chance he'd been offering a polite kiss and she'd gone after him like a sex-starved monkey.

"I, ah, don't know what to say," she admitted, not quite meeting his gaze.

"I shouldn't have done that," Finn mumbled. "You weren't… That's not why you…" He cleared his throat.

She frowned, not sure if he was apologizing or trying to escape. Hope shoved embarrassment out of the way.

"I'm glad that you did that," she said, telling herself that being brave built character. "You are?"

She forced herself to look at him and found him staring at her. Oh, yeah. That was some serious passion.

"Very glad."

One eyebrow raised. "Me, too."

Heat stained her cheeks, but she plunged ahead anyway. "We could do it again."

"We could. There's only one problem."

He was married? He used to be a woman? He was gay?

"I'm not sure I'll want to stop," he admitted.

The relief was nearly as good as the kiss had been. Dakota stepped toward him and didn't stop until her body was plastered against his. Which answered the question about his feelings on the subject.

"That works for me," she whispered.

She'd planned to say more, to suggest they move to her bedroom, but she didn't get the chance.

Once again, Finn kissed her. And while it wasn't as unexpected as the first time, she still found herself swept away.

She surrendered to his strong embrace, wanting to feel his arms around her. She parted her mouth, and he plunged inside, teasing her into passionate frenzy. Even as his mouth claimed hers, his hands were everywhere. He stroked her back, then dropped lower, to her rear. He cupped the curves, squeezing until she instinctively arched forward.

Her belly rubbed against his erection. He was hard and thick, and the image that contact painted made her whimper. Without thinking, she reached behind her and grabbed his hands, then brought them around to her breasts.

The second he touched her, she began to melt. His hands cupped her curves, caressing the skin as he learned every inch of her. His thumbs and forefingers found her nipples and teased them. Then he grabbed the hem of her sweater and tugged it over her head.

He'd barely had time to toss it away when she was pulling at the hooks on her bra. The bra went flying. Her only thought was to hope the stove was off so if it landed there, nothing bad would happen.

While she was doing that, Finn pulled off his shirt and kicked off his shoes. Then he bent down and drew her right nipple into his mouth. He licked the hard, sensitive tip before sucking deeply. She felt the connection all the way down her belly. Wanting tugged her center.

The combination of the movement, the heat, the moisture and the friction nearly drove her to her knees. She held on to him to keep standing. He switched to her other breast and used his fingers to caress the first. She ran her fingers through his hair, then brought his face to hers so she could kiss him again.

As their tongues tangled, he unfastened the button on her

jeans. She stepped out of her flats. Seconds later, her jeans and bikini briefs hit the floor. Finn followed, dropping to his knees, parting her thighs and kissing her intimately.

There was no warning, she thought frantically. No way to prepare herself for the gentle assault of his lips and tongue. She was defenseless as he explored all of her before returning again and again to her swollen center.

With each erotic lick, she felt herself getting closer. Her legs trembled until it was nearly impossible to stay upright. She dug her fingers into his shoulders, but it wasn't enough. She could feel herself starting to sink.

He caught her as she fell, pulling her into his embrace and against his chest. His skin burned hot against hers. As he stood, her feet left the floor, then he was carrying her through the small house.

She thought about giving directions, but as there were only two bedrooms on a single floor, she knew he could figure it out. Sure enough, he went directly into her bedroom, where he placed her on the quilt. Before he joined her, he sent his jeans and boxers skidding to the other side of the room.

He slid down next to her and put his hands on her body. He began at her forehead, lightly tracing her skin. He touched her cheekbones, her ears, her jaw. He traced her shoulders, her collarbone, before settling his hands on her breasts.

From there, he journeyed down her waist, over her hips, to the vee between her legs. She'd thought he might linger, finish what he started. But instead he continued down her thighs to her knees, her calves to her ankles.

He made the return trip more slowly. When he reached the soft skin of her inner thighs, he shifted between her legs, parted her and bent down to kiss her.

His tongue went immediately to where she was most sensitive. The steady stroking, a back and forth rhythm designed to drive her to madness, made her moan. Her body was not her own. He controlled every reaction, every sensation. Over and over again. Up and down.

Her muscles tensed. She felt herself straining toward the finish.

Not yet, she thought frantically. It was too good. She had to make it last. But it was impossible. The sureness of his touch, the feel of him against her. She felt herself nearing the end, nearing the inevitable.

Then he shifted slightly and inserted a finger deep inside of her. He pushed in once, twice, and she was lost. Her body dove into the pleasure. It swept through her, over her and around her. It was everywhere, and she never wanted it to end.

But gradually, the shuddering slowed. She felt herself resurfacing, returning to the real world. Lethargy battled with contentment. She hadn't felt this good in a really long time.

Just as the last of her climax faded away, Finn straightened, then put his hands on her hips. He entered her with one smooth, determined thrust. He was as big as she had imagined and filled her completely.

When he was all the way inside, she opened her eyes and smiled at him. "Nice," she whispered.

He managed a grin. "You like?"

"I do."

She wrapped her legs around his hips and drew him closer. When he withdrew and thrust in again, she urged him to go deeper. She wanted to take all of him. She wanted to get lost in what they were doing. This was life. This is what people who were alive did.

Every time he filled her, she found herself moving a little closer to who she had been before. Her body accepted him, widening and stretching to accommodate him. She felt him get closer. She felt herself getting more aroused.

Next time, she promised herself. Next time she would come again. But for now it was enough to feel him tensing. To feel him straining. To hold him as he lost himself in her.

SASHA AND LANI both sat cross-legged on the only bed in her motel room. The space he shared with his brother was bigger, but not by much. Once they'd been picked for the show, the production company paid for their food and lodging. Not that Geoff saw the need to pay for anything extravagant. So they were all stuck where they started.

When the show was over, they each got twenty grand. More than enough to finance his move to L.A.

Lani spread out several sheets of paper onto the bedspread. A few were new, but some of the pages looked old, with stains, tears and creases from being folded and unfolded again and again.

"I want to be a household name by the time I'm twenty-two," Lani said, her dark brown eyes bright with conviction. "Movies would be great, but TV feels like more of a sure thing. I flew to L.A. last year for pilot casting season." She paused and looked at him.

Sasha nodded. He knew enough about how the media worked to be familiar with pilot season.

Every year the networks and cable stations produced pilots for potential television series. Then the executives at the various stations decided which shows got a chance to be seen and which were dumped before they'd even begun. Casting was a big part of making a pilot, and unknowns were welcome to try.

Getting onto a pilot was huge, but once cast, there were no guarantees. Even if the show got picked up—a one in a million shot—your part could get recast with someone else. It was an actor's version of the lottery.

"How did you do?" he asked.

She sighed. "I got on two pilots. Neither went anywhere."

She raised her arms above her head and stretched. As she moved, her T-shirt pulled across her boobs.

Sasha watched, mostly out of habit. Lani was beautiful. Her features were exotic, and he would bet she would photograph great.

"What about modeling?" he asked.

"I'm too short," she told him. "Five-five. It's not going to happen. I've done some swimsuit stuff back home. Catalogues, that kind of thing. Of course I've had tons of offers to do nude shots, but there's no way. I wouldn't want those pictures to come back and haunt me when I'm up for an Oscar."

He wanted to get out of Alaska and be famous and very rich. Being a star was a way to make that happen. But Lani wanted it all. A serious acting career, awards and scores of paparazzi following her every move.

"We need to nail down our plan," she said, shuffling the papers. Her long, dark, wavy hair tumbled over her shoulders.

He supposed he should want to have sex with her or something. If she took off her clothes and offered, he wouldn't say no. But he wasn't really interested in her that way. Lani was the first person he'd met who wanted the same thing he did, only more. He understood that if they worked together, they would have a better chance of getting it all.

"You know, if we win, we'll each get a hundred and twenty-five thousand dollars," he said, leaning back against the pillows. "Plus the twenty. I want to rent a house in Malibu."

"Don't be an idiot," she told him. "That's before taxes. We'll be lucky to walk away with seventy thousand. And that has to last. I'm getting an apartment in the San Fernando Valley. Somewhere near the studios in Burbank, and an easy drive over the hills. That way I can be in Century City or Hollywood pretty fast. I know if I don't get picked up right away, I'll need to get a job." She looked at him. "Do you have your dream list of agents?"

Agents? "Ah, not really."

"I do. Once this show starts to air, I'm going to be making calls, asking their assistants to watch me. There's no way I'll get to the agent I want, but assistants love to take calls. They're looking for the next big thing. They want to find him or her and take that potential client to their boss."

Sasha stared at her. He and Lani might be about the same age, but he suddenly felt like a kid at the grown-ups' table. How did she know all this?

His questions must have shown because she grinned. "Don't look so surprised. I've been working the program since I was thirteen."

"I guess that should make me feel better."

She shook her head. "You'll catch on. It's not that hard. Everything is about capturing attention. Getting your fifteen minutes of fame and making it an hour. I've been thinking that we need a story line."

"What do you mean?"

"Regular dating isn't interesting. Who wants to watch that? What, we'll be sitting there talking?" She shook her head. "We need something better. We need a better reason for viewers to want us to win."

He leaned toward her. "Okay. Like what? Something from a movie?"

"I thought one of the classic love stories," she admitted. "But I'm not sure that's the way to go. Too many people will be familiar with the plot. Plus, it's not enough. It's not like we can have people kidnap us, although that would be fabulous."

She pulled out one of the pieces of paper and waved it at him. "I watched soaps. Some of the story lines are really great. When you think about it, people watch soaps because something is always happening. That and they care about the characters. So we have to get people to care about us and we have to give them something interesting to watch." She looked at him. "Sex sells."

"I can do sex," he said with a grin.

Lani rolled her eyes. "I already told you, no porn. But that doesn't mean we can't do romantic and passionate. People love that. I'm thinking we could have one of those great relationships where we're always falling in love and fighting and then breaking up and then getting back together. The camera loves drama. The camera loves action. If we give the director something interesting to film, we'll get the most TV time. And that's what we want."

"I can do action," Sasha said, still a little stunned by Lani's determination and willingness to do anything to get what she wanted. The most he'd done was walk away from college and his brother. At the time, that had seemed huge. Now he wasn't so sure.

"We'll be the couple everyone is talking about," she said eagerly.

"Absolutely. So what's the plan?"

Lani grinned. "I'm not sure." The grin widened. "Are you afraid of fire?"

THERE WAS A lot more to filming a television show than Dakota had realized. With ten couples, nearly as many locations and what seemed to her to be a very small crew, chaos reigned. Each couple was going to get a local date, and a few of them would get travel dates. It seemed to her that getting a travel date the first week made it a lot easier to stay on the show.

She'd always been a huge fan of shows like *Project Runway* and *Top Chef.* But she'd had no idea of all the work that went into forty-five minutes of air time. Today two couples were getting to know each other while they walked around Fool's Gold. A very nice first date in reality, but from what she could see on the monitors, it didn't make for exciting television.

She checked her clipboard to see how long the "date" was supposed to last. As she glanced back at the couple, she saw a tall, yummy-looking man walking toward her.

She hadn't seen Finn for nearly two days. Not since he'd been at her place and they'd engaged in acts that had the potential to send her to a higher plane. A quality she could really grow to like in a man.

As she wondered if she would be embarrassed or feel awkward around him, her body began a quivering dance of anticipation. As if her whole being had been invaded by sex-starved DNA.

"Morning," he said as he approached.

"Hi."

She stared into his blue eyes and found herself smiling. No bad feelings for her, she thought, relieved. The quivering got even better when he smiled back.

"How's it going?" she asked.

"Better," he told her. "I've been dealing with a few work-related crises back home, I flew some cargo to Eugene, Oregon, then spent most of yesterday trying to talk the twins into going back to Alaska."

"How did that go?"

"When we were done, I pounded my head against a wall just to make myself feel better."

"Ouch. Did you really expect your brothers to get on a plane and go back with you?"

He shrugged. "A guy can dream, right?" He shook his head. "No, I really didn't expect them to come with me. I knew it wasn't going to work, but I was compelled to try. Call me an idiot."

"Actually, I think you're someone who really cares about his family. You're misguided, but that happens to all of us."

He chuckled. "Thanks, I think."

"I was being nice," she told him.

"In a very subtle way."

She laughed. It was good to know she hadn't imagined that being around Finn was fun. The morning after could be an awkward time, even several days later, but she felt just as comfortable with him as she had before they'd made love.

"About the other night," he began.

Talk about being on the same wavelength, she thought. "I had a great time."

"Me, too. It was a surprise, not that I'm complaining." He looked at her. "Are you complaining?"

"I've never felt better."

The slow, sexy smile returned. "Good." The smile faded.

"What with it being unexpected and all," he said, "I didn't use anything. Is that a problem?"

It took her a second to realize what he was talking about. Protection, as in birth control.

"There's no problem," she told him.

"You're on the Pill?"

The easiest thing would be to say yes. It's what people expected the answer to be. But for some reason, she didn't want to lie to Finn.

"I don't need to be," she told him. "I can't have kids. It's a medical thing. Technically, if all the planets aligned, on the day of an eclipse, with the aliens landing, it could happen. The phrase 'one in a million' was tossed around."

She gave Finn credit. He didn't back away or even look ridiculously relieved. Instead, sympathy crossed his face and he said, "I'm sorry."

"Me, too. I always wanted kids. A regular family. I am at heart someone who planned to be a mother."

There it was, she thought, the sadness. When she first found out what was wrong with her, she thought she might drown in it. The sadness had overwhelmed her, sucking the life from her. Despite all her training, all the classes and papers and lectures, she'd never truly understood depression. She'd never understood how a person could lose all hope.

Now she knew. There had been days when she had barely been able to move. Taking her own life or hurting herself wasn't part of her personality. But pulling herself out of a constant state of apathy had been one of the hardest things she'd ever had to do.

"There's more than one way to get what you want," he told her. "But then you already know that."

"I do. I tell myself that all the time. On my good days, I believe me." She studied him. "You, on the other hand, aren't looking for a family at all."

"A good guess or your professional assessment?"

"Both. Am I wrong?"

"No. Been there, done that."

His words made sense, she thought. Finn had been forced to take on unexpected responsibility at a time in his life when he had planned to play. Why would he want to start over, with a new family?

A good reminder, she told herself. She liked Finn. They'd had fun together. But they wanted very different things, and if she continued to spend time with him, she needed to remember that. The last thing she needed right now was a broken heart.

"Have I freaked you out?" she asked.

"No. Were you trying to?"

She laughed. "No. Not really. I just don't want things to be awkward between us."

"They're not."

"Good." She moved a little closer, then looked up at him. "Because the other night was really fun."

One eyebrow raised. "I thought so, too. Want to do it again sometime?"

Sex with a man who definitely wasn't staying? All the fun with none of that commitment? She'd never been that kind of girl. Maybe it was time for that to change.

She smiled. "I think I would."

CHAPTER SIX

DAKOTA COULDN'T REMEMBER the last time she'd been this cold. Although the calendar claimed it was mid-spring, a cold front had blown through, dropping the temperature nearly twenty degrees and depositing over a foot of snow in the mountains.

She pulled her coat tighter and wished she'd thought to wear gloves. Unfortunately, she'd already packed away most of her winter clothes and had had to make do with layering. The thick blanket of clouds weren't helping, she thought, staring at the pale gray sky.

She heard someone call her name and turned. Montana waved as she hurried down the street, looking warm and comfy in a thick down jacket. A colorful knitted cap covered her head, and she had on matching mittens.

"You look cold," her sister said as she approached. "Why aren't you in something warmer?"

"I packed it all away."

Montana grinned. "Sometimes it pays to procrastinate."

"Apparently."

"It's supposed to warm up in a few days."

"Lucky me."

Montana moved close and linked arms. "We'll share body heat." She pointed to the lake. "What's going on?"

"We're filming a date."

"Outside? They're making contestants be outside on water when it's three degrees above freezing?"

"Somebody didn't look at the weather report. Worse, it's one of the older couples. They're supposed to be having a romantic picnic lunch. Last I heard, the sound guy is complaining he can't understand anything. Between the wind howling and their teeth chattering, there's not much conversation."

Montana studied the small boat in the middle of the black, choppy water. "TV isn't anything like I thought. It's not very interesting. Or romantic."

"Taping segments takes a long time. I won't miss this when they're gone."

"I can see why." Montana frowned. "There's no music. Do they add that later?"

"Probably." Dakota shivered. "The next few dates are out of town. Stephen and Aurelia are going to Las Vegas, then Sasha and Lani were supposed to go to San Diego, but Geoff freaked about the price of rooms, so they might be staying here."

Temperatures in both places were supposed to be well into the seventies. She was hoping for San Diego for sure.

"Those are the twin boys, right?" Montana asked. "They're gorgeous."

"A little young for you," Dakota said dryly.

"Oh, I know. I wouldn't be interested. I'm just saying, they're very nice to look at."

Dakota laughed. "Looking is allowed. Just don't let Finn catch you. He's still determined to get his brothers back home."

"How's the plan going?"

"Not very well, but not for lack of trying on his part."

Finn was determined. He was a lot of other things she really liked, but she wasn't going to share those with Montana. The last thing she needed was her sisters speculating about her personal life. While the attention would be well-meant, it would still be more than she could handle.

"So he's sticking around?" Montana asked.

"I suspect to the bitter end."

"Poor guy." Montana glanced to her left, then nudged Dakota. "Is that him?"

Dakota turned and saw Finn walking toward them. He wore a leather jacket. His head and hands were bare, but he didn't look the least bit cold. Probably because, compared to a brisk South Salmon spring, these temperatures were practically balmy.

"That's him," she said. "Don't embarrass me."

Montana freed her arm. "When have I ever done that?"

"We don't have enough time for me to start the list."

Montana started to say something, but mercifully stopped before Finn got close enough to hear.

"Whose fool idea was this?" he asked. "It's too cold for them to be out on the lake. Does anyone plan ahead?"

Dakota did her best not to smile. "Finn, this is my sister Montana. Montana, this is Finn. His two brothers are on the show."

Finn glanced at them both. "Sorry. I was distracted." He held out his hand to Montana. "Nice to meet you."

"Nice to meet you, too," Montana said. "It doesn't sound like you're having a good time."

"Is it that obvious?" He shook his head. "Never mind. I don't think I want you to answer that." He glanced between them, paused, then looked more thoroughly. "You really are identical, aren't you?"

Dakota laughed. "Because we'd lie about it?"

"Good point," Finn said. "My brothers are identical twins," he told Montana. "They've always said they have a relationship I can't understand. Are they telling the truth?"

"Sorry," Montana told him. "But they are. It's a weird thing to be identical to someone else. You kind of always know what they're thinking. I can't imagine life any other way, but I've been told it's not like that for other people."

"I figured you'd say that," he admitted. "Dakota said the same thing."

"But you didn't want to believe me?" Dakota asked, not sure if she should be annoyed or not.

Finn looked at her. "I believed you. I just wanted you to be wrong."

"At least he's honest," Montana said. "The last honest man."

"Don't say that," Finn told her. "I couldn't stand the pressure." He looked at Dakota. "I hear we're going to Las Vegas tomorrow."

"Have you ever been?" she asked. Las Vegas didn't strike her as a Finn kind of town.

"No. It's not my thing. I'm sure Stephen will love it, though." He sighed. "Damn show."

"You'll get it figured out," she told him.

"Want to tell me when so I have something to look forward to?"

"I wish I knew."

He turned to Montana. "It was nice to meet you."

"Nice to meet you, too."

Finn waved, then turned and walked away.

Dakota watched him go. She enjoyed the way he moved, his easy confidence. While she felt badly that he was worried about his brothers, there was a part of her that was looking forward to being with him in Las Vegas. She'd been there a couple of times with girlfriends, and it had been fun. She could only imagine what that town would be like with a man like Finn.

"Interesting," Montana said. "Very, very interesting. How was the sex?"

Dakota nearly choked. "Excuse me? What kind of question is that?"

"An obvious one. Don't try to pretend nothing happened. I know you. You and Finn have had sex. I'm not asking for a lot of details, I just want to know how he was. Hardly an unreasonable request. It's not like I'm getting any. Living vicariously through one's sisters is a time-honored tradition."

"I, ah…" Dakota swallowed. She knew better than to try to

fake her way out of telling the truth. With someone else she might have a prayer, but not with one of her sisters.

"Fine. Yes, I was with Finn. It was great." She smiled. "It was better than great."

"Are you going to do it again?" Montana asked.

"The possibility is on the table. I'd like to."

Montana studied her. "Is it serious?"

"No. Even if I was tempted, it can't be. Finn isn't staying. He practically lives on another planet and my life is here. Besides, neither of us is looking for anything significant or long-lasting. So we'll be fine."

"I hope you're right," her sister told her. "Because sometimes when things are going really well, we find the one thing we're pretending we're not looking for."

"WHAT DO YOU mean the shipment came in early? All three hundred and eighty boxes? Are you telling me there are three hundred and eighty boxes sitting in our warehouse?" Finn asked.

"Not boxes," his partner Bill said. "Crates. Goddamn crates. What is he building? An ark?"

This wasn't happening, Finn told himself. It couldn't be happening. Not now. Not while he was stuck here.

The air charter company survived on contracts. That's where the main money came from. The one-time deliveries were great, but the annual contracts paid the bills.

One of their largest customers had decided to build a boat. By hand. He'd ordered it from God knows where and had arranged to have the pieces delivered to South Salmon. Now they had to be airlifted to his property three hundred miles north of town.

When Finn had first heard about the project, he'd figured they were talking a half dozen boxes at most. Apparently, he'd been wrong.

"The weight's listed on the side of each crate," Bill said. "We're talking three to four crates per trip, at best. You want to do the math?"

Finn swore. One hundred trips? "It's not possible," he said, more to himself than to Bill. "We have other customers."

"He's willing to pay," Bill said. "Finn, we can't lose this guy. He keeps us going all winter."

His partner was right. The majority of their work came between April and October. But a hundred trips?

"I've already put the word out," Bill told him. "We've got the planes. I've shifted around the schedule. What we need is pilots. You have to come back."

Finn stared at the Southwest Airlines plane at the gate. The flight was already boarding. Stephen and the cougar were going to Las Vegas, and he had to be there to make sure everything was going to be okay. He didn't trust that woman, or Geoff or anyone associated with the show. Excluding Dakota. Like him, she was doing what she had to.

"I can't," he said. "Sasha and Stephen need me."

"That's bullshit. They're twenty-one. They'll be fine on their own. This is where you belong, Finn. Get your ass back here."

He'd been responsible for his brothers for the past eight years. There was no way he could walk away now.

"Who have you called? Did you try Spencer? He's a good pilot and is usually available this time of year."

There was a long silence before Bill spoke again. "So that's your answer? Hire someone else?"

Finn turned his back on the other passengers and lowered his voice. "How many times have you needed me to cover for you? Before you got married, how many times did you have a hot date down in Anchorage or want to go trolling for lonely tourists in Juneau? I've always said yes to whatever you asked me to do. Now I'm asking you to give me a break. I'll be back when I can. Until then you have to handle it."

"All right," Bill said, sounding pissed. "But you'd better get back here pretty quick. Or there's going to be a problem."

"I will," Finn said, wondering if he was telling the truth.

He closed his phone and shoved it in his pocket, then joined the line of passengers waiting to board. Guilt battled with annoyance. To make matters worse, he was flying commercial. He hated flying commercial. He hated flying when he wasn't in charge. But the tickets to Vegas had been cheaper than renting a plane, and Geoff was trying to save money.

Finn stalked onto the plane and shoved his small duffel into the first overhead compartment.

"Sir, you might want to take that with you," the flight attendant said. "That way it will be closer to where you're sitting."

"Fine," Finn growled between gritted teeth.

He grabbed the duffel and continued down the aisle. When he spotted Dakota with an empty seat next to her, he stopped. Of course there was no room for his carry-on here. Cursing under his breath, he stepped over her, dropped into the middle seat, and shoved his duffel into the space where his feet should go.

"Tell me this isn't a five-hour flight," he grumbled.

"Aren't you perky this morning." Dakota turned to him. "What has you all grumpy?"

He leaned back in his seat and closed his eyes. "Is grumpy the technical term? Are you asking me as a psychologist?"

"Do you want me to?"

"Maybe we could just skip the talk therapy and go directly to electric shock treatment." A few thousand volts of electricity coursing through his body would put everything else in perspective, he thought.

Dakota touched his arm with her hand. "Seriously? It's that bad? You're not blowing things just a little out of proportion?"

"Let's see. I just talked to my business partner. We have an unexpected delivery of nearly four hundred crates that have to be flown several hundred miles. We can get maybe four crates on each plane. I should be there helping. Instead I'm stuck on a plane I'm not piloting, going to Las Vegas. Why, you ask? Because my brothers decided to leave college in their last semester. Even as we speak, Sasha is planning to destroy his life by moving to Hollywood. And Stephen is about to be devoured by a cougar." He turned to her. "You tell me. Am I blowing things out of proportion?"

Her mouth twitched a little.

He narrowed his gaze. "This isn't funny."

"It's a little funny. If you weren't you, you would think it was funny."

He leaned back in his seat. "Go away."

"I'm sorry," she told him. "I'll take this more seriously, I promise. I really can't help with your business problem. Although the good news is, you have a lot of new business. Is your partner going to hire another pilot?"

"He has to. He'll probably charge me for it. I'd do it to him."

"You could go home. You don't really have to be here."

"I do. Someone has to look out for them." He hesitated, then glanced around to make sure no one was listening.

"Years ago, when our parents died, it was a mess. There was a plane crash and the media got involved. Reporters crawled all over town, we were the hot story of the week, at least up in Alaska. Some even sent money to help us out."

Dakota stared at him. "I have a feeling you hated that."

"I did. I knew it was a temporary thing, but that's not what Sasha got from it. He wants to be famous because he believes being cared for by the world at large will keep him safe. Sure, he's twenty-one, but that thirteen-year-old kid who lost his folks has never gone away."

He leaned back in his seat. "Stephen is going along with this. I'm guessing it's to make sure Sasha is okay. I know they're technically adults. But they lived in a small town until they went to college. They don't know about this world. They're too trusting and don't know enough to protect themselves. I have to be there for them."

"I'm sorry," she said, putting her hand on his. "I didn't know."

He shrugged. "I have to let them go. I'm good with that. But not like this. Not when they're dealing with men like Geoff."

"Agreed. But you do realize that at some point you have to

let go. At some point you have to trust them to make their own decisions."

"Maybe you're right. But not today." He looked around. "Have you seen her?"

"Who?"

"The cougar out to destroy my brother. The one you said was going to get pregnant to trap him." He wanted to think she would miss the flight, but his luck wasn't that good.

Dakota's eyes widened. At the same time, Finn heard something very much like a whimper coming from in front of them.

Dakota cleared her throat. "Ah, yes. Aurelia is on the plane. In fact, she's sitting in the row in front of us. Had you been paying attention, you would have noticed." She jabbed him in the side. "And I never said she was going to get pregnant. Oh, look." She pointed. "There's your brother. He's going to sit next to her." Dakota turned to him. "Perhaps he can explain why you're such an idiot."

Finn almost regretted what he said. Almost. He was sure that under normal circumstances Aurelia was a perfectly decent human being. But he couldn't trust a woman who had gone on a reality show to find a man. Who did that? She was too old for Stephen. He was going to do everything in his power to keep them apart.

He glanced out the window. "When does the flight leave?"

"I swear, if you plan to spend the entire hour flight asking, 'Are we there yet?' I'm going to drop something heavy on your groin."

Despite everything going on and his growing level of frustration, Finn laughed. "Okay, you win. I'll behave."

"Can I get that in writing?" she asked.

"Sure."

She settled back in her seat and took his hand in hers. "You are so lying."

"Maybe not."

"I'll believe it when I see it. So tell me, what would you be doing if you were back in Alaska? Flying?"

"Probably."

"You're on a plane now. That's practically the same thing."

He laced his fingers with hers. "It's not the same thing. When you're the pilot, you're in charge."

"We could ask the flight attendant if you can have a pair of those little wings they give kids. You could pin them on your shirt. That might make you feel better."

"You think you're pretty funny, don't you?"

"I *am* pretty funny."

"I'll give you pretty, but that's as far as I'm going."

She smiled. "I can live with that."

AURELIA HAD NEVER been to Las Vegas before. She'd seen it on TV and in the movies, but she found that real life was much, much better. The short plane ride had passed painfully slowly, as she'd desperately wished to disappear into her seat. Finn's cruel assumptions about her and why she was on the show had made her feel horrible. She'd spent most of the trip berating herself for not standing up to her mother more. Because if she had something close to a spine, she wouldn't be in this situation.

Now they'd arrived at the huge airport in Las Vegas, she was determined to shake off her bad feelings and simply enjoy the experience. She might never come back, and she had a feeling she would want these memories later.

Stephen stood next to her as they waited for their luggage. Geoff had said to pack for an evening on the town. That was tomorrow. This afternoon's agenda was supposed to be a lot of quick shots of them in the casino and around town.

As the luggage carousel started, she caught sight of Finn and Dakota walking toward the taxi stand. As they weren't going to be on television, they'd been able to pack light and only needed carry-on bags. Aurelia had been forced to borrow a couple of fancy dresses from women at the office, with the idea that at least one of them should be okay for their dressy evening.

As she watched, Finn put his hand on the small of Dakota's back. It was a simple, polite gesture, but one that made Aurelia long for a man in her life. Someone who would be there for her, just like she wanted to be there for him. Someone who would care.

"Point out your bag and I'll grab it," Stephen told her.

She nodded.

He was sweet, she thought wistfully. But too young. That's what she wanted to tell Finn—that she'd already come to terms with the fact that she and his brother could only be friends. But she was afraid if she told Stephen, he would act different and Geoff would notice. Aurelia didn't want to be voted off the show too soon. The longer she stayed, the more she didn't have to deal with her mother. Oddly enough, the more she was around Stephen, the stronger she felt.

She saw her bag, and Stephen lifted it off the carousel. He had his. Karen, one of the production assistants, ushered them toward a limo. The camera guy was already waiting for them.

"Don't look so scared," Stephen said, leaning toward her and speaking softly. "They're going to think you don't want to be with me."

"That's not true," she said, doing her best not to remember Finn's outrageous claim she would trap his brother by getting pregnant.

"Because I'm exactly who you've been waiting for all your life?" he asked, his voice teasing.

She smiled. "I've always had a desperate longing for someone who could tell me the difference between Hilary Duff and Lindsay Lohan."

He winked. "I knew it."

They were still looking at each other as they got into the limo.

She'd never been good at talking to men, let alone flirting, but Stephen made it easy. Maybe because she knew she was safe with him. He was…nice. Probably not a word to excite him, but for her, it was plenty.

They left the airport and drove toward the Strip. She could see all the hotels rising toward the sky, their various heights and shapes standing out against the sand-colored mountains. As they got closer, she made out the different structures. The big, black pyramid at the Luxor, the Eiffel Tower in front of the Paris Hotel and the vast expanse that was Caesars Palace.

"Do you know where we're staying?" she asked.

"There."

Stephen pointed to the right. As they rounded the curve in the road, Aurelia saw the tall towers of the Venetian Hotel. The limo pulled into the covered entry and their door was opened.

She was vaguely aware that the cameras were filming everything, but she couldn't seem to pay attention to them. Not when there was so much to see.

They stepped into a massive lobby with a painted ceiling. Every inch was beautiful—from the huge sprays of flowers to the gilded posts. Even the carpets were gorgeous.

There were people everywhere. She could hear a dozen different languages flowing around her, and the air was lightly scented with a slightly citrus fragrance.

"You're already checked in," Geoff told her, and handed over her keys. "Your rooms are next door to each other. If you decide to do anything interesting, call one of us. We want to be there."

Aurelia felt her eyes bug out. Call him? What? If any of the contestants decided to have sex, he wanted it on film?

"I can't really see that happening," she murmured.

Geoff sighed. "Tell me about it. Still, if you get drunk enough, we all might get lucky."

With that, he walked off.

Aurelia stood in the center of the lobby. The crowd moved around her, as if she wasn't there. Hardly a surprise. She'd spent most of her life being invisible.

"Ready to go to the rooms?" Stephen asked, joining her. "Geoff said we're already checked in."

She held up her key.

He glanced at the number. "We're next to each other. That's great. We can send coded messages through the wall."

She stared into his blue eyes and told herself it was enough that Stephen was nice. Going through this with a guy who was a jerk would have been unbearable.

"Do you know any codes?" she asked.

"No, but we could learn one. Or make one up. You're good with numbers, right?"

She smiled. "I'll work on it."

They made their way to the room elevators. Thankfully, the camera guy took a different elevator, leaving them alone for a few minutes.

Once they reached their floor, they made their way to their rooms. They were actually across from each other, rather than next door, but still close enough. A different camera guy was already waiting for them.

"Who do you want to go in with?" she asked.

He shrugged. "Your room. Stephen, go with her."

Like they were sharing a room? She blushed at the thought, then shoved her key into the lock and opened the door.

Aurelia hadn't traveled much and rarely stayed in a hotel. Still, she knew what a regular room looked like, and this wasn't it.

To her right was a beautiful bathroom done in marble and glass. There was a stall shower and a big tub, double sinks, a vanity and plenty of mirrors. It was like a movie set or something out of a fairy tale. Past the bathroom was the bedroom. Except it was more than a bedroom. There was a king-size bed with beautiful linens and big nightstands. Beyond that, three steps led to a sunken living room. Floor-to-ceiling windows offered her a view of the pirate boat floating in front of Treasure Island.

She turned in a slow circle, taking in the room again, then

looked at Stephen. "I don't understand," she said. "This can't be my room. It's so beautiful." She laughed. "Tell me we never have to leave."

"If we win big downstairs, we can stay as long as you like," he told her.

Aurelia smiled. "I'd like that."

They agreed to meet in half an hour and go down to the casino. Aurelia used her time to put her brown hair into hot rollers and pray that it came out okay. She changed into white jeans and a turquoise-colored silk blouse she'd bought on sale nearly a year ago.

She normally didn't spend much money on her casual wardrobe. All of her clothing budget was spent on work clothes, and everything she didn't spend on her own living expenses either went to her mother or her small savings account. But the shirt had been so beautiful, she'd been unable to resist it.

After spreading out her newly purchased cosmetics on the marble counter, she carefully applied moisturizer, then concealer. The powder foundation went on as easily as the girl at the makeup counter had promised. She kept her eye shadow simple by brushing on a light taupe color. After mascara, she applied blush, then lip gloss. The last step was pulling out the hot rollers and finger combing her hair. She bent at the waist and doused herself in hairspray. As she stood, she flipped her head back and surveyed the look.

In a bathroom full of mirrors, there was no escaping reality. But this time it wasn't so bad. Aurelia looked at herself from several angles. She would never be stunning, but for once in her life she was pretty. At least she felt pretty, and that might be enough.

She'd barely slipped into her shoes when Stephen knocked on her door. She picked up her purse and went to meet him.

"Hi," she said, hoping she didn't sound as breathless as she felt.

"Hi, yourself," he began, then stopped and stared at her. "Wow, you look great."

"Thanks."

She was aware of the man and the camera just beyond Stephen's shoulder. For a moment she wished it could just be the two of them. That even a small part of their time together could be real. But it wasn't. She had to keep reminding herself of that.

"What do you want to do first?" Stephen asked. "Slots, blackjack, or do you prefer roulette?"

"I've never gambled," she admitted. "What do you suggest?"

As they spoke they walked toward the elevators. Stephen pushed the button for them to go down. The doors opened immediately. As they stepped onto the elevator, she felt him put his hand on the small of her back.

It was nothing, she told herself. Men did that sort of thing all the time. She'd just noticed Finn doing it to Dakota. But she couldn't help being aware of how he touched her. The silk of her shirt seemed to intensify the heat from his hand. As the elevator started down, she felt a little light-headed and told herself it was from the vertical movement and nothing else.

They walked out of the elevator and into the craziness. It was fun and bright and loud. Aurelia didn't know where to look first.

"Are you hungry?" Stephen asked, pointing to the Grand Lux Café.

"Maybe later," she said. Right now she was too excited to eat. There was too much to see.

An older couple walked past them. "Don't you love seeing a family traveling together, George?" the woman asked. "She brought her baby brother to Las Vegas. Isn't that nice?"

Aurelia stepped away from Stephen. She didn't know if he'd heard the comment or not. The camera guy had his lens trained on the old people, so she knew that moment was going to make the show.

She started walking, not sure where she was going. Humiliation heated her cheeks and stole the pleasure she felt at being here. She thought about running after the couple and telling them what was going on, but what was the point?

Stephen kept pace with her. "You okay?" he asked.

His obvious confusion told her he hadn't heard their words, at least not yet. Reminding herself they were just friends didn't make her feel any better.

She stopped in the center of the casino and faced him. He was so nice, she thought. A good guy. But there was no way...

"Excuse me. What are you doing?"

Aurelia and Stephen turned toward the well-muscled man in the dark suit. The name badge said that he was with security. His expression told them he was very serious about his job.

He pointed to the camera guy. "You can't film here."

"We're doing a reality show," Stephen said. "Didn't the production company clear this with you?"

"No." The man from security moved toward the camera. "Turn that off now or I will turn it off for you."

"I'll get Geoff," the camera guy said as he turned and practically ran away.

"Is he coming back or do I have to chase him down?"

Aurelia wasn't sure if the security man was talking to them or not. Apparently, it didn't matter. He pulled a walkie-talkie out of his jacket pocket and spoke into it. She had a feeling that this wasn't going to end well.

"We'll go," she said taking Stephen's hand in hers.

Stephen glanced at the security guy's annoyed face and nodded. "I don't think either of us would like jail."

They turned.

For a second, Aurelia wondered if they would be allowed to simply walk away. But nothing happened as they dashed up an escalator. As the stairs carried them to another floor, she was able to draw in a deep breath.

"You okay? I thought you were going to faint," Stephen told her.

"I was terrified," she admitted. "I can't believe Geoff brought us all here without making arrangements with the hotel. It's not a surprise they don't want us filming. They don't know what we're going do with it. It could be a scam. Or a trick to cheat or something."

She had more to say but suddenly couldn't speak. Stephen was riding on the step behind her. Without warning, he rested one hand on her hip as he leaned toward her.

Aurelia did her best to act casual. Shrieking in surprise wasn't very appropriate. Besides, she'd taken his hand in hers to pull him away from the security guy—although that had been different. She couldn't explain why, but knew it was.

When they reached the top of the escalator, they stepped off. She planned to continue her analysis of what it all meant, only she couldn't. Not when it seemed as if they'd entered another world.

Above them, the ceiling was painted sky blue with clouds that almost appeared to float by. They were in the hotel, but she felt like they really could be outside. There were stores and restaurants and...

"Look," she breathed, pointing to the narrow boats floating on a man-made canal. "Gondolas."

"Want to ride?" he asked, then urged her forward. "Come on. It'll be fun."

There wasn't much of a line, so in a matter of minutes, she was carefully stepping into the gondola. It wobbled on the water, but she managed to sit down without falling. Stephen sat next to her.

There wasn't a lot of room, so he was close. Close enough for her to feel the softness of his long-sleeved shirt against her hand and the pressure of his thigh against hers.

"Ever done anything like this before?" he asked as he looked around. "No."

Never. Not even in her dreams.

They took the leisurely boat ride through a winding course. People walking by stopped to wave. Music echoed off the ceiling and reverberated all around them. She caught sight of stores whose names she'd only seen in magazines. Everything about the moment was perfect.

Then Stephen put his arm around her and it all got better.

When they rounded a corner, a man was waiting with a camera. He told them to smile, then snapped their picture. Once the ride was over, they went to check on the digital image displayed on a computer screen.

"You're beautiful," Stephen told her.

Aurelia knew he was being kind, but she was pleased with how the photo had turned out. They were both looking at the camera, with genuine smiles. She noticed they were leaning into each other and looked very much like a couple. If one ignored the age difference.

"We'll take two," he said, then paid for them.

"I should buy them."

"Why?"

Because she made more than him. Because he was still in college and this wasn't a date. But she didn't want to say any of that, so instead she simply said, "Thank you," when he handed her the thin bag containing the pictures in a paper frame.

"Hungry?" Stephen asked, pointing to one of the outdoor restaurants.

"Yes."

"Good. Me, too."

It was midafternoon, and there wasn't much of a crowd. They were seated immediately at a small corner table next to a plant. Despite being in the open, the space felt private. Intimate.

The server gave them menus. Even though she was hungry, Aurelia couldn't imagine eating. She chose a salad and iced tea. Stephen ordered a pizza and soda.

"You know why I decided to do the show," she said. "Why did you?"

He picked up his fork and turned it over in his hands. "A lot of reasons. I wanted to get out of South Salmon and this was a good way."

"A good way? You left college in your last semester. How is that smart?"

Stephan rolled his eyes but Aurelia persisted.

"Getting an education can't hurt. What are you going to do when the show is over?"

Stephen put down the fork and leaned toward her. "I don't want to fly."

"I don't understand. You want to drive back to Alaska?"

He laughed. "No. I mean I don't want to be a pilot, like my brother. I don't want to go into the family business."

"Oh." She knew all about family expectations. Despite the fact that she was nearly thirty, she had never once been able to please her mother. "Is that what Finn wants? He expects you to go into the family business?"

"It's implied."

"Have you told him how you feel?"

"No. He doesn't care about that."

Aurelia shook her head. "You're talking about a man who flew a thousand miles to make sure you and your brother were okay. I think he cares a lot about you."

"That's different. He wants me home so he can control me. If I were to tell him that I wanted to be an engineer, he'd fly me up to ten thousand feet and kick me out of the airplane."

"Now you're talking like a kid."

"Hey!" He straightened. "Where do you get off saying that?"

"Look at your actions. You're not willing to sit down and talk to Finn. Instead, you ran off. How is that mature?"

"You're supposed to be on my side."

"I'm a disinterested third party." Disinterested probably wasn't the right word. Embarrassingly enough, she found herself more than a little interested in Stephen. Why couldn't he have been thirty instead of twenty? Life was nothing if not karmically cruel.

"Besides," she continued. "If you're one semester away from graduation, he already knows your major."

"The major isn't important as long as I come back home." He shook his head. "When our folks died, things were bad. Finn took care of us. Now he can't let that go. He thinks we're still the little kids who needed him."

"You should talk to him," she said. "Why wouldn't he be happy that you wanted to be an engineer? It's a good, solid job."

"I've known him all my life, Aurelia. You're going to have to trust me on this. Finn would never approve."

She wanted to argue but didn't. After all, there were plenty of people who would tell her to simply stand up to her mother. From the outside it seemed so easy. But from the inside, everything was different. She couldn't seem to survive the waves of guilt every time she tried. It was as if her mother had been given an instruction manual on how to manipulate her and had memorized every page.

Stephen had been one of the few people to accept her limitations. "I do trust you," she said.

In the square, someone called their names. She and Stephen turned toward the sound of several people running. One of the production assistants hurried up to them.

"There you are," Karen said, sounding breathless. "We've been looking everywhere. Geoff is furious. We're all packing up and going home. You have to come right now."

Aurelia looked at Stephen, who shrugged. "I guess we'll get something to eat at the airport," he said.

"Hurry," the production assistant said. "We have to get to the airport. Geoff is furious that there wasn't a date."

Aurelia and Stephen walked out of the restaurant. As they followed the production assistant to the elevators, he leaned close.

"Geoff was wrong," he whispered in her ear. "There was a date and I had a great time."

Deep inside of her, she felt her heart give a little tug. "Me, too," she whispered back.

He smiled at her and took her hand in his.

CHAPTER SEVEN

DAKOTA OPENED HER front door to find Finn standing on her porch. It was a little after seven in the evening. She and Finn had managed to catch the four-thirty flight out of Las Vegas, which meant she hadn't even been home an hour.

"I know, I know," he said, shuffling his feet. "You have stuff to do. I shouldn't bother you."

"Yet here you are," she said with a smile. "It's okay. I didn't have any hot plans."

She wasn't sorry to see him. As for hot plans, he certainly qualified.

He stepped inside and handed her a bottle of wine. "I come bearing gifts, if that counts."

"It does."

"I'm spending so much time at the wine store, the guy there wants to know if he and I are planning to run off together."

She laughed. "You know he was kidding, right?"

"I hoped he was. People don't joke like that in South Salmon."

"Then people in South Salmon need to work on their sense of humor." She led the way into the kitchen and set the wine on the counter. "Is wine enough or do you want something to eat, as well?"

"You don't have to feed me," he told her.

"That wasn't the question." She walked to the refrigerator and pulled it open. There were salad fixings, some yogurt and a few raw almonds in a bowl. Not exactly man food.

She turned to him. "I'm going to have to take back my offer of food. I don't have anything you'd like. Want to order a pizza?"

He'd already opened the drawer where she kept the corkscrew. "Pizza sounds good. I'll even let you put something healthy on your half."

"You'll let me? How magnanimous."

He shrugged. "I'm just that kind of guy."

"Lucky me."

She ordered pizza, then they took their wine into the living room and sat down. She ignored the fact that she liked having Finn in her house. That was a road without a happy ending. Instead, she focused on why he'd shown up.

"There wasn't a date," she said. "So Stephen and Aurelia are in danger of being voted off. It doesn't make you happy?"

"Yes, as long as he goes back to college."

"You can't follow him around for the rest of his life. At some point you have to let him be an adult."

"When he acts like an adult, I'll treat him like one. Until then, he's just a kid."

Dakota leaned back in her chair and studied him over her glass. He still wasn't getting it. How his brothers acted had everything to do with how they had been raised and nothing to do with his presence in town. Whether he stayed or left, the twins' actions would be the same. But how to get him to believe that?

"Except for them going back to college without you dragging them, is there a win in this?" she asked.

"I don't know," he admitted. "I guess there has to be. What if they never go back to college? I need to know they're okay and that no one is taking advantage of them." He picked up his glass. "Something I don't want to think about. Let's change the subject. Are you sorry we left Las Vegas early?"

"I won't cry myself to sleep tonight, if that's what you're asking. But it would have been fun to stay. There's plenty to do. I heard there was great shopping at the hotel."

"You like shopping?"

She laughed. "I am a girl. It's practically genetic. You, on the other hand, buy the same shirt over and over again. And your socks come in a package of ten or twelve."

"It's easier that way," he said. "And what do you have against my shirts?" He glanced down at the light blue cotton shirt he wore. "I'm not wearing plaid. You should appreciate that."

"Oh, I do. I don't have anything against your shirt. I think you look nice."

"You're just saying that." He sighed dramatically. "Now you've hurt my feelings. I don't think I can talk about this anymore. It's just so hard when a man tries to look special and no one notices."

She put down her wine glass so she wouldn't spill it. Even as she tried not to laugh, she found herself chuckling. The teasing side of Finn was very appealing.

"Do you want me to say you're pretty?" she asked.

"If you mean it," he said primly. "Otherwise you're just messing with my feelings."

She stood and walked around the coffee table. After taking his wine and setting it down, she tugged him to his feet. She held both his hands in hers and stared into his eyes.

"I really, really like your shirt."

"I bet you say that to all the guys."

"No. Only to you."

She expected him to keep up with the game. Instead he drew her close and lowered his mouth to hers.

There was nothing playful about the kiss. He claimed her with an intensity that took her breath away. There was hunger in his touch, a need that echoed her own sudden, powerful passion. She wrapped her arms around him and gave herself over to the pleasure of feeling his body against hers.

He was strong and solid and powerful, she thought hazily.

Everything she needed from a man. When he tightened his hold, she parted her lips and welcomed him inside.

Want filled her. Her breasts swelled in anticipation of his touch. Her belly throbbed in an ancient rhythm that made her want to squirm to get closer. When he started backing her toward the sofa, she went willingly.

Her legs had barely bumped against the cushions when she heard something in the background. An insistent knocking.

"The pizza guy," she mumbled against Finn's mouth.

"Let him get his own girl."

She laughed. "I have to pay him."

Finn straightened. "I'll get it."

He released her and walked toward the front door.

When his back was turned, she hurried out of the living room and down the short hall to her bedroom. Seconds later, she was barefoot, and the small lamp by her bed was on. Finn appeared in the doorway.

"Is this your way of telling me you're not all that hungry?" he asked.

She tilted her head. "I am. Just not for pizza."

His slow, sexy smile made her toes curl.

"You're my kind of girl," he told her as he crossed to her.

"I'll bet you say that to all the women."

"Only you," he whispered, right before he kissed her.

"CHARLIE IS BLOND TO THE BONE," Montana said. "He's the sweetest guy, but I worry he's not bright enough to get into the program."

"When will you know for sure?" Dakota asked.

"Max will have a pretty good idea when Charlie is about six months old. Until then, I'll teach him the basics and we'll see how that goes." Montana rolled onto her side and rubbed Charlie's belly. "But you love everybody, don't you, big guy?"

The big guy in question was a three-month-old yellow Lab

puppy. Charlie had feet the size of softballs. He was not going to be petite by anyone's definition.

"What happens to him if he doesn't make it into the program?" Nevada asked.

"He's given up for adoption. Max's dogs are bred to be family friendly, so there's always a waiting list. Charlie will find a good home. I'd just hate to see him go. He would have been the first dog I trained from birth. Well, six weeks. They can't do much when their eyes are still closed."

The three sisters lay stretched out on blankets in Montana's backyard. It was a warm Saturday afternoon. Un-seasonable for this time of year and they were going to be back in the fifties tomorrow. Two other dogs played in the yard. An apricot-colored toy poodle named Cece and a labradoodle named Buddy sniffed in the grass and chased butterflies.

"I don't get the poodle," Nevada said. "Isn't she kind of small?"

"Cece is very well trained," Montana told her. "She works with really sick kids. Because she's so small, she can sit on their beds. A lot of times the kids aren't even strong enough to pet her. She sits close or curls up next to them. Having her there makes them feel better. Being a poodle, she doesn't shed like other dogs. She gets bathed before going to the hospital and carried in so she doesn't pick up germs on her feet. That means she can go into some of the special wards."

Dakota sat up. "Is that what you do with your day? Take dogs to visit sick children?"

"Sometimes. There are dogs that visit nursing homes. I take them there. And I spend part of the day training. The older dogs don't need much instruction, but the younger ones get regular reinforcement. The puppies take a lot of time. And I'm working on the reading program."

When Montana had said she was going to start working with therapy dogs, Dakota hadn't realized how much was involved. "You're very dedicated to your work."

Montana rolled onto her back, supporting herself on her elbows. "I think I've found what I'm supposed to be doing. You two have known for a long time, which is great for you but left me feeling inadequate. I'll never get rich doing this, but that's okay. I love the dogs, I love working with people. When you're lonely, having someone love you is really important. Even if that someone is just a dog."

Nevada sat up. "Now I feel like a slacker. All I do is design things."

"Houses," Montana said. "Everyone needs somewhere to live."

"I don't design houses. I work on remodels or I tweak existing designs."

Dakota looked at her sister. Nevada had always wanted to be an engineer. Was she regretting that decision now? "Don't you like working for Ethan?"

"I don't dislike it. It's just…" Nevada drew her knees to her chest and wrapped her arms around her legs. "Do you know I've never applied for a job? Sure, I had part-time jobs in high school and college, but I mean a real job. Once I chose engineering, everyone assumed I'd go to work for Ethan. I graduated and showed up at his office the next day. I didn't have to prove myself."

"Just because it was nepotistic, doesn't mean you aren't doing a good job," Dakota told her. "Ethan wouldn't keep you around if he didn't want you working there."

Nevada shook her head. "You really think Mom would let him fire me?"

Montana pulled Charlie onto her lap. "She has a point. Ethan can't fire her."

"Do you want him to?" Dakota asked.

"No. I work hard for him. I know he's happy with my work, but that's not the point. I went to work in the family business. I never thought about doing anything else. I just want to know if I'm in the right place. Doing the right thing."

"Is this a triplet curse?" Montana asked. "For so long I didn't know what I was doing. Now I'm finally happy and you're confused?"

"There's no curse," Dakota told her.

"I've been thinking about this for a while," Nevada admitted. "The thing is, I don't want to leave Fool's Gold. I like it here. It's my home. But it's not like there are a lot of other opportunities. I'm not comfortable working for another contracting firm. I don't want to be in competition with Ethan."

"So what's the solution?" Dakota asked.

Nevada straightened her legs and picked at a blade of grass. "Have either of you heard about Janack Construction?"

Dakota frowned. "The name is familiar. Wasn't there a guy in school named Tucker Janack? He was friends with Ethan and Josh. They went to a cycling camp together, way back when. I can't recall all the details."

"I remember," Montana said. "Tucker's father is super rich. Didn't he send a helicopter to pick up Tucker?"

"Yes and yes," Nevada said. "They're one of the largest construction companies in the country. Apparently, Tucker's father liked what he saw when he visited here all those years ago. He bought a couple hundred acres north of town."

"How could he do that?" Dakota asked. "Isn't that Indian land? They can't buy that."

"Tucker's father is one sixteenth Máa-zib. That's all you need to be. Apparently Tucker's mom is also part Máa-zib."

Dakota wondered how her sister knew so much about the Janack family. "Did you meet them sometime we don't know about?"

"The parents? No, I've never met them."

"What are they going to build there?" Montana asked. "Isn't two hundred acres a lot of land?"

"I've heard it's going to be an exclusive resort," Nevada said. "Big hotel, spa, casino and a couple of golf courses. There's some serious money going into the project. They're going to hire a lot of people."

"So you'd go work for them?" Dakota asked.

"I haven't decided. I might apply and see what happens. At least then I could say I've been on a job interview."

Dakota wondered if there was more going on than Nevada wanted to tell them. Was she not getting along with Ethan? Or was the situation exactly what she said—a need to prove herself?

"I haven't heard anyone talking about this project," Montana said. "I guess if they're on Indian land, they don't need City Council approval. But you'd think they'd at least talk to the mayor."

"Maybe they have and Marsha simply hasn't mentioned it to anyone," Dakota said. "There's plenty going on right now, what with the reality show and all the men still pouring into town."

"When are you going to decide what to do?" Montana asked.

"Not for a while," Nevada admitted. "They're still in the design stage. That could take months or even a year. Once I know they're actually moving forward with work, I'll think about what I want to do." She shifted on the blanket. "Please don't say anything to Ethan. It's not that I don't like working with him. I just need to know that I could work somewhere else, too."

"I'm not going to say anything," Montana said. "I've been flaky for years. I totally understand the need to figure out what you want to do."

"I won't say anything, either," Dakota promised. "If you need someone to listen, if you just want to bounce ideas off me, I'm always available."

"I know that," Nevada told her. "Thanks."

"Has it occurred to any of you that none of us have been on a date in months?" Montana asked. "Maybe there *is* something to this stupid man shortage."

"I'm dating," Dakota said.

"No. You're having sex with Finn. That's not dating."

"Did I know this?" Nevada asked. "When did you start sleeping with Finn?"

Dakota briefly explained her recent encounters with the

twins' brother. "It's not serious," she said. "When he figures out that his brothers are more than capable of taking care of themselves, he'll go back to South Salmon. This isn't a long-term relationship. And technically, as Montana said, it's not really dating."

"Point taken," Nevada said with a grin. "So the question is, do you want a date or do you want to have sex?"

"Can't I have both?" Montana asked. "Do I have to pick?"

"Find the right guy and you can have both," Nevada told her.

"Is that what you want?" Dakota asked.

Nevada laughed. "I'll take the sex, at least for now. Love is too complicated."

"Sometimes sex is complicated, too," Montana reminded her.

Nevada shook her head. "I'm willing to take my chances." She looked at Dakota. "What about you? Is sex enough?"

There were things they didn't know, Dakota thought. How she couldn't have children and how knowing that had changed everything. She would tell them eventually, just not today. Not when they were having fun, enjoying such a beautiful day.

So she smiled at her sisters and said, "Is sex with Finn enough? Absolutely."

FINN WAITED WITH SASHA in the lobby of the Gold Rush Ski Lodge and Resort. The place was nice enough, he thought. If one was into attractive tourist hotels. He would rather be home.

Once Geoff found out what carting everyone to San Diego would cost, especially for the beachfront hotel he preferred, he'd decided to keep Sasha and Lani in town.

The pool area of the Lodge had been transformed into a tacky tropical paradise, with fake palm trees, twinkle lights and tiki torches. Unfortunately, the weather was anything but tropical. While it didn't phase Finn, everyone else was running around wearing thick coats and shivering.

"What if I gave you ten thousand dollars?" he asked his brother. "To go home and finish college. Would you do it?"

Sasha grinned at him. "The show is paying twenty, bro."

"Fine. Thirty. Go back to school and you'll have a check that day." His business was successful, and he didn't have a lot of expenses. The house where he and his brothers had grown up was paid for.

"What did Stephen say when you offered it to him?" Sasha asked.

"To shove it up my ass."

Sasha's grin broadened. "He read my mind."

"I figured," Finn said glumly. "But I had to ask. What's the plan for today?"

"It's all going down tonight. We were going to have a city tour, but since we're pretending we're not in Fool's Gold, I don't see that happening."

Finn glanced around at the fake greenery. "This is a crazy business."

"I like it."

He thought about pointing out that Sasha's love of fame was tied to their parents' death, but he and his brother had had that conversation a dozen times before. He suspected Sasha had to go through the process himself and learn the truth the hard way.

That was the part Finn objected to. Not the learning, but the inevitable pain that would follow. If only he could be sure that his brothers were ready to be on their own, that he'd done all he could to keep them safe. Then he could walk away. But how to know?

"You should chill," Sasha told him. "You're wound too tight. Relax."

"You've been spending too much time with Hawaii girl."

His brother laughed. "I like Hawaii girl. She's fun."

Finn was sure Sasha liked Lani well enough but suspected their relationship was far more a means to an end than anything romantic. Sasha's idea of a steady relationship was a date that lasted two hours. On the other hand, Stephen had always preferred long-term relationships. Despite being identical twins, the brothers were fairly different.

"You should do something fun," Sasha told him. "Think of this as a vacation."

"Except it's not. I'll 'chill' or 'relax' or whatever you want when you and Stephen get back to Alaska and finish college."

Sasha sighed. "Sorry. No can do. I wish you could let it go."

Before Finn could say anything, one of the production assistants called for Sasha to get ready for a lighting check. His brother waved at him and followed the girl toward the hotel.

Finn checked his watch. He had a group of tourists to take on a flight in a couple of hours. They would be the second ones this week. The previous group had been a family, including a thirteen-year-old boy who'd been fascinated by the idea of flying a plane. Finn had talked to him about taking lessons.

"You're looking serious about something."

He glanced up and saw Dakota walking toward him. She carried a clipboard in her hands and stopped in front of him.

"For once, not the usual," he told her.

"Your brothers?"

"Work stuff."

"Everything okay back in South Salmon?"

"As far as I know."

She stood there, as if waiting for him to explain more.

"I was thinking about the tour I have later and the one I had a few days ago," he said slowly. "There was this kid. He was really into flying. Sometimes I think about opening a flight school, focusing on kids." He shrugged. "Who knows if it would work."

"Don't you have to be a certain age to get your pilot's license?"

"You can solo at sixteen, but training could start before that. Teaching a kid to fly gives him, or her, the ability to sense possibilities. You need math skills to do some of the calculations. There would have to be a way for them to raise money to pay for the lessons, or grants or something." He shook his head. "It's just something I play around with."

She tilted her head. "You should talk to Raoul. My boss. His whole thing is helping kids. His camp focused on bringing inner-city kids here to the mountains to get them out of their environment. He might have some ideas about how to get started."

"I will. Thanks." It beat worrying about the twins.

She gave him the contact information. "I'll let him know to expect your call."

He wondered if what he'd thought about doing was possible. There weren't a lot of inner-city kids in South Salmon. Of course, his cargo business was there.

But the thought of doing something a little different excited him. Cargo was paying the bills, but taking tours around was a lot more interesting. And doing something useful with kids appealed to him, as well. While he worried about his brothers, there was also a sense of satisfaction, of knowing he'd been the one to shape them into grown-ups. Of course, he had no idea yet if he'd done a decent job.

Dakota glanced around at the decorated pool area. "San Diego would have been a lot warmer. It's eighty there. I could have lain by the pool, ordered little drinks with umbrellas." She sighed.

"I thought you loved Fool's Gold," he teased.

"I do, but I love it more when it's warmer. It's spring. There should be plenty of heat." She shivered in her coat. "I had to dig out warmer clothes."

"It seems fine to me."

"You're from Alaska. Your opinion doesn't count."

He chuckled. "Come on. I'll buy you a cup of coffee."

"At Starbucks? A mocha latte would really help me feel better."

He took the hand that wasn't holding the clipboard. "You can even have whipped cream on it, if you want."

She leaned against him. "My hero."

CHAPTER EIGHT

A SHARP, INSISTENT ringing called Dakota out of a dream that involved a panda, a raft and ice cream. She rolled over in the bed and picked up the phone.

"Hello?"

"Dakota? It's Karen."

Dakota glanced toward the clock, wondering why the production assistant was calling her. "It's one in the morning."

"I know." Karen's voice was muffled, as if she were trying to be quiet. "I'm out by the pool at the lodge. There's a Tahitian dancing team here. Or maybe it's not a team. I don't know what they're called."

Dakota flopped back on the bed and closed her eyes. "I appreciate the news flash, but I'm really tired. I can catch the dancers tomorrow." Which was technically later today, she thought.

"I don't want you to see them. Sasha is here and so is Lani. I think she knows some of the dancers. Geoff's filming the whole thing."

"Then I can see it on the show broadcast. I'm sure Sasha and Lani are great dancers. Thanks for telling me, Karen."

"Don't hang up. I called to talk to Finn."

That got Dakota's attention. She sat straight up and clutched the phone tighter. "Why would you think he was with me?"

"Oh, please. Do you know how small Fool's Gold is? Everybody knows you're sleeping with him. Which isn't the point. I need to talk with him. I'm afraid this is gonna get out of hand. Sasha is dancing with Fire Poi."

Dakota wanted to go back to the "everybody knows you're sleeping with him" remark, but the words "Fire Poi" got her attention.

"Fire, as in flames?"

"They're lighting them right now. Geoff thinks it will be great for the show. I'm scared Sasha will get hurt."

Dakota was already getting out of bed. "Finn's at his hotel. Do you have his cell number?"

"No."

Dakota gave it to her. "Tell him I'll meet him at the hotel."

"I will. Hurry," Karen said.

There might have been more, but Dakota didn't bother to listen. She shoved the phone back on the base and turned on the light. Seconds later, she'd pulled on jeans and shoved her feet into athletic shoes. After grabbing her car keys and her cell phone, she was out the door and heading for her car.

DAKOTA DROVE AS FAST as she could up the mountain and pulled into the parking lot. A car jerked to a stop next to her, and Finn got out of his rental. He was already swearing.

"I'm going to kill him," he growled, taking off toward the back of the hotel, where the pool was located.

Dakota raced after him. "They're filming. Just so you know."

Finn scowled as he grabbed her hand. "Meaning Sasha will resist any attempts to help him." He swore under his breath. "I want to blame Geoff for this, but my brother is the real idiot." He looked at her. "They don't call it Fire Poi because it only looks like fire, do they?"

"Karen said there were actual flames."

Finn picked up the pace. By the time they got to the pool, he was almost at a dead run. She had no way to keep up with him and arrived a few seconds later, barely able to breathe.

Note to self, she thought as she gasped for air. In the morning, she was really going to have to consider some kind of exercise program.

Any other thoughts on the exercise issue disappeared the second she stepped onto the patio area by the pool. About a half dozen Tahitian dancers stood by the water. Two of the guys were spinning balls of fire at dizzying speed. Sasha held a single ball of fire, connected to a chain. As she watched in horror, he raised his arm level with his shoulder and began to turn the fire.

What should have been darkness was illuminated by the lights from the two cameras. All that was missing was an insistent jungle drumbeat. That, and someone who knew what he was doing.

Urged on by the other dancers and Lani, Sasha spun the chain faster and faster. The fire created eerie circles of light. Dakota thought of Geoff lurking by the bushes. If Finn got a hold of him, there would be hell to pay. Normally she didn't condone any kind of violence, but Geoff made it clear that all he cared about was the show. The fact that Sasha could be seriously hurt was of no interest to him.

Finn stalked toward the dancers. Dakota followed, not sure if she was going to interfere or not. While she strongly believed Finn should let his brothers live their own lives, this was different.

"What the hell are you doing?" Finn asked as he approached. "Do you want to get killed? Put that down."

Sasha turned toward his brother. It seemed as if, just for a moment, he forgot he was holding a chain with a ball of fire on the end. He stopped turning the chain and the ball swung toward the ground. The arc of movement swept perilously close to Sasha's side.

She wasn't the only one who noticed. Even as Finn dove toward his brother, Lani screamed and one of the dancers yelled out a warning.

But it was too late. Sasha's T-shirt caught fire. He instantly dropped the chain and yelled. In the time it took Dakota to register the horror, Finn barreled into his brother, and they both tumbled into the pool.

"I'M GOING TO KILL HIM," Finn said as he paced the length of Dakota's living room. He'd showered and dried off, but hadn't cooled down.

"I don't care about the consequences. I'll plead guilty. I'll face the judge. Do you think there is any judge in this country who wouldn't understand why I have to kill my brother? And Geoff. What the hell. If I'm going to jail for murder, what difference does the second one make? Doesn't everyone like a two-for-one sale?"

Dakota sat on the sofa. For once she wasn't sure what to say. She believed Finn was hanging on too tight, but tonight Sasha had crossed the line. Legally, he was an adult. Apparently a stupid one. What kind of idiot started swinging around a ball of fire in the middle of the night? Sure it made good TV, but he wasn't going to have a career if he ended up with third-degree burns.

Although the paramedics had said he was going to be okay, they'd taken him to the hospital to be checked out. Dakota had been relieved when Finn hadn't climbed in the ambulance. She'd been concerned about having them alone in such a small space.

"I can't do this anymore," Finn said. "I'm going to tie them up and throw them on a plane. I know you think that will land me in jail but I'm good with that. If I get them back to Alaska and back in college, I will happily go to jail."

"If you're in jail, they'll just leave college. As for tying them up, they're about your size, Finn. You could probably take one of them but you can't take both."

He paused by the window and looked at her. "Want to bet? I'm mad enough to take on a Kodiak bear."

This probably wasn't the time to point out that the Kodiak bear would win.

"I can't believe Sasha did that," she admitted. "I can't believe he was that stupid."

"Despite the visual demonstration?"

"Even then. I'm so disappointed."

"Imagine how I feel." He crossed to the sofa and sat next to her. "I know you think I'm being controlling, but now do you see that Sasha will risk his life to get that damn fame he so desperately wants? I have to stop him. He's my family." He shook his head. "I'm never going to be done raising them, am I?"

She laid her head on his shoulder. "Yes, you are. But you're never going to stop worrying. There's a difference."

"And here I thought I'd be done by now." He wrapped his arm around her. "This is why I don't want more kids. It never ends. You can't get away from the responsibility. How do you know you've done a good job? How do you know they're going to be okay? It's too much. God, I want to go home."

Unexpected emotion swirled inside her. The sharp pain from the reminder that children might not be in her future. Disappointment that Finn didn't share her dream of family.

She and Finn didn't have a future. The fact that he didn't want children and had plans to return to South Salmon wasn't news. She'd known from the first second she met him that he didn't want to be in Fool's Gold. As for the kid thing, she knew that, too.

But it was possible that sometime in the past week or so she'd allowed herself to forget that Finn wasn't a permanent part of her life. It was possible that he had managed to creep past her defenses, and now she cared about him. Which meant she had to get her feelings under control or she would be at risk of having her already fragile heart shattered.

"Sorry," he said with a sigh. "This isn't your problem."

"We're friends. I'm happy to listen. Besides, I'm something of a professional in this area. Feel free to pick my brain."

"I know what you think." He kissed her lightly. "You're not exactly reticent when it comes to sharing your opinion."

"I'm going to take that as a compliment."

"Good. That's how I meant it." He glanced at the clock on the wall. "It's late. We should get some sleep."

"You want to stay here?" she asked, before she could stop herself. What was she thinking? She just realized that she was at emotional risk with Finn, and now she was asking him to spend the night? It's not that she was afraid they were going to have sex. They were both tired and stressed. The real danger came from not having sex. From sleeping together. Sharing. Connecting.

"I'd like that," he said standing.

They walked into the bedroom and got undressed. She kept on her short-sleeved nightshirt, but took off her shoes and jeans. Finn dropped everything to the floor. They slid into her king-size bed and met in the middle. After she turned out the light, he lay on his back, she curled up next to him. He put his arm around her.

"Thank you," he murmured in the darkness. "You've been a rock."

"I'm happy to help." Which was the truth. Helping was easy. It was protecting herself that was going to be hard.

SASHA SAT ON A BED in the emergency room, waiting for the doctor to release him. He had minor burns on his right side and on the underside of his arm. Nothing that wouldn't heal in a few days.

They hurt like hell but had been worth it. On the ambulance ride over, Lani had told him that Geoff had already called a couple of reporters to tell them what had happened. His accident was going to give the show a lot of publicity, which was great for both of them.

The only downside in all the excitement was how pissed Finn was going to be at him. Like that was news, Sasha told himself.

He'd survived it before, and he would survive it again. Finn was an old man who couldn't remember what it was like to be young and have dreams. Sasha had his whole life ahead of him.

The curtain to his small alcove parted, and Lani stepped in.

"How are you doing?" she asked, her voice low.

He motioned her close. "Are the guys out there?"

She nodded. "Both cameras. They're not supposed to film in the hospital without written permission, but you know Geoff. He's telling them to get what they can."

She settled on the side of the bed and grinned at him. "This is so cool. We're going to get tons of airtime. I was thinking, when we get back, we should stage a big fight. They can edit that in to make it look like you wanted to do the Fire Poi to prove something to me."

He tugged on her long, dark hair. "Have you been talking to Geoff?"

"Of course. Come on. We all want the same thing. Huge ratings. This is one way to get that. Geoff said he's already had a call from *Inside Edition.* They're talking exclusive interview. That would be beyond amazing."

Inside Edition?

For years now, the thing he'd wanted most in life was to get the hell out of South Salmon. As a kid, the dream had been about only that. He hadn't had another destination in mind—just a fervent need to be anywhere but there.

As he'd gotten older, he'd started to realize he needed a better goal. A place to reach toward, rather than away from. Which was how his idea of being a star had been born. Now he wanted to get on a TV series, or be in movies. He wanted to be someone, to be loved and cared for by millions. And if the price of that was a couple of burns, so be it.

"So we'll stage the fight and then there will be these scenes?" he asked.

"Uh-huh." She lowered her voice even more. "So I'm thinking I should probably cry and beg you to live."

He chuckled. "Sure thing. Then some loud kissing?"

She nodded and stood. "Let me go tell the guys."

Sasha watched her go. She was pretty enough, he thought. But there wasn't any chemistry between them. There were a lot of other women he would rather kiss and then sleep with. But whatever it took for him to get to the next level...

Lani returned. She stood by his bed, drew in a few deep breaths, then started to cry.

"Sasha," she said, her voice thick with emotion. "Sasha, you have to be okay. Please, please live. S-Sasha?" Her voice broke on his name.

Her talent impressed him. He stared at her for a second, then imagined how all this would feel if he really loved her and thought he was going to die.

"Don't go," he said, his voice low and husky, as if he was in extreme pain. "Lani, I need you."

"I'm right here. You know I'm here." She sniffed. "I can't believe you got hurt. Do you need something for the pain?"

"They gave me something. It's not bad. I'm not going to give up, because I have you."

Her eyes twinkled with laughter as she said, "Really? You feel it, too? Our connection? I thought..." Another sob. "Oh, Sasha, I've been afraid to say anything and then when we fought before, I thought you didn't care about me."

"Of course I care. Getting matched with you was the luckiest day in my life."

"You mean that?"

"You're my girl."

"Oh, Sasha."

She covered her mouth to hold in a giggle, then climbed into the bed next to him.

"I don't want to hurt you," she told him.

"You couldn't. Just being next to you makes me know everything is going to be all right."

"I want to kiss you," she said, while sticking a finger down her throat and silently pretending to gag.

He had to swallow hard to keep from laughing. "Yes, baby," he murmured. "Just holding you makes it all better."

They began to kiss, going more for noise than passion. Sasha heard the sound of metal hooks on a pole as the privacy curtains were opened enough for the camera to get a shot of them.

He kept his eyes closed and thought about what he would do with his half of the money. How every woman would want him and every man would want to be him. Then he flipped Lani onto her back and put some tongue into it.

FINN WATCHED THE live feed of the show. The blend of what was happening on stage and taped pieces was interesting. Someone had to plan all that—figure out what to put where. Some of the taped pieces showed a contest with the various couples putting together bookcases. The kind that came in long flat boxes, with too many pieces and instructions written in awkward English.

Sasha and Lani laughed more than they worked and didn't finish in the allotted time. Stephen and Aurelia came in first. They worked together quickly and easily, sharing the tasks and ending up with a project that actually looked like a bookcase.

After the taped piece about Sasha and the Fire Poi, viewers were asked to vote for their favorite couple. The results would be announced in a couple of hours.

When the show ended, Finn knew Sasha and Lani would be staying. He had a feeling that building a bookcase wasn't enough to entice viewers, so Stephen and Aurelia might be at risk.

Dakota walked over to him. "How did it go?" she asked.

"Sasha and Lani are going to clean up this week," he told her. "I'm less sure about Stephen and Aurelia."

"Still think it's too soon for him to want to go home?"

"I'm sure of it."

"Have you asked Stephen what he would do?"

"I'm a guy," he said. "So is he. We don't have conversations."

"That's part of the problem."

"It must be nice to always have the answer," he said, annoyed by her certainty.

Dakota raised her chin slightly. "I'm not the bad guy here. I'm on your side."

"Then why are you always telling me what I'm doing wrong?"

"Because you're reacting as if you're trying to reason with yourself instead of your brothers. You're not looking at the situation from their point of view."

"I know them a hell of a lot better than you do."

"Which isn't the point. Your way hasn't changed their mind. Maybe another point of view would be helpful."

"But only if it's yours, right?"

She exhaled sharply. "I didn't say that. I care about you and them. I want you to stay close with your brothers so the family unit remains intact. I'm not sure why you can't see that. You're so determined to protect them from the world. And you can't."

"I can sure try."

"They're not seven. You keep saying that the twins are the ones who have to grow up, but maybe you're the one who can't let go of the past."

He glared at her. "Is this advice free or am I expected to pay for it? Because it's not worth shit."

She looked at him for a long time. "Fine. I thought that you wanted my opinion. My mistake. I can see you're only interested in being right."

With that, she turned and walked away.

Finn let her go. He didn't need her. He didn't need anybody. Only he knew he was lying. If he really didn't care, he could get on the next plane to Alaska and leave his brothers to their fate. If he didn't care, he wouldn't be wondering how badly he'd messed up with Dakota and how he could fix it without getting deeper into a relationship that wasn't meant to be.

CHAPTER NINE

"You'VE GOT TO give me something to work with," Karen said. "I think you're a cute couple with a lot of potential, but there's nothing there. No fights, no kissing and certainly no making up. There's nothing interesting to film. You know how Geoff is. You two came in second to last on the voting. That means you're at risk of being voted off."

"Do we have to come in last before we're let go?" Stephen asked. "Is that decision based on numbers or does Geoff make it?"

Karen sighed. "Technically you have to go if you come in last on the viewer voting. My point is, if you want to stay on the show, you have to give us something. Otherwise you're gonna be gone."

"Thanks for letting us know," Aurelia said.

She was doing her best to accept the information in the spirit in which it was given. But it was very difficult not to feel even more romantically inept than usual. Here she was, failing at a fake relationship. If she couldn't make this work, when it wasn't even real, how was she supposed to ever find a man and fall in love?

"I think you two like each other," Karen said. "Maybe you should think about that and stop worrying about the cameras."

Aurelia nodded. She knew that a lot of the couples had no trouble being around the cameras. But she was always aware of them, afraid of how she looked. Afraid of what people would say. After the show first aired, her mother called with her critique. It was not kind. She didn't like her daughter's clothes, or her hair or what she said. She also didn't like how young Stephen was but agreed there was nothing to be done about it. It wasn't as if Aurelia had picked him.

The only bright spot was the fact that Aurelia wasn't expected to visit her mother as much.

"I need to get back to the office," Karen said. "Please don't say anything. I'm not supposed to tell you, but I wanted to."

"We won't say anything," Stephen promised. "We'll do better next time."

Aurelia waited until the production assistant had left, then turned to him. "I guess we're done," she said. "The twin factor helped us the first couple of weeks, but the thrill is probably wearing off."

Or it was her. A conversation she didn't want to have with Stephen.

They were sitting on the grass in the large park in the center of town. The live portion of the show had been the previous night, and now they were on their own for a couple of days. For Aurelia, that meant going back to work. Show or no show, she still had clients.

"I'm not ready for this to be over," Stephen told her. "Do you want to be finished with the show?"

"No, but we're not like your brother and Lani. Do you want to play with Fire Poi to get more votes?"

"I would prefer to get out of the show unscarred," he said with a grin. "But we could do something."

"What I should do is grow a spine," she murmured. "Stand up to my mother. I'm a lot more afraid of her than I am of Geoff."

Stephen sat across from her. His blue eyes darkened with concern. "Why does she scare you?"

"Scared isn't exactly the right word. When I'm with her, I feel bad about myself. I feel guilty. Like I'm always doing something wrong. When I was a kid, it was just the two of us. We felt like a team. We did everything together. But then something changed. I'm not sure exactly when, but one day there were expectations. Rather than going off with my friends, I was supposed to come home and hang out with her. In high school, I didn't date. Some of it was me. I was bookish and not very pretty. Some of it was her, though. When I did get asked out, she always had a dozen reasons as to why I couldn't go."

"Because she wanted to keep you for herself?"

Aurelia hesitated. "I'm not sure. Although she's always complaining I'm not married or giving her grandchildren, I'm not sure she would be happy if I was. She has a sense of entitlement. She believes that it's my responsibility to take care of her."

"Is she sick?"

"No. She works, but she expects me to pay most of her expenses. It's as if I only exist to serve her. She doesn't like that I have a life. And somehow I've let that be okay. She talks about all the things she did for me and tells me over and over again that I should be grateful. I am. It's just, when do I get to have a life of my own?"

Stephen leaned toward her and took her hands in his. "Now," he said softly. "You get to have a life now. The longer you let her do this to you, the harder it's going to be to break away. Don't you want more?"

What she wanted was someone to look at her the way he was looking at her now. With caring and concern. With an intensity that made her fingers tremble.

She must be dehydrated or something. This was Stephen. He was young enough to be her baby brother. Nothing about him should make her tremble or even see him as anything but a friend. He was practically a teenager.

"I do want more," she said. "I want what most women want. A husband and children."

"That's not going to happen until you're willing to stand up to her. So which is bigger—your fear of her or your desire for your dreams? Because that's what it comes down to."

In the space of a few minutes, he'd managed to articulate everything she'd been thinking for the past five years. "You're right," she whispered. "I do have to confront her." She looked at him, then bit her lower lip. "Does it have to be today?"

He laughed. "No, it doesn't."

"Good. I need to work on my courage a little bit."

"So you're not ready for the show to be over yet?"

She shook her head. Even just another week with Stephen would be wonderful. He was so easy to be with, someone she could really talk to. He was…safe. Not a description he would like, but to her it meant the world.

"Then we're going to have to work on giving the camera something," he said, moving toward her. "I suggest we start with this."

Before she knew what he was talking about, he'd taken her in his arms and pressed his mouth to hers.

She didn't know which shocked her more—the kiss or the fact that they were outside, in the middle of the afternoon, where anyone could see. She wasn't a middle-of-the-day kind of girl. Not that she had a whole lot of kissing experience. There had been a few boys in college, but still. Those had all been night kisses.

Yet she couldn't seem to summon the indignation to protest. Not when he had one hand on her shoulder and the other on her thigh. Not when she could feel the heat from his body and feel how her heart bumped around in her chest. Not when his lips on hers felt so good.

Tentatively, she raised her arm so it rested on his shoulder. She slowly, very slowly, tilted her head and let her lips soften. She found herself straining toward him, wanting more than just a simple kiss.

Then it happened. Somewhere deep inside of her a small,

cold, empty space came to life. Instead of feeling inadequate, she felt powerful. Instead of wondering what everyone else was thinking, she found herself thinking about what she wanted. Instead of holding back and being scared, she leaned in and touched his bottom lip with her tongue.

Stephen responded by wrapping both arms around her, lowering her to the grass, then kissing her with a passionate intensity that stole her breath away.

She met him stroke for stroke, enjoying the warmth that poured through her, feeling long-numb parts come to life. At that moment it didn't matter that he was nine years younger or that she was a wallflower who hadn't been on a date in six years. In his arms, with the bright sun blessing them, she was a woman and he was a man and everything about this moment was right.

DAKOTA WALKED THROUGH the production offices, looking for Finn. She hadn't seen him in a couple of days and felt badly about their last conversation. In truth, he should be the one coming to look for her, but she wasn't going to wait for that to happen. She liked Finn and wanted to make sure they stayed friends.

She found him in one of the empty offices, working a column of numbers with a calculator.

"Hi," she said as she leaned against the door frame. "How's it going?"

He looked up. "Things are good." He grinned. "I talked to your boss about the flying school."

"How did that go?"

"Great. He had a lot of information on starting a nonprofit business. It's going to take a hell of a lot of money, but he gave me some ideas on where to start."

"You sound excited."

"I am. I've been playing with the idea for a while, but never thought anything could come of it."

"See what happens when you come down to the lower forty-eight?"

"Yes, I do. I have a lot to figure out. My charter business, the twins, this damn show. But I'm thinking I want to seriously consider the flight school. I'm not sure what the focus would be right now, or where I'd start it, but I know it's important."

He was enthused and not worrying as much about his brothers. At least not the way he had before. The flight school idea had some interesting consequences. As he'd mentioned before, there weren't a lot of inner-city kids in South Salmon. Which meant Finn had to be considering moving. Maybe Fool's Gold would make the list.

"I wondered if you wanted to come over for dinner," she said. "I have another chicken recipe that's pretty good."

He rose, shoved his hands into his jeans pockets, then rocked back on his heels. "Thanks for asking, but I'm going to pass."

"Oh. Okay. Sure."

The refusal surprised her. She told herself not to take his words personally, that she couldn't know everything going on in his life. Saying no wasn't a personal rejection. But psychological training didn't make it any easier to avoid feeling hurt.

"I guess I'll see you around," she said and turned to leave.

"Dakota, wait."

She faced him again.

"This isn't a good idea." He pulled one hand free of his jeans and motioned between them. "Us seeing each other. I'm not staying, which means this isn't going anywhere."

He was dumping her? They hadn't technically been dating. How could he be dumping her?

"I didn't expect it to go anywhere," she told him, doing her best to keep her voice even. So much for the hopes he would settle here. "I know that you're heading back to Alaska or wherever, and I'm staying here. This was always just going to be for fun."

"I thought you might be getting more involved."

"What gave you that idea?"

He shrugged.

She moved from hurt to pissed. This was so like a man. "I wasn't," she said coolly. "I was very clear on the parameters. Please don't worry about my feelings."

"I won't."

"Good."

Her anger grew. She wanted to scream or throw something, then told herself to keep breathing and take the high road. She might not like it now, but she would feel a whole lot better about herself later.

"Have a good night," she said between clenched teeth and left.

Once outside, she started home, then changed direction a block later and walked toward Jo's Bar. Tonight was definitely a margarita night. She would drink tequila, have a salad and watch HGTV. Later, when she was at her place, she would take a bath, go to bed, all the while reminding herself that Finn Andersson was an annoying jerk and that she was well rid of the likes of him.

In a couple of days, she would even believe it.

NEVADA'S INVITATION TO DINNER came at exactly the right time. Dakota appreciated the chance to get out of her house and spend time with her sisters. Three grilled steaks and one bottle of red wine later, they were all feeling pretty good. Dakota hated to upset the mood, but she knew it was time to come clean.

Her sisters were sprawled on the red sectional sofa. There was a fire in the fireplace and the soundtrack from *Mamma Mia* playing in the background. Montana had already mocked her sister for her choice in music, so Dakota didn't bother. But she did wait until the song about money was over, before introducing the topic of her infertility.

"I need to tell you something," she said in the brief silence between songs.

"We already know you're sleeping with Finn," Montana told her. "I can't decide if I want details or not. On the one hand, at least one of us is getting some. On the other hand, I don't know that I want to be made aware of how pathetic I am. It's a tough decision."

"I don't want to know," Nevada said. "I don't want the reminder of what I'm missing."

Eventually she was going to have to tell them that Finn had dumped her. But it wasn't what she wanted to talk about tonight. Instead, she had to figure out a way to explain that she would probably never have children. At least not the old-fashioned way.

Montana sat up and looked at her. "What's wrong?"

"What is it?" Nevada asked, at almost exactly the same moment.

It was as if they were reading her mind. One of the unique realities of being a triplet.

"I saw Dr. Galloway last fall." There was no reason to explain who the doctor was. All three of them saw her. Dakota would guess most of the women in town had Dr. Galloway as their gynecologist.

"The pain during my periods was getting worse. She did a few tests and it turns out I have some problems." She went on to explain the ramifications of having both polycystic ovarian syndrome and pelvic endometriosis.

"I actually have a better chance of being struck by lightning than getting pregnant the old-fashioned way," she said, keeping her tone light. "Even intervention is unlikely to help. I'm thinking of trying for the lottery instead. The lightning thing doesn't sound very fun."

Nevada and Montana moved as if one. They crossed the small living room and crouched in front of her chair.

"Are you okay?"

"Why didn't you tell us?"

"Can we do anything? Donate anything?"

"Will it get better over time?"

"Is this why you want to adopt?"

The questions overlapped. Dakota didn't worry about the turn the conversation was taking. What she felt, what healed the lingering ache in her soul, was the love that comforted her like an embrace.

"I'm fine," she told them. "Seriously. I'm perfectly fine."

"I don't believe that," Nevada said flatly. "How can this be? You've always wanted kids. A lot of them."

"Which is why I'm adopting. I'm on the list. I could get a call any day now."

That was a slight exaggeration. So far, her adoption experience had been less than perfect, but it could change. She refused to give up hope.

Montana hugged her. "There are other ways to get pregnant, right?"

"I'll definitely need help if I want to carry my own child."

Because of the scarring, there might not be any good eggs. And getting them out would be more difficult than for most women. But there was no point in getting into that.

"Have you given up?" Montana asked.

"On having a kid? No. I'll get there." She didn't know how, but it would happen. She had to hang on to that.

"This doesn't change anything," Nevada told her. "You're great. Smart and beautiful, with a great personality. Any guy would be lucky to have you."

She appreciated the vote of confidence, especially because she happened to know Nevada didn't think of herself as very attractive. An interesting mental schism. If Nevada thought Dakota was pretty and she and Dakota were identical triplets, how could she not admit the same about herself? Perhaps that should have been the topic of her thesis.

"Guys seem to be amazingly blind," Montana said. "It's very annoying."

"Who have you liked who hasn't liked you back?" Dakota asked.

Her sister's mouth twisted. "I can't think of anyone right now, but I'm sure it's happened." She sat on the carpet and rested her chin in her hands. "What's wrong with us? Why can't we find 'the guy' and fall in love? Everyone else seems to be in a relationship. Even Mom is thinking of dating. But here we sit—alone."

Montana looked at Dakota. "Sorry. I didn't mean to rant off topic. We can talk about the baby thing more."

Dakota laughed. "I'm okay with being done with it. As to the man question, I don't have an answer."

"You don't need one," Nevada grumbled. "You have Finn."

Not as much as they thought. "He's only here temporarily. As soon as he gets his brothers to go back home or figures out it's time to let go, he'll return to South Salmon."

"What about a long-distance relationship?" Montana asked.

Dakota shook her head. "Finn and I want different things. He's tired of being responsible and I want to get serious. In fact, he told me he's concerned I'm getting too attached, so I don't think we're going to see each other anymore."

Both her sisters stared at her.

"He didn't," Nevada breathed.

"He did."

"Butthead," Montana grumbled. "I liked him. Why do all the guys I like have to be jerks?"

"Max isn't a jerk," Nevada said.

"Would you lay off Max? He's old enough to be my father and while he's nice and everything, um, ick. He's my boss."

"The boss-secretary romance is very popular," Dakota said, her voice teasing. "What about that 'Ms. Jones, you're so beautiful' moment? That could be fun."

"I don't want to have sex with Max. Ever!"

Nevada looked at Dakota. "I hope she makes up her mind soon. All this indecision exhausts me."

Dakota sighed as she leaned back in her chair. "Me, too."

"I'm ignoring you both," Montana grumbled.

Nevada laughed.

"We'll all find someone," Dakota told her sisters. "Statistically, it's bound to happen."

"I love math as much as the next girl," Nevada said, "but I don't find it very comforting when it's applied to my love life."

"You could go to South Salmon with Finn," Montana suggested.

Dakota shook her head. "First, he hasn't asked." If anything, he'd made it clear he wasn't interested in keeping things going for the next two days, let alone twenty years. "Second, I don't want to. I'm sure it's a wonderful place to live, but my life is here. I love Fool's Gold. My family is here. My history, my friends. I belong here. When Geoff's show wraps up, I'm going back to work for Raoul and develop the curriculum for the program we want to start."

She was also thinking of opening a private practice. Just part-time, seeing a few patients a week.

"His loss," Nevada said firmly. "I'd thought the guy had a brain, but I was wrong."

"I wish I had a dog that liked to bite people." Montana wrinkled her nose. "A really big, scary, biting dog. That would show him. Maybe I could train one of the dogs to bite on command."

Dakota leaned forward and hugged them. "I love you both," she whispered.

"We love you, too."

She was lucky, she reminded herself. No matter what, she would never have to deal with the dips in her life alone. There were people who cared about her. People who would always be there for her. And eventually, because she refused to give up hope, she would have a child. And that would be enough.

CHAPTER TEN

FINN FOUND SASHA and Lani playing volleyball in the park. His brother had recovered from his minor burns and seemed to be doing just fine. Sasha spotted him and waved but didn't break away from his game.

After watching for a few minutes, Finn wandered away. It was Saturday afternoon on a warm spring day. Much of the town seemed to be outside taking walks, running errands. He saw parents with small children, old ladies walking little dogs. The fire department had pulled one of their trucks up to the park. Children scrambled over the shiny rig. Restaurants and coffee shops had set up tables outside, taking advantage of the mild weather.

Two of the other couples on the show were away on dates. Finn thought they might have gone to Lake Tahoe. Regardless of their destination, there was no filming in town today.

He walked through the park, remembering that Stephen had told him he and Aurelia were going to have a picnic by the lake. Twenty minutes later he found them on a blanket in the shade of a tall tree. Aurelia sat cross-legged while Stephen lay on his stomach, looking at her. Their expressions were intense, as if they were talking about something important.

Finn hesitated, torn between the normal polite response of

not wanting to interrupt and the need to come between a sophisticated older woman and his brother. Then Aurelia spotted him and waved him over.

"How's it going?" he asked, hovering at the edge of the blanket, not comfortable sitting down.

Stephen sat up. "Good. We were just talking."

"I have an overbearing mother," Aurelia admitted. "We're strategizing. I'm going to stand up to her and tell her to get off my back." She wrinkled her nose. "That sounds so brave. I'm fearless, right up until I see her. Then I crumble." She looked at Finn. "Any suggestions for gathering courage while facing a private demon? Not that my mother is a demon. She has her reasons for running my life. I'm the one with the problem."

Finn was having a little trouble following her conversation. "I'm sure you'll be fine."

Stephen laughed. "Typical guy response to an emotional situation. When in doubt, distance yourself, then run."

"You're not running," Finn said. "Why is that?"

"I like Aurelia. We have a lot in common." Stephen sat up. "We're both the quiet ones in our family, we like the same movies, we enjoy reading."

"I finished college and you didn't," Aurelia said with a quick smile. "Oh, wait. That's a difference."

Her teasing but effective dig surprised Finn.

"You're taking my side on the college thing?" he asked, incredulous.

"It does seem a little shortsighted to go all the way to your last semester and then quit." Instead of looking at Stephen, Aurelia looked at him. "Stephen's been majoring in engineering."

"I know," Finn told her. He didn't understand. She seemed to think the words were significant. He was Stephen's older brother. Of course he knew what he was studying.

Stephen shot her a look that silenced her. When she ducked her head, he reached out his hand and touched her arm.

Finn stood there, feeling like the odd man out. There was

an undercurrent he didn't understand and made him uncomfortable. Which made him miss Dakota. She would get it and smooth the situation over. She did that kind of thing.

"I, ah, have to get going," Finn said quickly. "You two kids have fun today."

He hurried away, not sure where he was going but wanting to get far away.

What was up with those two? As for Aurelia supporting the idea of Stephen finishing college, he couldn't tell if that meant she was an okay person, as Dakota had claimed, or if this was all part of her cougar game.

He kept walking. The park was filled with residents and tourists. Young children offered bread to the ducks by the pond. He caught sight of someone with blond hair and a familiar build. Dakota!

He turned toward her, frowning when the family between them moved. No. Not Dakota. One of her sisters walking several dogs wearing service vests. He stood in place until she was out of sight. His cell phone rang.

He checked the screen and recognized Bill's number. "How's it going?"

"Great. The new guy's a terrific pilot. There's no bullshit. He does the work and then he goes home. I like that. We've already got sixty boxes delivered."

"That's fast," Finn said, surprised they were doing so well.

"Tell me about it. If this guy wants to stick around, you can stay there as long as you'd like."

"Good to know. I didn't like leaving you shorthanded."

"Plenty of hands now," Bill told him. "I gotta run. Talk to you later."

Finn listened to his partner hang up, then stood in the center of the park and realized he had nothing to do with the rest of his day. He stepped into the sunlight and looked around at the bustling town. Everyone had somewhere to be. Everyone had someone to be with. Except for his brothers, the only other person he wanted to spend time with was Dakota. The problem was, the last time he'd seen her, he'd acted like an ass.

It hadn't been her at all, he admitted to himself. It had been him. He wanted to say he'd acted the way he had because he'd known the relationship wouldn't last and he was only trying to protect her. But that would make him a liar. Instead, he'd felt himself getting closer to her. The realization had scared the crap out of him. So he'd acted or, rather, reacted. He'd rejected her and sent her on her way.

Now he was left with the consequences.

Knowing that, whether or not she was willing to forgive him, he had to apologize, so Finn walked the short distance to Dakota's house. When he reached the front door, he knocked, then waited. If she wasn't home, he'd come back later.

The door opened a few seconds later. Dakota raised her eyebrows when she saw him but didn't say anything. She was wearing jeans and a T-shirt. Her feet were bare. Her blond hair tousled. She looked good. Better than good. She looked sexy and only slightly pissed at him.

"I should probably talk first, huh?" he said.

She leaned her shoulder against the door frame. "Sounds like a good idea."

"I have a good excuse for acting like a jerk."

"I can't wait to hear it."

He cleared his throat. "Would saying it's because I'm a guy be enough?"

"Probably not."

It had been worth a try, he thought. "I was frustrated and angry about my brothers. And starting to get involved with you. That last part wasn't supposed to happen. You know I'm leaving and I know I'm leaving."

"So you decided on the mature response," she said.

"I'm sorry. You didn't deserve that. I was wrong."

She stepped back and held the door open. "Come on in."

"As easy as that?"

"It was a good apology. I believe you."

He stepped into the house and she shut the door behind him and faced him.

"Finn, I have a good time with you. I like talking to you and the sex is pretty good, too." She smiled. "Don't let that last part go to your head."

"I won't," he promised. Although he wanted to take a second and enjoy the praise.

Her smile faded. "I'm very clear on the fact your stay here in town is temporary. When you leave, I'll miss you. Despite that, I'm not going to get crazy and try to make you stay."

"I know," he said quickly. "I shouldn't have said all that before. I'll miss you, too."

"Having cleared up how much we're going to miss each other, do you still want to spend time together while you're here?"

He hadn't dated much in the past eight years. Once his parents had died and he'd become responsible for his brothers, there hadn't been time. So he wasn't sure if her direct attitude was about dating a woman who was more mature, or if she was incredibly special. He had a feeling it was the latter.

"I'd like to see you as much as I can," he said. "And if you want to beg me to stay, I wouldn't mind that, either."

She laughed. "You and your ego. I'm sure you would love that. You in your plane, ready to fly away. Me sobbing on the edge of the runway. Very 1940s and going off to war."

"I like war movies," he said.

"Let me put on some shoes." She walked across the living room and slipped her feet into sandals. "I'll show you the town and later you can stay for dinner." She turned back to him. "And if you're very lucky, I might just use you for sex."

"If there's anything I can do to encourage that last one, just let me know."

"I'm sure there's something," she said with a smile. "Let me think on it."

DAKOTA SPENT THE afternoon showing Finn around town. They explored Morgan's Books, got a coffee at Starbucks and watched the last two innings of a Little League game. Around five, they headed back to her place.

"Want to get takeout?" he asked.

"I still have the ingredients for that chicken dish," she said, enjoying the soft breeze and the feel of his hand in hers.

"Who taught you to cook?" he asked. "Your mom?"

"Uh-huh. She's a great cook. We always had a tradition of big family dinners. We were all expected to show up every night, regardless of what else might be going on. As a teenager, I hated the rules, but now I appreciate them."

"Sounds like you were part of a close family."

She looked at him. "From what you said earlier, it sounds like you were, too."

"It wasn't the same. Dad and I were always flying off somewhere. We didn't have a lot of meals together. But you're right. We were close."

They'd reached her house and went inside. While he browsed through her music selection, she got the chicken ready to put in the oven. Once she'd slid it into place, she grabbed a bottle of wine and joined him in her living room.

They sat together on the sofa.

"How old were you when you learned to fly?" she asked.

"Seven or eight. Dad started taking me up when I was about four. He would let me take the controls. I got serious about studying to be a pilot when I was ten. There's a lot of written material, but I got through it."

She shifted so she was facing him on the sofa. "Why do you love it?"

"Part of it is growing up in Alaska. There are lots of places that you can only get to by boat or plane. Some of the towns in the far north are only accessible by plane."

"Or dogsled," she teased.

"A dogsled only works in the winter." He put his hand on her leg. "Every day is different. Different cargo, different weather, different destination. I like helping people who are depending on me. I like the freedom. I'm my own boss."

"You could be your own boss anywhere," she said.

"I could," he agreed. "As much as I like Alaska, I'm not one of those guys who can't see himself living anywhere else. There are things I like about being in the city. Maybe not a big one. But there's something to be said for tradition. My grandfather started the business. It's been in the family ever since. Sometimes there's a partner, sometimes it's just us."

Dakota knew all about belonging to a place. "My family was one of the original families here in town. Being there from the beginning can make you feel like a small part of history."

"Exactly. I don't know what's going to happen with the company," he admitted. "Sasha's not interested in flying. I always thought Stephen would take it over, but now I don't know. Bill, my business partner, has a younger brother and a cousin. They both want in. Right now they're flying for regional carriers. That's why he couldn't hire them to help while I'm down here."

He leaned forward and picked up his wine. "Sometimes I think about selling out. Taking the money and starting over somewhere else. It used to be important for me to stay in South Salmon, for my brothers."

"Less of an issue now?" she asked.

He nodded.

Dakota told herself not to read too much into the conversation. Finn was just talking. The fact that he wasn't determined to stay in Alaska forever didn't change their circumstances. He'd made it clear several times he wasn't going to stay in Fool's Gold. When a man spoke like that, he was telling the truth. It wasn't code for "try harder to change me."

But there was a part of her that wanted it to be. Which made her foolish, and Dakota didn't like being a fool.

"You don't have to make a decision today," she said. "Even if you don't stay in South Salmon, there are other parts of Alaska."

He glanced at her. "Trying to make sure I don't change my mind about leaving? That sounds a lot like 'don't let the door hit you in the ass.'"

She laughed. "I would never say that."

He chuckled. "Thinking it counts."

He put down his wine, then pulled her against him. She went willingly, enjoying the feel of his body against hers. As always, the combination of strength and gentleness aroused her. The man could make her melt without even trying. How fair was that?

He brushed his mouth against hers. "Dinner's in the oven?"

"Uh-huh."

"How long do we have?"

She glanced at her watch. "About fifteen minutes. I was going to make a salad."

"Or you could spend the next fifteen minutes making out with me."

She wrapped her arms around him and drew him closer. "Salad is very overrated."

He pressed an openmouthed kiss against her lips. She parted for him, enjoying the slow, enticing strokes of his tongue. Wanting grew. He put his hand on her knee, then moved it steadily up her body until his fingers caressed her breast.

Her nipples tightened and the pleasure began. Between her legs, she was already wet and swollen.

Were they really that hungry, she wondered. Couldn't she pull the chicken out of the oven and let it finish cooking later?

She drew back slightly, only to have the phone interrupt the question. Finn reached across to the receiver on the end table and handed it to her.

She sat up.

"Hello?"

"Dakota Hendrix?" an unfamiliar woman asked.

"Yes."

"I'm Patricia Lee. We spoke a few months ago about your adoption application."

"What?" She quickly cleared her thoughts. "Oh, yes. I remember." The international agency had been quick to approve her application. Unlike several of the others she'd tried, this one hadn't minded that she was single.

"I heard about what happened with that little boy," Patricia said. "I'm so sorry. I don't know if they told you, but there was a mix-up in the paperwork."

Dakota had been told the same thing, although she'd never been sure if it really was a mix-up or if the agency had preferred sending the child to a married couple. Either way, it was an odd thing to call about on a Saturday night.

"Of course I was disappointed," Dakota admitted.

"Then you're still interested in adopting a child?"

"Of course."

"I was hoping you would say that," the other woman said. "We have a little girl. She's six months old and quite adorable. I wonder if you would be interested in her."

Dakota felt the blood rush from her head and wondered if she was going to faint. "Do you mean it? You have a child for me?"

"Yes, we do. I'm emailing you her file right now. There are a couple of pictures, as well. I was wondering if you would call me back after you look at the pictures. We have one of our workers returning home late tomorrow. If you want to take the child, she can get on the same flight. Otherwise it might be a couple of months until you can have her. I know this is quick, so if you want to wait we all understand. It won't change your application status."

Dakota's head spun. They were offering her what she'd always wanted. The chance for a family of her own. And six months old. That was so young. She was somewhat familiar with the developmental problems of a child raised in an orphanage. The younger the child, the more easily those problems were overcome. The little boy she'd been offered before had been five.

"When would you need to know?"

"In the next couple of hours," Patricia admitted. "I'm sorry it's such short notice. Our contact has been called home with a family emergency. We try to send a child with every adult going home. But again, it's up to you. We're not trying to pressure you. If you're not ready, we'll call the next family on the list."

Dakota walked into the kitchen. She picked up a pen and some sticky notes, then sat at the kitchen table. "Give me your number," she said. "I'll look at the file and call you back within the hour."

"Thank you," Patricia said.

Dakota took the information, then hung up. She sat in her kitchen. She knew she was in a chair with her feet on the floor, but part of her felt as if she were flying. Flying and shaking and emotional beyond tears. She had to still be breathing because she was conscious, but she couldn't really feel her body.

Somewhere in the background there was a dinging sound. Finn walked into the kitchen and took the casserole dish from the oven. Then he turned to face her.

"You're adopting a child?" he asked, sounding stunned.

She nodded, still unable to focus on anything. "Yes. They have a little girl for me arriving in L.A." She looked at him. "She's from Kazakhstan. Six months old. They're sending me a file. I need to go turn on my computer."

She stood, then couldn't remember where her computer was. This wasn't happening, was it? She laughed. "They're going to give me a little girl of my own."

"I know you wanted kids…" His voice trailed off, then he nodded slowly. "You have a lot to deal with. Why don't I get out of your way?"

"What? Oh."

So much for their romantic dinner, she thought sadly. So much for him. Finn had more than made it clear he wasn't looking for another family.

"Thanks," she said. "I have to make a decision pretty quickly."

"No problem." He started to leave, then paused. "You'll let me know what you decide?"

"Of course."

"Good."

She watched him leave. There was a whisper of sadness, but it quickly faded as she hurried to her spare room and turned on her laptop. The machine seemed to take forever to boot, but when it finally did and she was able to open the file, she saw the picture.

And she knew.

CHAPTER ELEVEN

MAKING THE DECISION was easy, Dakota realized the next morning. The details, on the other hand, threatened to drown her. She'd barely gotten any sleep. Every time she'd closed her eyes, she'd thought of something else she had to do. Even putting a pad of paper and a pen on her nightstand hadn't helped very much.

It was barely after eight in the morning, and she was exhausted. She had lists, including supplies, and the names of who she was going to call. The last big issue to be resolved was whether to drive to Los Angeles or to fly.

Although flying would be faster, she had to face the reality of dealing with the six-month-old baby she barely knew. What if her new daughter cried the whole way? Dakota wouldn't know how to handle that. So driving made more sense. Except it was probably an eight-hour drive and wouldn't that be stressful on the child, as well?

Dakota tapped her pen on the paper, not sure what was the best solution. In a few minutes, she would call her mother. She wanted to tell Denise the good news and ask her advice on the transportation issue.

In the meantime, she could review her shopping list. Not only would she need diapers and a couple of blankets, there was the issue of formula. Dakota didn't know very much about babies, but she was relatively sure switching formula could cause an upset stomach. Hopefully, the person traveling with the little girl had brought plenty.

She crossed to the phone by the sofa, but before she could pick up the receiver, there was soft knocking on her front door. She changed directions and opened it, only to find Finn standing on her small porch. He had take-out coffee containers in each hand.

"What are you doing here?" she asked. "It's early."

He handed her the coffee. "Nonfat, right?"

"Yes. Thank you." She stepped back and shook her head. "Sorry, I'm a little fuzzy this morning. Why are you here?"

"You're keeping the baby."

"How do you know?"

He smiled. "I know you. You talked about the fact that you can't have kids and you're a kid person. Given the chance to adopt, you will."

"Oh, you're right." Unexpected insight, she thought. But nice. He followed her into the house.

"I don't know what I'm doing," she admitted. "I didn't get much sleep and it seems like there are a thousand things to do."

He followed her into the kitchen. "Sure there are. Most people get nine months to figure out what to do about a baby. You've had what? Nine hours?"

All of which was true, she thought. But she was still surprised to see him. He'd taken off so quickly the previous night.

"I'm doing the list thing," she said, pointing to the pages on the kitchen table. "I'm going to call my mom in a few minutes. She's had six kids. If anyone knows what to do, it's her."

"Have you picked a name?"

She smiled. "I was thinking of Hannah. It's the name that came to me when I saw her picture."

"Hannah Hendrix. I like it."

"Me, too," she said. "Everything is so surreal. I don't know what to think even."

"You're going to be fine," he told her.

"You can't know that."

"Sure I can. You're the kind of person who cares about other people. And isn't that what you're always telling me? That kids want to know you're there for them?" He smiled. "I'm really happy for you, Dakota."

His support was unexpected, but very nice. She was close enough to the edge that it could've made her cry, but she was determined to maintain control.

"For a guy who isn't interested in having a family," she said, "you're pretty sensitive and understanding."

He winced. "Don't let word get out. I have a reputation to uphold. How are you getting to L.A.?"

"To pick up Hannah? I can't decide. That's what I was going to talk to my mom about. Flying is faster, but I'm afraid to take an unfamiliar baby on a plane. Which means driving makes more sense, but it's kind of long. I don't know how she'll feel or what she's like. She could be really scared."

"Let's fly," he told her. "I'll rent a plane. She's coming into the international terminal, right?"

"Yes, but you can't fly me to Los Angeles."

"Why not? Don't you trust me?"

Her concern wasn't about his flying abilities. She was sure he was very good. "Isn't renting a private plane a big deal? And expensive?"

"Not that big a deal. It's going to cost more than flying commercial, but I'm talking about a four-seater plane. Not a jet. It'll be faster than a car, and when you consider going through security and having to get there two hours before your flight, faster than flying commercial. There's an executive airport just east of LAX. We'll land there and take the shuttle to the international terminal."

"That sounds perfect," she said, relieved to have her problem solved. "Thank you. This is a huge relief. How do I pay for the plane? Do you want my credit card number?"

"We'll work that out later," he told her. "Let me go arrange for the rental."

They decided on what time they were leaving in the morning, then Finn kissed her lightly. "Congratulations," he said.

"Thank you for everything."

"I'm happy to help."

After he left, Dakota stood in the center of the room, holding her coffee. She was still surprised by his offer of help, although very grateful. She wasn't sure why he was getting involved, but she knew better than to ask questions.

A quick glance at the clock told her it was time to call her mother. She only had one day to get her entire life rearranged. In less than forty-eight hours, she would be a mother.

BY NOON, her house was overflowing with well-wishers. Dakota had called her mother. Denise had called her other daughters, along with most of the people they knew in Fool's Gold.

Nevada and Montana had shown up first. Then her mother had arrived minutes later. Liz and Jo were joined by Charity and her new baby. Marsha, the town mayor, arrived with Alice, the chief of police. Friends and neighbors filled Dakota's small house.

She'd already printed out the pictures of Hannah the adoption agency had emailed, and they were passed from hand to hand.

"Are you excited?" Montana asked. "I would be terrified. The dogs take the best of my maternal skills. I'm not sure I could manage more."

"I am terrified," Dakota admitted. "What if I screw up? What if she doesn't like me? What if she wants to go back to Kazakhstan?"

"The good news is, she can't talk," Nevada told her. "So asking to leave is out of the question."

"Small comfort," Dakota muttered.

Her mother joined her on the sofa and put her arm around her. "You're going to do just fine. It's going to be difficult at first, but you'll get the hang of it. Your daughter is going to love you and you're going to love her."

"You can't know that," Dakota told her, fighting panic.

"Of course I can," her mother said. "I guarantee it. And the best part of all is I finally get a granddaughter."

Nevada smiled. "Because it's all about you?"

"Of course." Denise laughed. "Not that I don't love my grand-sons, but I'm dying to buy something pink and frilly. Please don't turn my only granddaughter into a tomboy, I beg you."

"I'll do my best," Dakota promised.

She looked around her crowded living room. Most of the women had brought food for the impromptu gathering. A few had brought casserole dishes that she could use later in the week. That was the way of life here. Everyone took care of their own.

A very pregnant Pia and her husband, Raoul, Dakota's boss, moved toward her.

"So typical," Pia said hugging her as tightly as her huge belly would allow. "Jumping to the front of the line. Here I am nearly two months away from giving birth and you're getting a baby first."

"Congratulations," Raoul said, kissing her cheek, while man-aging to keep his arm around Pia. "How you holding up?"

"I'm in a panic. I need to go shopping," she said. "I need dia-pers and a bed and a changing table." She knew there was more, but she couldn't think of what. One of those baby books would help, she thought. Didn't they have lists of what you needed? "Are there baby things that you don't need when the kid is six months old?" she asked.

"Not to worry," her mother told her. "I'll go shopping with you. I'll make sure you have everything you need for the flight home. You're going to give me your house key. By the time you get home tomorrow, everything will be waiting."

If anyone else had told her that, she wouldn't have believed her. But this was her mother. Denise knew how to get things done. You couldn't have six kids and not be an expert at management.

"Thank you," she whispered, then hugged her mother. "I couldn't get through this without you."

Emotions threatened to overwhelm her. None of this felt real, yet she knew it was happening. She was going to have a baby. A child of her own. Despite her broken body, she was getting her own family.

As she looked around the room, at all the friends and family who had dropped everything to stop by and wish her the best, Dakota realized she was wrong. She wasn't getting her own family. Her family had always existed. What she was getting instead was a wonderful, unexpected blessing.

DAKOTA HAD NEVER been in a small plane before. But even flying in something roughly the size of a tin can was nothing when compared with the reality of becoming the mother of a six-month-old child she'd never met.

As Finn flew them southwest toward Los Angeles, she frantically flipped through the book she'd bought the previous day. The authors of *What to Expect the First Year* deserved some kind of award. And perhaps a house on the beach to go with that. Thanks to them, she at least had a place to start.

"Diapers," she muttered.

"You okay?" Finn asked.

"No. Yesterday Pia went on and on about different kinds of diapers. I thought she was silly. I mocked her. But what do I know about diapers? I can't remember the last time I diapered a baby. Any babysitting I did in high school was with older kids."

She looked at him, trying to breathe through her panic. "This is crazy. What are those people doing, leaving me alone with a child? Shouldn't they have investigated me more? There were only two home visits. Should I have to take some kind of practical evaluation? I don't know what formula to give her or if she's had shots. Kids get shots, don't they? Shots are a big deal."

"Calm down," Finn said soothingly. "Diapers aren't that hard. I changed them when my brothers were babies. The disposable kind make it really easy."

"Sure. They were easy twenty years ago. Things could be different now."

He turned his attention back to the view out the front window. One corner of his mouth turned up. "You think they've made it more difficult to diaper a baby in the past twenty years? That doesn't make for a very good marketing plan."

Her chest felt tight. She told herself she was fine, but it seemed more and more difficult to breathe. "Don't use logic on me, mister. Do you really want me to get hysterical? Because I can."

"I don't doubt you," he said. "Dakota, you're going to have to trust yourself. As for the formula and shots, whoever has Hannah now will give you all that information. What did they tell you when they called?"

"Not that much," she muttered. "You heard most of the conversation."

"Didn't you have other interviews before?"

"Yes. Several. There was paperwork and we talked and they came to Fool's Gold and checked out me and my family. The process was very lengthy."

"So they've checked you out thoroughly. If they trust you, then you should try trusting yourself."

"Okay." She inhaled. "That could work."

"Remember, you have your mom for help. Your sisters and your friends. You can ask me anything you want."

She clutched the book tightly against her chest. "Would you please turn the plane around?"

"Anything but that. You know you want this baby."

He was right. Sure, it was going to be tough in the beginning, but she would learn. Mothers had learned for thousands of years. She was considered to have above average intelligence. That had to help.

She opened the parenting book and tried to read. The words were a blur. The illustrations frightened her, and the lists made it difficult to keep from screaming.

"I need more time. Can't I have more time?"

"We'll be landing in about forty minutes. Is that enough?"

She glared at him. "That's not funny."

"I wasn't trying to be funny." He clicked on the microphone and spoke to the tower.

Dakota didn't know much about flying, but she realized Finn had been telling the truth. As she looked out the window she saw the vastness of Los Angeles spread out before them.

She could do this, she told herself. She wanted to do this. She glanced at the notes her mother had given her. She knew she had the right supplies, even if she didn't know what all of them were. She was prepared for Hannah to be tired and cranky. There were soft blankets and diapers and stuffed animals in the baby bag. A couple of changes of clothing in different sizes, in case Hannah's clothes were damp.

Finn had promised to help her with the first couple of diaper changes. There would be a family restroom in the airport terminal. Everything was going to be fine. She just had to keep telling herself that.

As promised, forty minutes later the plane rolled to a stop. Finn grabbed the diaper bag and stepped out of the plane. Dakota followed. She felt light-headed, and if her heart pounded any harder, it was going to jump out of her chest. That wasn't going to be pretty.

Finn checked in with the office and explained they were only going to be on the ground about an hour. Dakota had already called on the flight from Europe. Hannah and her escort were probably clearing customs right now.

They took the shuttle from the chartered airport over to the LAX international terminal. Finn had the diaper bag over one shoulder and held on to her hand. She clung to him, aware she probably looked pathetic, but not caring.

The main floor of the terminal was crowded with waiting families. People from dozens of countries spoke different languages. She wasn't sure how they were supposed to find a woman they'd never met, carrying a baby she'd never seen in person.

"I wish they'd sent me her picture as well as Hannah's," she said. "That would have made this easier."

"Dakota Hendrix?"

Dakota turned and saw a small nun with gray hair holding a crying baby. The little girl was the same one in the picture, she realized. Her face was flushed and she was much smaller than Dakota had expected. Even so, everything inside her went still, as if each cell in her body knew this was one of those extraordinary moments out of time.

"I'm Dakota," she whispered.

"I'm Sister Mary and this is your little girl."

Instinctively, Dakota held out her arms and took the child. Hannah didn't struggle. Instead her slight weight settled into Dakota's arms, and she gazed up at Dakota with dark brown eyes.

Hannah wore a pink jumper with a T-shirt underneath. Both were wrinkled and had a few stains on them. Not surprising, given how long she'd been traveling. Her dark hair was cut in an unflattering bowl style, but she was still beautiful.

Her full cheeks were deep red, and her mouth moved as if she were gathering her energy to cry. Even through her clothes, she felt warm.

Finn led them to a relatively quiet corner of the terminal. As people bustled around them, Sister Mary checked Dakota's identification. They both signed paperwork, and then it was done.

"Someone from the agency will call you in a couple of days, to set up an appointment," Sister Mary said. "Have you named her?"

"Hannah."

"A beautiful name," the nun said. "She's had a difficult journey. She has a low-grade fever and you'll want to get her ears looked at. I think she has an ear infection." The other woman sighed as she passed over some baby Tylenol. "This is all we have. Money is so limited. There are so many children and so few resources. The doctor cleared her for the trip but that was more so she could come here. She's due for another dose in an hour."

Hannah's eyes had closed. Dakota stared at her, torn between the beauty of her daughter and the fear that she might be sick.

"Is she small for her age?"

"Not compared with some of the other children. I've brought a supply of her formula, a few diapers and her clothes." The nun glanced at her watch. "I'm sorry but I have a flight to catch."

"Yes, of course," Dakota said. "Please feel free to go. I'll get Hannah into a doctor as soon as possible."

"You have all the numbers for the agency," Sister Mary told her, handing Finn a small suitcase. "Call anytime, day or night."

"Thank you."

Finn stood and shook hands with her. When the nun had left, he turned to Dakota. "Are you okay?"

"No," she said softly. "Did you hear what she said? Hannah might be sick." The baby's eyes were closed. Her breathing was regular, but her skin was so red. It burned Dakota's fingers when she stroked her cheek. "I need to get her to a doctor."

"Do you want to do that here or do you want to go home?"

"Let's get her home." Dakota checked her watch. She already had an appointment with the pediatrician late that afternoon. Better to take care of things there.

They went back the way they'd come. Fortunately, the shuttle driver had waited for them. It only took Finn a few minutes to check the plane and then get clearance. Less than an hour after they'd landed, they were airborne again.

This time, she sat behind the passenger seat with Hannah

strapped into a car seat next to her. Dakota watched her anxiously, counting every breath.

"You doing okay?" Finn asked.

"I'm trying not to freak."

"She'll be okay."

"I hope so." She kept her gaze on her daughter. "She's so small." Too small. "I know she comes from a very poor part of the world, that the orphanage doesn't have much money or many resources. I knew there could be problems. They warned me about that."

When she'd first applied, there had been several live interviews where she'd seen videos of the different orphanages the agency worked with. She'd also spoken with other parents. They'd told her about children who were small for their age, but quickly caught up. They'd glossed over any initial difficulties.

Now, as Dakota felt her daughter's fiery cheek, her own eyes burned.

"I don't want anything to happen to her."

"You're taking her to a doctor. It's only a few hours."

She nodded because it was impossible to speak. Her new daughter might be desperately ill, and she didn't have any way to make her better. Not medicine or even the experience to know how to make a poultice.

"Do you know what a poultice is?" she asked Finn.

"No. Why?"

"I thought it might help."

"Dakota, you have to relax. Wait until there's a reason to get upset, okay? You're going to need your energy to keep up with Hannah once she's crawling around."

"I hope you're right," she said, her voice oddly thick. It was only then, she realized she was crying.

She dropped her head into her hands and gave in to the tears. A couple of seconds later, Hannah woke up and started crying, too. The baby rubbed at her ears, as if they hurt her.

"It's okay," Dakota said quickly. "It's all right, sweetie. I have some medicine right here."

She dug out the Tylenol and measured the dose. The plane was amazingly steady, for which she was grateful.

"You're saving my life," she told Finn. "I couldn't have done this on my own. I don't know how to thank you."

"Just hang on."

She nodded, then offered Hannah the baby spoon. The little girl turned her head.

"Come on, sweetie. Take the yummy medicine. It will make you feel better."

After offering it a couple more times, Dakota lightly touched the girl's nose, then stroked her cheek. Hannah parted her lips, Dakota slipped the medicine inside, and the girl swallowed.

But whatever bothered her was too much for an over-the-counter remedy. Or the child was tired, or maybe scared. After all, she was surrounded by strangers. Whatever the reason, she cried louder and harder, her whole body shaking with her sobs. Dakota tried rocking the car seat and rubbing her tummy. She sang to her. Nothing helped.

Through the rest of the flight and the car ride to the pediatrician, Hannah screamed. The sound wrenched at Dakota's heart and made her feel nauseous. She didn't know what to do and knew that her ignorance could put an innocent child at risk. What had the agency been thinking—giving her a child?

Finally they pulled up in front of the pediatrician's office. She got Hannah out of her car seat, wrapped her in a blanket and carried the still-screaming infant into the waiting room, Finn close behind her.

Dakota, crying as well, could barely speak her name. The receptionist took one look at the two of them and motioned to the door on her left.

"Vivian will show you right into a room."

"Okay. Thanks."

Dakota looked at Finn. "I don't know how to thank you," she

said over the baby's crying. "You don't have to wait. I'll call my mom and she'll come get me."

Finn brushed her cheek with his fingers. "Go. I'll wait. I'm not going to leave you now. I have to see how this all ends."

"You're a good man. Seriously. I'll talk to someone about getting you a plaque."

One corner of his mouth curved up. "Nothing too big. You know I'm all about it being tasteful."

Despite everything, she managed a smile, then turned and followed the nurse into the examination room.

CHAPTER TWELVE

"THE KEY TO good parenting is to keep breathing," Dr. Silverman told Dakota. "Seriously, if you pass out, you're no good to anyone." The pediatrician, a petite blonde in her late thirties, smiled.

Dakota wanted to shriek at her. Did the doctor think this was funny? Nothing about this was funny. It was horrifying and potentially life threatening, but not funny.

As soon as Dr. Silverman had walked into the examining room, Hannah had stopped crying. She'd submitted to the detailed exam with barely a sound and now lay in Dakota's arms, her hot body limp.

"She's exhausted," the doctor said. "That trip wouldn't be easy on anyone. I'm sure she's scared and confused. Her life hasn't been easy. Adding to that are the other problems."

Dakota braced herself for the worst. "The fever?"

The doctor nodded. "She has an infection in both ears and she has her first tooth coming in. She's way too small for her age, which isn't surprising given her circumstances. I don't love the formula they've been using, either."

She looked at the can of powder Dakota had given her. It was the same one Sister Mary had left with Hannah's things.

"All right," the doctor continued. "We're going to start her on a course of antibiotics. I don't like to use them for ear infections, but under the circumstances, she needs the jump to get better."

Dr. Silverman explained how to administer the medicine and told her what to expect with the combination of fever, first tooth and potential digestive upsets. They went over how to slowly transition Hannah to a more easily digested formula, and she offered suggestions on how much to feed her and how often.

"Normally at six months she'd be starting on solid foods, but I want you to hold off on that for at least three weeks. Let's get her healthy and her weight up a little. Then you can begin the process." Dr. Silverman explained how to make sure Hannah didn't get dehydrated.

"Do you have someone to help you?" the doctor asked. "The first few days will be the most difficult."

"My mom," Dakota said, trying to absorb all the information. "I have sisters and friends." Not to mention all the women in town who would step in.

"Good." The doctor pulled a business card out of her white coat pocket. "I'm on call this weekend. If you need me, the answering service will be able to get in touch with me."

Dakota took the card and sighed. "Thank you. Is there any way I could convince you to move in with me for the next couple of years?"

Dr. Silverman laughed. "I think my husband would object, but I'll ask him."

"I really appreciate all of this."

The doctor touched the top of Hannah's head. "From what I can tell, she's basically healthy. Once we get her ears cleared up and her baby teeth in, your life will calm down. Try to stay relaxed and sleep when you can. Oh, and keep breathing."

They discussed when Dakota should bring her new daughter in for a follow-up visit, what circumstances would require a phone call to the doctor and what to look for that could be dangerous.

"I think you're going to be fine," the doctor told her. "Both of you."

Dakota nodded. "I understand and I appreciate all the information." Now if only she could figure out a way to keep it straight in her head.

She carried Hannah back into the waiting room. Finn stood when he saw her and closed the distance between them.

"What did she say?" he asked.

"Hopefully not more than I can remember." Dakota walked to the receptionist and made her follow-up appointment.

As she and Finn walked to his car, she told him about the visit and what the doctor had said. "I have to get a prescription filled," she said. "And change her formula, but I'm supposed to do that over time. Otherwise she could get really sick. Right now tummy trouble is the last thing she needs."

Getting overwhelmed seemed easy enough, she thought. Talk about going from zero to sixty without a whole lot of warning. Everyone was encouraging her, telling her she could do it, but at the end of the day, she was going to be the one left with the baby.

"I'll take you home," Finn told her. "Then I'll go get the prescription filled. One less thing for you to do."

Dakota finished strapping Hannah into her car seat, then closed the back door and straightened. "You've already done so much for me. I don't know how to thank you."

"I'll send you a list."

The drive back to Dakota's place didn't take very long. She kept looking over her shoulder, checking on Hannah. Exhaustion seemed to have set in, and the baby was sleeping.

She told herself that once Hannah started on the medication, everything would be better. At least that was her hope. There were—

"Somebody's having a party," Finn said as he pulled into her driveway.

She followed his gaze and saw there were at least a dozen

cars parked on the street. She recognized a few of them and had a feeling she knew the owners of the others.

Warmth and relief chased away a good portion of the fear. She really wasn't alone. How could she have forgotten that?

"It's not a party," she told him, then got out of the car. "Not in the way you're thinking."

He faced her across the roof of the vehicle. "Then what is it?"

"Come see."

She collected Hannah from her car seat. The baby barely stirred. Finn grabbed the diaper bag and followed her into the house.

She'd seen all the cars, but was still surprised by the number of people in her living room and kitchen. Her mother was there along with her sisters. Mayor Marsha and Charity, a very pregnant Pia. Liz and the feuding hairdressing sisters, Julia and Bella. Gladys and Alice, and Jenel from the jewelry store. There were women everywhere.

"There she is," Denise said, hurrying toward them. "Are you all right? How was the trip? How's your sweet little girl?"

Dakota handed her daughter over to her mother. But that was all she could do. Anything else was impossible. Her throat was too tight, her heart too full.

From where she stood, she could see stacks of presents. The packages were yellow and pink and white, topped with ribbons and bows. There was a high chair in the dining room and stacks of diapers on the chairs. She could see two steaming crockpots on the counter in her kitchen, a large basket of fruit and a bouquet of balloons.

As Denise rocked her new granddaughter in her arms, Nevada and Montana led Dakota into the spare room. Her small computer desk had been pushed to the far wall. Once-white walls had been painted the softest of pinks. New curtains hung at the windows. A thick rug covered the hardwood floor.

A crib sat in the center of the room. The linens were a cheerful yellow and white background with ballerina rabbits. A mobile of bunnies and ducks spun lazily overhead. There was a changing table and a dresser. The closet doors were open and tiny clothes hung on white hangers.

"It's some special paint," Nevada said. "There aren't any fumes, so it's safe for the baby. Everything else is organic or nontoxic."

Dakota didn't know what to say, so it was good that her sisters simply hugged her. She'd seen the town in action before, had been a part of it several times, but she'd never been on the receiving end of Fool's Gold love. The sense of connection and belonging nearly overwhelmed her.

"I didn't expect any of this," Dakota whispered, fighting her happy tears.

"Then our work here is done," Nevada teased.

Finn walked into the baby's room. "You people know how to throw a party," he said. "I'm going to get the prescription filled. I'll be back as soon as they're finished."

She nodded, rather than speak. From her perspective, she'd already spent much of the day crying. If she tried to thank him, she would only resume the waterworks. The man deserved a break.

Dakota allowed her sisters to lead her back to the living room. Her mother still held Hannah, and the baby seemed more relaxed in experienced arms. Several of the women jumped up to make room for her on the sofa. Dakota collapsed onto the cushions. A plate was put in her hands and a glass of something that looked like Diet Coke was placed on the coffee table in front of her.

"Now start at the beginning and tell us everything," her mother said. "Is Hannah all right? Finn mentioned he had to go out for medicine."

"She's going to be all right," Dakota said poking her fork at the pasta salad on her plate. "It might take a little while for us to get there, but Hannah is going to be just fine."

AURELIA STOOD ON the sidewalk in the warmth of the early evening. Some people were just plain gifted. As she watched,

Sasha and Lani stood in the park, fighting. They weren't just having an argument, they were yelling and waving their arms. At one point, Sasha grabbed Lani by her upper arms, hauled her close and kissed her.

Lani resisted at first. She twisted away, then raised her hand as if she were going to slap Sasha. He held her in place and kissed her again. This time, she surrendered. Her body went limp against his, and her hands drew him closer. From several feet away, it looked as though the young lovers had averted a crisis.

Aurelia knew better. She knew the fight was staged, a little scene for the cameras. "You have to admit they're really good," she told Stephen. "Whether or not they make it to the end of the show, they obviously have what it takes to be successful actors."

Stephen rested his hands on her shoulders. She wasn't sure why, and thinking about the possible reasons made her head hurt. He was a good guy. He was smart and fun to be with and really caring. Being with him was easy, even though it didn't show on camera. Every time she and Stephen were filmed together, the situation became awkward.

She couldn't say what was wrong. Her nature was to accept all the blame, but if that were true, then their time on camera should only be half bad. Instead it was, as Geoff had said the previous morning, truly awful.

"Hello, Aurelia."

Aurelia turned at the sound of her name and saw her mother walking toward her. Between work and the show, there hadn't been much time to visit. She'd called regularly, although her mother explained that was hardly the same and not nearly enough.

"Your mother, I presume," Stephen whispered in her ear.

Before she could agree, he stepped past her and introduced himself. They shook hands. While keeping her mother's hand in his, Stephen thanked her for insisting Aurelia go on the show.

"Your daughter speaks of you frequently," he continued. "I can see how much she cares about you.

"No, she doesn't." Her mother sniffed, then withdrew her hand and glared at them both. "If she really cared about me, she would stop by to see me more."

"She's busy with her job and the show."

Aurelia stepped between them. She could see where the conversation was going, and while she appreciated Stephen looking out for her, she knew it was time for her to stand up for herself.

"Stephen, could you give us a minute?"

He nodded and moved back.

She led her mother over to a bench. But before she could speak, her mother jumped in.

"I can't believe how young he is. I'd hoped they were exaggerating, but now I've seen him in person. Obviously, they weren't. It's humiliating. Do you know what my friends are saying? The people at work? Don't you care about me at all?" Her mother sighed and shook her head. "You've always been selfish, Aurelia. And while we're on the subject, where's my check for this month?"

Aurelia stared at the woman who had raised her. It had always been just the two of them, and for so long, that had been enough. She had been brought up to believe that family was everything and that taking care of her mother was her responsibility. She'd told herself that her mother's bitterness could be excused, if not explained. Now that she thought about it, she wasn't exactly sure why her mother was so angry all the time.

Stephen didn't appreciate Finn's interference and saw it as nothing more than irritation. She knew better. Finn had put his life on hold because he was worried about his brothers. He wanted nothing for himself. Everything he did was for them. It had never been that way with her mother.

In Aurelia's family, her mother came first. Her mother was the important one. Somehow Aurelia had allowed herself to be manipulated. Part of the blame lay with her mother, but part of it lay with her. She was nearly thirty years old. It was time for her to change the rules.

"Mom, I really appreciate you encouraging me to go on the show. You were right—I haven't been doing anything to move on to the next stage of my life. I want to get married and have children. Instead, I hide myself at work and I spent all my free time with you."

"Not recently," her mother snapped.

"I'm sorry you feel that I haven't been paying enough attention to you. The time on the show has allowed me to get a little perspective. I'm your daughter, and I will always love you, but I need to have my own life."

"I see," her mother said icily. "Let me guess. I no longer matter."

"You matter very much. I don't want it to be an either/or. I think I can have a life, and you and I can still be close." Aurelia sucked in a breath. Now came the hard part. There was a knot in her stomach, a ball of fear and guilt.

"You have a really good job," she said slowly. "The house is paid for, as is your car." She should know. She paid off both loans herself. "Obviously, if there's an emergency, I want to help. But otherwise, you need to be responsible for your own bills."

Her mother sprang to her feet and glared at her. "Aurelia, this is not how you were raised. I'm the only mother you'll ever have. When I'm dead and gone, your selfishness will haunt you forever."

Aurelia watched her walk away. She knew her mother expected her to run after her, but she couldn't. The relationship they'd had before had been twisted and difficult. If she wanted it to change, she would have to be strong.

Stephen walked over to her and put his arm around her. "How do you feel?"

"Nauseous." She pressed her hand to her stomach. "We're not done. She'll be back. But I feel like I've taken the first step and that's something."

"It's great."

She looked up at him and smiled. "Great is healing some freakish disease. All I did was stand up to my mother."

"When was the last time you did that?"

"I was probably five."

"Then it's a big deal."

"You're too nice to me."

"Not possible."

They walked through the park, going away from the direction her mother had chosen. Aurelia told herself to ignore the guilt, and that in time, it would fade.

The reality was her mother was more than capable of supporting herself. But for some reason, she wanted to be taken care of.

"Maybe she thinks that having me pay for things proves that I love her," she said, thinking out loud.

"Or she wants to be able to tell all her friends. That gives her status with them. After all, what do their kids do?"

"I hadn't thought of that," she admitted. "On my good days, I tell myself to feel sorry for her rather than be angry or resentful."

"Does it work?"

"Sometimes."

They stopped by Lake Ciara. The sun had set and the sky was dark. She could see the first stars appearing. As a little girl, she'd wished on the stars, wanting them to make her dreams come true. Back then, most of her dreams had been about a handsome prince who would rescue her.

Now, looking back, she realized the rescue was about escaping her mother. While she'd appreciated having someone to care about her, that relationship had too many rules and strings. Even as a child, she'd felt the need to be loved for herself.

That desire was still there, but she knew it wouldn't come from the stars. Instead she would have to grow enough as a person to be able to accept that kind of love. Tonight had been a good first step. If her mother returned and tried to suck her back into their old relationship, she would do her best to stand strong.

"You're looking serious about something," he said.

"Reminding myself to stay strong."

He gazed into her eyes. "I really admire you."

She blinked. "Excuse me?"

"You've had to deal with so much. You're standing up to the only family you have. You're on this show."

While she appreciated the praise, she didn't feel especially worthy. "I'm nearly thirty years old. It's long past time for me to take on my mother. Besides, you stood up to your brother. I think you inspired me."

He shook his head. "It was just the two of you. Changing that relationship isn't easy." He grimaced. "I didn't stand up to my brother, in fact. I ran."

"That's different."

Without warning, he leaned in and kissed her. The feel of his mouth against hers made every part of her weak with longing. She kissed him back, knowing she shouldn't, telling herself she would stop any second now.

He wrapped his arms around her and pulled her hard against him. She went willingly, surrendering to a force bigger than her doubts. He was tall and strong and made her feel safe. Stephen always made her think that, as long as he was there, nothing bad could happen.

When his tongue touched her bottom lip, she parted for him. She met him stroke for stroke, feeling the heat grow. His hands moved up and down her back, then dropped to her hips. She surged toward him and felt his erection against her stomach.

The physical proof of where this was going shocked her

into pulling away. She stepped back, her breathing ragged, and stared at him.

"Stop," she gasped, then shook her head and held up a hand. "You have to stop. *We* have to stop. This is crazy."

His blue eyes were bright with passion as he reached for her again, but she stepped back.

"I mean it," she said as forcefully as she could. It was difficult to be stern when all she wanted was to throw herself at him, to be held by him, to make love with him.

"I don't understand," he told her. "I thought…" He looked away. "My mistake."

"No." She grabbed his arm to keep him in place. "I'm sorry. I'm saying this all wrong. Stephen, this isn't about you. It's about me and us and where we are in our lives." She stared at him, willing him to understand.

"You're twenty-one years old. You need to finish college and go live your life. You have so many firsts, so many new experiences ahead of you, and I don't want to get in the way of that."

He didn't look the least bit understanding or appreciative of her attempt at self-sacrifice. "What the hell are you talking about? You're acting like you're a hundred years older than me. What first do I have in front of me that you don't have, too? Sure, you're a couple of years older, but so what? I like being with you. I thought you felt the same."

He liked being with her? It was hard to focus on what was important and not revel in that information. As for the firsts… "What about falling in love for the first time? You need to do that with someone your own age."

He stared at her with the expression of a confident male. At that moment there wasn't nine years between them. They were equals—or maybe he was a little in charge.

"Who have you been in love with?" he asked.

"Um, well, technically I haven't been in love, but we're not talking about me."

"Your point is that you have a whole world that I haven't experienced. But that's not true. You told me that even during college you were coming home every weekend. It's not like you had a great love affair. And since then, you've been involved with work and dealing with your mother."

Aurelia began to regret all the things she'd told Stephen. She hadn't realized he would use the information to win an argument.

"You're not a virgin, are you?" he asked.

She flushed but managed to keep looking at him. "No. Of course not." She'd had sex. Once. Back in college. The night had been a disaster. For once, she hadn't gone home for the weekend. She'd stayed on campus and gone to a party where she'd gotten drunk for the first time in her life. Not to mention the last time.

She remembered going to the party and meeting a guy. He'd been cute and funny and they'd spent a couple of hours talking. Then he'd kissed her and... She'd never been sure what had happened next. Events were blurry. She remembered him touching her everywhere and being naked and that sex had hurt a lot more than she'd thought it would. But there were no details, just vague images.

She'd spent the next three weeks sweating whether or not she was pregnant, and the next few months waiting to see if there was anything else she had to worry about. She'd managed to escape relatively unscathed, but nothing about the encounter had made her want to repeat it. Until now. Until a twenty-one-year-old boy held her and kissed her. Suddenly there were possibilities.

Life was nothing if not unexpected, she thought sadly. She'd finally found someone she could care about, and everything about him was wrong. She supposed it could be worse. He could be married or eighty or gay.

"I know what I want to do with the rest of my life," she said. She had to do the right thing. "I have an established career and something resembling a life. Yes, I have issues with my mother, but I'm working on them. I'm going to keep working on them. You need to go finish college and find out what you want to do with the rest of your life. You need to find a girl your own age and fall in love and get married and have beautiful babies."

It was difficult to talk. Her throat tightened, and her eyes began to burn. "You're really special, Stephen. I want the best for you."

"This is bullshit. You think I care what other people think? What does age have to do with it? Why can't you be that girl? As for what I want to do with my life, why can't I figure that out with you?"

"Because you can't."

"There's an argument." He grabbed her by the shoulders. "You're the one that I want."

"You say that now. But you could change your mind tomorrow."

"So could you," he told her. "I should trust you because of your age?"

What she wanted to say was that he could trust her because he knew her. But she knew he would tell her the same applied to him. The part that scared her was that she knew he could be right. Which left her exactly where?

"You scare me," she admitted in a shaky whisper.

He immediately dropped his hands and took a step back. "I'm sorry. I didn't mean to—"

"Not that way," she said quickly. "I'm not afraid *of* you. I'm afraid of what I feel when I'm around you. I'm afraid of what I want." She shook her head. "I don't want to see you again privately. We'll go out on our dates for the show but that's all. I can't do anything else."

"Aurelia, no!"

She turned and walked away. It wasn't easy, but it was the right thing to do. She heard him start to come after her, then he seemed to change his mind. It was for the best, she told herself. It didn't feel like it right now, but eventually she would get over him and move on. He needed to be with someone else. As for what she needed, she'd always been very good at thinking about others first.

FINN HELD THE front door open as the last of Dakota's guests left. When he'd returned with the prescription, the house had still been full of helpful friends. As he watched, they'd shown her the best way to feed the baby. That had been followed by a diapering demonstration and lots of other advice.

Denise, Dakota's mother, had offered to stay, but her daughter had refused.

"I need to know if I can do this," Dakota said, sounding brave.

"Call me if you need anything," her mother said. "I can be here in ten minutes."

Dakota looked like she was going to change her mind and ask her mother to stay, then shook her head. "We'll be fine."

Finn led Denise to the door.

"If things look desperate," Denise whispered, "you call me."

"I will," he promised. Although if things looked desperate, his plan was to stay the night. It might have been a long time since his brothers were babies, but Finn remembered the drill.

He returned to the living room only to find it empty. Making a logical assumption, he went down the short hallway and into the baby's room.

Hannah lay in her crib. Earlier, Dakota had changed the baby's clothes. Everyone had agreed that she could wait on the bath. There had already been enough new experiences for one day.

Hannah stared up at the gently turning mobile. She was mesmerized by the rotating bunnies. But even as she stared, her eyes slowly drifted closed.

"I didn't expect her to be so beautiful," Dakota whispered as she brushed her daughter's cheek.

He came up behind her and put his hand on her waist. "In about fifteen years, you're going to have guys lined up around the block."

Dakota smiled at him. "Right now I'd settle for getting through the night."

"She's on her medicine and seems to be feeling better. Her tummy is full, you know how to change a diaper."

She stepped away from the crib. He followed her into the living room.

"You're right," she said brightly. "I've had a crash course in parenting. I'm going to be fine." She smiled, which didn't fool him. "You've been great. I really appreciate all your help. It's been such a long day, you must be exhausted."

She was working the program, he thought. Faking it with the best of them. He could see the terror in her eyes, but she was determined to be brave. At least on the outside.

This was where he told her he was leaving, he reminded himself. What they'd had before had been great. Fun and uncomplicated. Hannah changed everything. Dakota was now a mother. There were new rules, and he wasn't going to screw with them. Getting out while he could made the most sense.

Except he couldn't seem to leave. Her pretend bravery touched him. Her willingness to throw herself into a situation for which she was desperately unprepared made him admire her. Add that to the fact that he already liked her, and there was no way he could walk out. Even though it was the smart thing to do.

"I'm staying," he told her. "You can't change my mind, so don't bother trying. You're stuck with me for the night."

"Really?"

He nodded.

She sank to the sofa and covered her face with her hands. "Thank God. I was trying to make everyone think I know what I'm doing. I don't have a clue. I've never been so scared in my life. She's completely dependent on me and I don't know what I'm doing."

He sat down next to her and pulled her against him. "Here's what we're going to do. You're going to get the baby monitor and put it in the bedroom. Then we're going to get ready for bed. I'll be here, so you're going to sleep as much as you can."

"I'd like to sleep," she admitted, leaning her head on his shoulder.

"Then here's your chance."

She raised her head. "Thank you for everything. You're my hero."

"I've never been anyone's hero before."

"I doubt that."

He stood and pulled her to her feet. Together, they walked toward the bedroom.

Inside of him, a voice screamed that this was trouble, but he silenced the words. He wasn't getting involved. He was staying for one night and then things would go back to the way they'd been before.

CHAPTER THIRTEEN

"WE NEED TO make the show more interesting," Geoff said. "I want to use one of the festivals as a backdrop. This town has them every other week."

"Sometimes more," Dakota agreed. "I think the Tulip Festival is next. I'll talk to the mayor and see what she says about you filming there."

She had a feeling Mayor Marsha would be less than amused at the idea but would still probably agree to it. After all, keeping Geoff in plain view was safest for everyone.

"Good," Geoff told her. "We need to add some drama to the show. I've been getting complaints from the executives. I'm not sure the festival is going to be enough. Do you think we could get a police band radio and follow the cops? Maybe if there was an explosion or something."

"We don't have an explosion rate here," she told him, doing her best not to roll her eyes.

"Too bad," he muttered.

Dakota wasn't sure what to say to that.

Geoff glanced at the pad in his hand, as if checking to see if there was more. Just then, Hannah made a cooing sound.

The producer turned toward the noise and saw the baby in

her playpen. Hannah was on her back, staring at the mobile Dakota had attached to the side of the crib.

"Is that a baby?" Geoff asked.

"Uh-huh."

"Yours?"

She hid a smile. "Yes."

He turned to leave, then looked at her again. "Were you pregnant and I missed it?"

"She's six months old."

"So that's a no?"

The smile escaped. "I wasn't pregnant before."

"Okay. Because I've been told that I'm not very observant when it comes to anything other than the show. But I would have noticed if you were pregnant."

"I'm sure that's true."

He looked at Hannah. "She's yours, right?"

Dakota thought about explaining about the adoption, but decided he really wasn't that interested. "She's mine."

"Okay, then. You'll ask about the explosion?"

"No, but I'll ask about the festival."

Geoff sighed. "I guess that will have to do."

"I guess it will."

He left.

Dakota laughed, then crossed to the playpen and picked up Hannah. "What a silly man," she said, holding her daughter in her arms. She felt the girl's forehead and was pleased that it was cool. The antibiotic was working quickly.

Her mother had stopped by that morning to check on her and warn her that Hannah's fever could climb during the day. Dakota was prepared with Tylenol drops. So far, though, everything was going well. Hannah had been eating and seemed less frightened of all the new experiences.

While Dakota sat in her chair, holding the baby, she called the mayor and explained about the festival.

"If I say no, will he take his show and go away?"

"Probably not."

"Then I suppose he can film it. How's Hannah?"

"Doing well. She slept for a few hours last night. She's eating well."

"Good. You know you can call me if you need anything."

"Yes, I know. Thanks."

Dakota made a couple more calls, then walked around the production office with her daughter. No one seemed overly interested in the child, which was fine. These people didn't know her.

When they got back to her desk, she put the baby in her car seat and placed her so that she could see the morning filming out the window. Dakota did her best to work but found herself glancing at Hannah every few seconds.

She had a baby. A child of her own. The true miracle of it all had yet to sink in.

A few minutes later, Bella Gionni, one of the feuding Gionni sisters, walked into her office.

"I wanted to see how things were going," the dark-haired, forty-something woman said. "We were all worried about your first night. How was it?"

"Good," Dakota told her. "Hannah slept relatively well. She's doing better. I don't think her ears are bothering her as much."

What she didn't admit was that Finn had spent the night with her. Every time Hannah had whimpered, Dakota had jumped to her feet and raced into the baby's room. Finn had been right there with her, helping with the formula, getting her settled in the rocking chair. She couldn't have done it without him.

"Can I hold her?" Bella asked.

"Of course," Dakota said. The doctor had told her to make Hannah's life as normal as possible. In Fool's Gold, that meant knowing lots and lots of people.

She took the baby out of the car seat. Bella held out her arms, and Hannah seemed to lean into her. From what Dakota could tell, the little girl was enjoying the attention. Perhaps there hadn't been enough at the orphanage.

"Who's that beautiful little girl?" Bella asked, cooing softly. "That's you. Yes, it is. You're going to be a heartbreaker."

Dakota knew this was the first of many visits. Not only would Bella come back again, but there would be others. The women in town would take care of them both.

While she appreciated the support and knew she could depend on it, she knew that last night it had been Finn who had kept her sane. Having him stay had meant everything to her. It had been better than sex. Not that she would say so if he asked, because the sex was amazing. But last night had been about taking care of her. About being the man she needed.

She'd never been able to depend on a man before. The experience was new, and she found she liked it. Still, it wasn't something she should get used to. After all, Finn was leaving. He'd made that very clear.

Even so, she was determined to enjoy what she had while it lasted.

AURELIA KNEW THERE was a problem when three more days passed and she hadn't heard from her mother. Normally they didn't go an entire day without speaking at least twice. While she knew she had to learn to stand on her own, there was no reason she also had to lose contact with the only relative she had. After work the following Friday, she went by her mother's house.

Her mother answered the door right away.

"Hi, Mom."

"Are you here to see me?" her mother asked, feigning surprise.

"Yes. We haven't spoken in a few days. I wanted to check on you."

"I can't imagine why. You've made it clear that you care nothing about me. I could drop dead in the street and you would simply step over me."

Aurelia told herself to be patient. She had established new boundaries that her mother didn't like, and they were going to be tested. If she respected herself, her mother would learn to respect her, as well.

Instead of getting angry or frustrated, she smiled. "You have such a way with words. You always create the most amazing visuals. I wish I'd inherited that ability from you." With that, she slipped past her mother and entered the house.

"Have you made tea yet?" she asked as she made her way to the kitchen. Her mother always made tea after work, unless she was going out with friends.

There was no kettle on the stove, which meant her mother was going out that evening. Good. Conversation couldn't drag on for hours.

Her mother followed her, then came to a stop in the middle of the kitchen. Her arms were folded tightly across her chest and her mouth was pinched.

"Did you come here to mock my poverty?"

Aurelia raised her eyebrows. "There you go again. Mom, have you ever thought of writing fiction? You'd be so good at it. Maybe short stories, you know, for those women's magazines?"

"I don't appreciate you making fun of me."

"I'm not," Aurelia said gently. "I wanted to check on you and make sure everything was all right. I'm sorry you don't feel comfortable calling me. I hope that will change."

"It will change when you stop acting so selfishly. Until then, I want nothing to do with you."

There it was. The gauntlet. In the past, Aurelia had always given in. The thought of being abandoned by her mother had crushed the little spirit she had left. But today was different. Sure, she felt like throwing up, but that would pass. She meant what she'd said before. She was happy to help in an emergency, but she was done being a financial and emotional convenience.

She'd had plenty of time to think about her actions. Stephen had respected her wishes. She hadn't heard from him once. Why did her mother find it so easy to ignore her while Stephen found it so easy to do exactly what she asked? A dilemma for another time, she told herself.

"I hope you have fun tonight with your friends," she said quietly. "It was nice to see you, Mom." She turned to leave.

Her mother caught up with her in the hallway. "You're leaving? Just like that?"

"You said you didn't want to have anything to do with me unless I went back to the way I was. I can't do that. I'm sorry if you think that makes me selfish. I don't think it does."

"I'm your mother. I should come first in your life."

Aurelia shook her head. "No, Mom. I need to come first in my own life. I need to take care of myself."

Her mother put her hands on her hips. "I see. Selfish to the end. I know what you're saying to yourself. When in doubt, blame the mother. I suppose this is all my fault."

"I didn't say that and I'm not thinking that. But if you're first in your life and you're first in my life, where does that leave me?"

She didn't expect an answer, but she waited for a few seconds anyway. It seemed polite. Her mother opened her mouth and closed it.

"I'll talk to you soon," Aurelia said, then left.

On the walk home, she replayed the conversation in her head. For once, she was happy with what she'd said. She might not be where she needed to be, but she was making progress.

She found herself wanting to call Stephen and tell him what had happened. Only she couldn't. They were seeing each other on the show and nowhere else. She knew she'd made the right decision, but that didn't make the loneliness any easier to bear.

DAKOTA WRAPPED THE towel around Hannah. Her daughter was warm and rosy after her bath. Denise stood at the end of the changing table and gently tickled her granddaughter's toes.

"Who's a beautiful baby girl?" Denise asked in a singsong voice. "Who's special?"

Hannah waved her fingers in the air and laughed.

"She's feeling much better," Dakota said. Knowing her daughter was healing was such a relief. Getting used to dealing with a baby was hard enough, but when that baby was sick, it was a nightmare.

She and Hannah had been together nearly a week now. They'd established something of a routine. The follow-up visit to the pediatrician had been much better than that first encounter. The doctor had said Hannah was doing well. Her weight was up, and her ears were clear. Hannah had to finish the course of antibiotics and there was still teething to get through, but all that was doable.

"She's eating well," Denise said. "I can tell she's feeling better. Do you have her on the new formula?"

"Yes. We were lucky. Her tummy handled the change well. The doctor said to start her on solid food in another week, which is a whole week sooner than we expected. That will help her gain more weight and catch up with her age group."

She finished drying the little girl, then put a new diaper on her and slipped her into her pajamas. By then, her daughter was half asleep. Her eyes sunk closed and her body relaxed.

"Go ahead," she told her mother. "You put her to bed."

Denise smiled at her. "Thanks," she whispered, and picked up the baby.

Hannah snuggled close. Denise crossed the room and settled the little girl on her back in the crib. After starting the mobile, they dimmed the lights and stepped out of the room.

"I'm so lucky with her," Dakota said, as she adjusted the volume on the baby monitor. "Hannah enjoys being with people. I've heard that some of the children from orphanages are cautious around anyone new. In this town, that would be a problem."

They settled on the sofa. Her mother looked at her.

"You're doing well," her mother told her. "I know you're

terrified half the time, but it doesn't show. Soon you'll be terrified only a quarter of the time, which is something to look forward to."

"Thanks," Dakota said. "You're right. I am scared. It's getting a little better. Knowing that she's healing helps a lot. As does all the company. Ethan and Liz stopped by a couple of days ago and I'm getting lots of visits at work." She smiled at her mother. "You're helping a lot, too."

"I love having her here. Finally a grandchild who lives close to me. You'll have to tell me if I become one of those annoying, interfering grandparents. I'm not saying I'll change my behavior, but I will at least feel guilty about it."

Dakota laughed. "As long as you feel guilty, then I guess it's okay."

"So you're handling the stress? You're sleeping?" her mother asked.

"Better than I was." Finn had stayed with her the first couple of nights. Just having him around had made everything better. But she'd realized that at some point she had to face motherhood on her own. She hadn't slept at all the first night he'd been gone, but since then she'd been sleeping more and more.

"Sometimes I freak out for no reason," she admitted. "Does that get better?"

"Yes and no," her mother said. "You freak out less and then they become teenagers. That's when the real nightmare begins." Denise smiled brightly. "But that's some time away. Enjoy Hannah while she's still young and rational."

"We weren't that bad," Dakota told her.

"You didn't have to be that bad. There were six of you."

"I guess you have a point there."

Her mother studied her. "At the risk of interfering, how are things going with Finn? I haven't seen him around. Or is he here when I'm not?"

"Finn has been a great help with Hannah," Dakota admitted. "Which has been wonderful. But romantically..."

It was difficult to explain the relationship, mostly because she didn't understand it herself.

"He's a great guy, but we want different things. We were having fun together, only it started to get complicated. He's here about his brothers and..." She shrugged. "I don't actually have an answer to that question."

"I got that," her mother said. "I'd wondered if it was getting serious with him."

"It wasn't," Dakota assured her, then wondered if she was lying.

She thought about Finn a lot and missed him. She knew he was working at the airport and told herself that was why he hadn't been around. There were plenty of tourists to keep him busy. And Raoul had mentioned he'd had another meeting with Finn about starting a nonprofit program.

"I see." Her mother studied her. "None of my girls are married. Sometimes I think it's my fault."

"As much as I would love to put all this on you," Dakota told her, "I don't think I can. I've never been in love. I've always wanted to be, I always thought I would be. There were guys in college who were great but I couldn't see myself spending the rest of my life with them. Maybe it's me."

"It's not you. You have a warm and giving heart. You're completely adorable. I think the men in this town are stupid."

Dakota laughed, then leaned close and hugged her mother. "Thank you for your unwavering support. As for the men in this town, I don't have an answer for that, either."

"And you're sure about Finn?"

"He's looking for less responsibility, not more. Once he gets his brothers settled, however that works out, he's going back to his regular life. Even if I'd been tempted before, having Hannah changes everything."

Dakota was very aware of the fact that having a baby, being a single mother, was only going to make the man thing more difficult. But they were two different animals—she didn't want to give up one kind of love for another.

"I want what you had," she told her mother. "I want a great love. A love that will sustain me for the rest of my life."

"Is that what you think?" her mother asked. "That we only get one great love?"

"Do you think differently?"

"Your father was a wonderful man and I loved him very much. But I don't believe there is only one man for each of us. Love is all around us. Maybe I'm foolish and too old to be thinking that, but I would like to be in love again."

Dakota did her best to keep from showing her shock. Dating was one thing, but falling in love? She'd always assumed there wouldn't be anyone for her mother but her father.

Now, looking at Denise, she saw her for what she was. An attractive, vital woman. There were probably a lot of men who would be interested in her.

"Do you have anyone in mind?" she asked.

"No, but I'm open to the possibility. Does that bother you?"

"It makes me envy you," Dakota admitted. "You're willing to take a chance again."

"You've taken a chance on that little girl. The right man will come along. You'll see."

"I hope so."

She wanted to fall in love, too. The problem was, thinking about being in love made her think about Finn. Was she truly interested in him? Or was it just easier to distract herself by wanting the one man she couldn't have?

CHAPTER FOURTEEN

DAKOTA SAT ON the floor with her daughter. They were on a blanket, in the middle of her living room. There were several age-appropriate toys scattered around. Dakota had a large picture book in her hand and was slowly reading the story to Hannah.

"Lonely bunny was happy to have found a friend." She pointed to the drawing on the page. "See the bunny? He's not lonely anymore. He has a friend now." She pointed to the fluffy white kitten, nose to nose with the formerly lonely bunny.

"See the kitten?" She pointed to the kitten. "He's white."

From all that she had read, Hannah needed plenty of verbal and visual stimulation. Hannah seemed interested in the story. She would look where Dakota pointed, and the bright colors of the picture book kept her attention. Dakota was about to turn the page when someone knocked on her front door.

She stood and collected Hannah. She felt her breath catch in her chest as she saw Finn standing on her small front porch.

He looked as sexy as ever, especially when he gave her a slow grin that made her thighs heat. "Hey. I should have called first, shouldn't I? Sorry. I've been doing a lot of flying and this was my first break. How are you?"

"Good. Come on in."

He stepped into the house, then reached for Hannah. "How's my best girl?" he asked.

The baby reached toward him. He pulled her against his chest, and she settled in as if she, too, had been missing him.

"You're growing," he murmured, kissing the top of Hannah's head. "I can see the difference already." He turned his attention to Dakota. "You look good, too, by the way."

She grinned. "Gee, thanks. I appreciate the compliment, even if it is an afterthought."

She led the way into the living room. Finn settled on the blanket, with Hannah on his lap. Dakota sat across from him.

He'd always had the kind of looks that made her think of tangled sheets and late mornings spent in bed. But there was something about seeing a strong, confident man holding a baby. She'd never experienced it before but now she totally got the appeal.

"How are things on the show?" he asked. "I talked to Sasha a couple of days ago and he was complaining that they needed to go on a hot date."

"Bad choice of words. After the fire incident, I'm thinking even Geoff is hesitant to let those two loose."

"I think that's why they're staying close to home. Nothing's been scheduled with Stephen and Aurelia. I don't think they're interesting enough for Geoff."

"Probably not. He's getting frantic about keeping the ratings up. He mentioned he would love an explosion at the Tulip Festival. I told him there was no way that was going to happen. So how's the flying? Miss those Alaska mountains?"

"Not as much as I would have thought. There are plenty of people who would rather fly to Fool's Gold than drive. I don't get it—the drive is beautiful, and I say that as a pilot. Still, it's keeping me busy. I've flown a few cargo flights and had an interesting afternoon taking a whooping crane from San Francisco to San Diego. The bird I flew is supposed to be a hot breeder." He chuckled. "He didn't look any different to me, but I'm not a girl whooping crane."

As he talked, Hannah reached toward one of the small stuffed animals on the floor.

"Do you want that?" Finn asked. He picked up the small pink stuffed elephant and handed it to her.

"Ga ga ga."

Dakota stared at the little girl. "Did you just say ga?" She turned to Finn. "You heard that, right? She spoke."

Finn rolled onto his back and held the little girl up in his arms. "Look at how smart you are. You can say ga."

Hannah squealed with delight as Finn continued to hold her in the air. When he rolled back to a seated position, she reached for her elephant. He handed it to her.

Dakota couldn't stop grinning. "I know I had nothing to do with it, but I feel so proud."

"It's a parent thing."

That's right. She was a parent now. "I need to remember what this feels like so that when she's fourteen and driving me crazy, I have something to fall back on."

He chuckled. "You are a woman with a plan."

They watched the little girl. She seemed mesmerized by her pink elephant.

"One of the guys I flew in told me there's talk of building a casino just north of town," Finn said.

"I heard about that. Apparently it's going to be a very upscale facility. More tourists are always a good thing."

"I also heard plenty of talk about the man shortage. You know the world thinks Fool's Gold is filled with desperate women."

Dakota winced. "It's been an ongoing problem. I told you about the grad student who wrote about the man shortage in her thesis. The media picked it up and went crazy. That's why we have Geoff here, doing his show. Demographically, men might be outnumbered, but we are hardly desperate women." She looked at him. "Although it does explain my attraction to you."

"You'd want me no matter how many men were in town."

"There's certainly nothing wrong with your ego."

"Or any other part of me."

He was right about that, Dakota thought, remembering the feel of his body against hers. But she wasn't going to admit it.

"There seem to be plenty of guys in town," he said. "Is there still a shortage?"

"I'm not sure. They were coming in by the busload last fall, but I don't know how many of the men stayed. Still, the town is fine. That's what made all the media attention so frustrating."

"It's a good town," he told her. "You'll get through this."

"Mayor Marsha is counting the minutes until Geoff and his production company leaves. She's afraid of what they'll want to do next. I'm pretty sure Geoff finds Fool's Gold quiet and boring. We don't want him writing our tourist brochure, that's for sure."

As they were speaking, Hannah started to lean more heavily against Finn. Her eyes began to close in that familiar way.

"Someone's getting sleepy," Dakota said, scrambling to her feet. She glanced at the clock. "It's a little past time for her nap. I don't want to put her down too late. She's nearly sleeping through the night."

Finn handed her the baby, then stood. "Not something you want to mess with."

"Exactly. Sleep is still precious. More so for me than for her."

Dakota headed for her daughter's room. Finn trailed along behind her. She checked the baby's diaper, then put her in her crib and turned on the mobile.

Finn moved next to her and touched Hannah's cheek. "Sleep well, little girl."

The baby sighed and then drifted off to sleep. Dakota picked up the monitor and stepped out of the room. Finn closed the door behind them.

"How long does she sleep?" he asked.

"About two hours. Then we have dinner and I read to her some more. The evenings are—"

She had more she was going to say but never got the chance.

They were barely in the living room when Finn put his hand on her waist and drew her to him. She went without thinking and was glad she did when his mouth settled on hers.

Her first thought was that it had been too long between kisses. He'd been busy with flying, and she'd been adjusting to being a mother. But when she felt his tongue on her bottom lip, her thoughts faded as she lost herself in the fiery passion that lurked whenever he was near her.

He tasted of coffee and mint. His body was strong and hard against hers. She wrapped her arms around his neck, trying to get closer, to feel all of him. His heat surrounded her.

More, she thought hungrily. She wanted more.

Still holding on to the monitor, she led the way into her bedroom. She put the monitor on her dresser and checked the sound, then turned to him.

Neither of them had said anything. She suspected neither of them had planned this moment. But if the desire in his eyes was anything to go by, he wasn't going to object, and she knew she wanted everything he had to offer.

He stepped toward her. She moved into his arms.

Perhaps this wasn't the smartest decision she'd made that day, but she was okay with that. There might be consequences for giving herself to Finn when she knew that eventually he would leave. She would worry about that later, she promised herself, getting lost in his kiss and the feel of his hands on her body. For now, there was only the man and the way he made her feel.

FINN WAS AWARE of Dakota's even breathing. It might only be four in the afternoon, but she was exhausted. He would like to take credit, but an hour of passionate lovemaking was nothing when compared to caring for a six-month-old baby.

He doubted she slept for more than four hours at a stretch. So when he heard the sound of Hannah stirring, he got up from the bed and turned down the monitor.

After pulling on boxers and jeans, he walked barefoot into

the baby's room. Hannah smiled when she saw him and raised her arms, as if she wanted to be picked up. He obliged her and held her tiny body against his bare chest.

"Did you sleep well, pumpkin cheeks? Your mama is getting some rest right now. So we're going to be very quiet."

He walked over to the changing table. After taking care of her diaper, he carried her into the kitchen and checked the refrigerator. Knowing Dakota as he did, he wasn't surprised to see several bottles already prepared.

"You have to admire a woman who knows how to take care of business," he told the baby.

A pan of water sat on the stove. He turned on the burner and waited for the water to heat. He briefly glanced at the microwave. A pan of water might be old-fashioned, but it was more reliable.

While they waited, he rocked the baby in his arms. She kept eye contact with him and offered a tentative smile.

"You are going to be a heartbreaker one day," he told her. "Just like your mother."

Dakota was more than that, he thought, remembering the taste of her, the feel of her skin. She was a temptation. Not just because of how she got to him in bed, but because he enjoyed her company. She was the kind of woman a man looked forward to coming home to. Under other circumstances...

No, he told himself firmly. She was not for him. He had a life, and it didn't include a woman and a baby. He'd been the responsible guy for the past eight years. Now that his brothers were nearly grown, he was going to be free. And he had plans. A new business to build. The last thing he wanted was to be tied down.

When the bottle was heated, he tested the milk. Assured that the temperature was correct, he returned to Hannah's room and settled in the rocking chair.

The little girl latched on to the bottle eagerly. As she ate, he watched her watch him. There was something about her big brown eyes. He smiled at her. She raised her hand and grabbed on to his little finger, holding tight. Deep inside, he felt something shift, almost as if making room.

Ridiculous, he told himself.

When she'd finished eating, he grabbed a towel from the pile by the rocker, put it on his shoulder and burped her. She snuggled close. He held her as he rocked, humming tunelessly.

"Your mom said that she reads to you now. I saw the book about the bunny. I guess that's more appropriate than *Car and Driver*. Although you might be into cars. It's probably too soon to tell. And we should check on your mom. Last I saw, she was naked." He grinned. "She looks good naked."

"I'll have to take your word on that."

Finn looked up and saw Dakota's mother standing in the doorway. He stood, then wondered if that was a mistake. He was wearing jeans and nothing else, holding Dakota's baby in his arms. Dakota was in her room, probably still asleep. And naked, as he'd so helpfully pointed out.

Although he was usually good on his feet, he couldn't think of a single thing to say.

Denise approached and took the baby. "I suppose I should have called first. Dakota's asleep?"

He nodded.

He felt like a seventeen-year-old caught making out with his girlfriend. Except he wasn't seventeen, and they'd done a whole lot more than kiss.

Getting dressed seemed to be the first priority, he thought, wondering how he could get around Denise without being obvious. Then he heard a sound in the hall.

"Did you take care of Hannah?" a very sleepy Dakota asked, walking into the room.

She'd pulled on a robe and nothing else. Her hair was mussed, her mouth swollen from his kisses. She looked rumpled and satisfied, and then completely shocked when she spotted her mother.

"Mom?"

"Hello. I was telling Finn that I should have called first."

"I, ah…" Dakota grinned. "At least you didn't show up two hours ago. That would have been awkward."

Her mother laughed. "For all of us." She stepped out of the way. "I think Finn was trying to get past me without being obvious."

"I thought I'd get dressed," he murmured.

"Don't put on a shirt on my account," Dakota's mother told him and winked.

"Mom, you're going to frighten him."

"I can handle it," he said, wondering if he was telling the truth.

He excused himself and escaped into Dakota's bedroom. Once there, he dressed quickly. He was stepping into his boots when Dakota showed up.

"Sorry about that," she said. "She didn't have a habit of stopping by before I had Hannah. I didn't think she would today."

"It's okay."

She shrugged. "It's embarrassing."

"I'll survive." He pulled on his boots, then straightened and kissed her. "You okay?"

"Uh-huh. Thanks for letting me sleep."

"You needed it. Hannah is fed."

"I could tell. She has that look of happy contentment."

He touched her cheek. "So do you."

He was a good man, Dakota thought, as she walked Finn to the door.

Her mother was hiding out in the kitchen, which Dakota appreciated. Saying goodbye in private would be a lot easier. Of course, she still had to face her mother and explain what was going on.

"I'll see you soon," Finn said.

She nodded and hoped he was telling the truth.

Dakota returned to the kitchen where she found her mother playing with Hannah.

"I'm glad you got some rest," her mother told her. "I know how tired you've been."

Dakota waited, but her mother didn't say any more. "You have to want to know about Finn."

"I think I know enough already. He's the kind of man who looks good holding a baby. Should I worry about you?"

"No. I'm protecting my heart." For a moment, she allowed herself to wish that she didn't have to. That, in addition to looking good holding a baby, Finn was the kind of man who stayed. But she knew the truth.

"Are you sure you're not already in love with him?"

Talk about a crazy question. "Of course I'm sure. I would never let that happen."

AURELIA STOOD AWKWARDLY on the sidewalk. Karen, one of the production assistants, had emailed her the time of her next date with Stephen. Aurelia had hoped everyone would just forget about her and Stephen, but that was too much to ask. Now she had to not only go on a date with him, but she had to do it in front of the camera crew and who knew how many people watching on television.

If only they'd been voted off sooner, she thought, shifting her weight from foot to foot. But that was the coward's way out.

In truth, she owed Stephen an apology. Not that they would ever be right for each other, but that didn't excuse how she'd handled the situation. She hadn't been very nice. Probably because there was a part of her that didn't want to give him up. There was a part of her that didn't care about the age difference or the fact that he deserved someone who was where he was in life.

Somehow everything had gotten so complicated, and she didn't know how to make it simple again.

"Aurelia?"

She turned toward the voice and found Stephen standing behind her. Despite her best attempt, he'd still managed to sneak up on her. For a single heartbeat, she felt only happiness at the sight of him. So tall and strong, so handsome. She smiled and knew he could read everything she was thinking.

Then reality returned and, with it, the realization that she could never be right for him.

"I guess we have a date to get through," she said. "If we continue to be the most boring couple, I'm sure we'll get voted off this week."

"Is that what you want?" he asked.

"It makes the most sense."

She found it difficult to talk. When she was that close to him, her brain didn't work right. She could only think about him holding her and how she felt when he kissed her.

Why did it have to be like this? Why couldn't he be older or her younger?

"I didn't want to hurt you," she blurted. "I never wanted to be someone you would regret. I'm not afraid for me. I'm afraid for you."

She clamped her hand over her mouth and wished there was a way to call back the words. She should never have told him that, never have admitted the truth. He would think she was an idiot. Or worse, he would feel sorry for her.

Without thinking, she started walking away. She had no destination in mind, just a burning need to escape the situation. But before she could go anywhere, he was in front of her, his hands on her shoulders, his intense blue eyes staring into her face.

"I could never regret you. Us."

How she wanted that to be true. In this moment, it probably was, but one of them had to think beyond today.

"Let's say I believe you," she said. "So what happens next? What are you going to do?"

He grinned. That happy, easy grin that made her toes curl.

"Go back to college."

She stared at him. "Excuse me? Go back to college? That's

what your brother wanted all along. Why would you agree to it now?"

"Because I know it means you'll take me seriously."

She opened her mouth, then closed it. "Really?"

He nodded. "I liked college. I enjoyed studying engineering. I've been taking classes in bioengineering, with an emphasis on alternative fuels. It's a growing industry. College was never the problem—it was Finn. He knows Sasha isn't interested in the family business, so he's expecting me to be the one to join him." He shrugged. "I like flying, but I don't want to make it my career. I've never wanted that."

"I know that, but Finn doesn't. You have to tell him."

His mouth twisted. "Would you tell him if you were me? Finn has a bug up his ass about the business and college. I think it has more to do with our parents dying and him having to raise us. He's done a good job, but he's gotten too used to running our lives. I knew he expected me to go into the family business. I didn't know how to tell him I didn't want that. So I did something drastic—I came with Sasha to be on the show. I never expected to find you."

She stared at him. "I don't understand." Her voice was a whisper.

"I thought I was looking for something. Now I get that I was looking for some*one*. You. I'll go back to school and get my degree because it will make you happy. But also because it will make me the kind of man you want. This is all about you, Aurelia. Don't you get that?"

All she heard was a faint buzzing sound. The world seemed to move around her, and it took her a second to realize she was on the verge of passing out. She couldn't catch her breath, but then Stephen was kissing her and little things like breathing didn't matter.

She kissed him back, losing herself in the feel of his mouth on hers. The moment was everything she'd ever wanted. Better than that, the man was everything she'd ever wanted.

He raised his head and stared at her. "I love you, Aurelia. I think I have from the first moment I saw you."

"I love you, too."

She hadn't been sure she would ever get to say those words to a man. Now, as she spoke them, she knew the rightness of each syllable.

Sure, there were complications. Things to be worked out. Explanations to be made. But that was for later. Right now there was Stephen and the fact that he loved her.

He kissed her again. She moved closer and—

"Now that's what I'm talking about," Geoff said. "This is good television."

Stephen straightened, looking as shocked as she felt. She stared at him, horror growing inside of her. The cameras. How could they have forgotten about the cameras? They weren't having a private conversation. They were on television.

Stephen swore softly. "I'm sorry. I forgot they were there."

"Me, too."

There was no point in going to Geoff. He wouldn't understand the concept of keeping a private moment private. He was interested in ratings. The boring couple had just given him a blockbuster of a teaser.

It wasn't just that Geoff and the crew had seen it all. Soon everyone would be a witness.

Stephen cupped her face. "Want to change your mind?"

"No."

"Me, either." He smiled. "We should probably brace ourselves for the worst. What's that line from that movie? If you jump, I'll jump."

"It's a long way down."

"Don't worry. I'll catch you."

CHAPTER FIFTEEN

DAKOTA AND FINN sat on her sofa, watching that week's install-ment of *True Love or Fool's Gold*. The teaser right before the commercial break was of Aurelia and Stephen, standing some-where in town, looking intense.

"I didn't know they were going to be featured this week," Dakota said. "They didn't have a date, did they?"

"Not that I know of," Finn said, passing her the bowl of popcorn.

He'd come over for dinner. She'd made steaks and salad. They'd sat at her table and laughed and talked, taking turns holding Hannah. A good evening, she thought, telling herself not to read too much into it. Sure, she enjoyed Finn's company, but as a friend. What was that phrase? Friends with benefits?

Hannah had gone to sleep, and Dakota was hoping that after the show, she and Finn would also go to bed. Although the sleep part wasn't what interested her.

The commercial ended, and the show resumed. A long shot of Aurelia and Stephen made her think the camera was some distance away. The sound seemed enhanced, too, as if the two of them hadn't been miked.

It took Dakota a second to realize what Aurelia was saying. Something about not wanting to hurt Stephen, that she didn't want him to have regrets. The look on his face when he said he could never regret their relationship stunned Dakota.

"I didn't realize," she began, then pressed her lips together. Oh, crap. So much for them being the quiet couple. When no one was looking, they'd gone ahead and gotten involved. If she didn't know better, she would swear they'd fallen in love.

Finn wasn't going to be happy about that.

She glanced at him out of the corner of her eye and saw him staring intently at the screen. Before she could figure out what to say, or even if she should say anything, the topic of the conversation shifted.

"I knew Finn expected me to go into the family business. I didn't know how to tell him I didn't want that."

Finn handed her the popcorn bowl and stood. "Well, hell."

Dakota set the bowl on the coffee table and rose. "Take a breath," she said. "This can't be news."

Finn glared at her. "Of course it's news. We've been talking about this for years. When Stephen finishes college he's coming into the family business. That was always the way it was going to be."

She didn't actually believe that. From what she could tell, Stephen had never shown any interest in the family business. He was majoring in engineering in college. If he wanted to join forces with his brother, wouldn't he have been studying business or something flying-related?

"You're not upset because he doesn't want to be in the family business," she said gently. "It's that he didn't tell you himself. You had to find out this way."

"Sure, that's some of it. Why the hell couldn't he come talk to me? I'm his brother. Why wouldn't he tell me the truth?"

She put her hand on his arm. "Maybe because you're not interested in the truth. You only want to hear the story you want to hear. I suspect both your brothers have been telling you things for a long time. They didn't decide to come here on a whim.

They've been looking for a way out for a while. The show offered them that in an easy way."

"You don't know as much as you think you know." His voice was low and angry, although she had a feeling he was more angry at himself than at her.

"I know you're pushing them. I know you've been pushing them for a long time. You want to run their lives because you believe it's the only way to keep them safe." She drew in a breath. "Finn, you've done an amazing job with your brothers. Everyone can see it. There is no arbitrary line that you cross that says it's okay to stop worrying. That it's okay to stop taking care of them. That's what you're looking for. Someone somewhere to tell you it's okay to let go."

He shook off her hand and backed up a couple of steps. "You don't know what you're talking about."

"Yes, I do. Let them be. You've given them everything they need to be successful. Trust yourself and trust them."

"Even if that means not finishing college?"

"Yes."

"Not possible." He shoved his hands into his jeans pocket.

"So what are you going to do?" she asked. "Force Stephen into the family business? Are you going to guilt him into it? That's not you. You don't want him living a life of duty, doing things because he has to."

"That's what I had," Finn growled. "Nobody asked me what I wanted. Nobody gave a damn about my life. One day my parents were alive and everything was fine. The next they were dead. I was there. Did you know that? I was flying the plane when it crashed. There was a storm and my mother didn't want to fly, so we were going to wait. But she was worried about my brothers, so we took off anyway. The plane was hit by lightning and we went down. They were both injured. I had to hike out, and by the time I got back with help, they were dead."

He'd never told her how his parents had died beyond the fact that it had been a plane crash, and she hadn't thought to ask for details. She'd assumed it had been some kind of accident but nothing this bad. Nothing he'd been a part of. No wonder he held himself together so tightly. No wonder he didn't want to get involved or have more responsibility.

Everything made sense now. His intensity with his brothers. His concern about their future and safety. He was trying to control fate, and that wasn't possible.

She stepped in front of him and stared into his dark blue eyes. "You did what you had to do. You took care of your own. Your parents would have been very proud of you."

He started to turn away, but she grabbed the front of his shirt and held him in place.

"You're right," she said. "No one asked you if you wanted to take on that responsibility. You did it because they're your family and it was the right thing to do. You understood that. Just like you know, deep in your heart, that you don't want Stephen in the business if he doesn't want to be there."

Finn stared at her for a long time, then opened his arms. She stepped into his embrace and hung on as if she would never let go.

"He should have told me," he whispered. "He should have told me himself. I would have understood."

She doubted Finn would have made the conversation very easy. Even so, his point was a good one. This was not how he should have found out.

She could argue that Stephen was still a boy, although that wouldn't help her case of Finn letting them grow and live their lives. Besides, she understood his pain, even if she couldn't feel it herself. He had given up so much, and now he felt betrayed.

Families were hard. They were great, but they were hard. Or maybe it was just loving someone that made things complicated.

As she held on to him, she realized that her mother had been right. Falling in love with Finn would be easy. Too easy. She was going to have to be very, very careful.

DAKOTA AND HER sisters lay sprawled on several blankets in the backyard. Hannah sat between them, laughing at their various antics. The sun was warm, the sky was blue, and Buddy, one of Montana's rescue dogs, a pale cream labradoodle, monitored them anxiously.

"I can't believe you're really a mother," Nevada said. "It happened so fast. Last month you were single and now you have a kid."

"Tell me about it," Dakota said, rolling on her side and facing her daughter. "Obviously I've been thinking about adopting ever since I found out how difficult it would be for me to have children. But that was a theory. This is real." She grinned. "Of course, I'm still single."

Hannah reached for her pink elephant. It was slightly out of reach, and she tumbled to her side as she stretched. Montana scooped her up and held her in the air. The baby laughed while Buddy whined nervously.

"It's okay," Montana told the dog. "She's fine."

Montana put the little girl back on the blanket. Buddy crawled toward her. When he was next to her, he angled his body to provide support and maybe protection.

"He's really good with her," she said.

Montana nodded. "He does great with little kids. Although he's a bit of a worrier. He gets crazy when they fall. But he's so patient. He doesn't mind if little kids crawl all over him and pull his fur and tail. Some of it is the training, but most of it is his personality. He's a nanny dog." She leaned over and rubbed Buddy's head. "Aren't you, big boy?"

The dog kept his attention on the baby. He whined a little, as if concerned they weren't paying enough attention to what was going on.

"I want a baby," Nevada murmured. "At least I think I do, but not like this."

"You wouldn't consider adopting?" Dakota asked, a little surprised by her sister's reaction.

"Sure I would, but not so quickly. Yes, this was a deliberate act, but you had to make the final decision quickly. Didn't that scare you?"

"It terrified me, but that's part of the process. I suppose if I'd been picked by a woman who was pregnant, I would have had more time to get used to what was going to happen." She touched her daughter's soft, dark hair. "Except I wouldn't change any of this."

"You're braver than me," Montana admitted. "The dogs are about all I can handle. Besides, I don't think I'd be a very good mother."

"Why not?" Dakota thought her sister would be great. "You're caring and nurturing. You give everything you have. Look at how you are with the dogs."

"That's different."

"I don't think it is," Nevada said. "You're not as flaky as you think."

Hannah dropped her elephant again, then reached to pick it up. Buddy nudged it toward her, as if wanting to make sure she was careful.

"How is Finn taking all this?" Montana asked in a not-so-subtle attempt to change the subject. "He flew you to Los Angeles to pick her up. That was nice."

He'd done plenty of other nice things, she thought. And they weren't all about transportation.

"He's a good guy. The baby thing doesn't freak him out. His brothers are a lot younger and that helps. He remembers the baby stage."

He was also careful not to get too involved, she reminded herself. That kept stress at a minimum for him.

As she watched her daughter laugh, she wondered what it would be like if Finn weren't the kind of man who planned to walk away. Having him want to settle down would be pretty amazing. Especially if he wanted to do that settling with her.

"Dakota?"

She looked up and saw her sisters staring at her.

"You okay?" Nevada asked.

"Fine. Just daydreaming."

"About a certain handsome pilot?" Montana asked with a grin. "He looks like he's a great kisser."

"He is, but we're just friends. Anything else would be foolish."

"On his part or yours?"

"You know why he's here," Dakota reminded them. "When he figures out his brothers are doing fine on their own, he'll leave. After all, he has everything he needs in Alaska."

"You're not there," Montana said loyally. "Or Hannah. Plus he has to like the town. Who wouldn't want to live in Fool's Gold?"

"I'm sure there are hundreds of people," Nevada murmured.

Dakota decided she was tired of talking about herself. "Anyone know if Mom's been on a date?"

"No," Nevada said. "There are a couple of guys I know— contractors who are really nice. They're about her age. I suppose if I were a better daughter, I would offer to set her up. Only I can't seem to do it."

"Do you think it's a bad thing?" Montana asked, frowning slightly.

"No. I want her to be happy and it's been over ten years since Dad died, so I'm not thinking it's too soon."

"Then what?" Dakota prompted.

Nevada grinned. "I think I'm afraid she'll find someone in thirty seconds. That would be so depressing. I can't remember the last time I was on a date."

"Tell me about it," Montana said with a sigh.

"What about those contractors?" Dakota asked. "Any of them young enough to be interesting?"

"I work with them. It's not good to date someone you work with."

"Why not?" Montana asked. "If you work with them, then

you get the chance to see them in all kinds of circumstances. You'll know a lot about their character. Isn't that a good thing?"

Nevada shrugged and turned to Dakota. "I suppose you're not interested in dating."

"I have a new baby."

"And a man." Montana flung herself on Buddy. "Admit it. The sex is pretty fabulous."

Dakota didn't hide her grin. "It's even better than you could imagine."

FINN DID HIS best to avoid his brother. There was nothing Stephen could say that he wanted to hear. But two days after the broadcast, his brother cornered him out at the airport. He looked up from loading boxes into the plane and found Stephen standing there.

"I'm busy," Finn said brusquely.

"You have to talk to me sometime."

"I haven't seen you in a week. Don't make it sound like you've been dogging my heels for days."

"You know what I mean," his brother said, glaring at him. "You're pissed."

Finn put the box in place, then straightened. "Because you went on national television and told the world I was a jerk? Why would I be pissed?"

"I didn't say that. I said…" Stephen shook his head. "Forget it," he said, turning away. "It doesn't matter. You're not going to listen. I don't know why I bother trying."

Stephen started to walk away. Finn's instinct was to let him go. The kid was acting like a spoiled brat. He'd made one attempt to get his point across, and when that didn't work, he gave up. So much for Dakota's theory that his brothers were ready to be on their own.

Except he was supposed to be the mature one in the relationship.

"All you had to do was tell me," he said.

Stephen came to a stop but didn't turn around. "You wouldn't have listened. You would have told me to get my ass back to college and to plan on being in the family business. You always knew Sasha wasn't interested, and that left me."

Finn felt frustration building, but he did his best to ignore it. Communication, he reminded himself. That was the point of a conversation. Not to yell. Not to win.

"I wouldn't want you to do something that made you unhappy," he said. "I thought you were studying engineering because it was interesting, not because you wanted to be an engineer."

His brother faced him. "I took an introductory class my freshman year and got hooked."

Stephen shoved his hands into the front pockets of his jeans. "Don't take this wrong, but I don't want to be you. I like flying. It's fun and it gets me places, but it's not my life. Not wanting to be part of the business doesn't mean I don't appreciate what you've done. You gave up a lot when Mom and Dad died. You were there for us. I'm only a couple of years younger than you were when it happened and I can't imagine doing what you did."

Finn shifted uncomfortably. "You don't have a couple of kid brothers depending on you. That changes things."

"You took care of us," Stephen said earnestly. "I really appreciate that. We both do." He gave him a halfhearted smile. "Me more than Sasha."

Finn found himself relaxing his shoulders. "Dad wanted the business to stay in the family. Bill's always on me about selling and I didn't want to, because of you two."

"I thought you loved flying. I thought the business was everything."

"I do love flying, but carrying cargo back and forth isn't my idea of a good time. I want to start a charter company and take people places. Maybe teach flying to kids." Finn drew in a breath. "Sometimes I've thought about going somewhere else. Starting over. The world doesn't begin and end in South Salmon."

"I didn't know you realized that."

"I have my days."

Stephen's humor faded. "I'm sorry about what happened on the show. We didn't know the cameras were there. We were just talking."

"I kind of figured that out," Finn admitted. "I just wish you'd come to me before and told me. It might have changed things."

"You're right. I'm sorry."

Words he didn't hear very often, Finn thought. Good words. "I'm sorry, too. I didn't mean to push you into something you didn't want to do."

"Thanks. I guess it worked. I'm going back to college."

Finn stared at him. "Since when?"

"That's how the conversation with Aurelia started." Stephen looked confused. "I said I was going back to college and then we were discussing engineering."

"Okay. I remember that."

"Let me guess," his brother said, rolling his eyes. "You heard the part about me not wanting to go into the family business and got mad. Did you hear anything else?"

Finn shook his head. "Apparently not. I guess I should've listened harder."

Stephen looked uncomfortable again. "About Aurelia," he began.

"I'm really grateful to her," Finn told him. "I don't know how she got you interested in school again, but I'm glad she did."

"It's more… You're right," his brother said. "She, ah, has really been talking to me about the importance of an education."

There was something else. Finn could tell Stephen was either hiding something or trying to distract him. What he didn't know was what the something was.

He thought about pushing, then decided to let it go. Dakota was right. His brothers were grown-ups. They could handle their own lives. At least Stephen was going back to college. Finn knew Sasha was headed for Los Angeles or maybe New York. But Stephen would complete what he'd started, and that was a win.

WHAT HAD BEGUN as a quiet lunch with her sisters had somehow grown into a chickfest. It seemed that nearly every woman Dakota knew in town had come into the Fox and Hound that day for lunch. Tables had been pushed together in the center of the restaurant. The tourists sat in booths, watching the loud group.

Dakota sat at one of the square tables. She and Hannah were the center of attention. Actually, it was mostly Hannah. The baby was passed from arm to arm. She was cuddled and cooed at and rocked and held.

"At least you're not dealing with baby weight," Pia said. As she spoke, Pia shifted in her chair. She was about six or seven months pregnant, with twins. Just looking at her made Dakota uncomfortable.

"How do you sleep?" Dakota asked.

"Restlessly. If I can get comfortable I sleep really well. The problem is getting comfortable. That and wanting to eat Cincinnati. I'm hungry all the time. What is it about being pregnant and wanting food? Sure, I'm eating for three, but two of them weigh less than five pounds. You'd think I was giving birth to linebackers."

"It will be worth it," Mayor Marsha told her.

"I'm excited about the babies," Pia said. "It's the baby weight that has me nervous. I've been doing some reading. I think if I breast-feed, that helps."

"Breast-feeding twins is going to be a challenge," one of the women said with a laugh. "But it will help you lose the weight. Plus it's better for the babies. Something about the immune system and bonding. Everybody gets to bond."

"Raoul is already bonded," Pia muttered. "I wish he could breast-feed."

Dakota grinned at the thought of the former football player nursing a child. "He can be supportive in other ways."

"He's certainly trying," Pia admitted. "He loves these babies and they're not even born yet."

"And you love him," Nevada told her from across the table.

Pia smiled slowly. "I do. He's pretty amazing. I got so lucky when he fell in love with me. Of course, I tell him he got lucky when I fell in love with him. I think it helps to keep him humble. I just know it would be so hard to be doing this alone."

"Twins are a challenge," the mayor said. "Still, you would have had all of us. Just like Dakota does."

Dakota nodded. "I definitely don't feel alone in this." Which was true. While it would be nice to have a man around—a partner to be there and pick up the slack—she knew she could always ask for help and it would be there.

Although she had to admit to a twinge of envy when Pia talked about Raoul. Her friend's eyes lit up, and her mouth curved into a special smile. Her mother looked the same way when she talked about her late husband. Being in love did wonderful things to a woman, Dakota thought wistfully.

She'd always told herself that she would find that special someone eventually. Now she was less sure. Hannah was wonderful, and she was so grateful to have her, but being a single mother would make the whole "falling in love" thing more complicated.

Had she been holding her baby, she would have whispered that she was more than worth it. As it was, Hannah was on the opposite side of the table with Gladys, one of the older ladies in town.

"So, does breast-feeding keep you from getting pregnant?" Pia asked.

"I think so," Denise said, then tilted her head. "Or is it not breast-feeding? It's been too long for me and tragically, I'm not having sex with anyone."

"Tell me about it," Gladys said, reluctantly passing Hannah

to Alice Barns, the police chief. "Sure there are more men than there were, but they're all too young. How about shipping in a few older guys?" She grinned. "But not too old."

Everyone laughed.

"I know you don't get your period for a while after you're pregnant," Denise said. "I remember that much. But I think you can get pregnant before it starts. It seems to me that at least one of my boys was the result of that lack of information." She chuckled. "Not that I'm complaining."

"About the boy or the sex?" Gladys asked.

"Both."

Dakota leaned back in her chair and enjoyed being with the women she loved. This town was special. Whatever happened, there was support and understanding. Look at her situation. Everyone was there for her as she adopted Hannah. If she'd chosen to become a single mother the old-fashioned way, they would have been there for that, too.

Not that it was likely, she reminded herself. One in a hundred. It might as well be one in a million. If she ever did get pregnant, she should go buy a lotto ticket. There was absolutely no way—

Dakota sucked in a breath. Everything inside of her went still as she realized she hadn't had her period in a while. Certainly not since she'd gotten Hannah and even some time before that.

Thoughts swirled as she tried to figure out what was going on. The obvious answer was that she was pregnant—except she couldn't be. Her doctor had been very clear on that. She could still hear Dr. Galloway delivering the harsh news.

"It's very unlikely you'll ever conceive through intercourse. I won't say it's impossible, but statistically the reality is it's not going to happen."

She placed her hand on her belly and wondered what on earth was going to happen if the doctor was wrong.

CHAPTER SIXTEEN

"I DON'T UNDERSTAND," Dakota murmured, despite having said the same thing about six times already. "I can't be pregnant. I can't. It's supposed to be impossible."

Dr. Galloway, an older woman with a sensible haircut and a kind smile, patted her leg as she removed Dakota's feet from the stirrups and helped her sit up.

"I would say it's a miracle," she told her patient. "Or is this not good news?"

Dakota took a deep breath, trying to clear her spinning head. The home pregnancy test she'd used the previous evening had confirmed what she'd begun to suspect. Driving to the next town to buy it had taken more time than waiting for the results. As she'd played with her daughter, she'd watched the time, then had read the clear message.

Pregnant.

A single word that was difficult to misunderstand, although she was having a whole lot of trouble absorbing it. Pregnant? Impossible. And yet, she was.

"It's good news," she said slowly. "Of course I want more children." Hannah and her sibling would be close in age. But now? "I just didn't think…"

"You didn't think it would happen," Dr. Galloway told her.

"That's life. I've seen it many times in my office. Although I should lecture you on the foolishness of not using a condom, young lady. Pregnancy isn't the only reason for protection."

"You're right, of course." Dakota wanted to grab her head and scream, more from the surreal nature of the conversation than because she was upset. "You're really sure?"

"I'll do a blood test to confirm, but I'm sure. Based on my exam, I would say you're about six weeks along."

Dakota opened her mouth, then closed it. Six weeks ago? That would mean it had happened the first time she and Finn had made love. They'd been so frantic for each other, so lost in passion. If any event was going to defy the odds, it made sense that was the one.

"I'm in shock." She shook her head, wondering if she would ever feel normal again. "I didn't think this could happen. I thought if I were to get pregnant I'd need medical intervention."

"So did I. When I said it was unlikely for you to conceive naturally, I was being kind. I thought it was impossible. Yes, there was the smallest of chances, but I never thought I would see it happen." She smiled. "Your young man must have impressive swimmers."

"I guess." Dakota looked at her. "I just adopted a baby girl. She's six months old."

"Good for you. This is excellent news. I've always thought siblings should be close in age. Harder for the parents, but better for the children." Dr. Galloway wrote on a pad. "What about the father?"

"I have no idea what he'll think," Dakota said honestly, wondering if the swirling she felt in her stomach was nerves, panic or hormones. "Finn isn't looking to get involved seriously or to take on more responsibility." He'd nearly gotten his brothers on their way. A baby would completely freak him out.

"Men often talk that way, but when faced with a child of their own, they come around. You're going to tell him, I hope?"

"Yes." Eventually. First she had to be able to grasp the information.

Even now, sitting in her doctor's office, naked from the waist down after peeing on a stick and having a pelvic exam, the information wasn't real to her. She could say the word *pregnant,* but she couldn't feel it in her heart.

Dr. Galloway opened a drawer and pulled out several brochures. "Some information to get you started. Pick up some sample prenatal vitamins and a prescription for more on your way out." She rose. "You're a healthy young woman. The problem was never about your carrying the baby. Now that you've conceived, we'll do everything we can to make sure you have an uneventful pregnancy. Enjoy your blessing, Dakota."

"I will."

Dakota waited until the doctor had left to stand and then reached for her clothes. She set the paperwork on the exam table and drew on her bikini briefs. As she picked up her jeans, her gaze fell on a drawing of a pregnant woman. The side view showed a sketch of how the near-term baby was positioned inside of her.

As she studied the simple picture, she touched her own still-flat belly. Her heart began to beat faster, and her breath caught in her throat.

She was pregnant! After all the pain and heartache, after thinking she was broken and could never be like anyone else, she was pregnant.

She stood in the center of the examining room and laughed, then felt tears burning her eyes.

"Happy tears," she whispered. "Happy, happy tears."

She dressed quickly, eager to tell her mother, who was watching Hannah. Denise would be thrilled. Dakota hung on to the happiness, knowing the freak-out at the thought of being a single mom to two small children would hit her any second.

Could she do it? Handle it? Did she have a choice?

There was so much to think about, to consider. She had to go by the airport and...

And what? Tell Finn?

She sank onto the edge of the examining table and shook her head. This wasn't going to be good news for him, she thought sadly. There was no way he wanted to take on a baby.

Sure, he was good with Hannah and very supportive, but not in a way that meant he was interested in more than a temporary "uncle" relationship. He enjoyed the baby, but being a guy who liked kids did not a father make.

Finn had been clear about what he wanted from the first second they'd met. He'd never tried to convince her he was interested in anything but getting gone. If she wanted more, then she was only fooling herself.

Thinking that made her remember the name of the show. *True Love or Fool's Gold.*

She knew which she wanted. That was easy. But finding it was more complicated. As for the fool's gold—an artificial and unsatisfying substitute for the real thing—maybe she'd accepted a little of that, too. Allowing herself to believe there was more between her and Finn than there really was.

He was a great guy, and she knew she was in danger of losing her heart to him. But she also knew he'd been honest with her, and that, when he said he didn't want to stay, he meant it. Which left her in an uncomfortable dilemma.

How and when did she tell Finn she was pregnant?

She didn't think he would believe she'd lied about her condition to trick him, at least not when he'd had a chance to think about it. But she wouldn't be surprised if he went there at first, so she had to be prepared.

There was also the issue of coparenting. Did he want to? If so, how would they manage? Would he fly in from South Salmon? What about the winter, when the small town was practically cut off from the world? What would happen later if one or both of them fell in love with someone else? It wasn't anything she could imagine for herself, but Finn was the kind of man nearly every woman would want.

Too many questions, she told herself as she stood and picked up her purse. She took a cleansing breath. They didn't all have to be answered today. She was about six weeks pregnant. That meant she had months and months before any decisions had to be made. She could take her time and figure out the best way to tell Finn what had happened. As for his part in raising their baby—if she had to do it alone, she would. She might not have a life partner, but she had family and a town, and they both loved her.

Sensible words, she thought as she walked toward the reception desk to pick up her samples and prescription. Words that should have made her feel better and stronger. Instead there was an emptiness inside, a sense of longing for the very thing she couldn't have.

Finn.

SASHA LEANED BACK on the bench. "I thought I'd hear from an agent by now," he grumbled. "What if none of them are watching the show?"

Lani sat on the grass in front of him. She looked up and smiled. "They're watching."

"You can't know that."

Most of the time Sasha liked Lani. She was easy to get along with, and, because neither of them wanted to sleep with the other, there was none of that tension between them. It was like hanging out with his sister. If he had one.

But sometimes she really bugged him. Especially when she acted as if she knew everything about being on TV and he knew nothing. Maybe he hadn't been to Los Angeles for pilot season, but that didn't mean he didn't read and talk to people. He'd studied a lot on the internet.

Lani rolled onto her stomach. Her long, dark, wavy hair

brushed against the grass. She was beautiful and all, he thought. But not his type.

"I told you," she said, her voice sounding smug. "I sent notices to all the best agents in L.A. Well, to their assistants. I suggested they watch us."

He'd forgotten about that. "You don't know that they're watching."

She rolled her eyes. "Don't be so negative. You have to believe. You have to see what you want in every detail and then do the work to make it happen. That's how we're going to become stars. Do you think I like being on this stupid show? It's a great concept, but Geoff's a pain in the ass. He has no vision. But it gets me in front of people. It gets me seen. That's why I'm here."

Lani was so sure of herself, Sasha thought. She had a plan. All he had was a dream and the need to get out of South Salmon. That was the difference between them, he realized. Instead of complaining about her, he should learn from her.

"So what do we do now?" he asked.

"Close your eyes."

He looked at her. "I don't think so."

She pushed up into a kneeling position. "I'm not going to do anything bad. Trust me. Now close your eyes and start breathing real deep. Like from the bottom of your stomach."

He did as she instructed, leaning back against the bench and closing his eyes. He consciously slowed his breathing and felt himself start to relax.

"Okay. Now picture your dream house in L.A. It's on the beach right?"

"Malibu," he said with a smile, still keeping his eyes closed. "I can see the ocean." What he could see was girls in bikinis, but he didn't say that to Lani. "And I know how to visualize."

"You know how to daydream," she said. "There's a difference."

He wanted to push back but reminded himself she wasn't playing at any of this.

"Okay," he said, his eyes still closed. "Go on."

"Now imagine your house has a deck and there are stairs down to the beach. Ten stairs. They're wood. Your feet are bare. It's warm and sunny. You can feel the railing in your hand and you can feel the wooden deck below your feet. There's a light breeze."

Sasha was surprised to realize he actually could feel the deck. The wood was smooth and warm from the sun. He could feel the loose sand under his toes. The light breeze she described blew against his face. He felt his hair move.

"Now imagine yourself walking down the stairs," she said, her voice low and soothing. "You're getting closer to the beach. You can smell the ocean and hear the sound of the surf. You can see people on the beach." She laughed. "Let's change that. You can see girls on the beach."

"Maybe just a couple," he said with a chuckle. "Okay. I'm walking down the stairs."

"Go slow," she said. "Imagine everything about it. The railing. Don't forget that. You're walking down and down. There's only one more step and then you'll be on the beach. So stop at the last step. Can you see yourself there?"

He nodded. He could see everything, and he could feel it, too. The moment was so real, he could taste salt on his lips.

"Now step onto the sand," she said. "Feel the warm sand. It's just the right temperature. Not too hot, but warm on top and cooler underneath. Three of the girls see you. They whisper to each other and then start running toward you. They know exactly who you are and they are so excited to meet you. Because you're on their favorite show. One of them is holding a copy of *People* magazine. And you're on the cover."

Sasha grinned. Everything about it was real, right down to the picture of him on the magazine. With his eyes still closed, he squinted, then laughed. There it was, in bold print. *Sexiest man alive.*

He opened his eyes and looked at Lani. "That was great. How do you do that? I want to do it more."

"You're such a baby. Why aren't you visualizing every day? It's the best way to get what you want. Sure, you have to do the work, but this allows you to be in the right place at the right time. When you visualize and practice, you prepare yourself for success. I've been visualizing myself winning an Oscar since I was fourteen years old."

She stood and walked over to the bench, then sat next to him. "I don't know anyone in the business," she told him. "I don't have a lot of experience or friends I can ask. I'm doing this all on my own. This is how I make it real. This is how I get through the day. If you want it, Sasha, you have to believe in yourself. Most of the time no one else will believe in you."

"I get it. I need to come up with what I want and then imagine it already happening."

"Yes. But do it every day. That's what makes it powerful." She sighed. "I imagined myself on a reality show. I should have been more specific. I can't get anyone to tell me ratings numbers. Have you heard anything?"

"What are you talking about?"

She groaned. "How is the show doing? Are the advertisers happy with the number of viewers? That kind of information is important. We want the show to be successful."

"What does it matter if it isn't? We'll be gone."

"It's important because if we're going to put it on a resume somebody has to have heard about it. There is no point in claiming stardom on a show no one saw." She stared at him. "You make me crazy, and not in a good way."

"Part of my charm," he told her and grinned.

"You are not all that." She looked past him. "For all we know, one of the camera guys followed us. We should probably make out for a little bit just in case."

While there wasn't any chemistry between them, kissing a pretty girl was never bad. But instead of thinking that he wanted her, he found himself remembering her lesson on visualization. He would get started on that right away. The first thing he was going to visualize was his big brother flying back to Alaska and leaving him the hell alone.

FINN PICKED UP his two bags and left the grocery store. He barely made it onto the sidewalk when a tall older woman stopped him.

"You're that man," she said, peering at him. "The one dating Dakota."

He wasn't sure if she was telling him or asking a question. Either way it wasn't her business. Except this was Fool's Gold and he'd learned that people got involved whether you wanted them to or not.

"I know Dakota," he admitted.

"How is she doing? Her baby is just so precious. Hannah—that's her name, right?"

"Um, yes." Finn wanted to hurry her along to ask her why they were having this conversation, but he knew better. This stranger would get to her point when she was good and ready. His job was to wait and listen.

"Do you know if she still has a lot of food in the freezer?" the woman asked. "I always prefer to wait before bringing over a casserole. In the beginning of any family crisis, everyone rushes in with food and it all has to be frozen. It's never as good when it's thawed and heated. I think we should make a schedule. People could sign up and bring food on an ongoing basis. But no one listens. So I do it myself. I wait a couple of weeks and then bring by food. So do you know if she has enough?"

"Olivia."

Finn turned and saw Denise, Dakota's mother, approaching. Her smile looked amused rather than friendly, as if she knew he were trapped and she was trying to decide if she was going to help him escape. As he had been practically naked in her daughter's house, he understood her need to make him squirm. He could only hope that in the end she helped set him free.

"Hello, Denise," the older woman said. "I was just talking to Dakota's young man here to find out if I should bring over a casserole."

"Olivia is known for her casseroles," Denise told Finn. "She's a member of another of the founding families here in Fool's Gold. Olivia, this is Finn."

"We've met," Olivia announced. "He doesn't say much, does he? I can respect that. I, too, enjoyed a quiet man. I assume he has other attributes that recommend him."

Finn couldn't remember the last time he'd worried about blushing. He figured he had to have been in his teens. But here he was, standing on the streets of Fool's Gold, trying not to turn red.

Denise's brown eyes danced with amusement. "I'm sure he does. Not that Dakota discusses them with me. Perhaps if you ask one of her sisters."

Finn nearly choked and started to inch away. Denise grabbed him by the arm to hold him in place.

"Perhaps I will," Olivia said. "In the meantime, if you think she would enjoy something to eat, I'll take Dakota a casserole."

"I wish you would," Denise said. "I know you'll enjoy meeting Hannah. She's wonderful. An adorable little baby girl. She was small for her age when Dakota got her, but she's growing fast. She's starting to eat solid food."

"I remember what a mess that was," Olivia said with a smile. "All right. Thank you for the information. If you see Dakota, please let her know I'll be by later today."

"I will," Denise promised. She waited until the older woman had walked away, then turned to Finn. "I wasn't sure you were going to make it," she said.

"I respect your need to torture me."

"A mother's prerogative. But it really wasn't that bad. Most everyone in town is nice, if a bit inquisitive." The dancing humor was back in her eyes.

He found himself smiling. "People don't go through many things alone around here."

She took one of the bags from him, and they started walking toward his rented room.

"We don't believe in self-sufficiency," she told him. "But you grew up in a small town, so you under stand."

"We were always ready to help a neighbor, but we were expected to manage pretty much on our own."

"When I gave birth to the girls, I had some complications." Denise shook her head. "I was pretty sick. I don't remember very much. My husband, Ralph, didn't want to leave me alone in the hospital. But he had three little boys at home and a business to run. Not to mention triplet infants and it was Christmas. It was a stressful time. When I finally came home, I was weak. It took me a couple of months to recover. The women in town took care of us. Someone was in the house every single day for the first six months. I don't think I changed a diaper until the girls were at least three months old."

"Impressive."

"I want you to know that we take care of our own. If you choose to stay here, then you would become one of us, and we would take care of you, too."

"I don't need a lot of taking care of."

"I'm sure that's true. I'm just letting you know how it would be. But from what my daughter tells me, you're not thinking about staying."

He glanced at her, wondering what was coming next. As he wasn't sure what Denise thought of him, he couldn't guess her preference. Did she want him to stick around? Or would she prefer he left sooner rather than later?

"I'm not looking to add more responsibility to my life," he admitted. She might not like the truth, but he wasn't going to lie to make her happy. "Dakota is great, though. I like her a lot."

"But not enough to stay." Denise wasn't asking a question.

ONLY MINE

"You don't have to worry. If you wanted to stay, that would be great. But if you don't, she'll be fine."

She was giving him permission to walk away. There wouldn't be any guilt or games. In a way, it was the perfect situation. So why didn't he feel better about it?

They had reached his motel room. Finn felt funny about inviting her in but wasn't comfortable standing in front of the door. Denise solved the problem by handing him back his second bag.

"I hope you find what you're looking for," she told him.

"What makes you think I'm looking for anything?"

"Because you don't seem very happy." She tempered her observation with a gentle smile.

With that, she turned and left. Finn watched her go, then let himself into his small room and shut the door. He put away the groceries, filling the tiny refrigerator. Then he paced restlessly in the room.

He wanted to go after Denise and tell her that she was wrong. Of course he was happy. He'd spent the past eight years raising his brothers, and his job was finally done. He could go home, knowing they would be okay in the world. Why the hell wouldn't he be happy?

He flung himself on the bed and stared at the ceiling. Who was he kidding? He wasn't happy. He hadn't been for a long time. He wanted to blame his brothers but knew it was more than that. It was him.

A next step seemed logical, he thought. If only he knew what it was.

His cell phone rang, saving him from the pain of introspection.

"It's Geoff," a familiar voice said when he answered. "You'll want to watch the show tonight. I think it will make you happy."

"Not if Sasha plays with fire again," he grumbled.

"It's better than fire," Geoff promised him. "Make sure you watch."

CHAPTER SEVENTEEN

ALTHOUGH DAKOTA HAD seen most of the episodes of *True Love or Fool's Gold* with Finn, tonight was different. While he was comfortably sprawled on the sofa, with Hannah on his chest, Dakota found herself restless and uneasy. No doubt it was the secret she was keeping. Being pregnant had a way of changing a woman's perspective. She was thrilled about the thought of having a baby. Two months ago she'd thought she might never have a family, and now she had a beautiful baby girl and another child on the way. What was that old phrase? An embarrassment of riches?

But there was always another side to any situation. In this case, it was telling Finn that *he* was the father of her child. Something she knew he didn't want.

· "Have I mentioned Geoff isn't one of my favorite people?" Finn asked. "He specifically told me to watch tonight's episode and so far it hasn't been very interesting. Or maybe that's just me." He glanced at her. "Am I the wrong demographic?"

It took Dakota a second to realize what he was talking about. "I've heard the ratings aren't very good. Karen, one of the production assistants, told me that Geoff was really sweating the numbers. I think it's the show's premise. I'm a big fan of reality television, but this concept doesn't make sense to me. We all want to see people falling in love, but this feels fake."

He raised his eyebrows. "I don't want to watch people falling in love."

She smiled. "Okay, okay. It's a girl thing. A while ago on *Biggest Loser* two of the contestants fell in love. It was just the best. My sisters and I couldn't stop calling each other about it."

"But you don't know them. Why does it matter if they get involved?"

"It just does. It's fun to watch people fall in love. Which should make the show more interesting. I guess that's the problem. No one is falling in love."

She glanced back at the screen and saw Sasha and Lani. "Here they are," she said.

Finn turned his attention to the television. Dakota found herself watching him rather than the show. He was a good man. Kind and responsible. He was also pretty fabulous in bed, but that shouldn't matter. She smiled. Even though it sort of did.

He turned up the volume on the remote with one hand while keeping the other on Hannah's back. The baby was sleeping on his chest, her head on his shoulder, her nose pressing against his neck. It was the kind of image that turned even the most sensible of women's hearts to mush. She wasn't sure how she was supposed to resist.

"This is interesting," Finn said.

Dakota glanced at the screen. Sasha and Lani were in the park. Sasha sat on a bench while Lani sat on the grass in front of him. They were in deep conversation.

"You're such a baby," Lani said. "Why aren't you visualizing every day? It's the best way to get what you want. Sure, you have to do the work, but this allows you to be in the right place at the right time. When you visualize and practice, you prepare yourself for success. I've been visualizing myself winning an Oscar since I was fourteen years old."

She stood and walked over to the bench, then sat next to

Sasha. "I don't know anyone in the business," she told him. "I don't have a lot of experience or friends I can ask. I'm doing this all on my own. This is how I make it real. This is how I get through the day. If you want it, Sasha, you have to believe in yourself. Most of the time no one else will believe in you." She sighed. "I imagined myself on a reality show. I should have been more specific. I can't get anyone to tell me ratings numbers. Have you heard anything?"

Dakota blinked. She didn't know a whole lot about the entertainment business, but she was pretty sure contestants on a show weren't supposed to talk about ratings.

"What are you talking about?" Sasha asked.

She groaned. "How is the show doing? Are the advertisers happy with the number of viewers? That kind of information is important. We want the show to be successful."

"What does it matter if it isn't? We'll be gone."

"It's important because if we're going to put it on a resume, somebody has to have heard about it. There's no point in claiming stardom on a show no one saw." She stared at him. "You make me crazy, and not in a good way."

"Part of my charm," he told her and grinned.

"You are not all that." She looked past him. "For all we know, one of the camera guys has followed us. We should probably make out for a little bit, just in case."

As Dakota watched, they went into each other's arms with practiced ease. But little or no romance. It was painfully obvious that they were simply going through the motions to get more show time.

She winced. "Geoff made a huge mistake in showing that. I'm sure he's going to think it will get people talking, but the viewers are going to feel like they've been tricked."

"Which means my brother is about to be voted off," Finn said. She couldn't tell if he was happy or not. "And then what?"

"Hell if I know." He kissed Hannah's head. "Sorry, little girl." He settled more deeply in the sofa and sighed. "If I had to guess,

I would say that Sasha is going to head to Los Angeles. There is no way he's coming back to South Salmon. Stephen told me he was going to finish college. I guess I'm going to have to be happy with one of them getting through school."

Before she could point out that he had a fifty percent success rate, the scene shifted to Stephen and Aurelia. They were locked in what looked like a very passionate embrace. This wasn't fake, Dakota thought, feeling her mouth drop open. This was hot and sexy and very real.

"Oh, my," she murmured. "I didn't know Aurelia had it in her."

Finn sprang to his feet. She had to give him credit—he held Hannah so securely, the baby didn't even stir. But Dakota saw the fury in his eyes.

"She lied. She made it sound like all she was interested in was getting Stephen back to school. He lied to me, too. Damn him, he never said a word about this." He turned to Dakota. "I'm going to kill them both."

FINN DIDN'T CARE about breaking the law. He knew it was wrong to kill anyone, especially a woman. He knew he would go to jail, and he accepted that. He wasn't sure how this had happened, but he was going to make sure it stopped. And while he was out ravaging the countryside, he was going to find Geoff and put a fist through his face.

In the back of his mind, he acknowledged that for the second time in as many months, he was contemplating murder. In his normal life, the one he liked back in South Salmon, he never had those kinds of feelings. He simply went about his day, fat, dumb and happy. Well, not fat or dumb, but still. He didn't think about crushing another human being.

It wasn't him, he told himself. It was this damn town.

Dakota took Hannah from him. The baby stirred and murmured a protest before falling back asleep. For a second, staring at her sweet face, he felt himself grow more calm. Rational thought took over. Then he looked at the television screen where his brother was making out with some cougar, and the rage returned.

"Don't go out there mad," Dakota told him. "I know you're not happy about this."

"Not happy?"

He did his best to keep his voice level, more for the sleeping baby than because he didn't want to shout. Right now yelling sounded pretty damn good. As did throwing something or maybe putting his fist through a wall. Of course, if he put his fist through a wall, he ran the risk of breaking something and right now the only thing he wanted to break was Geoff's face.

"If I can't imagine hating her, how am I going to kill her?"

"Are you talking about Aurelia?" Dakota's eyes widened. "You can't kill anyone. Not only is it wrong, it's not in your nature."

"It could be. I'm very capable of protecting my own. I knew she was a cougar. I knew it and I should have done something right away. She was so sweet the last time I talked to her, pretending she cared about Stephen going back to college. It was all an act."

"You're going to protect your brother from the woman he's probably in love with? That makes sense. Finn, sit down. Take a breath. This isn't the end of the world."

"She's nearly ten years older than him. Her life is established. What is she doing with my baby brother?"

"I'm sure she's asking herself the same question. I don't know Aurelia well, but I've met her several times. I saw her in school. She's not aggressive. She has a horrible mother and lives a very small life. I'm sure she's as upset about this as you are."

He deliberately looked at the television screen where the couple in question was still kissing. "Yeah. I can see she's really broken up about it."

Dakota shifted the baby in her arms. "Maybe she's not upset right now, but I'm sure..."

"She wants something from him. Whatever it is, she's not going to get it. She's using him. She's probably been planning this from the beginning."

Dakota didn't look convinced. "Don't do anything rash."

He ignored her request. "Are you going to tell me where she lives?"

"No. And you shouldn't go looking for her or your brother until you've calmed down."

"That's not going to be for a very long time." He started for the door, then turned around and came back. He kissed Dakota on the cheek and Hannah on the top of her head, then stalked out.

Once outside of Dakota's house, he paused, not sure which way to go. He had no idea where Aurelia lived. He'd have to start with Stephen.

He moved toward the center of town. His brothers shared a room in a small motel opposite the park, just off the lake. Fifteen minutes later, he was knocking on the door to the motel room, but no one answered. No doubt Stephen was hiding from him. A smart move, considering Finn's mood.

He started back across the parking lot, only to see Stephen and Aurelia approaching. The couple was holding hands and came to a stop when they saw him.

He stood his ground, waiting.

About forty feet separated them. Stephen whispered something to Aurelia, then the two of them walked closer. As they passed under a streetlight, Finn could see that Aurelia had been crying.

The information didn't change anything, he told himself. She was a good actress. Too bad she hadn't been paired with Sasha. They could have found fame and fortune together.

"Obviously we have to talk," Stephen said when they were close enough to have a conversation.

"We can have it out here or in your room." Finn glared at

Aurelia. "Or we could go back to your place and you could tell me your plan."

Aurelia's eyes widened. More tears slipped down her cheeks. "It's not what you think," she whispered.

"Do I look like I believe that?"

"Don't," Stephen told him, then led the way to the motel room. After using his key, he pushed open the door.

Aurelia went in first. Finn followed.

The space was small. Two double beds, a long dresser with an old television sitting on top, a chair in the corner and the door leading to an even tinier bathroom. The digs weren't impressive, but then Geoff didn't feel the need to pamper his contestants.

"I know you're upset," Stephen began.

"You think?"

His brother ignored that. "Despite how angry you are, you'll treat Aurelia with respect. If you don't, this conversation is over."

"You're going to make me?"

Stephen stepped between him and Aurelia. "Yes."

There was quiet determination in his brother's voice. A strength in the way he stood. Finn was careful not to let his surprise show. Neither of his brothers had ever tried to stand up to him before. They preferred to sneak off rather than confront him directly. Maybe Stephen was finally growing up.

"All right," he said, folding his arms across his chest. "Tell me why I shouldn't believe the worst."

Aurelia and Stephen looked at each other. Finn was aware of silent communication between them, but he couldn't interpret it.

"We never meant for this to happen," Aurelia said quietly.

"You came on the show," Finn reminded her. "It's a show about meeting someone. Obviously, you wanted to meet someone. I agree that you probably had no control over who you were matched with."

He could feel his fragile control slipping. The anger returned and with it the need to lash out. "Look at him," he demanded.

"He's twenty-one. He's still a kid. His running away to be on this show proves that. If you think there's anything to be gained, any money, you can forget it."

Stephen stepped between them again and put his hand on Finn's chest. "Don't," his brother growled. "Don't push her, don't threaten her, don't make this end badly."

On the one hand, Finn appreciated Stephen's maturity. On the other hand, this was the wrong time for it to show up.

"Stop," Aurelia said. She stepped between them and separated them, holding them at arm's length. "You're family. Try to remember that." She looked at Stephen. "Please let me do this. Finn doesn't mean anything bad. He's worried about you and that's a good thing."

"I'm worried about you," Stephen told her. "I don't want him to upset you."

Aurelia shook her head. "It's not him. It's what's happening around us." She turned to Finn and dropped her arms to her sides. "You're right. I did come on the show looking for something. A lot of it was about my mother, which I'm not going to get into now." She managed a slight smile.

Her whole face changed when she smiled, Finn thought. She went from plain to pretty. There was an intelligence in her eyes. He could see why Stephen found her so appealing. But that didn't make the relationship right.

"I should have thought this through," Aurelia admitted. "When they first put me with Stephen, I was so embarrassed. He's younger and attractive and outgoing. Everything I'm not. But I was afraid to walk away. It would just be another rejection. I also wanted the twenty thousand. I want to buy a house of my own."

She clutched her hands together in front of her waist. "I know you can't understand. You've always been successful. Look at what you've done with the family business and with your brothers."

She glanced at Stephen, then back at Finn. "I've never had

the courage to stand up for myself. I've always been so afraid. Being around Stephen has shown me who I can be if only I'm willing to take the risk. He's taught me to be brave. I didn't know I could be."

"I'm sure this would be very compelling to someone who gave a shit," Finn told her. "But I—"

"I wasn't finished," she told him firmly, staring directly into his eyes. "I would appreciate it if you would let me finish what I have to say."

"All right," Finn said slowly, surprised she was willing to take him on. He was pretty sure he had intimidated her, so this act of courage was unexpected. It was possible it made him like her a little.

"I'm not a cougar. I wasn't looking for a younger man. I don't know what I was looking for, and maybe that's the problem. I never thought I would find anyone. I never thought I was good enough. But I am. I deserve love as much as anyone else."

She raised her chin slightly. "It was never my intention to be caught in a passionate embrace on television. I apologize for that and any embarrassment it may have brought your family. But I don't apologize for loving your brother. I don't apologize for caring about him and wanting the best for him."

She drew in a breath. "I know he's too young. I know he has a lifetime of experiences waiting for him and I shouldn't get in the way of that. God has nothing if not a sense of humor, because I can't help being in love with him."

Finn had been with her right up until she said she was in love with his little brother. But before he could speak, Aurelia turned to Stephen.

"Your brother is right. You don't belong here with me. Go home. Finish your degree. Get a job doing what you love. Live your life."

She sounded sincere, Finn admitted, if only to himself. Under any other circumstances, he would've believed her and been impressed as hell.

Stephen moved toward her. Finn knew what was going to happen. His brother would yell and stomp and pout until he got his way, his actions proving that he wasn't ready to be in a relationship. But it turned out Finn was wrong.

Stephen cupped Aurelia's face in his hands. "I know that's what you believe. I know you think being with me only hurts me. But you're wrong. You are everything I have ever wanted. I *will* go to college and finish my degree. I *will* get a job. But I'm going to do it here. With you. There is nothing you can say to make me go away. I love you."

Finn could feel the emotion between them. He felt like an outsider caught staring at something intimate.

Stephen turned to him. "I was wrong to run away. Coming here the way I did only reinforced your idea that I wasn't a man. I was acting like a kid and I deserve to be treated like one. I'm sorry for screwing up. I'm sorry you had to come after me. I know you have a business and responsibilities. But I didn't think of any of that. I only thought of myself."

Finn wouldn't have been more stunned if Aurelia had morphed into a squirrel and started dancing. "It turned out okay," he said roughly.

"Not yet, but it will." Stephen faced Aurelia again. "I want to marry you. I know it's too soon, so I'm not asking. I'm just letting you know where I think this is going. I'm going to finish school and get a job. I'm going to keep on seeing you. A year from today I'm going to ask you to marry me. And on that day, I'll expect an answer."

Finn waited for the fury, but there wasn't any anger. There wasn't even a mild annoyance. If he had to name the emotion surging through him, it was regret. Not because his brother had grown up, but because he, Finn, didn't have anything close to what Stephen had with Aurelia. His kid brother had won the prize.

It wasn't that he wanted to be in love. Not exactly. What he wanted was something different. Still, he couldn't escape the sense of having missed out on something important.

"I'll get out of your way," Finn said.

"You don't have to go," Aurelia told him. But she was looking at Stephen as she spoke.

"You two have a lot to talk about."

He thought his brother might want to make sure things were okay between them, but Stephen was too busy kissing Aurelia. Finn backed out of the room, stepped onto the walkway and closed the door behind him. One brother's situation solved, another to go.

He walked down the street, wondering what to do about Sasha. How to get him—

He stopped by Morgan's Books and stared blindly at the display in the window. There was nothing to do about either of his brothers. Dakota had been right all along. His job was done. He'd parented them as best he could, and keeping them safe forever wasn't an option. He had to trust they were ready to make their own decisions. It was time.

DAKOTA STARED AT all the clothes spread across the bed. It was as if a department store had exploded in her mother's bedroom.

"I didn't know you owned this many things," she said, putting Hannah into her playpen. "When was the last time you cleaned out your closet? Are those leg warmers? Mom, the eighties were a long time ago."

"You're not funny," her mother snapped. "If you think this is humorous, you're wrong. I'm in crisis here. A really, really big crisis. I feel sick to my stomach, my head hurts, I'm retaining enough water to sink a battleship. I'm a woman on the edge. You need to respect that."

Her mother sank onto the bed where she sat on several outfits, crushing them.

"I'm sorry," Dakota said, trying to keep the humor out of her voice. "I won't be funny again."

"I don't believe you. But that's not the point. I can't do this." Her mother covered her face with her hands. "What was I thinking? I'm too old to do this. The last time I dated, dinosaurs roamed the earth. We didn't even have electricity."

Dakota knelt in front of her and pulled her hands away from her face. "I happen to know nearly all the dinosaurs were extinct and there was electricity. Come on, Mom. You know you want to do this."

"No, I don't. It's not too late to cancel, right? I can cancel. You could call and tell him I have some kind of typhoid fever. Imply that it's very contagious and I'm going to be shipped off to one of those federal medical facilities in Arizona. I hear the dry air is very good for typhoid fever."

Just then, Dakota heard voices in the hall. "Are we too late?" Montana called. "I don't want to miss the fun part."

Montana and Nevada entered the bedroom. They looked around at the array of clothing and accessories.

"I didn't hear about a tornado on the news," Nevada said cheerfully. "Was anyone hurt?"

"I can see I raised you girls with too much freedom and affection," their mother snapped. "I should have repressed you more. Maybe then you'd treat me with more respect."

"We love you, Mom," Nevada said. "And we respect you. I didn't know you had this many clothes."

Dakota chuckled. "Don't go there. She'll bite your head off."

Montana lifted Hannah from the playpen and cuddled with her. "Who's a pretty girl? We're going to ignore all those sniping grown-ups, aren't we?"

"I was telling your sister that I can't do this," Denise said. "I can't go on a date. We were discussing telling him I have typhoid fever."

Nevada rolled her eyes. "Right. Because he'll never guess you're lying if you say that. Come on, Mom. It's one evening. You need to get out there and see if you're interested in dating. Right now it's just a theory. If it's horrible, you never have to go again. Besides, you're making us all nuts. None of us are dating." She glanced at Dakota. "Well, Dakota might be. No one can pin her down on her relationship with Finn. For all we know, they're running off to the Bahamas tomorrow to get married."

"You're getting married?" her mother asked.

Dakota sighed. "Don't pretend to be distracted by something you know isn't true. Nevada is right. Try the date." She carefully avoided asking what the worst was that could happen. That question never went well.

"Who's the guy?" Montana asked, still holding Hannah.

"A friend of Morgan's," Denise said.

"We like Morgan," Nevada said. "That's a good sign."

Denise stood and pressed her hands against her stomach. "His friend may be nothing like him. He may be a serial killer. Or a cross-dresser."

"At least you have enough clothes to support his habit," Montana offered.

Dakota and Nevada laughed. Their mother glared at them.

"You're not helping," Denise informed them. "I'm going to have to ask you three to leave. Hannah can stay. She's very supportive." She looked at the little girl. "Never have daughters. Trust me. They only break your heart."

Nevada walked to the bed and stared at the clothes strewn across it. After a second she reached into the mess and withdrew a white-and-blue floral print wrap dress.

"Wear this," she said. "It will work nearly anywhere. You look great in it and it's comfortable. It's perfect for the season. You have those gorgeous blue shoes. He'll be wildly impressed."

Denise stared at the dress, then at the three of them. "Really?"

Dakota nodded. "You know how I hate to admit that Nevada is right, but this time she is. That dress is perfect. You'll look lovely, and more important, you'll feel good." She walked over to her mom and put her arm around her. "I know this is scary, but it's important. Dad's been gone for nearly eleven years. It's okay for you to move on. You deserve to be happy."

Her mother drew in a shaky breath. "Okay," she said. "I'll go on the date and I'll wear the dress. My makeup is done and this is as good as my hair is going to look. So all I have to do is get dressed." She glanced at the clock. "Oh, God. I have two hours until he gets here. I think I'm going to be sick." She waved her hands in front of her face. "Quick. I need a distraction. Somebody say something that will make me forget I even have a date."

Montana and Nevada looked at each other and shrugged, as if they didn't have anything to offer. Dakota figured this was as good a time as any to spill her news.

"I'll give it a try," she said with a smile. "Mom, I have something to tell you. I'm pregnant."

CHAPTER EIGHTEEN

DAKOTA'S SISTERS LOOKED at her with identical expressions of surprise. Her mother lunged forward and hugged her close.

"Really?" Denise asked, still holding on. "You're not just teasing me to get my mind off my date?"

"I wouldn't do that. I'm pregnant. It's kind of unexpected, given my medical history. I wasn't planning on this, but I can't help but be happy."

"Finn must have some great swimmers," Montana said. "It is Finn, right?"

Dakota laughed. "Yes, it's him. There hasn't been anyone else. I know there're complications and I know this isn't anything he wanted, but I can't help being happy. I'm going to have a baby and I never thought I could."

"You're probably having enough sex to defy the odds," Nevada told her. "Statistically it was always possible. You just needed the right set of circumstances."

Dakota stepped back and turned in a circle. "I don't care whether it was his swimmers or the moon or an alien landing. I'm so excited." She was having trouble grasping the reality of the situation, but so far there was no downside. Sure, having two kids so close together would be a challenge, but other women got through it and she would, as well.

"When you decided to become a mother, you did it in a big way," Denise said with a laugh. "If you're happy, I'm happy."

"I am. Hannah is going to love having a baby brother or sister."

Montana and Nevada exchanged a glance. Dakota knew exactly what they were thinking. She drew in a breath.

"No, I haven't told him," she said, answering their unasked question. "I will. I know I have to. And I know he's not going to take it well. Finn has made it very clear what he wants from life and it isn't more responsibility. He's been great with Hannah, but she's not his. He can walk away at any time. A baby is going to change everything for him."

There was an emotional storm coming. As much as she wanted to believe he would be happy, she knew better. He might even think she'd tried to trick him. Whatever happened, she would get through it. Even if he walked away, she would be fine. Broken hearts healed. Hers would, too. Because no matter what, she was having a baby.

"He might surprise you," her mother said. Although her expression was hopeful, her tone was thick with doubt.

"I don't think so." Nevada looked uncomfortable but kept on talking. "When it comes to things like this, men tend to tell the truth. If the guy says he's never been faithful, a woman needs to listen. And if a man says he doesn't want a family, he's probably not lying." She turned to Dakota. "I'm sorry. I really want to be wrong. But I don't want to see you hurt more."

"I know." Dakota understood the risks. She and Finn had started their relationship for a lot of reasons that were about attraction and hot sex. Along the way, she had discovered he was a pretty great guy. She'd felt herself starting to fall for him and figured that was the biggest problem she would face. Being in love with a man who only wanted to leave.

Now she had to explain how her claim of being unable to conceive might not have been completely true. Not a conversation designed to go well.

"Maybe he'll surprise you," Montana said. "Maybe he'll be mad at first, but then he'll realize this is what he's wanted all along. Maybe he's wildly in love with you and doesn't know how to tell you."

"If wishes were horses…" Denise said, then sighed. She looked at Dakota. "I'm sorry, honey. Nevada's right. Men tend to tell the truth, even when they don't mean to. I don't think Finn is going to be happy about this."

"I know." Dakota smiled. "I'll be fine, whatever happens. I know I have all of you and the town. I have Hannah. And I'm having a baby. That's the miracle. Whatever else happens, I have my miracle. Most people don't get to say that. Most people go their whole lives without experiencing something like this. Having Finn around would have been an amazing bonus, but I'm okay with what I have."

"You love him," Nevada murmured. "Did I see this before?"

"No, because I didn't want to admit it to myself." Love? Dakota told herself not to be surprised. Considering the man in question, it was probably inevitable.

Love. She turned the concept over in her mind and found that it fit. She loved him. No doubt she had for a long time.

"It will be an unconventional happy ending," she told her sisters and her mother. "I won't get the guy, but I'll get everything else. That's going to be enough for me."

They moved toward her as one, embracing her and holding her close. She felt their love wash over her and through her, strengthening her. There were people who had to go through much worse situations alone. She was lucky. She had her family, and they had her.

FINN CHECKED THE cargo manifest against the boxes he loaded. It was a good day to fly. The winds were light, the sky was clear and he was going to Reno. Sure, it was a turnaround trip, with him on the ground less than an hour, but it was always interesting to fly somewhere he'd never been.

He was enjoying the airspace of the West Coast. The weather was more predictable, and there were a lot more airports to be had. Even moderately sized communities like Bakersfield lay sprawled in all directions. There were people everywhere, little towns and big cities. Instead of dodging mountains and arctic storms, he had to find his way through commercial flight paths in the wake of a 757 jetliner. Different challenges, same thrill.

Flying was in his blood. He couldn't escape it, and he didn't want to. He regretted that neither of his brothers were as interested, but he accepted it. He wouldn't have wanted to be pushed into some other career.

He finished the paperwork and started toward the office. If he got back early enough, he could take a second trip that day. That would make Hamilton happy. The old coot reminded Finn of his grandfather. Both men were smart entrepreneurs, patient with honest mistakes and unfailingly generous. They were men from another time.

"Finn?"

He stopped and turned. Sasha was walking across the tarmac. His younger brother had been voted off the show the previous night. Given what he and Lani had admitted on camera, it wasn't a surprise that viewers had been disappointed in them and wanted them gone.

He'd wondered if Sasha would be disappointed. Now as he watched his brother approach, he recognized the other man's excitement. Sasha had good news.

Finn knew without being told that Sasha was not going back to South Salmon. Even so, he paused and waited for his brother to speak.

"Did you see the show?" Sasha asked, sounding more happy than sad. "I can't believe we got caught like that. We've been so careful." He shrugged and grinned. "I guess not careful enough."

"You don't sound upset."

"I'm going to L.A. I got a call this morning from an agent.

One of his assistants has been watching the show and she thinks I'm really hot." The grin broadened. "Hot is good. So he wants me to come down to L.A. We're going to talk. He already has a few ideas of where he's going to send me. There is a show looking to replace an ongoing character and a small part in a movie."

Sasha kept talking, going on about how he and Lani were driving down that afternoon. She knew of a cheap apartment where they could stay. It seemed she, too, had an audition and interested agent.

Finn knew it was time to let go. Sasha no longer belonged in South Salmon. His brother needed to be other places.

"This is what I really want," Sasha told him earnestly. "I know you're disappointed."

"A little," Finn admitted. "But not surprised. You've been heading in this direction for a while."

"That almost sounds like you're not mad."

"I'm not. I won't say I didn't wish this had turned out differently. I would rather you finish college. But you have to make your own decisions and live with the consequences. I hope this turns out for the best. I hope you get to be on TV or in a movie."

"Thanks!" Sasha sounded both happy and surprised. "I thought you'd be furious."

"You wore me down, kid." Finn pulled his wallet out of his back pocket and counted out the money he'd withdrawn from his account that morning. "Here's three hundred dollars and a check for a thousand more. Get yourself a decent place to live. Try to eat regularly."

"I don't know what to say," Sasha admitted, taking the money. "I really appreciate this. It's gonna make a big difference."

"Your brother is going back to college. The money is still there, in your education fund. If you decide to go back, you'll be able to finish whenever you want."

Sasha's mouth twisted. "You're the best brother a guy could have. I know I've been a pain. It wasn't on purpose."

Finn felt his throat tighten. "Most of the time it was."

Sasha laughed. "Maybe fifty percent." His humor faded. "You did a good job with us. Mom and Dad would be proud. I have a plan. You can stop worrying about me."

"That's not going to happen, but I'm ready to let you go."

They moved toward each other at the same time. There was some back slapping and a brief hug. About as much emotion as either of them were comfortable with. Then Sasha put the money in his pocket, waved and walked away.

Finn had come to Fool's Gold to force his brothers to return home. He'd believed the only place they belonged was in college or in South Salmon. He'd been wrong on all counts. Neither brother was coming home, and oddly enough, he was just fine with that.

DAKOTA ARRIVED AT WORK the next morning with a burning need for coffee and a promise to herself that she would tell Finn about the baby before sundown. Or maybe by the end of the week.

She wasn't trying to be a coward or even keep the information from him. It was just that she was so happy. She wanted to stay happy for a little longer. She wanted to have her fantasies about the future and pretend everything was going to work out fine. She wanted to imagine a house with a big tree in the yard and two children playing together and Finn beside her.

Because as much as she wanted this baby, she also wanted to be with that baby's father. The big surprise wasn't that she had fallen in love with him, it was that it had taken her so long to figure it out.

She walked toward the temporary production offices and was surprised to see large trucks pulled up in front of them. As she approached, she saw guys in T-shirts carrying boxes and furniture into the trucks. If she didn't know better, she would say everyone was leaving.

She saw Karen, one of the production assistants, sitting at a table in the middle of the sidewalk.

"What's going on?" Dakota asked as she approached. "Why are you working out here?"

Karen looked up at her. Her eyes were swollen and red, as if she'd been crying. "It's over. The show's canceled." She sniffed. "We were shut down late last night. Geoff called me from the airport. He's already back in L.A."

"Canceled? How can they do that? We're not even through this cycle. Who wins?"

"No one," Karen told her flatly. "No one cares. The numbers suck. We started out okay but then plummeted in the third week. It's a disaster."

Dakota was having trouble taking in the information. "What happens to the contestants?"

"They go home."

"What happens to you?"

Tears filled Karen's eyes. "I work for Geoff. Right now that's not a good thing. I have a lot of friends in the business and they'll help me. I need to get work with another company or producer." She sighed. "I have savings. This sort of thing happens all the time, so if you're going to survive, you have to be prepared to deal with weeks of unemployment. But it's not fun and I know people are wondering if I knew. I didn't. But nobody gives a crap about that."

"I'm sorry," Dakota said, feeling awkward. She didn't know what else to say. She didn't understand how so much money could be put into a show and then the show simply canceled within a few short weeks.

"If you need a recommendation or if I can help in any way, please let me know," Dakota told her.

"Thanks." She glanced at her watch. "You'd better get into your office. If you have anything personal, I'd get it in the next five or ten minutes. Your part of the office is going to be dismantled by nine."

"Okay. I will." Dakota stood there awkwardly for a few seconds, but Karen returned her attention to her work and didn't look up again.

As Dakota walked toward her small corner of the production office, she pulled out her cell phone and left a message for the mayor. She had a feeling that word had already spread all over town. She looked around at the cameras being loaded onto trucks and people getting in cars and driving away. The TV show had tried to take over the town. She had a feeling that in a matter of hours, it would seem as if it had never been there. Maybe that was just the nature of the business. It was all an illusion and nothing ever lasted.

BY NOON, Dakota was back in her old office, ready to tackle the curriculum planning for which she'd been hired. She'd had a quick meeting with Raoul Moreno and, as he put it, a game plan. She let him call her schedule a game plan for two reasons. First, because he was a former NFL quarterback and sports terms made him feel happy. Second, because he signed her paycheck.

Before his summer camp had been transformed into a temporary elementary school, his dream had been to open a facility for kids in middle school. The emphasis would be on math and science. They would come for three or four weeks at a time, have extensive study in either math or science and, in theory, return to their regular schools enthused about what they could accomplish. As the elementary school would need the camp for at least two years, they had ample time to develop their program.

Montana arrived at the office exactly at two. She had a leash in one hand and pushed the stroller with the other. Buddy, the intense and worried labradoodle, kept pace with the stroller. Every few seconds he looked at Hannah, as if making sure she was all right.

"I can't decide if Buddy would make a good dad if he were human," Montana said, "or if he would be on Prozac half the time."

"He's a pretty good-looking guy," Dakota said, rising and coming around her desk. "He'd probably discover women and forget to pick up his kids from day care."

Montana bent down and patted the dog. "Don't you listen to her, Buddy. I know better. I know you'd never forget to pick up your children from day care. Who's that handsome puppy? We'll ignore my mean sister."

Dakota laughed. "I'm sorry, Buddy. I was teasing." She picked up Hannah and pulled her close. "How's my girl?"

Montana straightened. "She was great. She's eating much better. I swear I can see her growing. I can't say I love poopy diapers, but I'm getting good at them."

"I really appreciate you looking after her," Dakota said. "Now that I'm back here, I should be able to bring her to work with me at least three days a week. So I'm not going to need as much day care. Mom's going to take her one of those days and I've had about five calls from different women in town wanting her the other day."

"It must be nice to be popular."

"It's not me. It's Hannah. She's more popular than any of us."

Montana sat on the edge of the desk. "I don't think I could do what you do."

"Plan curriculum?"

"Have a baby by myself." Montana's gaze dropped to her sister's stomach. "Make that two babies."

"It wasn't planned," Dakota admitted, telling herself not to panic at the thought of being a single mom to two young children. "I'll admit I'm scared, but I'm not going to think about that. Both children are a blessing."

"What is Finn?"

A good question and one she couldn't answer.

"I love him," Dakota said quietly and shrugged. "I know it's stupid, but I couldn't help myself. I just…" She smiled. "He's the one."

"Wow. You found him."

"I'm not saying it was an intelligent choice."

"It could work out," Montana told her.

"I appreciate your loyalty, but do you really believe that?"

"He could surprise you."

Dakota gave her a skeptical look. "He's made it clear that he wants his old life back. With his brothers moving on, he's finally free. I know he cares about me, but that's not the same as love or taking on more responsibility."

"So you're not going to ask?"

"I'm not going to make myself crazy wishing for something that might never happen."

Montana started to speak, then stopped. "Tell me what I can do to help."

"What were you going to say?"

Her sister shifted. "That you're giving up without trying. If you love him, if he's the one, shouldn't you at least try to make things work? Fight for him? Only he hasn't said no yet, because you haven't told him. So there's no fight to be had."

"I'll tell him. I'm waiting because I know what's going to happen and I don't want to ruin what we have. Trust me. When Finn finds out I'm pregnant, there will be burning skid marks on the road."

"If you say so."

The conversation wasn't going the way Dakota had intended, and she found herself annoyed. She told herself that this wasn't Montana's fault. She didn't understand. Wanting something didn't make it happen.

"You need to give him the chance to surprise you," Montana murmured. "Maybe he will."

Dakota nodded because she didn't want to fight, but she knew the truth was very different.

THAT NIGHT DAKOTA FELT RESTLESS. She couldn't forget her argument with her sister, and she couldn't ignore the voice in her head saying that she was hiding rather than being honest. That both she and Finn deserved better.

When she let him in that night, she had a marinara sauce simmering and soft music playing. Hannah had already drifted off for her dinnertime nap.

"Hey," Finn said, as he walked into her small house. "How was your first day away from TV? Do you miss the excitement of working in the entertainment industry?"

He smiled as he spoke, his blue eyes crinkling slightly. He was tall and handsome and strong. He was someone she could lean on.

Maybe she'd never fallen in love before because she hadn't found the right guy. There had always been a nagging sense of something missing. With Finn, she felt full...complete.

If only.

She waited until he closed the front door, then stepped into his arms. As she wrapped her arms around him, she drew his head down so she could kiss him. Telling him how she felt was a one-way road to disaster, but showing him... That might be different.

She pressed her mouth against his, letting all the frustration, the love, the worry, spill into her kiss. He held on tight, as if sensing she needed to be close. He kissed her back, his tongue tangling with hers, his body surging close.

Hunger flared to life, but it was about so much more than sex. It was about him and what they could have together.

Wordlessly, she reached for his hand and tugged him through the living room, down the hall and into her bedroom. With the door open, they could easily hear Hannah if she cried.

Once in the dimness of her bedroom, she turned to him. There were questions in his eyes, but he didn't ask anything. Apparently he knew she needed more than conversation.

He put his hands on the hem of her T-shirt and pulled it over her head. She unfastened her bra. When she was naked to the waist, he bent down and drew her already tight nipple into his mouth. He used his hand to tease her other breast.

His mouth was warm. His tongue aroused her, flicking the tip over her nipple. With each deep tug, she felt herself swelling and readying. Only it wasn't enough. She wanted more than this. She wanted all of him, on top of her, filling her, taking her. She needed him. She needed the connection.

Again, he read her mind. He reached for the button on her jeans. She undid it for him, then pushed down her clothes. Immediately he slipped his hand between her legs. She was already wet. With his thumb, he found her center. As he rubbed that sensitive knot of flesh, he pushed two fingers inside of her.

Sensations assaulted her. From his mouth at her breasts to his hand stroking, massaging, pushing. He went in deeper, finding all the places that made her gasp. Even though she hung on to him, her legs began to tremble. She was having trouble staying upright. But she didn't want him to stop. She didn't want anything to distract him from the way he made her feel.

Tension filled her. Tension and pleasure and an unrelenting desire to be swept away into an ocean of satisfaction. She was getting closer and closer, so close that—

He stopped. She cried out her protest, not sure what was happening. Before she could say anything, he'd pushed her back onto the bed. She sat on the edge of the mattress, and then he was on his knees, parting her legs, replacing his thumb with his tongue. He kissed her intimately, even as he thrust his fingers back inside of her.

The feel of his tongue, his breath, the fullness was too much. She barely had time to register the pleasure when she was tumbling into her release. She cried out as her body shuddered.

The waves came again and again until she was limp. Then he was standing and tumbling with his clothes. As he sent his shirt, shoes, socks, jeans and boxers flying, she scrambled up a little higher on the bed. He joined her seconds later.

"Dakota," he breathed, as he pushed into her.

She welcomed him, wrapping her legs around his hips and drawing him closer. Usually she closed her eyes, but this time she kept them open, watching him watch her. They were connected. She felt what he felt, knew his anticipation, experienced the tension. As he got closer, so did she. The need for more grew until there was nothing to do but come together.

She clung to him as he held on to her. The night closed around them until it seemed as if they had always been together and that they could never ever be apart.

I love you.

She thought the words but didn't speak them. She knew once she said them, she would have to tell him the truth, and then those words would be a trap. A way to make him feel obligated.

If only.

The wish was like a prayer, sent out into the cosmos. Was having the one man she'd waited her whole life to find too much to ask?

Even as the question formed, she heard Hannah's soft sigh and had her answer. She'd already been given so much. There was no way she could have it all.

She might not be able to keep Finn, but she would have his baby, and somehow, she would make that enough.

CHAPTER NINETEEN

"YOU'RE KILLING ME," Bill said, his voice surprisingly clear considering he was twelve hundred miles away. "We're starting our busy season, Finn. You've got to get back here or you've got to cut me loose."

"I know," Finn said, clutching the cell phone. "Just give me another week."

"To do what? You said the show was over. That your brothers were done with it. What more is there to do in that damn town?"

An excellent question, Finn thought. He should be jumping on the first plane back to Alaska. And he wasn't. He kept having this feeling that there was more to do here.

"It's that woman, isn't it?"

"Dakota? Some of it is her." He hadn't meant to get involved. He didn't want to get close to anyone. But there was something about her. Something that appealed to him. Walking away was going to be harder than he'd expected.

"Are you thinking about staying?"

"I don't know. I'm not sure of anything. Look, Bill, I know this is unfair. I know you're working your ass off. Just give me a week. I'll have an answer then."

His friend sighed. "Fine. A week. But no longer. And you are going to seriously owe me."

"I know. Whatever you want, it's yours."

Bill chuckled. "Like I believe that. Talk to you in a week. If you don't call me, I'm selling your half of the business to the first person who offers me a nickel."

"Fair enough." Finn ended the call.

He stood on the tarmac of the Fool's Gold airport and looked at the planes. He could make a life here, if that was what he wanted. The question was, did he? He'd been responsible for so damn long, and he'd told himself that when he got his brothers raised, he was done. He was only going to think about himself, do what he wanted.

Now that he was free, being alone wasn't quite so appealing. He'd gotten used to being part of the family. Part of something. Did he want to walk away from that? Did it have to be all or nothing?

"What did your partner say?" Hamilton asked.

Finn had mentioned having to phone Bill. "He's not happy I'm still here. I told him I'd make a decision within the next week."

Hamilton raised his bushy gray eyebrows. "You thinking about buying me out? I can have some papers drawn up."

The old man offered him the business nearly every time he reported for work. The price was fair, and there was plenty of potential to grow. Finn had some ideas about scheduled shipping routes and passenger service. If he wanted to stay.

"I'll let you know in the next week, as well."

"What's so special about the next seven days?" Hamilton asked. "You reading tea leaves or something?"

"Not yet. I need to figure some things out."

Hamilton shook his head. "You young people today. Never wanting to make a decision. I know what's keeping you here. It's that girl in town. She seems pretty enough to me, but then what do I know? I've been married nearly forty years." He grinned. "Take it from an old man. Marriage is a good way to go."

Marriage? Is that what they were talking about? He knew in

his head it was a logical next step, but the thought of it made him take a step back. Dakota had a daughter. Was he ready to be a father? Hadn't he already done that with his brothers?

He supposed it came down to his feelings for Dakota. He knew he liked her. She had been an unexpected find in what could have been a terrible situation. She was supportive and caring. He liked watching her with Hannah. She was a good mother and a good friend. She would probably make a great wife. The thing was, he didn't think he was looking for one.

"A week," he repeated.

Hamilton raised his arm. "Fine by me. Take as long as you want. I think you like it here. I think you're looking for an excuse to stay. If you were so hot to get back to Alaska, you'd already be gone. But then I'm just an old man."

Finn grinned. "You say that a lot. That you're an old man and what do you know, but you seem to have an opinion about everything."

Hamilton laughed. "When you're my age, boy, you'll have an opinion about everything, too."

SUNDAY MORNING, Dakota joined her sisters at her mother's house for an informal brunch. It was getting warmer and warmer as they headed for the summer months. Today, Denise had set the table on the patio. There was a bowl of fresh fruit, juice, pastries and an egg casserole. The scent of fresh coffee competed with the delicate aroma of flowers in the morning.

Dakota held Hannah on her lap. The little girl was doing well in her high chair, but this many people would be a distraction. It was easier to keep one arm around her squirming body as she reached out toward her aunt and her grandmother.

"So how was the date?" Nevada asked. She poured herself a cup of coffee, then passed the pot to Montana. "Did you do anything wild and get arrested?"

Denise sipped her juice, then put the glass on the table and leaned back in her chair. "It was fine."

Montana laughed. "I don't think he's going to want your endorsement in a campaign. Fine? Did you have a good time? Did you like him? Start at the beginning and tell us everything."

"He's a perfectly nice man. We talked about a lot of different things. He's funny, sort of. He's well-traveled. It was fine. I wasn't exactly expecting a life-changing event. It was just a date."

Dakota thought about the time she spent with Finn. "Sometimes 'just a date' can be life-changing."

"I'm not sure I believe that," her mother said. "You have to get to know someone. Is there really love at first sight? I'm not sure. Maybe that's only something that happens when you're really young. When you don't have to be cautious and careful."

"Why do you have to be careful?" Nevada asked.

"A lot of reasons. I haven't dated in over thirty years. I don't know how the rules have changed. Plus I'm not a kid. I have responsibilities. I have children and grandchildren and a place in the community. I'm not going to run off with some biker just because he sets my thighs on fire."

"I think I'd run off with the biker who set my thighs on fire," Nevada said. She smiled. "Assuming you mean setting them on fire the good way and not with a match."

"Well, of course. I'm not interested in dating a pyromaniac." Denise shook her head. "It's very complicated at my age. You girls don't understand. You're still very young. The rules aren't the same for you."

"Are you saying you were sexually attracted to him and you're afraid to act on it?" Dakota asked, oddly terrified of the answer. She told herself that they were all adults here, and her mother was as much a sexual being as the rest of them. But it was still strange to be having this conversation with a parent.

"No. I was speaking theoretically." Denise picked up her coffee. "There wasn't any chemistry. We kissed." She shuddered delicately. "Maybe I'm too old to have a man's tongue in my mouth."

Dakota did her best not to flinch. Nevada stiffened and Montana shrieked, then covered her ears with her hands.

"I can't," Montana said. "I know it's not mature, but I just can't have you talking about this. It's icky." She dropped her hands. "Not icky exactly, but just too much information."

Hannah clapped her hands and laughed at her aunt's antics.

"At least you're amused," Dakota told her little girl, then kissed the top of her head. She turned her attention to her mother. "While I'm willing to be more mature about this than my sister, I will admit that it's strange to talk about you having a sex life. But as a trained professional, I will listen."

Denise laughed. "You girls are ridiculous. I'm talking about French kissing. It's not like I described twenty minutes of intercourse."

Montana covered her ears again and started humming. Nevada looked like she was ready to bolt.

"It's probably best you didn't have sex on the first date," Dakota said, hoping she sounded calm and reasonable. She was completely with her sisters. Anywhere but here. Parental sex discussions should be illegal. "It's been a long time for you. You were married to Dad for all those years and now you've been a widow for a decade. Starting the dating game slowly makes the most sense."

"That's what I thought," her mother said primly. "The kissing was really just an experiment. I wondered what it would be like with another man. It wasn't that great."

Montana dropped her hands again. "Maybe it wasn't the kissing, maybe it was the guy. Chemistry matters. There has to be that spark."

"Maybe he was a nice enough man," their mother said. "But there was no spark. I'm not going out with him again. I want to say I'm never going out again but it would be silly to make that decision based on a single date. I'll think about it."

She turned to Dakota. "And while we're on the subject about

thinking about things—have you told Finn about being pregnant?"

"Is Finn pregnant, too?" Montana asked, grinning.

"I'm ignoring you," her mother said. "Eat your breakfast."

"Yes, ma'am." Montana reached for her fork.

The other two looked at Dakota. She shifted on her feet. "I haven't told him, exactly."

Her mother's expression turned disapproving. "This is not information you keep to yourself. Finn has the right to know he's going to be a father."

"I know, and I'm going to tell him. Soon." She drew in a breath. "Every time I think about telling him, I get a knot in my stomach. He's still here. He doesn't have to be here, but he is. Everything is settled with his brothers and he hasn't said when he's leaving. Which makes me think I might be the reason he's staying."

"You're afraid if you tell him about the baby, he'll run," Nevada said gently.

"Yes," Dakota whispered, knowing it was cowardly and still the truth. "I love him. I want him to stay. Having him go would break my heart."

"Then tell him that," Montana suggested. "Knowing how you feel could change his mind. And you don't know that he won't be happy about the baby. He might surprise you."

Dakota would like to believe that, but she wasn't holding her breath. As for telling Finn that she loved him...

"I don't want him to see my feelings as a trap," she admitted. "I don't want him to think I'm telling him I love him to get him to stay. I'm not sure I can tell him those two things together. But if I tell him I love him and then tell him about the baby, it's still a trap. If I tell him about the baby, I probably won't get a chance to tell him that I love him. I don't know how to fix this."

"That's because it can't be fixed," her mother told her. "There is nothing to be resolved. There is information to be shared and plans to be made." She paused. "As for which you tell him first,

I understand your dilemma. However you choose to handle this, he needs to know that you're pregnant. Every man has the right to know he's going to be a father. Don't wait for the right time, because there isn't one."

It had been many years since her mother had scolded her, Dakota thought. No matter how old she got or how mature she felt, those chiding words still had the power to make her feel small. She wanted to protest that she had her reasons, but she knew her mother was right. She was hiding from the situation, avoiding what had to be done. Whatever the outcome, she had to tell him.

"I'll tell him today."

And by tomorrow he would be gone.

"Sasha called from L.A. He's found an apartment, and sharing it with two other guys. I guess they take turns sleeping. I'm not sure what happened with Lani, but whatever. He sounds happy."

Dakota found it difficult to concentrate on Finn's conversation. While she was usually happy to listen, this was different. The need to tell him the truth pressed in on her. She still hadn't figured out the best words to use, but she was done procrastinating.

"I have to tell you something," she said, interrupting him. "It's important." They were sitting on her living-room floor, Hannah on the carpet between them. The little girl held a set of baby keys in her hand and was delighted by the noise when she shook them.

Finn drew his eyebrows together. "Is everything okay? Is it Hannah?"

Dakota drew in her breath. She just had to say it, she told herself. Just blurt it out. Then hope for the best. "It's not Hannah. It's me." She shook her head. "No, I don't mean it that way. I'm…"

She swore silently. It wasn't supposed to be this hard.

"You've been really great to me," she said, forcing herself to stare into his dark blue eyes. "I know you didn't want to come here. But I'm glad you did. I'm glad I got to meet you and spend time with you. You're really special to me."

She swallowed. There she was—about to say the word she'd never said to a man before. She'd never even come close. She loved her family, but this was different. This was romantic love. And this was the rest of her life.

"I'm in love with you. I didn't mean for it to happen, but it did. And I know you probably don't want to stay here, but you're not gone yet and I'm hoping Hannah and I are part of the reason. There are a lot of complications, your life in South Salmon, my life here, but I thought maybe we could figure it out together."

She couldn't tell what he was thinking. He kept looking at her, but his expression was unreadable. She didn't know if that was good or bad.

Now came the hard part. "There's just one more thing."

FINN WASN'T SURE what the one more thing could be. Having Dakota spell out her feelings was a surprise. No one had ever been that honest with him. One more point in her favor, he thought, turning her words over in his mind and finding he liked them.

She was right. He'd never planned on staying in Fool's Gold. He'd never wanted to come here in the first place. But he was glad he had. Being here had taught him to trust his brothers. Being here had allowed him to see they were adults and he could let go. Being here had even given him the opportunity to fall in love with Dakota.

His gaze drifted to Hannah. Sure, he didn't want to take on any more responsibility, but this was different. She was a great kid, and he already knew her. Plus the idea of a little girl was fun. There would probably be a whole lot fewer broken windows. He hadn't thought he would get seriously involved for a while, if ever, but life wasn't always tidy.

"I'm pregnant." She bit her lower lip. "I know this is a shock.

I know I told you I couldn't get pregnant and it was true. Well, obviously not completely true, but the doctor said it was unlikely and it was a one in one million chance and it's probably because you have really good swimmers and…" She stared at him. "I'm pregnant."

Pregnant.

He knew what the word meant intellectually. He knew where babies came from. He'd known that since he was ten. But pregnant?

He wanted to stand and raise his fist to the heavens. This was not supposed to happen. She'd told him she couldn't get pregnant, and he'd believed her.

She was still talking, but he wasn't listening. The occasional word slipped through. Something about a small chance. Something about them getting lucky.

He stared at her. "Lucky? You think this is lucky?" Now he did rise to his feet. "This isn't lucky. This is a scam. Was there ever anything wrong with you? Or were you just trying to trick me?"

Even as he asked the question, he already knew the answer. Dakota wouldn't trick him. That wasn't her style. She'd been honest from day one. But damn. Why the hell had this happened?

She scrambled to her feet and pulled Hannah into her arms. The baby gurgled and held out her hands to him.

"I didn't do this on purpose." Dakota's voice was quiet with determination.

He shoved his fists into his jeans pockets and stalked across the room. "I know that," he said, nearly yelling. "But this isn't what I wanted. Not now. Not again. I just got free and now I'm trapped again."

"You're not trapped. You're not anything. Feel free to walk away." She raised her chin. "We don't need you here, Finn. I'm telling you because it's the right thing to do. Not because I want anything from you."

Which sounded good but wasn't the least bit believable. After all, she'd started this conversation by telling him she loved him. Was that even true? Maybe it was all a way to lull him into a false sense of security. Or to make him feel obligated, so when she sprung the pregnancy on him, he would instantly want to be a part of things.

"How do I know this wasn't just a big game to you?" he asked her.

"There are no winners here." She shrugged. "I thought you'd want to know that you're going to be a father. But don't concern yourself. I can see it in your eyes. You want to run. Fine. Go ahead. There's the door and I'm not stopping you."

IN THAT SECOND when he just stood there, Dakota held her breath. She desperately hoped she was wrong, that Finn would want to stay. That somehow he'd realize he loved her back and that they belonged together.

As she watched, she saw the emotional door swing shut and knew that she'd lost. Before he bothered walking out, she knew he was already gone.

CHAPTER TWENTY

TREE-COVERED MOUNTAINS stretched for as far as Finn could see. The sky was blue, the sun bright, even though it was after nine in the evening. This time of year, the northern parts of Alaska got close to twenty hours of daylight.

He'd already completed two flights in the past twenty-four hours. When he flew back to South Salmon, he would rest for a while, then do it all over again. Orders were backed up, and he owed Bill. His partner had been damned understanding about his extended absence.

The controls of the plane were familiar. He didn't have to think to fly—being in the sky, defying gravity, was as natural to him as breathing. This was all he'd ever needed.

In the distance he saw storm heads. The thick, dark clouds could have been a problem, but he knew the weather as well as he knew the sky. The clouds would pass west of him. By the time he was leaving again, the weather would have moved on.

Despite the steady drone of the engine, there was a relative silence. A sense of peace. No one sat next to him. No one waited for him when he landed. He could do what he wanted, when he wanted. He finally had the freedom he'd spent the past eight years longing for.

As he got closer to the South Salmon airport, he reported his approach and headed in to land. When the wheels touched down, he steered the plane toward the hangars he and Bill owned. His partner was waiting for him by the main building.

Bill was a tall, thin guy in his early forties. His father and Finn's father had worked together in the business. There was a lot of history between them.

"How did it go?" Bill asked. "You've been flying a lot of hours."

Finn handed over the clipboard containing the signed delivery receipts, as well as the plane's log. "I'm going to get some rest now. I'll be back about four."

He meant four in the morning. Shifts started early in the summer. They wanted to take advantage of as much daylight as possible. Flying was a whole lot easier when you could see everything.

Bill took the clipboard. "You adjusting okay?"

"Sure. Why do you ask?"

His partner shrugged. "You're not the same. I don't know if you're missing something or someone, or if it's having your brothers gone. There's a lot of new business, Finn. A couple contracts and other folks interested in signing. I've got them for you to look at. The thing is, if you're not going to be here, then I need to hire new pilots. Maybe bring in my cousin."

His partner looked at him. "Do you want me to buy you out? I can. My in-laws have offered me the money. I could pay about half in cash and get a bank loan for the rest. If you're not sure, this is the time to tell me."

Sell the business. He couldn't say he hadn't been thinking about it. Three months ago he would have sworn everything he wanted was in South Salmon. Now he wasn't so sure. His brothers had left and they weren't looking back. They'd found it surprisingly easy to make a life somewhere else. He had new ideas about what he wanted to do with his life. Run charters, teach kids to fly.

And then there was Dakota. He missed her. As much as he

didn't want to, as much as he was pissed and wondering if she'd done her best to trick him—even though he knew in his gut she hadn't—he wanted to be with her. He wanted to see her and hold her and laugh with her. He wanted to watch Hannah grow from a baby to a toddler, then into a little girl with bright eyes and a ready smile.

As for the baby… He couldn't go there. The thought of it overwhelmed him. He'd never considered the idea of more kids. From the day his parents had died, he'd always told himself that when his brothers were finally ready to walk away, he would do all the things he'd missed. He would go where he wanted, do what he wanted. He would be free. He never wanted to "have to" do anything again.

As much as he'd loved his brothers, there had been days he'd resented having to take care of everything. At a time when most guys his age were screwing everything that walked and partying with friends, he was checking homework, doing laundry and learning how to cook. He'd balanced work and parenting. He'd had to be both mother and father, and every single day he'd wondered if he'd been messing it up.

"Finn?"

Finn looked at his partner. "Sorry."

"You were somewhere else."

"The past."

"About the business?" Bill asked. "Can you get back to me by the end of the week?"

"By Friday," he promised.

Bill nodded and walked away.

Finn stayed where he was. There was a post-flight check to be done on the plane and paperwork to finish. But instead of moving on that, he found himself thinking about Dakota and how she would have to be both mother and father to her two children. She'd sought out the adoption, but the baby was as unexpected to her as it was to him.

He was sure she'd meant what she'd told him—that she had

no expectations. That he could walk away. She would probably draw up one of those agreements where he gave up all rights to the kid and she gave up all rights to financial support. She wouldn't want him to feel trapped.

Which should have made him happy. It had taken eight long years, but he was finally exactly where he wanted to be. Free. He could go anywhere, do anything. Hell, if he sold the business to Bill, he would have freedom and cash. Life didn't get any better than that.

"I'M FINE," DAKOTA INSISTED, speaking the words for the fourth or fifth hundredth time. "Completely and totally fine."

Both her sisters stared at her, as if not convinced. The statement would probably have been a little more believable if her eyes weren't red and puffy from all her crying. During the day she managed to be brave, but as soon as she was alone at night, she kind of lost it.

"You're not fine and you shouldn't be," Nevada told her. "You told Finn you loved him and he left. He didn't say anything, he just walked away. You're left here, pregnant with his baby and completely alone."

"Thanks for the recap," Dakota murmured. "Now I sound pathetic."

"You don't," Montana said quickly. "You sound like you've been through a lot and you have. You're strong. You'll be okay." She and Nevada exchanged a quick look.

"What?" Dakota demanded. She wasn't surprised they'd been talking about her behind her back, but she was concerned that they'd reached a conclusion that hadn't occurred to her.

They were at Jo's bar, with *Project Runway* playing on the big screen and HGTV on the smaller TVs. Denise had insisted Hannah spend the night, probably to give the sisters time to be alone. As the baby adored her grandmother, Dakota wasn't worried about her daughter.

"It's a big thing, finding out about the baby," Montana said carefully, as if expecting Dakota to blow up at her.

"I know that."

"He probably needs a little time. You needed time."

"I was willing to give him time," she said, doing her best not to clench her teeth as she clutched her glass of cranberry juice. "This isn't a time thing. He *left*. It's the leaving I object to. He stayed in town after his brothers had moved on right up until I told him I loved him and that I was pregnant. That's when he walked out. Left for Alaska that night. No call, nothing."

She'd never been left before. Not like this. The closest feeling she had was when her dad had died. That, too, had been unexpected. There was no arguing, no bargaining. There was just absence and pain.

"It's so like a guy to walk away," Nevada said. "Now you know he's that type."

"What type?"

"He disappears rather than faces responsibility. He only cares about himself."

Dakota shook her head. "That's not fair. Finn doesn't do that. He's spent the past eight years raising his brothers. He had to give up everything to take care of them."

"Look how that turned out," Nevada muttered.

"What do you mean? They're great guys."

"One of them wants to be an actor and the other is dating a woman nearly twice his age."

Dakota straightened. "That's not true."

"Sasha doesn't want to be an actor? He didn't move to L.A., abandoning his college education one semester from finishing?"

"Yes, but—"

Nevada shrugged. "You're better off without him."

"No, I'm not." The unfair assessment startled her. "There's nothing wrong with Sasha following his dream. Should he have finished college? Maybe. But he can go back later. It's not going anywhere. As for Aurelia, she's nine years older than Stephen, as you very well know. She's sweet and they're great together. Stephen is going back to college. He's studying engineering, something you can relate to."

She felt herself getting angry. "Where do you get off being so judgmental? Finn is a good man. He's proven that over and over again. I don't regret our relationship and I sure as hell don't need you making unfounded comments about him and his brothers."

Nevada picked up her drink and smiled. "Just checking."

"Checking what?"

"To see if you're still in there."

Dakota opened her mouth, then closed it. "What does that mean?"

"You're too accepting of this," Montana said, leaning toward her. "You can't be happy Finn left, but you're all Zen about it. What's up with that? Why didn't you fight for what you wanted?"

"Fight? I can't force him to want to be with me."

"No, but there's a whole ocean between doing nothing and forcing him."

Nevada nodded. "Come on. When you wanted to get into that special grad program so you could get your masters and Ph.D. at the same time, did you just put in your application and wait? No. You pestered the department chair until he nearly put a restraining order out on you. When you needed a classroom of kids for your thesis research, you knocked on teachers' doors for weeks until you found exactly what you were looking for, then you got her to agree."

"When you found out you couldn't have kids without help," Montana added, "you put in your application for adoption, went through all the studies and home visits and adopted a kid. You do things, Dakota. You're quiet about it and you don't expect people to notice, but we do. You've always gotten things done. So why are you being so passive now?"

She felt both praised and scolded. "I'm not being passive. I'm giving Finn time to come to terms with what he wants to do."

"What about what you want?" Nevada asked. "Isn't that important?"

"Sure, but..."

"There are no buts," Montana reminded her. "Remember what Yoda said? 'Do or do not. There is no try.'"

"You can sit on your butt and wait for him to decide," Nevada said. "Or you can take control of your destiny. I know you're scared."

"I'm not scared."

They both stared at her, eyebrows raised in identical expressions of disbelief.

She sighed. "I'm a little scared," she admitted. Confronting Finn did mean taking charge of her life, but it also meant facing the fact that he might tell her he just plain wasn't interested. That she wasn't for him.

She didn't think he was going to walk away from his child. It might take him a while, but eventually he would show up and want to be a part of his or her life. Finn would be a great father, but was he interested in being a husband?

"I thought the people on the show were stupid," she said slowly. "I thought they were desperate and that I should feel sorry for them. But they were simply looking to fall in love. Something nearly everyone wants. At least they did something about it. What have I done?"

She half expected her sisters to defend her, but they were both silent. Talk about truth in communication, she thought, both bemused and a little hurt. Then she reminded herself that it didn't matter what anyone thought but her and Finn. They were the ones this was all about.

She knew what *she* wanted. She wanted a happily-ever-after kind of ending with the man she loved. She wanted to marry him and raise children with him. She wanted a house full of kids and dogs, with a cat or two and carpooling and soccer practice. She wanted a little of what her parents had, with a twist that made it all their own.

But what did Finn want? She knew that eventually he would figure it out and tell her. But was giving him the time he needed being mature or being afraid?

He'd heard her say that she loved him and that she was pregnant, but she'd never had the chance to tell him the rest of it. About how she saw their future and that being responsible wasn't all bad. There were many wonderful rewards.

"I'm not going to wait," she said as she slid out of the booth. "I'm going to South Salmon to talk to him."

"There's an Alaska Airlines flight out of Sacramento at six in the morning," Nevada told her. "You connect with the flight to Anchorage in Seattle." She pulled a piece of paper out of her pocket and handed it over. "I made a reservation earlier. You can pay for it when you get to the airport."

Dakota couldn't believe it. "You planned this?"

"We hoped," Montana told her. "We were also arguing with Mom about who gets Hannah tomorrow night."

Dakota felt tears filling her eyes, but for the first time in days, her crying wasn't about being sad or having lost what mattered most. She waved her sisters out of the booth, then hugged them.

"I love you," she said as she held them close.

"We love you, too," Nevada told her. "Warn Finn that if he's an idiot, we'll send all three of our brothers after him. He can run, but he won't be able to hide forever."

Dakota laughed.

Montana kissed her cheek. "We'll keep it all together here. Don't worry. Just go find Finn and drag his butt back here."

"COIN TOSS?" BILL ASKED.

Finn stared out the office window. The first storm had blown through, but there had been a second one behind it. This one was bigger and headed directly for South Salmon.

Storms out here weren't like those down in the lower forty-eight. They were a lot less polite and plenty more destructive. Normally all flights would have been grounded, but a call had come through from a desperate father. His sick child needed to be flown out as soon as possible. The medical planes were all out on other calls. No one else could get there.

Now dark clouds rose fifty or sixty thousand feet into the heavens. There were wind shears and flashes of lightning. Flying in something like that was like daring the hand of God.

"I'll go," Finn said, grabbing his backpack and walking toward the parked planes. "Radio the family that I should be there in about three hours. Maybe a little longer."

"You can't go around the storm." It was too big. There was no "around."

"I know."

Bill grabbed his arm. "Finn, wait. We'll give it a few hours."

"Does that kid have a few hours?"

"No, but…"

Finn knew the argument. People who chose to live outside the civilized world risked situations just like this. Most of the time, the gamble paid off. Every now and then, fate exacted a price.

"That kid isn't going to die on my watch," Finn said.

"You don't owe them anything."

He owed them trying. That's what this job meant to him. Sometimes you had to take a risk.

He crossed to the plane and walked around the outside. The preflight routine was something he could do in his sleep, but today he took extra time. The last thing he needed was a mechanical problem complicating an already difficult situation.

By the time he was ready to take off, the first fingers of the storm were trying to grab him. Wind gusted and there were raindrops on his windshield.

The problem wasn't the flight out. He would be heading away from the storm. It was getting to Anchorage that was going to be the trick.

Six hours later, he knew he was going to die. The parents and the kid were in the plane, the worried father next to him, the mother sitting next to her son. The winds were so strong, the plane seemed to be standing still instead of moving forward. They were buffeted and tossed. A few times they were caught in a small wind shear and dropped a few hundred feet.

"I'm going to be sick," the mother called to him.

"Bags are next to the seat."

Finn couldn't take the time to show her. Not when all their lives depended on him getting them safely landed.

Despite the fact that it was afternoon, the sky was black as night. The only illumination came from the lightning strikes. Wind howled like a monster out to get them, and Finn had a feeling that this time the storm might win.

He watched his warning lights, checked the altimeter and made sure they were on course. Without wanting to, he found himself mentally drifting to another flight very much like this one. A flight that had taken his parents and changed his world.

There'd been a storm, dark and powerful. The lightning had flashed around them, dangerous shards of destruction. Finn remembered one cutting so close, he'd been able to feel the heat. He'd been flying, his father in the copilot's seat. The wind had growled and thrown them around like a kid with a softball.

They'd swooped and bucked, and then a single flash of light had hit their engine. The plane had shuddered as the engine was fired into a useless molten part, and the plane had dropped like a rock.

There'd been no controlling the descent. It had been too dark to know where to land, assuming there had been somewhere safer than the forest where they'd crashed. Finn didn't remember much about the impact. He'd awakened to find himself lying on the ground, in the rain.

His parents had both been unconscious. He'd cared for them as best he could, then he'd hiked out to get help. By the time he returned, they were gone. They'd probably died within an hour of his leaving, but he didn't like to think about that.

Lightning flashed next to the plane, jerking Finn back to the present. The mother screamed. The boy was probably terrified but too sick to make a sound. Next to Finn, the father clutched his seat.

No one asked if they were going to die, although he was sure they were thinking the question. Probably praying. Finn waited for a sense of regret, a voice that said nothing was worth this, that he should have waited.

And then he felt it. A sense of something other than himself. Even though he knew it was impossible, he would swear his parents were there with him, helping him. It was as if someone else took control of the plane, guiding his hands.

Not knowing what else to do, he listened to the silence, turning left, then right, dodging lightning and the wind shears, finding the calmest part of the storm. He flew lower when the invisible forces indicated he should, veered left, then up.

For the next hour he flew as he'd never flown before, and gradually the power of the storm faded. Fifty miles outside of Anchorage, he saw the first hint of sunlight. A voice from the control tower crackled in his headset.

They landed less than thirty minutes later. An ambulance was waiting to race the boy and his family to the hospital. At the last second, the father turned back to him.

"I don't know how to thank you," the man said, shaking his hand. "I thought we were going to die. You saved us. You saved him."

Then he was running after his wife and climbing into the back of the ambulance.

Finn stood by his plane and watched the sun break through the clouds. Automatically, he checked the plane. Everything was fine. There wasn't a single mark to indicate what they'd been through. He climbed back inside, knowing whatever he was looking for wasn't there.

Maybe it had been his parents, maybe it had been something else. Flying was like boating. If a man did it long enough, he experienced things that couldn't be explained. For whatever reason, he'd been spared the night of the crash. He'd always thought it was to raise his brothers, but maybe there was another purpose. Maybe he'd been saved so that he could find his way to Dakota.

He loved her. Having to go through a near-death experience to figure that out made him an idiot, but he could live with that. As long as at the end of the day he got the chance to tell her.

He loved her. He wanted to marry her and have lots of babies with her. Hell, he needed to call Hamilton and tell the old coot he wanted to buy the business. Then he should let Bill know he was selling. Most important, he had to get back to Fool's Gold and tell Dakota how much he loved her and wanted to be with her.

He pulled out his cell phone and called Bill.

"I've been worried," his partner said. "I had to hear it from the tower that you arrived? You couldn't call?"

"I'm calling."

"You've been on the ground ten minutes. What have you been doing? Shopping?"

Finn chuckled. "Getting my passengers into the ambulance. Look, Bill, I'm out. You can buy me out of the business. I have to go back to Fool's Gold right away."

"This is about that woman, isn't it?"

Finn thought of Dakota and grinned. "Yeah. I'm going to figure out how to convince her to marry me."

There was a pause, then Bill said, "She's going to be really happy to hear that."

"How do you know?"

"Because she's standing right next to me. If her smile is anything to go by, I'm going to guess she'll say yes."

DAKOTA USED BINOCULARS to scan the sky. Bill had told her in which direction to look, and when she saw the tiny speck of a plane appear, she began to jump up and down.

Finn landed and guided the plane off the runway. She was already running toward him.

They met on the grass by the tarmac. While there were a thousand things she had to say, right now she only wanted to be in his arms. Then she was, and he was holding her and kissing her and nothing had ever felt so right.

"I love you," he told her, then kissed her. "I love you, Dakota. You and Hannah and our unborn baby. I should have told you that before."

She was so happy, she wasn't sure she even needed to breathe. "You needed time."

"I got scared and then I took off." He cupped her face in his hands. "I want to marry you. I want us to be a family."

She searched his face. "Even though that means a lot of responsibility?"

He nodded, then kissed her again. "Who am I kidding? I was born to be responsible."

"You were a wild guy."

"For about fifteen minutes. I want to be with you."

Beautiful, amazing words, she thought happily. Perfect words, from the man who was exactly right for her.

"I love you, too," she whispered.

"You'll marry me?"

"Yes."

"We'll live in Fool's Gold?"

She wanted him to be happy. "Your life is here."

"No, it's not. I'm selling my half of the business to Bill. My brothers don't want it and I can use the money to buy Hamilton's company. I belong where you belong and that's Fool's Gold."

She flung herself against him. Being in his arms felt right.

"Hannah is going to be thrilled," she whispered. "She's really missed you."

"I've missed her, too." He touched her belly. "Soon she's going to have a baby brother or sister to boss around."

"One day you're going to have to show us all Alaska," she told him.

"I will, but right now, I'm ready to go home."

* * * * *

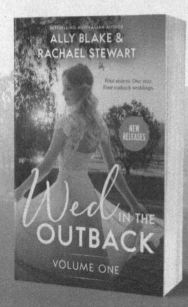

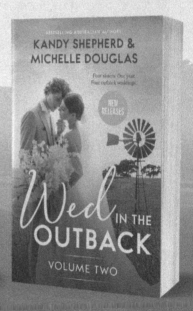